About the Authors

Cat S____d lives in Minnesota with her daughter, their opi____ ____urmese cats and a silly Doberman puppy. Wi____ ____ the Romance Writers of America 2010 Gol____ ____eart® for series contemporary romance, whe____ not writing sexy, romantic stories for Mills & E____ ____esire, she can be found sailing with friends on t____ ____roix River or in more exotic locales like the Cari____ and Europe. You can find out more about her ____ at www.catschield.net

Eliz____ Bevarly is the award-winning, nationally num____ ____e bestselling author of more than seventy nove____ ____d novellas. Her books have been translated into ____ ____ozen languages and published in three dozen count____ An honours graduate of the University of Lou____ ____e, she has called home places as diverse as San ____, Puerto Rico and Haddonfield, New Jersey, but ____ resides back in her native Kentucky with her ____ ____ her son, and two neurotic cats (as if there ____ere ____ other kind).

____res____ ____ill tells people if they want to be writers, to f____ ____ ____pouse who's patient, understanding and interested i____ ____in____ a patron of the arts. Lucky for her, she found a ____ ____ust like that, who's been with her through all the u____ ____d downs of being a writer. Along with their son a____ ____aughter, they live in Travelers Rest, SC, in the foo____ ____ls of the beautiful Blue Ridge Mountains, with two be____tiful, spoiled dogs and two gigantic, lazy cats.

American Affairs

COLLECTION

July 2020
Manhattan Money

August 2020
Florida Secrets

September 2020
New Orleans Opulence

October 2020
Rocky Mountain Rumours

November 2020
Los Angeles Love

December 2020
New York Nights

American Affairs: Manhattan Money

CAT SCHIELD

ELIZABETH BEVARLY

TERESA HILL

MIX
Paper from
responsible sources
FSC
FSC C007454

This book is produced from independently certified FSC™ paper
to ensure responsible forest management.

For more information visit www.harpercollins.co.uk/green

Printed and bound in Spain
by CPI, Barcelona

MILLS & BOON

First Published in Great Britain 2020
By Mills & Boon, an imprint of HarperCollins*Publishers*
1 London Bridge Street, London, SE1 9GF

AMERICAN AFFAIRS: MANHATTAN MONEY © 2020
Harlequin Books S.A.

The Rogue's Fortune © 2012 Harlequin Books S.A.
A Beauty for the Billionaire © 2017 Elizabeth Bevarly
His Bride by Design © 2011 Teresa Hill

Special thanks and acknowledgement to Cat Schield for her contribution to *The Highest Bidder* series.

ISBN: 978-0-263-28178-1

THE ROGUE'S FORTUNE

CAT SCHIELD

To my Aunt Sophie

One

He sauntered through the well-dressed crowd, bestowing his lazy smile on those who gushed their congratulations. Tall and powerfully built, he'd been ogled by half the women he'd passed. He, in turn, seemed uninterested in the stir he created as he charmed his way through the two hundred guests assembled for the premier wine auction.

As he scanned the room like a secret service agent, only his penetrating eyes gave away the fact that he wasn't as relaxed as he appeared.

Most people wouldn't have noticed Roark Black was on edge. Most people didn't have super-sensitive radar for the dangerous types.

Elizabeth Minerva did.

"The shrimp is running out!"

Jolted out of her ruminating by Brenda Stuart, her quick-to-panic "assistant" on this event, Elizabeth ripped her gaze away from the handsome adventurer and skimmed damp palms from her waist to her hips.

"I just checked and there's plenty of shrimp left," Elizabeth told Brenda. Annoyance with herself fed her impatient tone. There was also plenty of champagne and canapés and a dozen other things Brenda had fussed about in the last hour. "Why don't you make yourself a plate and go relax in the back?"

Anything to get rid of the former wedding planner to the middle class. Josie Summers, Elizabeth's boss, had saddled her with Brenda because as always Josie had underestimated what Elizabeth could handle. It was the woman's second event as Elizabeth's second in command, and rubbing elbows with Manhattan's rich and famous was spotlighting exactly why Brenda wasn't ready to be here. Instead of projecting a confident, capable vibe as she moved invisibly through the party, Elizabeth's assistant had badgered a server in front of Bunny Cromwell, one of the city's most prolific hostesses, and scolded a bartender for not making a city councilman's drink properly.

"I can't relax," Brenda exclaimed, her sharp tone catching the attention of two nearby guests. The women exchanged disgusted expressions. "And you shouldn't either."

Plastering on a serene smile, Elizabeth seized Brenda's arm above the elbow, fingers pinching ever so delicately. "I've got everything under control here. The auction will be starting in a half an hour. Why don't you head home?"

"I can't." Brenda resisted Elizabeth's grip as she was hauled toward the screens set up at one end of the enormous loft space to conceal the food prep area from the party-goers.

"Sure, you can." Elizabeth used her soothing voice as she marched the older woman away from the party. "You've put in so many hours this week. You deserve to get out of here. I can handle the rest."

"If you're sure."

As if Elizabeth hadn't handled larger parties in the three years since she'd graduated from college and taken a job with Josie Summers's Event Planning. Granted, this was Eliza-

CAT SCHIELD 9

beth's first A-list crowd. The first event that had given her butterflies before the guests arrived and began to murmur their approval over the way she'd transformed a dull, empty loft space into a sophisticated, elegant venue.

"I'm positive," Elizabeth said. "Go home and tuck your beautiful daughter into bed."

It was well past ten and Brenda's six-year-old daughter was probably already fast asleep, but Elizabeth had figured out the first day she'd worked with the woman that everything Brenda did was for her little girl. It was the only thing about the woman Elizabeth liked. And envied.

"Okay. Thanks."

Elizabeth waited until Brenda had gathered her purse and disappeared down the long hallway toward the elevator before she headed back to the party.

"Well, hello."

She'd almost managed to forget about Roark Black in the ten minutes she'd been dealing with Brenda, but here he was, less than five feet away, leaning his broad shoulder against one of the two-foot-wide columns that supported the ceiling.

Damn. Up close the energy of the man was astonishing. He practically oozed lusty masculinity and danger. He'd forgone the traditional bow tie with his tux and left the top buttons undone on his white shirt. Rakish and sexy, he set her pulse to purring.

You swore off bad boys forever, remember?

And Roark Black was as bad a bad boy as they got. Even his name gave her the shivers.

Yet earlier, there she'd stood, daydreaming about what it would be like to slide her fingers through his thick wavy hair. Brown in color, the shade reminded her of her great aunt's sheared beaver coat. She'd loved the sensual drag of the soft fur against her bare skin.

"Can I get you something?" she asked.

One side of his mouth lifted. "I thought you'd never ask."

His tone invited her to smile at his flirting. His eyes dared her to strip off her black dress and give him a glimpse of what lay beneath.

She swallowed hard. "Is there something you need?" The second the question passed her lips, she wished it back. Was she trying to play into his hands?

"Sweetheart—"

"Elizabeth." She shoved out her hand all professional like. "Elizabeth Minerva. I'm your event planner."

She expected him to take her hand in a bone-crushing grip. Instead, he cupped it, turned her palm upward and dragged his left forefinger down the middle of it. Her body went on full alert like a state penitentiary with a missing prisoner.

"Roark." He peered at her palm, the skin glazed blue by the indirect lighting that illuminated the space. "Roark Black. You have a very curvy…" His attention shifted and the next thing Elizabeth knew, she was drowning in his penetrating gaze. "Head line."

"A what?" Her dry mouth prevented anything more from emerging.

"Head line." His fingertip retraced its invigorating journey across her palm. "See here. A curvy head line means you like to play with new ideas. Do you, Elizabeth?"

"Do I what?" The air in the loft had grown thin in the last sixty seconds. Light-headed, she was having trouble getting enough oxygen.

"Do you like playing with new ideas?"

Bad boy. Bad boy.

Elizabeth cleared her throat and retrieved her hand in a short jerk that made Roark's crooked smile widen and heat rush to her face.

"I like creating unique party spaces, if that's what you mean."

It wasn't. His smirk told her so.

"I like what you've done with the place."

More comfortable talking about her job than herself, Elizabeth crossed her arms over her chest and surveyed all she'd accomplished in the past twenty-four hours.

"There wasn't much to it when I got started. Just a concrete floor and white walls. And those incredible arched windows with that spectacular view." She pointed out the latter, hoping to steer his unnerving stare away from her.

"I heard you came up with the idea of a slide show to honor Tyler."

Tyler Banks had died the year before. A thoroughly disliked human being, no one had any idea that he'd been behind twenty percent of all major New York City charitable donations in the past decade.

"While he was alive, he might not have wanted anyone to know all the wonderful things he'd done, but so many people were helped by his generosity. I thought he deserved a proper tribute."

"Beautiful and smart." His eyes devoured her. "Okay, I'm hooked."

And so was she. Naturally. Bad boys were the bane of her romantic existence. The worse they were, the more she wanted them.

From everything she'd heard and read about Roark Black, she'd expected him to be an arrogant, unprincipled jerk. Gorgeous and sexy, to be sure, but with questionable ethics. The sort of guy she'd have tumbled head over high heels for a year ago.

But after what had happened with Colton last October, she'd sworn on her sister's grave that she was done with all bad boys.

Unfortunately, since those seemed to be the only sort that tripped her trigger, her love life had been in sad shape these past twelve months. Which explained why her hormones had jerked to attention the instant Roark strolled into the party.

"I suggest you get unhooked, Mr. Black," she said, hoping her tart voice would counteract her sweet, gooey insides. Honestly, it was embarrassing to let a man, even a sexy, gorgeous one, turn her into a marshmallow.

"You don't like me?" He didn't appear particularly concerned that she didn't. In fact, he seemed as if he might just relish the challenge.

"I don't know you."

"But you've formed an opinion. How is that fair?"

Fair? He wanted to play fair? She didn't believe that for a second. In fact, she suspected if she gave him the slightest encouragement, she'd find herself in a bathroom with her hem above her ears.

To her dismay a tingle erupted between her thighs. Annoyance added more heat to her next statement than she intended. "I've read things."

"What sort of things?"

He was the reason this party was happening. If he hadn't talked Tyler's granddaughter into letting Waverly's auction off the rarest of Tyler's vast wine collection, there would have been no reason for this event and she would not have been selected as the planner.

All at once she wished she'd just kept her mouth shut. The man was too confident. His personality too strong. And she'd overstepped her role as event planner the second she'd let him engage her. "Things."

Bold, dark eyebrows twitched above keen green-gray eyes. "Oh, don't get all coy with me after throwing down the gauntlet."

No one had ever accused her of being coy before. "Look, it's none of my business, and I really need to make sure everything is all right with the party."

He moved to block her path. "Not before you answer my question."

At six feet three inches, he was a big barrier as he crowded her against the concrete pillar that had hidden their encounter from the prying eyes of the rest of the guests. To Elizabeth's dismay, her body reacted positively to his intimidating size. Lightning flashed in her midsection and zinged along her nerves, leaving a disquieting buzz in its wake.

"You have an opinion." He placed a hand on the column above her shoulder. "I'd like to hear it."

"I don't understand why."

From what she'd heard about him, he didn't really care what anyone thought. Or said. He did his thing and to hell with the rules or what was proper. And to the detriment of her anti-bad-boy pledge, his absolute confidence excited her.

"Let's just say you're the first woman in a long time that's not just playing hard to get. I believe you mean it." He leaned closer. "I'd like to know why."

Rattled by the way his nearness affected her heart rate, she blurt out, "Waverly's is in trouble. If it goes down, you could be the biggest reason why." Mortified by what she'd just said, Elizabeth held her breath and waited for the fallout.

"And where did you read that?" He looked neither surprised nor annoyed with her blunt proclamation.

"I'm sorry," she muttered. "It's none of my business. I should be getting back to the party."

"Not so fast." He surveyed her through narrowed eyes. His charm had vanished. Mouth tight, every tense muscle promising dire consequences if she denied him, he said, "I think you owe me an explanation."

"I spoke out of turn."

"But with a fair amount of knowledge." The dashing man of adventure had given way to a flint-eyed hunter.

Elizabeth quivered, but not in fear. The reckless part of her she'd worked so hard to refine responded to Roark's dangerous vibe. "Look—"

Before she had to explain herself, she was saved by the appearance of Kendra Darling, Elizabeth's old school friend and assistant to Ann Richardson, CEO of Waverly's.

"Mr. Black, Ann sent me to find you."

"Can it wait? Elizabeth and I were having a little chat."

Behind her tortoise-shell glasses, Kendra's large hazel eyes widened as she recognized whom Roark had cornered with his charismatic presence. "It's important," she said. "Some men showed up to talk to you." Kendra's slim body practically quivered with anxiety as she clasped her hands at her waist. "They're with the FBI."

Teeth clenched in irritation, Roark pushed away from Elizabeth and nodded to Ann's flustered assistant. "Tell her I'll be there in a couple of minutes."

"I think she'd like you to come right now."

In other words, the assistant didn't want to return without him. She was used to dealing with wealthy, sometimes difficult clients, not law enforcement. Otherwise she'd know that the FBI liked to chat with him whenever something questionable happened with Middle Eastern antiquities. He'd been both the subject of inquiries and the expert that helped them take down the thieves.

Before heading back to the party, Roark gave Elizabeth one last look. The stunning blonde hadn't moved during his brief exchange with Ann's assistant. In fact, she looked as if she'd like to melt right into the concrete support behind her.

He considered how many times he'd held a relic in his hands and immediately known whether the artifact was genuine or an excellent forgery. His gut had never been wrong, and he'd backed up every authentication with careful, detailed analysis.

This encounter with Elizabeth had hit him the same way. He'd held her hand in his and recognized she was the genuine article. No artifice. No games. Pure attraction. And he intended to have her.

"We'll continue this conversation later," he assured her.

Her eyes said: *don't count on it.*

"Mr. Black?"

He strode away from the petite event planner with the lush figure and unforgettable indigo eyes and made a bee-line toward the two obvious outsiders bracketing Ann. Unlike her assistant, Waverly's CEO wasn't in the least bit flustered that FBI agents had crashed the party. Her calm under pressure was one of the things Roark liked most about the head of Waverly's.

Her gaze locked on him as he neared. Eyes hard, she offered him a neutral smile. "Roark, these are Special Agents Matthews and Todd. They would like to ask us a few questions in private."

Roark eyed each in turn, recognizing Todd as an agent he'd seen in passing, but had never had any direct interaction with. Agent Matthews was brand-new. Tall and lean with black hair that spilled over her shoulders in abundant waves. Her dark brown eyes had tracked his progress across the room toward them, and Roark knew this one looked at him and thought career advancement.

"We can speak out on the terrace." Whipping off his tux-edo jacket, he draped it over Ann's shoulders as they headed to the door that led out onto a small outdoor space. Elizabeth's deft touch could be seen here, as well. With white lights tangled in white pine boughs and candles in modern hurricane lanterns, the terrace oozed romance.

After three months in the jungle, Roark appreciated the cool November evening as he enjoyed the glow of Manhattan visible beyond the terrace's cement half wall. Most of the time he found the city too tame for his taste. But there was no denying it sparkled at night.

As soon as the door shut behind them, Roark spoke.

"What can we help you with?"

"This is about Rayas's missing Gold Heart statue," the first FBI agent said. "We've had a new report from Prince Mallik

Khouri that a masked man with Mr. Black's exact build stole the statue from his rooms at the royal palace."

"You can't possibly think Roark stole the statue," Ann protested, but it was all for show. She didn't look a bit surprised that Roark was being accused of theft.

"We have reports that he was in Dubai at the time," said Agent Matthews. "It wouldn't be impossible for a man of his talents…" the FBI agent twisted the last word to indicate what she thought of Roark's abilities "…to slip into Rayas, get into the palace and steal the statue."

"It's completely within my power to do so."

Ann's grim glance told him to let her handle the accusation. "He wouldn't."

"Just like a thousand other illegal things are in my power to do," Roark continued, staring Agent Matthews down. "But I don't do them."

"Sorry if we can't take your word for it," Special Agent Todd said.

"There's no proof that Roark was involved." Ann showed no sign of believing otherwise and Roark appreciated that whatever her opinion of him, she hadn't thrown him to the wolves.

"The thief made the mistake of cursing during the scuffle." Matthews nodded. "The voice was deep and very distinctive." Her gaze locked on Roark. "He claims it was your voice, Mr. Black."

"We met briefly once in Dubai years ago. I can't imagine that he'd remember my voice."

But Roark recognized that he was the perfect scapegoat. And Mallik had another reason to suspect that Roark would break into his rooms at the palace.

"Why is this the first we're hearing about this thief?" Roark demanded.

"Prince Mallik was embarrassed to explain his failure to

stop the thief to his nephew, the crown prince." Matthews arched her brows. "But he's convinced it was you."

"He's mistaken," Roark snapped.

Ann put her hand on his arm and spoke in a calm, but firm voice. "I've met Prince Mallik. He seemed like an honest, gracious person. However, in the midst of a fight, I imagine being overwhelmed by adrenaline, with heightened senses, he may only think he heard Roark's voice. Didn't you say the thief wore a mask?" Ann didn't wait for the FBI to confirm her statement. "Perhaps his voice was distorted by the cloth."

Roark was working hard to keep his temper at a low simmer. "Have you questioned Dalton Rothschild about the theft?" The rival auction house owner had been a thorn in Waverly's side for years. "He's got a bone to pick with Waverly's and I wouldn't put it past him to send one of his minions to Rayas to steal the statue and pin the blame on me."

"Dalton Rothschild doesn't share your controversial methods for procuring artifacts, Mr. Black," Agent Matthews said. "We would have no reason to question him in this matter."

Of course they wouldn't. It wouldn't surprise Roark to find out that Rothschild was the one that pointed the FBI to Waverly's in the first place. The guy was a slick operator, but as greedy as they came.

While Ann escorted the FBI out, Roark stayed on the terrace and let the chilly fall air cool his ire. Through the large half-circle windows he searched the party for Elizabeth Minerva. She drifted through the well-dressed guests like a wraith, her blond hair confined in a neat French twist, stunning figure downplayed by the simple, long-sleeved black dress.

Hot anger became sizzling desire in seconds. From the moment he'd set eyes on her an hour ago, he'd been preoccupied. Petite, curvaceous blondes weren't really his type. He preferred his women long and lean with flashing black eyes and golden skin. Passion ruled him when it came to antiquities and lovemaking.

His sexual appetites would probably break a dainty, graceful creature like Elizabeth.

"Roark, what are you staring at?"

Without his notice, Ann had returned to the terrace and stood beside him. Roark cursed his preoccupation. Being caught unaware could get him killed in many of the places he ventured.

"How can I get in touch with your party planner?" he asked.

"My assistant made all the arrangements." She sounded surprised that he'd asked. "I'll have her email you the contact information."

"Wonderful. In a few weeks we're going to have reason to celebrate."

"You mean because of the Gold Heart statue?" Ann paced toward the terrace wall. "Are you sure it's not the one stolen from Rayas?"

"Are you asking me if I stole it?" He'd grown weary of her lack of trust in him these past few years.

"Of course not," she said, her tone smooth and unhurried. "But you're sure your source for the statue is completely legitimate?"

"Absolutely." He touched her arm. "You can trust me."

Some of the tension seeped out of her. "I know, but with this new accusation, we have to be more careful than ever."

And careful wasn't something he was known for.

"I need you to bring me the statue," she continued. "The quickest way to resolve this issue is for me to take the statue to Rayas and have the sheikh verify that it isn't the one stolen from the palace."

"It's not."

"Neither the FBI nor Crown Prince Raif Khouri are going to take your word for it." A determined firmness came over

Ann's expression. "You've been missing for three months, Roark. Waverly's is in trouble."

He might have been off the grid, but that didn't mean he was out of the loop. Roark knew about the collusion scandal that had rocked Waverly's and Ann Richardson's link to it. His half brother, Vance Waverly, was convinced the CEO had never been romantically involved with Dalton Rothschild and that there was no truth to the rumor of price fixing between the rival auction houses. Roark trusted Vance's faith in Ann where illegal practices were concerned, but he wasn't as convinced that Rothschild's hostile takeover of Waverly's was just hearsay. Nor was he sure Ann hadn't fallen for Dalton. Which meant Roark wasn't sure how far he could trust Ann.

"It's important to clear up the matter of the statue," Ann continued, handing him back his tuxedo jacket.

"I understand, but getting the statue here quickly is going to present a problem."

"What do you mean?"

"I mean with all the publicity surrounding the statue and Rothschild's obvious determination to cause a problem with the auction, it's more important than ever to safeguard it."

"Get it here as fast as you can. Or it may be too late to save Waverly's."

Ann Richardson's resolve resonated with Roark. He faced difficult situations with the same strength of purpose. It was part of the reason why he was willing to do what it took to help her save Waverly's.

In a thoughtful mood, he escorted her inside. While Roark slipped back into the jacket, he noticed a pair of eyes on him. They belonged to a very influential member of Waverly's board. Something behind the man's stare piqued Roark's curiosity. He snagged a glass of champagne from a passing waitress and strode over to shake the man's hand.

"Nice collection you secured," George Cromwell said. "I had no idea Tyler was such a connoisseur."

"He was a man of many secrets."

Cromwell lifted his glass. "Here's to hoping he takes most of them to the grave."

Roark offered a polite smile while impatience churned in his gut. Was he seeing trouble where there was none? Had his instincts been wrong about what he'd glimpsed in the man's manner? Or was he growing paranoid after years of dodging danger and the past three months spent in a deadly game of hide and seek with a bloodthirsty cartel?

"What were the FBI doing here tonight?" Cromwell asked.

Reassured that his instincts were right on track, Roark offered the board member a dismissive smile. "They'd received some bad information and came to clear up the matter." In its own way, this concrete jungle was just as perilous as the tropical one he'd left behind.

"And was it cleared up?"

Roark wasn't going to lie. "I believe they still have some doubts."

Cromwell grew grim. "I'm concerned about Waverly's future."

"How so?" Roark sipped at his champagne and played at nonchalance. He hated all the political maneuvering and missed the familiar danger inherent in guns, knives and criminals who didn't hesitate to kill anyone who got in their way.

"A number of Waverly's shareholders have been approached about selling our shares."

"Let me guess," Roark said, annoyance flaring. "Rothschild?"

"Yes."

"Selling to him wouldn't be in anyone's best interest."

"With the troubles of late, there is concern that Waverly's is being mismanaged." Cromwell was both stating his opinion and digging for information.

Roark's true connection to Vance Waverly wasn't mainstream knowledge, but a few people knew Vance and Roark shared a father. If Cromwell assumed Roark would divulge what he knew about Waverly's problems, he'd be wrong.

"That's ridiculous. Ann is the perfect choice to run Waverly's. Any troubles we've had recently can be attributed to one person. Dalton Rothschild."

"Perhaps. But your activities of late haven't helped."

Roark remained silent. It would do no good to protest that what he did had no bearing on Waverly's, but as long as he remained connected to the auction house, anything he brought in would be suspect. Being someone accustomed to operating alone, Roark found a sense of discomfort stirring in him to have others relying on him.

"What I do is completely legal and legitimate."

"Of course." The board member nodded. "But the world of business is not always interested in facts. Markets rise and fall on people's perceptions of what's going on."

"And I'm being perceived as…?"

"Too freewheeling in both your professional and personal lives."

Roark couldn't argue. He based his actions on his needs and desires. Taking others into consideration wasn't part of the equation. But the older man's assessment poked at a tender spot, bruised earlier by the scathing opinion of a petite blonde.

His attention wandered in her direction. He knew exactly where she was. Her presence was a shaft of light to his senses.

Pleasure flashed like lightning along his nerve endings when he caught her staring at him. He winked at her and grinned as she turned away so fast she almost plowed into a passing server.

Oblivious to Roark's momentary distraction, the board member continued, "I think if you could demonstrate that you're committed to Waverly's, I could convince the other board members that you, Vance and Ann are the future we want."

"And how would you suggest I do that?"

"Show us and the world that you've settled down."

In other words, postpone any dangerous operations for the near future. That could be problematic. Roark was now in pursuit of a new rare artifact—the second half of a pair of leopard heads that had once graced the throne of Tipu Sultan, an important figure in Indian and Islamic history. The first head, encrusted with diamonds, emeralds and rubies, had been discovered in a long-forgotten trunk in Winnipeg, Canada, and auctioned several years earlier.

The buyer was a collector of Middle Eastern art and had offered Roark access to the one-of-a-kind documents in his private library if Roark could find the second leopard. The knowledge locked up in the collector's home was worth way more to Roark than the half million dollars that the man had originally offered as a finder's fee.

Roark's gaze swept the party guests until he located Ann Richardson. "I'd planned to leave New York in the next few days."

"That's not a good idea if you're at all concerned about the future of Waverly's."

Roark tensed as the jaws of responsibility clamped down on him. "I have business in Dubai."

"Do you think that leaving town is a good idea while the FBI is interested in you?" George Cromwell nodded sagely at Roark's scowl. "Stay in New York. Demonstrate that your personal life has stabilized."

"Stabilized how?"

"Your romantic exploits are legendary. If you could settle down with one woman, that would convince everyone you're the man we need at the helm."

Roark ignored the sensation of a noose being tossed over his head and kept his body relaxed. Settle down with the love of his life. Not so easy for a man whose one true passion involved dangerous, globe-hopping adventures. No woman, no matter how lush, blonde and adorable, could compete with the thrill of discovering what had been lost for centuries.

But the prospects of Waverly's depended on his ability to project a stable, reliable image. What he needed was a woman who could play the part of his adoring girlfriend. Someone who understood this was for the good of Waverly's.

That way, when it ended, he wouldn't need to worry about breaking her heart.

Roark grinned. "It's funny you should bring this up now because I've been seeing someone for a while and we're very close to taking our relationship public."

"Wonderful." The board member covered his surprise with a relieved smile. "Bring her around for dinner tomorrow night and we'll discuss your future in more detail."

"We'll be there."

"Looking forward to it. What's your lady's name?"

"Elizabeth." Roark glanced toward the screened-off section of the loft. If he had to be settled down by a woman, he intended to choose one who intrigued him. "Elizabeth Minerva."

Two

Elizabeth barely noticed the exuberant buzz filling the offices of Josie Summers's Event Planning as she navigated the halls. A large coffee clutched in her hand, she thanked the coworkers who congratulated her on the success of the previous night's wine auction. Normally, the well wishes perked her up. She'd worked hard to become Josie's top earner and enjoyed the prestige it brought her.

Success had come easily since she had started immersing herself in her work a year ago, to keep despair at bay after her sister's death. If she was busy, she had no time to fall prey to the depression that lurked in the shadows. It wasn't long before she discovered that running herself into a state of exhaustion wasn't something she could do forever.

She needed a personal life, but thanks to her rotten taste in men, dating brought her more heartache than happiness.

What had struck her hard after losing her sister, brother-in-law and niece in a car accident was how alone she was. Her parents had moved from upstate New York to Oregon right as Elizabeth started her freshman year of college. In the seven years they'd been gone, they'd never returned to the East coast. It was as if with both their children grown, they'd started this whole new life for themselves.

When they'd first announced that they were moving Elizabeth had been bothered by their abandonment. But after she moved to New York City and started college, she'd fallen in love. Not with a man, but with the city. The excitement and the possibilities of living in such a wonderful place. And she'd never once felt lonely.

It had helped that her sister was a couple hours away by train. But with Stephanie's death, a hole had appeared in her heart. What she wanted was a family. That's when she decided to make a family of her own. Unfortunately, as fabulously as her career was progressing, things on the baby front weren't going so well. Two rounds of in vitro had failed.

She was all out of money. Her dreams of motherhood wouldn't be coming true this year.

Elizabeth's heart wrenched in dismay.

She should be flying high. Last night's triumph was yet another step upward professionally. She was crossing career goals off her list ahead of schedule. But what good did all her success do her when the reason she was working so hard was to provide for the child her body refused to conceive?

Maybe if she'd been more positive during the second in vitro try. Kept her hopes up. Spent her days and nights visualizing a baby in her arms rather than bracing herself for disappointment. Maybe then things would have turned out better.

If her sister could hear her thoughts, she'd agree. Stephanie had been an advocate for positive thinking since she was a freshman in high school. Top of her class. Head cheerleader. Captain of the women's volleyball team the year they won state. Whatever Stephanie visualized, she made happen.

And what would her sister say about Elizabeth's pity party for one? Stephanie would tell her to pull out a piece of paper and write her goal at the top, then list all the things she could do to move forward.

Elizabeth settled her purse in a drawer and hung up her coat. Flopping into her desk chair, she set a yellow legal pad in front of her and wrote *Motherhood* at the top. Below that she doodled dollar signs.

How to afford more in vitro treatments? Save money until she could afford to try again. Economizing wasn't the answer. She already lived in the smallest apartment she could stand, a tiny studio in Chelsea with a view of the neighboring building's wall. What she needed to do was increase her income. And the fastest way to do that? Demand that Josie make her a partner. She was already bringing in more money than all of Josie's other planners combined. It was time she reaped some of the benefits of all her hard work.

Feeling more determined than when she'd left her apartment an hour ago, Elizabeth headed for her boss's office. With each step she took, she gained confidence in her plan.

It was the perfect opportunity to make her pitch. Last night's party had been a huge success. She'd made a dozen contacts and fielded interest from at least eight people who wanted her to help with their holiday parties. Her career was about to go from fast track to supersonic.

"Josie, do you have a second?"

The fifty-eight-year-old head of Josie Summers's Event Planning sat like a queen on a cream damask sofa in her enormous corner office. A silver tray with an elegant coffee-pot sat on the low table before her. On the round table that stood halfway between the door and her boss's ornate cherry desk was a vase overflowing with the most gorgeous long-stemmed red roses Elizabeth had ever seen. Things must be going better between Josie and her boyfriend of twelve years.

Her boss waved Elizabeth in. "Darling, we're a triumph."

"Everyone seemed to enjoy themselves," Elizabeth said. "The auction raised three million for children's cancer research." She sat beside Josie and accepted the cup of coffee her boss handed her. "Kendra called me this morning and said her boss was pleased with our handling of the event."

Even though Josie hadn't been involved with any aspect of the planning, she claimed credit for every success.

"Well, I should say so." Josie crossed her legs and leaned forward to pour coffee into a second china cup. She sipped and eyed Elizabeth over the rim. "Josie Summers's Event Planning offers nothing but sublime perfection."

"Absolutely." Having her boss take credit for her successes didn't sit well with Elizabeth, but she needed her job and wanted to keep it.

Until coming to work for Josie, she'd never been one to tout her accomplishments. She'd always done her best without expecting anyone to praise her. But it hadn't taken more than six months in the cutthroat world of event planning for her to realize that if she wanted to get ahead, she not only needed to be the best, she had to make sure everyone knew it.

"I've already received a half dozen calls this morning about upcoming events thanks to the work we did last night." The diamonds in Josie's ears winked. "Josie Summers's Event Planning is the best in New York. It's about time everyone recognized that."

Thanks to all Elizabeth's hard work. She forced a smile. "That's great. And part of what I wanted to talk to you about this morning…"

"Oh, and those came for you." Josie indicated the roses. "They were delivered to me by mistake."

Elizabeth regarded the extravagant bouquet. She felt oddly light-headed. It was the sort of thing a man sent the woman he loved. "For me?"

Josie picked up a small white card and handed it to Elizabeth. "Another admirer, from the looks of it."

Stifling her resentment that her boss had already read the

card, Elizabeth slid it out of the envelope and stared at the bold script.

I have a proposal I'd like to discuss with you. RB

She had no trouble imagining the sort of *proposal* Roark Black had in mind. Proposition was more like it. Remembering the way his gaze had slipped over her last night, heat rushed into her cheeks. Conscious of her boss's avid curiosity, she mastered her expression and held very still. Difficult when she wanted to run from the room and the implications of that message. But fleeing would do her no good when the danger lay inside her. The searing curiosity about the enigmatic treasure hunter. What would it be like to have those mobile lips capture hers? His hands gliding over her skin as if she was a priceless artifact he'd been searching for all his life?

"Elizabeth?"

"Hmm?"

Josie's voice held amusement. "Who is RB?"

She dug her nails into her palm to disperse the sensual fog that she'd gotten lost in. Lying would do her no good. Josie's curiosity was fully engaged. She would dig until she was satisfied she knew everything that was going on with Elizabeth.

"Roark Black."

"Really?" Interest flared in Josie's brown eyes. "I didn't realize you knew him."

"He was at the wine auction last night." Elizabeth could see her boss jump to the wrong conclusion. "He was impressed with the work I'd done for the party. Perhaps he wants to hire me."

"This is a first," Josie purred, her opinion about the true reason for the bouquet already formed. "I've never seen two dozen red roses accompany a job offer before."

"Mr. Black is a unique individual."

"With unique tastes, I imagine."

Elizabeth responded with a tight smile. "I'd better go give

him a call." She stood, eager to escape her boss's keen gaze. She was halfway to the door when Josie stopped her.

"Don't forget your roses."

"Silly me," Elizabeth said, her teeth gritted together.

"And let me know what he has in mind. This is the opening I've been waiting for. A chance to move Josie Summers's Event Planning into a whole new level. Event planner to the rich and famous."

"Thanks to me," Elizabeth muttered into the sumptuous roses.

It wasn't until she returned to her office that she realized Roark Black's *proposal* had distracted her from her plan to ask Josie about making her a partner. How much longer was she going to build Josie's business without getting the rewards she deserved?

Setting the roses on her desk, Elizabeth perched on one of her guest chairs and dialed the number on the back of Roark's card.

"Hello, Elizabeth."

His deep voice, rich with amusement, sent a tingle up her spine. With two words he'd sparked a chain reaction inside her. She flopped back in the chair and closed her eyes to better concentrate on his seductive voice.

"Hello, Mr. Black," she responded, her tone less professional than she wanted. "Thank you for the roses."

"Roark," he corrected, his tone somewhere between a command and a request. "I'm glad you like them."

She hadn't said that. "They're beautiful."

"Beautiful roses for a beautiful lady."

His smooth compliments were having a detrimental effect on her professionalism. Flutters attacked her stomach. Warmth flooded her as delight scampered along her nerve endings. Her body appeared to have a mind of its own, wanting to curl up in the chair and cradle the phone like some smitten teenager.

"The card mentioned you had a job for me?"

"A proposal," he corrected, caressing the word.

"What sort of proposal?"

"I'd like to discuss it in person."

And she'd prefer to arrange everything over the phone so his enticing sex appeal wouldn't prove her undoing. "Would you like to come to my office this afternoon?"

"I was thinking perhaps you could meet me at my apartment. Say in an hour?"

"Your apartment…" She trailed off, at a loss for words since she didn't dare accuse him of hitting on her when she wasn't completely sure what was going on.

"Don't you visit a client's apartment when you're planning a party for them?"

"You want me to plan a party?" Her relief came through loud and clear.

"Of course." He sounded amused. "What did you think I wanted?"

The arrogance of the man.

Elizabeth fumed for about five seconds and then reminded herself that this was business and she was a businesswoman. She'd worked with demanding clients before. Just because Roark Black was sinfully handsome and dangerously exciting was no reason to let her baser instincts get the better of her. He was a client. Nothing more.

"An hour and a half," she countered, feeling ridiculous the second the words were out of her mouth. It was silly to try to play power games with this man when all he had to do was hit her with his crooked grin and every sensible thought fled her mind.

"I'll text you my address."

At one minute to ten, she stood outside Roark's loft in Soho. She recognized her nerves had gotten the better of her when she'd gone home to change into a sweater dress in a silvery blue. She loved the color. It intensified the gold tones of her hair and drew out the flecks of cobalt in her eyes. But most important, the outfit gave her confidence.

Briefcase clutched before her, weight on the balls of her feet, she awaited the appearance of the first man in a year who'd imperiled her no-bad-boys edict. Pulse hammering, she dredged up every hurt and disappointment caused by the men she'd chosen over the years. Remembering past injuries took the edge off her unwelcome excitement at seeing Roark again.

And then, the door opened, revealing him in all his male splendor. He was dressed casually in worn denim and a long-sleeved gray shirt that intensified the smoky tones in his eyes.

"Elizabeth." Her name sighed out of him like a lover's exhalation. "You are even more beautiful than I remembered."

Crap. Her heart fluttered like some idiotic debutant at her first cotillion.

"And you are more charming than ever." Her voice snapped like a whip, snatching the compliment right out of the words.

He grinned at her, unfazed by her tartness. "Come in."

The loft was as incredible as she'd expected. Sixteen-foot ceilings, enormous arched windows, exposed brick everywhere she looked. Wood floors gleamed beneath couches slip-covered in white. The living space was so huge he was able to have three separate sitting areas. One flanked the stone fireplace at the far end. One clustered in front of the floor-to-ceiling bookshelves near an opening that she guessed led to the bedrooms. A third near the open kitchen with its dark granite countertops and stainless-steel appliances.

"This is nice," Elizabeth murmured, reflecting on the shoebox she lived in. "Perfect for entertaining. How many people are you inviting?"

"I was thinking about a hundred or so."

Elizabeth pulled out an electronic tablet and began jotting notes. "Did you have a date picked out?"

"I was thinking next Saturday."

"That is short notice."

Mentally running through her bookings, she keyed up her schedule, already knowing she had the Hendersons' tenth wedding anniversary on that evening. The arrangements were all made. It was the sort of party Brenda could handle on her own.

"I'm happy to compensate you for any inconvenience it might cause."

Elizabeth offered him a bright smile as she mentally calculated her commission. "What sort of party did you have in mind?"

"It's an engagement party."

"How nice." And how surprising. She'd never pictured Roark Black hosting something like that. The man had commitment issues written all over him. "Who's the lucky couple?"

"We are."

Incomprehension fogged her indigo-blue eyes as she looked up at him. "We are what?"

"The happy engaged couple I'm throwing the party for."

Her crisp professionalism wrinkled beneath the weight of her confusion. "We're not engaged."

"Not yet."

The expression in her eyes went from shell-shocked to resolute. "Not ever."

"I'm crushed." He shouldn't enjoy teasing her so much, but it seemed the only way to get past her guards and reach the woman behind the event planner.

"I doubt it." She'd recovered her equilibrium and now regarded him with open skepticism. "Perhaps you should explain what's going on."

"Last night you jumped all over me about how I was going to be the downfall of Waverly's."

"I merely suggested you might be a contributing factor."

"You weren't the only one thinking that way."

Her eyes narrowed. "Not surprising. But what does that have to do with why I'm here?"

"A certain member of the Waverly's board mentioned that he's been approached by Dalton Rothschild about selling his shares and has been asked to persuade others on the board to follow suit. He doesn't want Rothschild to take over Waverly's, but needs a good reason to continue to support the current leadership at Waverly's."

She nodded, but remained silent while her steady gaze encouraged him to proceed.

"He thinks that leadership needs to include me, but recent events have raised questions about my activities. He indicated if I could demonstrate that I'm leaving behind my proclivity for trouble, the board would feel more confident about the stability of Waverly's."

"And you think an engagement will make you more respectable."

"It was suggested a stable personal life would inspire confidence in my upstanding behavior."

"Why me?"

While his address book was bursting with women who would jump at the chance to play his fiancée, Elizabeth was unaffected by his money or his charm. She intrigued him.

"After last night's passionate denouncement of me and your concern for the future of Waverly's, I thought you would be the perfect choice for a pretend engagement."

His last two words caused a profound reaction. Her muscles relaxed and she almost smiled. "Find someone else."

"I've already decided on you."

"Surely there are more suitable women in the circles you frequent that would be happy to perpetrate this ruse with you."

"None more suitable than you." And he meant it.

The concern she'd shown for Waverly's had inspired him to make her his co-conspirator in his scheme to improve his image. And the active dislike she was struggling so hard to maintain intrigued him. Winning her over presented an enchanting challenge. And if he was going to be stuck in New York for the uncertain future, he would need something exciting to occupy himself. Elizabeth Minerva fit the bill.

"Does it strike you at all counterproductive that you're trying to inspire confidence in your upstanding behavior by presenting a fake fiancée to your friends and family?"

"See, this is why I need you. Not one other woman I know dives straight to the heart of my shortcomings the way you do."

Her full lips twitched. "And somehow you perceive this as a good thing?"

Despite her skepticism, Elizabeth hadn't slammed the door on his proposition. Or at least, she hadn't stormed out of his loft and put an end to the conversation. If he could keep her around for a few more minutes, he knew he could convince her how much he needed her help.

"Last night you were right. Waverly's is in trouble. Dalton Rothschild is after the board members to sell. I'm in a perfect position to stop him." He hit her with all the seriousness in his arsenal. "And you are in a perfect position to help me do so. Think of what will happen to all the employees who've been with Waverly's for years. If Rothschild takes over, what do you think he's going to do with them?"

"You aren't playing fair." Her gaze skidded away from his.

At that moment, he knew he had her. "We'll make this a business arrangement. Consider it a contract job. Six months and you're free of me. In the meantime, think of all the contacts you'll make as my fiancée. Manhattan's elite will be vying to have you as their event planner."

"A business arrangement," she echoed, eyes narrowing as she searched his expression. "Nothing more?"

"Well, of course there will be public appearances and equally public displays of affection."

She chewed on her lower lip, attention fixed on the far side of the room where floating shelves housed some of the less valuable artifacts he'd brought back from around the world.

"But just public displays of affection. Don't expect to reap any benefits of our engagement in private."

Keeping her in the dark about all his intentions was completely necessary if he hoped to secure her agreement. There would be plenty of time later to demonstrate all the ways their arrangement could be mutually beneficial.

"I promise not to do anything you don't want me to."

Her brows came together. "That didn't answer my question."

"I assure you, anytime I'm involved in a relationship it's the women who have expectations, not me."

"No wonder people find you untrustworthy." Elizabeth shook her head. "You couldn't give a straight answer if your life depended on it."

"And I assure you, from time to time, it has."

"Let me be blunt. I'm not going to sleep with you."

"Who said anything about sleeping." He knew he should stop teasing her, but she was so damned adorable when she got riled up.

"If you think I'm some sort of weak-minded bimbo who will tumble into your bed at the first snap of your fingers, you've picked the wrong girl."

"Easy, sweetheart, I think you're no such thing. I fully expect you to resist me at every turn."

With her blue eyes snapping in ire, color flooding her cheeks and her soft lips parted to deliver scathing retorts, it took all his significant willpower not to draw her into his arms and take advantage of that simmering passion.

His facial muscles twitched as smiling became irresistible. "In fact, I'm counting on it."

Most single New York women would be flattered that Roark Black had chosen them to play the part of his fiancée.

Elizabeth suspected a whistle launched from his loft window would bring a dozen or so running. They'd scoff at her reluctance to get cozy with a handsome, eligible bachelor of Roark's financial and social standing even as they trampled her in their rush to vie for his attention.

Was she crazy to hesitate?

There'd been an intense light in his eye as he said he expected her to resist him at every turn that told her she was smart to be wary. Her heart hadn't stopped its distressed thumping the entire distance to Chinatown where her best friend lived. Allison and Elizabeth had been roommates freshman year and had bonded over their pathological need for organization and their mutual dislike of the girl across the hall, Honey Willingham.

"Elizabeth." The leggy woman with dark blond hair and dark circles under her eyes looked at her with delight. "Your timing is perfect. I just got Prince Gregory down for his nap."

"Sorry to stop by without calling." Since Allison had given birth five months ago, Elizabeth hadn't seen her friend more than once a month. To Elizabeth's shame, it stung that Allison was so happy being a mom when Elizabeth struggled to conceive.

"No. It's fine. I'm happy to take any time you can spare."

Her friend didn't mean anything by the remark, but Elizabeth flinched anyway. "I'm a terrible friend."

"No. You're just busy."

So was Allison. She had her hands full with a colicky baby, but she managed to call three times a week. Elizabeth felt even worse.

"How's Greg?"

"Getting better." Allison led Elizabeth into the tiny kitchen and fetched a couple diet sodas out of the refrigerator. "He sleeps almost four hours a night now."

"Yikes."

Elizabeth tried to imagine how she was going to make

things work on her own with a baby and no help. She glanced around the kitchen. Dishes were piled in the sink and baby bottles sat upside down in a drying rack. Beyond the break-fast bar, where once there had been a pristine living room with glass tables, expensive accent pieces and tons of plants, only the black leather couch remained and it was piled with a basket of unfolded baby clothes. Colorful toys and a baby swing competed for space on the hardwood floors.

"Can I babysit for you and Keith one night? Maybe you could go out for a nice dinner?"

Allison looked so hopeful, Elizabeth's heart clenched.

"That would be great. Get you ready for your own bundle of joy." This last was said with such weariness that Elizabeth wondered if her envy over her friend's perfect life had been a tad off base. Gasping, Allison leaned forward and grabbed Elizabeth's hands. Her eyes burned with hope. "Is that why you're here? To tell me you're pregnant?"

"No." Elizabeth shook her head. "The last round didn't take."

"Damn." Allison's mouth turned down at the corners. "I'm so sorry. What are you going to do?"

"Try again."

"But I thought you didn't have enough money."

"I'm going to ask Josie to make me a partner."

Allison blew out a breath. "Good luck with that." She looked immediately contrite. "I'm sorry. That wasn't what you needed to hear. How are you going to approach it?"

In the face of Allison's doubt, Elizabeth pushed aside her frustration and squared her shoulders. "I just handled my first A-list party and it was a huge success. All sorts of bookings are coming in and they all want me."

"How wonderful. Does Josie know they all want you?"

On the topic of Elizabeth's career, Allison had all sorts of strong opinions about Josie Summers. All of them negative.

"In her own way, she knows." But that didn't mean Josie would ever admit it.

"You could quit," Allison suggested with a far too innocent expression. "Start your own event planning company."

"You know I can't do that." It was a conversation she and Allison had engaged in often in the past three years.

"I know you're afraid to do that."

"I like the security of a job with a steady paycheck."

Allison didn't appear convinced by Elizabeth's determined tone. "You could put off having a baby for a couple years while you get your business going."

Elizabeth rejected her friend's suggestion with a firm shake of her head. "I'd rather put up with Josie for the next five years than wait to have a baby."

"You're so sensible." The baby monitor on the counter next to the sink erupted with cries. Allison stared at the device and held her breath as if even that small noise would further disturb the restless child.

"Do you need to go check on him?"

"No. He should settle down." But the cries became more insistent and Allison heaved a weary sigh. "I guess fifteen minutes is going to be all he can handle today. I don't know why he doesn't collapse with exhaustion. I'm tired and he gets less sleep than I do. I'll be right back."

Elizabeth expected to have to finish her conversation with Allison over the wails of the baby, but almost as soon as she vanished into her son's room, the monitor stopped emitting noise. She returned with her son in her arms.

"Can you hold this momma's boy for a second?" Without waiting for Elizabeth to answer, Allison handed her the baby. "I swear he lives to drive me crazy. Just like his father." The last she muttered, the words almost intelligible, but Elizabeth heard.

And grinned.

She buried her nose in the baby's neck and inhaled his

scent. This is what she was working toward. Why she'd accept Roark's offer to pretend to be his fiancée. She needed to bring in more clients and strengthen her position as Josie's top producer. Becoming a partner would assure her financial security and she could afford to try in vitro again.

Her phone vibrated, reminding Elizabeth that she had work to do. As much as she wished she could linger for the rest of the afternoon, there were clients to contact and arrangements to oversee. If she was gone too long from the office, Brenda might take it upon herself to organize something and that would be extremely bad.

The sun fell across Elizabeth's shoulders as she made her way to the nearest subway station. Visiting Allison's domestic haven had done her good. The parts of her psyche that had seemed frantic and out of control were calmer. She was thinking clearly instead of freaking out. Before she headed down the stairs to catch her train, she pulled out her cell phone.

Almost as if he'd been expecting her call, Roark picked up before the second ring.

"Okay, Mr. Black, we have a deal."

"Just like that?" Despite his words, he almost purred with satisfaction. "We haven't even discussed what you want in return."

"All I want is the chance to make the sort of connections that will further my career."

"And you'll meet plenty of people who will want to hire you. But I'm going to take up a significant amount of your time and I intend to compensate you for it."

"How much time?"

"To be credible we need to be seen together four hours a night, twice maybe three times a week for six months. Twenty thousand dollars is a nice round number, don't you think?"

She stared at the sky and blinked back a sudden rush of tears. Her relief was so profound, for a moment she couldn't breathe. With that much money she could afford to try in vitro again almost immediately. A twinge of conscience returned her to reality.

"That's too much. I wouldn't feel comfortable."

"The money is for your time, nothing more."

And although every one of her brain cells told her she was crazy, in her heart, she believed him. "It's still too much."

"Very well." A hint of exasperation entered his tone. "What sort of number did you have in mind?"

"Thirteen thousand, four hundred twenty-eight dollars and ninety-seven cents."

A long hesitation followed her words. When he spoke, his voice was rich with laughter. "Are you sure you don't want that rounded up to twenty-nine dollars?"

"No, thank you."

"Care to share what you're going to do with that particular sum?"

She smiled as she imagined the look on his face as she said, "I'm going to use it to get pregnant."

Three

A brisk November wind snatched at Elizabeth's breath as she exited the town car and stared up at the Fifth Avenue apartment building. She shivered in her wool coat. Nine hours ago she'd agreed to Roark's mad scheme, proving once again that whenever she was in the presence of a bad boy, she and common sense took divergent paths.

Roark lifted her hand and brushed warm lips across her chilly fingers. "Have I told you how beautiful you look?"

Several times. "Are you sure everyone is going to believe we're a couple?"

"They will if we seem smitten with each other."

"Smitten." The old-fashioned word struck her as odd coming from someone as masculine as Roark.

"Can you do smitten?"

Given the way her pulse fluttered in giddy delight every time he flashed his wolfish grin, she was pretty sure all she had to do was let nature take its course. "I guess."

"Just follow my lead." He tucked her hand into the crook of his arm and led the way into the building.

The urge to gape at the building's opulent entry almost overpowered her nervousness about the dinner party. It wouldn't do for her to act like some rustic just off the farm. She'd been in New York City since graduating from high school and had planned parties for many wealthy people. But she was about to step up to the big time. Any false move and she would have wasted her chance.

"How exactly are we going to break up?"

Roark shot her a wry glance. "We just started going out and you're already thinking about how things are going to end?"

"A girl has to be practical." So she claimed. Too bad she'd never been able to behave sensibly when it came to her love life.

"Why don't you forget about being practical for a while?"

"Tempting." She offered him a counterfeit smile. "But unrealistic. This is a business deal, remember?"

"I doubt I could forget with you reminding me every ten minutes," he mused. They'd stopped before a door. "Can we discuss the demise of our relationship on the way home?"

"Of course."

A woman in her early forties, wearing a maid's uniform, opened the door for them. Elizabeth stepped through and slipped out of her best winter coat. Because Roark was using her to tone down his reputation as a ladies' man, she wore a conservative wrap dress the color of claret.

With her hair's natural wave flattened by a straight iron and her grandmother's simple garnet drops dangling from her ears, Elizabeth knew she presented a classic, elegant picture.

"Absolutely beautiful," Roark murmured as he placed his hand in the small of her back and escorted her toward the living room where the rest of the guests had gathered.

Their engagement might be a sham, but there was nothing phony about Roark's flattering words or his affectionate tone.

The chemistry between them was real. She felt the tug of it every time he took her hand or caressed her with his gaze.

Man, oh man, she was in trouble.

"Good evening, Roark. And this must be the woman who captured your heart. I can understand why. I'm George Cromwell."

Elizabeth recognized the man from the wine auction, but doubted he'd remember her. She worked hard to be a ghost at the events she planned. Always around, but invisible to the guests.

"Elizabeth Minerva," she said. "You have a lovely home."

"My wife has exceptional taste. She picked me after all." He laughed at his own joke. "Let me introduce you."

By the time dinner was announced, Elizabeth had become way too conscious of her tall, handsome companion. He wouldn't stop touching her. Simple brushes of his fingertips at her waist, his palm against the small of her back, his lips across her temple. Grazing contact that demonstrated his adoration for the benefit of all onlookers. If it had been any other man, Elizabeth would have endured it without a blip in her heart rate.

But Roark Black wasn't any other man. He was dangerous, charismatic and intelligent. A lethal combination where her common sense was concerned.

"I just love the way you two can't keep your eyes off each other," murmured Elizabeth's dinner companion. An elegant woman in her mid-fifties, she was on the board of several charities and had promised to call Elizabeth about upcoming events. "Roark is such a favorite of mine. I'm glad he found someone who makes him happy."

Elizabeth smiled to hide her dismay. It was way too easy to act like a woman in love with Roark. Before tonight she'd believed him to be nothing more than a bad boy who charmed women and left a trail of loneliness behind him. But she'd watched him impress everyone with his wit and wry humor and realized there was more to Roark than what the papers printed. Had she taken on more than she could handle?

"That went well," Roark commented as he handed her into the back of his black town car. "I think we managed to convince everyone that you've tamed me."

Her lips twitched. "You're mad if you think anyone believes you tamed."

"Perhaps you're right." Upon entering the car, he'd let his head fall back against the rich leather. Now, he glanced her way, his eyes sparkling. "But they all can see that I've been leashed by the power of my feelings for you."

Despite the fact that his words were completely untrue, Elizabeth couldn't stop the thrill they awakened. Her proclivity for bad boys had its roots in the fantasy that one day she'd meet one she could tame. It was a frustrating dilemma because she wasn't at all attracted to the good guys. They were boring. So what happened if she tamed a bad boy? Would she grow bored?

Elizabeth knew she'd never find out.

"Now can we discuss what happens when those feelings end?"

"You're like a terrier with a rat, aren't you? Pursuing the thing past the point of exhaustion."

She regarded him, unaffected by his mockery. "Something like that."

"Do you want me to be the villain?"

She wasn't completely sure if he was the hero, but he'd been placed in the role of bad guy far too often.

"Since the engagement is supposed to repair your reputation," she said, "that would be counterproductive. Can't we mutually decide it's not going to work?"

"I really think it would be better if you broke my heart." Roark took her hand and placed it on his chest.

Her emotions tumbled as his heart thumped hypnotically against her palm. "And why is that?"

"Because I don't want to ever hurt you."

The tone of the conversation had gone from flirtatious to serious so fast it took her brain a second to catch up.

"That's chivalrous of you." She tugged to free her hand, but not hard enough to break his grip.

His fingertips trailed along her cheek, setting her skin ablaze. "I mean it."

"I know you do," she assured him, pulling his hand from her face. "But you don't need to worry about me. I'll be just fine."

Roark stood in the middle of his living room and marveled. Chased out at eight that morning by the phalanx of workers that had descended on the loft, he'd stayed away until he could no longer bear the curiosity.

In seven hours, Elizabeth had transformed the monochromatic, sterile space into a Moroccan dream. Using the room's height, she'd fashioned a tent of sorts. Gold-shot, jewel-bright fabric, attached to the ceiling and walls, masked the room's industrial feel. She'd removed his white couches and replaced them with chaise lounges. A hundred pillows, all different sizes and colors, covered the plush oriental rugs. Three large punched-metal lamps hung down the center of the room, spilling soft light over the décor.

At the center of all the decadent color and texture stood Elizabeth, classically elegant in a simple navy pantsuit, her hair smoothed into her signature French roll, as she directed last-minute touches of lavish flower arrangements and bowls of apples, dragon fruit, mangos and star fruit.

The urge to ease her down onto a spill of floor pillows and mess up her perfection overtook him. In fact, he took three steps in her direction before he awoke to the realization that they were not alone in his loft. His intention must have been written all over his face because a slim brunette in her mid-thirties stared at him with wide eyes.

"Hello," he said, reeling in his lust. "I'm Roark Black."

"S-Sara Martin. I'm helping Elizabeth with your event."

At the sound of her name, Elizabeth turned and noticed him for the first time. Her serene satisfaction, so dissimilar to the chaotic emotions thundering through his body, increased his craving for her.

"What do you think?" Elizabeth questioned, obviously pleased by the results she'd achieved. "Hard to believe it's a loft in Soho, isn't it?"

The longing to feel a smidgeon of her delight caught him off guard. That whole stop-and-smell-the-roses thing had never been on his agenda. He'd jumped from one adventure to another without pause, almost as if he was running from something. What? Boredom? Loneliness?

What had he gained from his travels except for questions about his character and a bunch of trinkets?

"You've done a wonderful job."

"I hope your friends think so." The tiniest flicker of uncertainty clouded her deep blue eyes.

"They will love it." And her. Conscious of their audience, he stepped into her space and felt her muscles tense. "Relax," he murmured. "Everyone is going to know about us after tonight."

"I know." She lifted her chin and gave him a wobbly smile.

Her soft rosy lips practically demanded his attention, but he kissed her cheek instead, lingering over her fragrant skin, listening to the uneven cadence of her breath. He disturbed her. Good. That was only fair since she made him mad with wanting. He couldn't wait to set her on fire and lose himself in the moist welcome of her body. With effort Roark mastered the urgent craving to sweep her into his arms and mark her as his.

Time enough for that later.

"Can you take a break?"

She nodded. "The caterers should be here any minute, but Sara can supervise their setup."

"Wonderful. Let's go talk in my study. I have something for you."

He guided her into his favorite room in the loft, a cluttered space lined with overflowing bookshelves. It was here that he spent most of his time, surrounded by the ancient texts that helped him unlock secrets to treasures hidden for centuries.

Plucking a black box off a pile of photographs, he opened it to reveal her engagement ring. Her shocked silence lasted until he slid the three-carat diamond onto her finger.

"I've never worn anything so expensive."

"It suits you."

Her slender fingers appeared even more delicate weighted down with the thick band of diamonds. Roark rotated her hand and watched fire dance in the gems, enjoying the slight tremble of her fingers.

"It'll take some getting used to."

"The ring or me?"

Her lips quirked in a wry smile. "Both."

Before either of them saw it coming, he brushed his lips against hers, capturing her amusement for himself. His heart hammered against his ribs at her sharp *oh* of surprise. The texture of her lips fascinated him. He explored the plump contours with the same focus he might use when evaluating a precious artifact. This woman deserved to be treated with all the reverence he reserved for the things he pursued with such single-minded determination.

"Roark."

His name, whispered out of her, sparked his impatience. As lust sliced away at his control, he spread his fingers against the small of her back and drew her tight against his aching body. "Say it again."

She pulled back at his command, her torso arching. Passion-drenched and dreamy, her eyes met his. "What?"

"My name." He kissed her nose. "Just put a little more heat behind it." It was a dangerous request. His passion might be simmering now, but it wouldn't take much to push it into a roiling boil.

"Is this how you plan to be tonight?"

"And every night hereafter."

She rolled her eyes. "Roark." More a warning than a caress.

He hummed and shook his head. "No one's going to believe you're madly in love with me if you use that tone. Try again."

"Roark." Exasperated.

"They'll believe we're together if you sound impatient. But I had something more like this in mind." He cupped her face, snared her gaze and held her immobile with his steely will. "Elizabeth."

To his amusement, her eyes widened and her mouth popped open. He rarely spent time with women that couldn't handle his brand of seduction. Sophisticated women knew the score. Understood that he might be in it for the short-term, but that he would make it worth their while.

Elizabeth possessed an innocence that both captivated and concerned him. She hadn't signed up to be seduced. And it was all he could think about doing.

"Do women fall for that?"

Her question shattered the sensual mood.

He frowned. "What do you mean do women fall for that?"

"The sexy voice. The take-off-your-clothes look."

No one had ever called him on it before. "I've never had any complaints." He cocked his head and regarded her. "Why aren't you falling for it?"

Her lashes lowered, concealing the secrets in her eyes. "Because I'm wise to your type."

"My type?" Unsure whether to be amused or annoyed, he prompted, "What type is that?"

"Bad boys."

"How is it you're immune?"

"Fool me once, shame on you," she quipped. "Fool me twice, shame on me."

"The best way to learn is by making mistakes."

"And yet I continue to make them. It's pretty apparent I have terrible judgment where men are concerned."

This intrigued him. She gave the appearance of a woman who knew exactly what she wanted and went after it. "Forgive me if I don't believe that."

"It's true." She twirled the diamond ring on her finger, but he could see her mind was far from the jewelry. "In high school, college and a year ago. The last one was the worst. I really believed if I loved him enough he would settle down and want to be a husband and a father." A harsh laugh broke from her, filled with self-loathing. "It was idiotic of me to believe he could change, that he might care enough about me to change. A scorpion is a scorpion. They behave according to their nature."

"If you want to get married and have kids why not pick the sort of man that wants the same thing?"

"Because those aren't the ones I'm attracted to." Her eyes were cool as they met his. "As much as I fought against it, I couldn't stop falling for unavailable men. The ones who don't show up when they're supposed to. Who forget to call you. Can't remember birthdays or special occasions."

Roark knew he'd been guilty of every one of those things at one point or another. How many women had become disillusioned with love because of him?

"But despite every disappointment, I didn't leave because occasionally there's a brief, exciting moment when he'd focus on me and for a while everything would be all right. And when the moment ended, I would spend all my energy trying to make it happen again. Eventually I decided that if the only man I want is bad for me, I'm just not going to be with anyone."

The shadows in her eyes bothered him. "I'm sorry those men hurt you."

She shrugged. "I let it happen. But never again. I'm done with bad boys. Done with disappointment. From now on, I'm going to focus on what I want. A fabulous career and motherhood."

And heaven help the man that got in the way.

Still disturbingly light-headed from Roark's intoxicating kiss, Elizabeth wiggled into the strapless silver sheath she'd bought for her "engagement" party, wondering what had possessed her to lay out her past romantic troubles for Roark. She could have acted the part of his fiancée for six months and kept things strictly business between them. Instead, she'd been so rattled by his seductive power that she'd been compelled to toss an overabundance of obstacles in his path.

She was a fool for panicking.

Flirting was like breathing to a playboy like Roark. As natural to him as following a scent was to a hound. She needn't worry about being the target of his chase. They had a business arrangement. She would just have to keep reminding him about that.

Hair up or down? She regarded her reflection in the bathroom mirror as she smoothed a comb through her blond curls. Did her eyes seem brighter tonight? Perhaps she was dazzled by the size of the diamond on her left hand? She admired the ring. Its heavy awkwardness on her finger reminded her of the weight of what she was doing with Roark. No one must suspect they weren't a happily engaged couple.

Could she put on a good enough show?

Lying wasn't something that came easy to her. Maybe if she simply lost herself in the fantasy of being the woman he adored. At least for a few hours a couple nights a week. As long as she lived in the real world by day, everything should work out just fine.

Or so she hoped.

Roark's guests had arrived while she primped. If she'd lingered overly long over her appearance, she could blame it on wanting to make a good impression on his friends. But in fact, she was grappling with her conscience and a minor case of nerves.

This would be the first party she'd organized where remaining invisible wasn't part of her job description. It was an odd sensation to walk into a room full of people and feel a dozen pairs of eyes bore into her.

As if aware of her discomfort, Roark intercepted her before she'd taken three steps into the room. He pulled her into his arms and kissed her lightly on the mouth.

"Breathtaking," he murmured, following up the first brush of his lips with a second, less fleeting contact. "Let's tell everyone to go home so I can have you all to myself."

His gaze gripped hers, deadly serious, but he'd raised his voice loud enough so those around him could hear. Elizabeth's heart jerked in her chest, but she pasted on a bright smile.

"Stop that," she scolded, keeping her tone light. It disturbed her how much she enjoyed his obvious desire for her. She couldn't let the chemistry between them flare. Playing along with his charade was one thing. Falling for his shenanigans would only leave her heart bruised when they parted. "What will your guests think?"

"That I haven't spent nearly enough time alone with you."

She put her hand on his cheek. "We can rectify that later."

His nostrils flared. Eyes widened in surprise and appreciation. He caught her hand and placed a searing kiss in the palm. Like when he'd traced her head line at the wine auction party, her body burst into glorious life.

"I'm counting on it."

Despite the fact that she knew this was for the benefit

of the people who'd been invited to the party so they could spread the word of Roark's engagement, for a couple seconds she had a hard time catching her breath.

Damn the man for being so convincing. She was starting to believe their charade.

"In the meantime, could you introduce me to some of your friends."

She knew her color was high as Roark drew her toward the first knot of guests. The next hour flew by in a blur of names and faces. Many she recognized. Keeping up on the society pages made sense for an ambitious party planner. A few she didn't recognize. About halfway around the room, Elizabeth realized Roark's guest list included almost all the board members from Waverly's. Since his goal was to put a positive spin on his personal life, naturally, his engagement party would include the people he needed to sway.

Given her coworkers' shock when she'd announced her engagement to Roark and their countless questions about why she'd been keeping such a juicy secret, Elizabeth had expected similar reactions from Roark's guests. To her surprise, everyone had greeted her warmly.

Well, not quite everyone.

Hostility radiated from a sultry, dark-eyed woman in her early twenties. She'd arrived late on the arm of an equally tall and striking young man who must be her brother—such was the resemblance between them. The exotic attractiveness of the pair snared the interest of those assembled.

"Who is that?" she asked Roark, indicating the beauty.

"Sabeen. And her brother Darius. He's the reason I spent the last three months in the Amazon."

Was it her imagination or did Roark sound disgruntled? "I thought you were there because you'd run into trouble with local drug lords."

"Darius ran into trouble. I went there to get him out of it."

"What was he doing in South America?"

"Looking for a temple I'd mentioned seeing years ago. It happens to be in a territory occupied by a very dangerous man."

"So, he's an antiquities hunter like you."

"No, he's not like me. He was after treasure that he intended to sell and become rich." A crease appeared between Roark's brows.

"Did he find the temple?"

"No. He was captured first." Roark grimaced. "I warned him what the temple held wasn't worth risking his life."

"Then why did he go?"

"He's in love with a girl. They grew up next door to each other in Cairo. Her father refuses to let them marry. He's ambitious and wants to marry his daughter to a very wealthy man. Darius hoped that by selling what he found in the temple he could become rich enough to change her father's mind."

"That's very romantic."

Roark shot her a dubious glance. "It's foolish. And he continues to pine for Fadira even though he can never have her."

"Maybe the father will change his mind."

"It's too late. While we were in Columbia, her father arranged her marriage. The wedding is set for the end of the month."

"Someone rich?"

Roark nodded. "And powerful. Sheikh Mallik Khouri of Rayas."

Elizabeth's head spun. "Doesn't his family own the missing Gold Heart statue?"

"Yes."

"Is this just a huge coincidence, or…" Elizabeth was gripped by a strong sense of foreboding.

Roark's expression was grim. "I don't know."

She mulled the situation, sensing there was something Roark was holding back.

"But Fadira's not married yet," she insisted, rooting for

Darius to get his heart's desire. "There's still a chance for love to conquer all."

"It doesn't work that way."

Elizabeth could see she was wasting her breath trying to convince Roark that love wasn't a crazy, imprudent emotion. Her attention shifted back to Darius, and discovered Sabeen's gaze on her. Contempt flickered in their dark depths.

To feel that much hostility from a stranger put Elizabeth on full alert. "What about Sabeen?" Elizabeth cursed the tight tone in her voice.

"What about her?"

"Is there a reason why she looks as if she'd like to crush me like a bug?"

"Don't read anything into it. She can be volatile. I'm sure all you're seeing is that she's annoyed with me for springing this engagement on her."

Elizabeth searched his bland expression, sensing that he wasn't telling her everything. Did Sabeen's antagonism stem from jealousy? How close were she and Roark? What had Elizabeth gotten in the middle of?

"Why didn't you ask for her help?"

His lips twitched. Amusement brightened his eyes as his gaze captured hers. He lifted her hand to his lips. "Because I can't trust her."

The implication being he could trust Elizabeth. Her traitorous heart skipped in delight until his next words.

"She's far too passionate. She'd get swept up in the romance. I'd never get her to accept that the engagement was a business arrangement."

"She's in love with you." Elizabeth's spirits dipped.

He shrugged, but didn't deny her claim. "I knew her father for twenty years. He taught me Arabic and Persian. He was a brilliant man. Everything I know about Middle Eastern antiquities I learned from him. Before he died, he asked me to look after his children."

Only they weren't children. They were a passionate, sultry woman ripe for love and an adventure-seeking young man who looked like he was bursting with boredom at such a tame event as this.

"They don't appear as if they need looking after."

Roark's lips quirked. "Looks can be deceiving. Earlier this year I chased off a fortune hunter. She loses all common sense when it comes to love."

"Good thing she has you around to teach her how to be sensible." Elizabeth rolled the engagement ring around her finger.

"Are you trying to tell me something?"

"Only that you seem to have an overabundance of skepticism about falling in love."

"It's not skepticism," he retorted. "It's practicality. Few women are going to be happy with a man who's gone most of the year. They need constancy, want a partner. I can't provide either."

Was he warning her off? If so, he was wasting his breath. She recognized his type. Exciting. Challenging. But in the end, unavailable.

"And I'm not in the market for a man in my life," she spoke more to herself than him.

"So you say."

"So I mean." Elizabeth made sure he recognized the firm determination in her expression before she continued. "I won't deny you are exactly the type I used to go for, but those days are behind me. All I want now is to become a mother and excel as an event planner. I'm done with romance." With men, she added silently.

"Pity." Half-lidded, his striking eyes perused her body with sensual intensity. "I have plans for you."

"What?" A startled laugh escaped her at his bluntness. Her skin tingled as if he'd touched her. The sensation delighted her even as her mind scolded her for succumbing to his flirtation. "What sort of plans?" She winced at the husky timber of her voice. Damn the man for being so appealing.

A slow, predatory grin curved his chiseled lips. "Why don't you stick around after the party and I'll give you a preview."

Wicked man.

"Why don't you just tell me now."

"Because a demonstration is worth a thousand words," he quipped. "And I think we would scandalize this staid group if I showed you what I had in mind for you."

"You seem pretty sure of yourself." *Stop flirting with the man.* "What if I'm immune to your charm?"

He brushed his fingertips down her bare arm, thumb grazing the side of her breast. She gasped. Her nipples hardened in anticipation.

"Are you?"

A ragged breath escaped her. "Apparently parts of me are not."

"It's those parts I'm interested in." He bent his head and kissed her cheek, his lips gentle and cooler than her overheated skin.

She was in trouble if he could set fire to her with nothing more than a series of provocative declarations. "And here I thought you wanted me for my keen mind."

"I like my women well-rounded."

Before she could reply to his double entendre they were approached by George Cromwell and his wife, Bunny. Despite knowing that impressing the socialite would help open doors in the future, Elizabeth had a hard time focusing on the impeccably dressed woman as she congratulated them on their engagement. Roark's right palm rested on her hip, his fingers cupping her curves possessively. His solid presence bathed her left side in warmth. Relaxing into his strength would be the easiest thing in the world. Her body was already melting against the hard planes of his muscular frame.

"What a beautiful ring," Bunny exclaimed, giving Elizabeth's hand a little turn so she could admire the diamond. She shot Roark a questioning look. "A family heirloom?"

"Only the diamond. It came from my grandmother's wedding ring. Elizabeth is a modern woman," he said, bestowing a wry smile on her. "I knew she would prefer a modern setting."

"A blend of old and new." Bunny nodded in complete understanding. "It's perfect."

As the conversation shifted to the inevitable questions of whether they'd set a wedding date and where they intended to marry, Elizabeth dodged specifics as best she could and smiled up at Roark, all the while hiding her dismay at the deception she'd allowed herself to become entangled in.

Roark must have sensed her disquiet because he gave her a gentle squeeze and kissed her cheek. "You're doing great," he murmured.

A second earlier she'd been ready to break free and run screaming from the room. With his words, some of her anxiety eased. And permitted her to notice a disastrous sensation. Delight. She hummed with it. Deep inside her, where an abundance of foolish inclinations frolicked, she was giddy over Roark's attentiveness and swamped with the longing to feel his strong hands roam over her body.

Her mind rebelled. This was the exact sort of thing she needed to guard against. Easier said than done.

After the party, when all the guests had departed and the catering crew had cleaned up and left, Elizabeth stood in the middle of the living room and told her racing heart to slow down. Every fond glance Roark had sent her way for the benefit of the board members had carried a sensual promise with it. Even from the opposite end of the room, she'd been caressed by his intent.

"Alone at last," he said, coming up behind her. His fingertips drew a line of goose bumps down her arm. His breath slipped warm and provocative against her neck.

"I think the party was a success." Was that her voice sounding all breathy and turned on?

"We achieved what we set out to do. The Waverly's board knows that beauty has tamed the beast."

Despite the way his fingers wandered along her waist with turbulent results, Elizabeth managed a chuckle. "I think I'd characterize you more like the big bad wolf."

He spun her around so abruptly, her mouth dropped open in a startled huff.

"Prepare to be gobbled up."

And his lips captured hers, robbing her of breath, torching her senses. It was magic.

A wave of longing crashed into her, drowning all thought. Thank goodness his strong arm banded her body to his powerful frame or the weakness that attacked her knees would have left her puddled at his feet. She opened to his questing tongue and groaned at the sexy slide of his free hand over her butt. He kneaded her curves and lifted her against his hungry erection. Where moments earlier there'd been an unsatisfied ache between her thighs, a raging storm of desire shot from her heart to her loins. In the grip of fierce anticipation, she clutched his shoulders as he broke off the kiss.

His smooth lips drew a line of fire down her neck. "Sweetheart, you taste like heaven."

The intensity of his rough murmur thrilled her. From his playboy reputation she'd expected a masterful display of his seductive powers, not this hungry assault. His raw sensuality seeped beneath her skin, awakening the sort of primitive urges she swore she'd never give in to again.

In a flash all her past romantic disappointments came back to her. Her days of making poor choices were behind her. She had a plan. Career. Motherhood.

Elizabeth's willpower thrashed against the whirlpool of carnal sensation sucking her downward. With a deep breath she put her hands against Roark's chest and pressed. "I've got an early morning tomorrow. I really should be going."

And to her amazement, Roark let her go without a single protest. She chastised herself for being disappointed. No more getting involved with boys, especially the naughty ones. And Roark was as naughty as they got.

"Have dinner with me tomorrow," he said, catching her hand as she turned to go.

With his thumb stroking the erratic pulse in her wrist, she nodded. "Somewhere we can be seen together."

The suggestion was only half because they were supposed to be taking their engagement public. Now that she'd discovered the powerful chemistry between them, she had limited confidence in her ability to fend off his kisses. Worse, she couldn't count on her ability to keep her hands off him.

Even now, blood pounded hot and insistent through her veins, persuading her to put down her purse and garment bag and shove him down into the nearby nest of pillows.

"I'll pick you up at seven."

With a nod, she fled.

The cool night air did little to reduce the simmering emotions Roark's kiss had aroused. What was she thinking kissing him like that? This was supposed to be a business arrangement.

Elizabeth stepped to the curb to hail a taxi and caught a movement to her left. The rear door of a limo opened and Sabeen emerged. She caught Elizabeth's gaze on her and let her coat fall open to reveal her low-cut evening gown.

After a heated exchange with Roark, Darius had dragged his sister away from the party an hour ago. Why had she come back?

"I am surprised that you are leaving so early," Sabeen called, striding forward. "From the way you looked at Roark all evening, I didn't think you'd leave his bed before dawn."

The implication being that Elizabeth must not be able to

keep her man happy if he was willing to let her go before midnight.

"I have an early morning." And now she was making excuses. "Did you forget something at the loft?"

"I didn't get a chance to thank Roark properly for returning my little brother to me unharmed."

Elizabeth had no trouble reading the sort of "proper" thank you Sabeen had in mind. At that moment, she felt sorry for the younger woman. No matter how beautiful or how hard she threw herself at Roark, he was never going to see her as anything but the daughter of his former friend and tutor.

"I'm sure he knows how much you appreciate his help, but go on up and thank him now. I know he'll enjoy seeing you. He told me you and your brother are like family."

She hadn't given Sabeen the sort of reaction the younger woman was hoping for. It was hard to be jealous when she was only pretending to be engaged to Roark, and she knew he wouldn't jeopardize the future of Waverly's for an indiscretion.

"And I will still be in his life, long after he tires of you."

Elizabeth didn't doubt that a bit. "Good evening, Sabeen."

Four

At three in the afternoon, only seven climbers scaled the rock wall at the Hartz Sports Club. With one of the most challenging climbing walls in the country and the largest in Manhattan, the facility was usually more crowded.

"You've been practicing while I've been gone," Roark called across to Vance, splitting his attention between his half brother and the difficult route he'd chosen.

"I wasn't going to let you embarrass me again," Vance returned, keeping his eyes on the wall in front of him.

"You should come with me to Pakistan and climb the Trango Towers."

Vance snorted. "I'm pretty sure I'm not ready for anything like that."

"How about something closer to home? There's Shiprock in New Mexico."

"Maybe when this business with Rothschild and the stolen statue goes away we can talk about it."

Roark nodded, sobering. For most of his life, the only

family he'd known had been his mother. Then four years earlier, Vance had approached him with a tale of being his half
brother. At first Roark had been skeptical. The story Vance
had told him about finding a letter from his father that directed him to track down his half brother had seemed too
far-fetched to be true.

With his mother's reclusive lifestyle, Roark had a hard time
imagining her taking a lover. But Vance's story that they'd
met when Edward Waverly had come to see her about a coin
collection she wanted to sell made sense. Throughout Roark's
childhood his mother had deflected all his questions about
his father, leaving Roark to indulge his active imagination.
He could see how his mother might have fallen in love with
the charismatic Waverly.

But why had it ended?

Perhaps Edward had abandoned her after discovering she
was pregnant. Perhaps she had broken things off because
she knew she could never have been the sort of society wife
a man like Edward would have wanted. Perhaps they'd just
fallen out of love.

Roark turned his thoughts from the past to the present.
"What are you and Ann planning to do about Rothschild?"

Vance stretched his left arm until his fingertips could just
curve around his next hold. "We have to keep our stock price
from dropping any lower. Otherwise we won't need to worry
about board members selling to him—he will be able to pick
up all the shares he wants on the open market."

"And the quickest way to stabilize the stock price is to
clear up this mess about the Gold Heart statue."

Roark's thoughts ran over the questions raised by the FBI
agents. He had no worries that Rothschild's machinations
would land him in jail. He'd been nowhere near the palace
on the night the Gold Heart statue disappeared. Of course, he
couldn't prove that since his activities the evening in question were not the sort he wanted law officials poking into.

"That may present a bit of a challenge," Roark said. "The statue may bring in well over 200 million. With the theft of Rayas's Gold Heart statue the owner of our statue has grown quite paranoid about security."

"And you're sure it's neither stolen nor a fake?"

"I'm staking my reputation that it's not."

"You're staking the reputation of Waverly's that it's not."

"No, I'm not. Originally there were three statues created by the king of Rayas for his three daughters. Each one is marked with its own unique stamp and I have a document that distinguishes which statue belonged to which daughter. Currently, one statue resides with a branch of Rayas's royal family. The one the FBI believes I stole belongs to the current king. The last one disappeared over a century ago. Stolen or sold, no one knows, and the family has since died off. It ended up in Dubai and became part of a collection of a hundred other artifacts belonging to a wealthy sheikh who died recently. His son has little interest in anything old. He prefers cutting-edge technology, young beautiful women and expensive cars and real estate. Selling the collection is going to fund his dream of building the finest resort in Dubai."

"So when the statue arrives, you can prove both its authenticity and its ownership?"

"Exactly."

"Then we have nothing to worry about."

"Not a single thing."

Roark pondered the break-in that had happened in his Dubai apartment while he'd been in Colombia. The thief had disabled a state-of-the-art safe and stolen all the documentation Roark had on the Gold Heart statue including the statue's provenance. He'd made copies, but doubted these would satisfy the FBI experts.

He'd often been in situations where he needed others to trust him. Dealing in antiquities was the sort of business that came with a lot of questions. Black marketers thrived and the technology that should have made it easier to tell real from fake also made it easier to create replicas that appeared authentic.

For the next twenty minutes the men climbed in silence, each occupied with their own thoughts. As their hour ran down, Roark returned to the floor and unfastened his harness. As usual, climbing left his mind clear. When your life depended on the security of your next hand- or foothold, it was hard to clutter your thoughts with worrying about things you couldn't control.

"Your fiancée certainly made a splash with the board the other night," Vance said as he stored his gear.

"I'm glad to hear it."

Elizabeth had charmed everyone. A dozen people had informed Roark how lucky he was to have found such an exceptional woman.

"I had no idea that you'd gotten so serious with someone of late," Vance continued, his tone neutral. "How long have you two been together?"

"Not as long as you might think."

Vance must have heard something in Roark's tone because he glanced his way, eyes sharp. "She must have been worried when you disappeared for three months."

"It definitely tested our relationship, but she understands my need to be gone a fair amount."

"A fair amount?" Vance echoed, eyebrows raised. "It seems to me that you've been in New York a total of twenty days in the last year."

"Sounds about right." Roark focused on storing his gear. "But Elizabeth is very committed to her career. I'm convinced she didn't miss me at all."

"Quite a love match then." A thread of sarcasm wove through Vance's voice. Ever since falling for Charlotte, he'd become a champion of committed relationships.

"Exactly."

"Tell me how you came to be engaged." Vance drank deeply from his bottle of water, giving Roark a chance to decide what exactly he was going to tell his brother.

Deceiving Vance left him with a heavy conscience and a bitter taste in his mouth. Past experience had taught him to trust no one. That mantra had kept him alive more times than he could count. But Vance wasn't a shady antiquities dealer with questionable associates. He was a well-respected businessman and Roark's brother. Having family to guard his back was changing Roark from a solo operator into a team player, and adapting to the new dynamic wasn't easy.

"We're not really engaged," Roark admitted, deciding that being truthful with Vance was best. "Cromwell approached me at the wine auction and told me Rothschild is after him to sell his shares and convince everyone else to do so, as well. He believes you, Ann and I are the future of Waverly's. But with the near scandal surrounding Ann's alleged relationship with Rothschild and my wild ways where women are concerned, he wasn't feeling confident about our judgment."

"That old man should talk. He's got more than a few skeletons in his closet."

As much as he would have loved to hear more about Vance's allegations, Roark stayed focused on his story. "Anyway, he thought if my love life settled down, I would demonstrate an ability to behave responsibly."

"So, you got engaged?"

"Elizabeth agreed to act as my fiancée until the situation at Waverly's stabilizes."

For a moment Vance looked mildly stunned, then he shook his head. "Did it occur to you that this is exactly the sort of thing that gets you into trouble?"

"Yes. But what else would you have me do? Waverly's is going to end up in Rothschild's hands if we can't keep our board members from selling. And you have to admit that the buzz about the Gold Heart statue being a fake or stolen has died down with the announcement of my engagement."

"Agreed." Vance scrutinized him a moment longer. "And speaking of you being the future of Waverly's, have you given any more thought to my proposition?"

"That I officially join Waverly's management and go public with our connection?" Roark shook his head. "It's not a good time."

"Don't be ridiculous. With Uncle Rutherford off doing who knows what, Waverly's needs you. Besides, you have the same rights to the company that I do."

"You seem to forget I'm the illegitimate son," Roark pointed out. "The black sheep of the family, if you will."

"I'm sure if my father had had his way, he would have married your mother." Vance picked up his gym bag. "He loved her."

"You don't know that." Not once had his mother named Edward Waverly in her journals. When she wrote of her lover, she talked about his thick brown hair and the unhappiness she'd glimpsed inside him. "And there's no proof he was my father." Despite the rumors, Roark never bought an artifact without authenticating its provenance. He was damn well not going to claim to be Edward Waverly's son without a declaration from his mother that it was true.

"The DNA test—"

"Proves we're related. We could be cousins." Roark knew his statement was ridiculous before Vance shot him a wry smile.

"You think you're Rutherford's son?"

"I don't know." Roark tempered his impatience. "And that's why I'm not keen on a public announcement."

"Fine. But I think if you come forward as a Waverly, it would go a long way toward bolstering our stock."

"Let's see how things progress with my engagement and I'll let you know."

* * *

Elizabeth swayed on her feet, half asleep as she waited for the elevator door to open. At seven o'clock on a Friday evening, the office housing Josie Summers's Event Planning was abandoned. Most of her coworkers were working events. The rest had left around five, eager to head home or swing by their favorite bar for happy hour.

Today had been a particularly difficult day. Not only because her newest client was a demanding perfectionist and unable to make a decision, but because she'd had a frustrating conversation with her mother about plans for Thanksgiving. With the number of parties booked around the holiday, Elizabeth couldn't get away from New York and she'd been unable to convince her parents to leave Portland and come for a visit.

Elizabeth really could have used her parents' support. A year ago she'd lost her sister, brother-in-law and niece. The ache of the loss rarely left her, but the pain had eased over the past twelve months. She no longer had days where it was nearly impossible to get out of bed in the morning, but not a day went by when she didn't see or hear something and pick up the phone to dial her sister. And now, it looked like she'd be spending Thanksgiving and the anniversary of their death alone.

Damn. Tears piled up in her eyes. She blinked away the moisture and willed the elevator to arrive. Already she was running late for her evening with Roark. He was expecting her at his loft in ten minutes. She'd give just about anything to be heading home.

They'd been out every night this week. Dinner with friends. A launch party for a socialite's shoe line. A special gala to raise money for diabetes research. And last night, he'd taken her to a Knicks game at Madison Square Garden.

Anywhere and everywhere they could be seen together.

As the elevator deposited her on the first floor, Elizabeth pulled out her phone and dialed Roark's number to let him know she was on her way at last. For a man who claimed to prefer an unfettered personal life, he'd demonstrated a protective streak.

At some point in the past fifteen minutes since she'd looked outside, a snowstorm had kicked up outside. Fat, quarter-sized flakes drifted down. If she hadn't been so darned tired, she might have enjoyed the beautiful scene. Instead, all she saw was the traffic snarled on the street before her. Catching a cab was going to be harder than she expected.

Flinching at the damage she was about to do to her favorite pair of shoes, Elizabeth pushed open the door and was surprised to see Roark's driver heading her way.

"Good evening, Miss Minerva."

"Hello, Fred." At the warmth of his smile, her throat tightened and tears sprang to her eyes. She was obviously more tired and overwrought than she thought.

"Mr. Black sent me to fetch you. He thought you might have trouble catching a cab tonight."

She gave him a watery smile. "I was just thinking that exact thing."

They'd agreed to meet at his loft tonight rather than have him pick her up at work. Until her day fell apart, she'd hoped to get out at three, go home and grab an hour's sleep before heading out for tonight's clubbing.

"Can you take me to my apartment so I can change?"

"Mr. Black requested I bring you to him directly."

And so she was being kidnapped. Elizabeth settled back into the comfortable leather and watched the city slide past her window. The slow journey lulled her into closing her eyes. The sound of Fred's voice awakened her.

"We're here, Miss Minerva."

She covered a jaw-cracking yawn with a gloved hand and swung her feet onto the pavement. "Thanks."

Groggy from her short nap, she half stumbled across the

sidewalk and nodded to the doorman as she passed. When the elevator door opened, she was surprised to see Roark.

"You were supposed to leave work at three."

Her heart thumped at his concern. She liked the way he worried about her. "Margo Hadwell is a demanding, difficult woman to plan a party for."

He tugged her into the elevator and pushed the button to take them to his floor. "You work too hard."

"I'm going to have to if I want Josie to make me a partner."

"How did your meeting with her go today?"

Thanks to Roark, when she'd approached her boss about her future with Josie Summers's Event Planning, Elizabeth had been ready to counter her boss's speculation about Elizabeth's surprise engagement.

"She swallowed our story that we met at a club the last time you were in New York, and that we had a whirlwind affair. How we fell in love by email. The roses you sent me after the Banks wine auction helped sell it." Elizabeth grinned in triumph. "After that, I was able to keep her focused through my entire proposal. She agreed to bring me on as partner, but only if I land Green New York's spring gala."

Sponsored by the largest conservancy organization in the city, the gala was one of the must-attend events of the spring. Josie had pitched on it three years in a row without success. This year she'd challenged Elizabeth to do the impossible.

"Whatever introductions you need, let me know."

"Thanks, but there's more to winning the gala than just knowing the right people. I need to present the perfect proposal."

"You can do it."

Roark's confidence in her abilities raised her spirits. He'd been so supportive, exactly the way she'd dreamed the man in her life would be. Only Roark wasn't the man in her life. At least not in the traditional sense.

Filled with conflicting emotions, Elizabeth twisted the engagement ring around her finger as Roark opened the door to his loft. She needed to keep her head in this game and ignore the messages from her heart. And by the looks of what Roark had planned for the evening, that was going to prove challenging.

Candlelight illuminated the dining table, barely making a dent in the darkness filling the large open space. Soft music played. Intimate, romantic, staged for seduction.

Elizabeth swallowed hard. "I thought we were supposed to go out tonight."

"You sounded tired when I spoke to you on the phone earlier. I figured we'd stay in tonight. Have a quiet dinner, just the two of us."

She should struggle to free herself from the spell he wrapped around her so effortlessly, but his hand, sliding into the small of her back, and her exhaustion undermined her willpower.

"What about the club hopping we were supposed to do? You want us to be seen."

"We've been seen enough this week. Tonight, I want you to myself."

Treacherous delight stole through her. She cautioned herself to resist, but the intense light in Roark's eyes weakened her resolve. "Dinner sounds nice, but I'm so tired I might fall asleep over dessert."

A crooked smile bloomed. "Sweetheart, if I have my way, you'll be dessert."

His words seared through her like lightning, bringing her body to vibrant, tingling life.

"That's not funny." Her voice shook.

"It wasn't meant to be."

"Roark." Elizabeth's feet remained glued to the floor as he headed toward the kitchen. "We've talked about this. I'm not going to sleep with you."

"Don't make any decisions until you've tasted my lamb stew."

"You cooked?"

Honestly, how much more could one girl withstand?

"It relaxes me."

Without further argument, she let him tow her toward the table. The man was nearly impossible to resist. But she would keep up the battle until the last of her strength left her. She'd made a promise to herself. No more bad boys.

But was Roark as bad as his reputation made him out to be?

Or was she fooling herself instead of confronting reality? How many times had she coated her doubts about a boyfriend in iridescent layers of hope, transforming ugly and uncomfortable truth into pretty falsehoods she could live with. Trouble was the bad stuff wasn't gone, only covered up by her optimism. Not this time.

"That was delicious." Elizabeth gathered their plates and headed for the kitchen. "When did you learn to cook?"

"Before I learned how to sneak out, I used to spend a fair amount of time in the kitchen with Rosie. Our cook." Melancholy settled over Roark as it always did when he talked about what it had been like to grow up in a penthouse high above the bustle of New York.

"What was your mother like?" Elizabeth looked contrite as soon as the words were said. "I'm sorry. If you'd rather not talk about her, I understand."

He shrugged. Talking about her had never been easy. His shame in leaving her the way he had was tied up in his resentment of how fiercely she'd sheltered him from the world, not understanding that an energetic boy needed activity and adventures.

"She was smart and tough. I never understood why someone with her head for business and her iron will became like a terrified child outside her front door."

"Did something traumatic happen to her?"

"Not that I ever found in her journals." The square stem of the crystal wineglass felt cool against his fingertips as he spun the goblet and observed the play of candlelight in the facets. "She wrote about everything else."

"If she never left her penthouse, how did she…"

"Conceive me?" Even in the dim light, Roark couldn't miss the color splashed over Elizabeth's cheeks. "Unlike what we're doing, I imagine she had sex with my father."

Her lips thinned at his mild censure. "But how did they meet?"

Until Vance had entered his life four years ago with the tale that they were both sons of Edward Waverly, Roark hadn't realized how deeply he'd buried his longing for a father. The hole in his psyche had gone unnoticed before he'd left for the marines, but he now understood that it had been a persistent ache he'd learned to ignore. After his military career ended, he'd focused his energy on the hunt for antiquities and used the thrill of success to keep all disquiet at bay.

"My grandfather collected coins, some of them extremely valuable. After he died, my mother decided to sell his collection. She approached both Rothschild's and Waverly's. The representative from Waverly's convinced her to let him auction the coins."

"You mean Edward Waverly."

Roark thought back to the journal entry from that day. His mother's normally bold, confident penmanship had wobbled. Her crisp, matter-of-fact recounting of the day's events had become somewhat disjointed when describing her meeting with Edward Waverly.

"She never named him." Roark thought about those passages. He'd scrutinized them over the years, looking for answers to his father's identity. "A week later they were lovers."

"So fast?"

"When he saw something he wanted, he went after it."

Roark caught Elizabeth's hand and tugged her onto his lap. "That's something we have in common."

She made no attempt to hide her dismay. "Strictly business, remember?"

He bent down and kissed her tight lips. Almost immediately her spine lost its stiffness. Her hand crept over his shoulder and tangled in his hair. He smiled at her soft sigh of surrender. They'd been circling this moment for days, flirting with the attraction between them, testing the limits of restraint.

"Forget business," he murmured against her lips. "I want you."

Her body trembled. "I want you, too. But I'm not sure this is a good idea."

"This is a great idea. I thought so from the first second I laid eyes on you. Somehow, even from across the room I knew it would be like this between us. So damned hot."

He pulled her blouse free of her narrow skirt, fingers skimming past the silk hem. She gasped at the skin-on-skin contact. Her muscles tensed as he spread his fingers over her rib cage.

His lips fastened over hers, swallowing her groan. With tongue and teeth he explored her mouth. The taste of her, the abandon with which she kissed him back. He wanted more. So much more. And so did she.

Swirling sensation stole all rational thought. He focused all his attention on the woman in his arms.

Blood pounded in his ears, driving his need for her higher.

"Roark." Elizabeth shifted on his lap. Her chest pumped as she sucked in an irregular breath. "Your phone is ringing."

"I don't care." He nuzzled her neck and smiled when she quivered.

She got her hands between them and used his chest to lever herself off his lap. "What if it's important? You should answer it."

Cursing, he let Elizabeth back away, but held her gaze. "You're the only thing that's important to me at the moment."

The phone stopped ringing before she could respond. They stared at each other for a series of heartbeats, anticipation building once again. His palms still tingled with lingering pleasure from the exploration of her lush curves. His chest burned from contact with her full breasts. If pressing against her drove him wild, what the hell was going to happen to him when he made love to her?

He might never be the same.

Roark took a single step in her direction and the silence was shattered by another round of ringing.

"See." Elizabeth looked toward the phone. "They've called back. You'd better find out who it is.

He snatched up the phone. "Yes?"

"Good evening, Mr. Black," said the doorman. "Sorry for the interruption but the FBI is here. They want to speak with you."

Any hope Roark had of resuming their earlier activity vanished. "Send them up."

Elizabeth was watching him with a frown. "Should I go?" Her fingers shook as she stuffed her blouse back into her skirt and smoothed her hair.

"No need." He headed toward the door. "They won't be here long."

"Who won't?"

"The FBI."

She stiffened. "Nine o'clock on a Friday night is a little past regular office hours." Suspicion darkened her eyes. "What do they want with you?"

"There are some questions surrounding the Gold Heart statue Waverly's will be auctioning."

"What sort of questions?"

"Whether it's the same one stolen from Rayas."

"Is it?"

Her distrust cut him like the sharpest dagger. "No."

Walls slid into place around his heart. The guarded sensation was familiar and reassuring. Talking to Elizabeth about his mother had been like unlocking a vault sealed for centuries. Some things were meant to remain undiscovered.

"Why is the FBI talking to you?"

Roark knew he'd lose ground with her if he brushed off her question. "Mallik Khouri accused me of stealing the statue from the palace." Annoyed with the interruption and frustrated by the suspicion that shadowed Elizabeth's eyes, he flung open the door. Voice dripping with sarcasm, he asked, "How can I help the FBI?"

"We've had some new developments regarding the missing Gold Heart statue we need to discuss with you tonight." Special Agent Matthews smiled at him from the hallway. Her lips bore a predatory curve.

Behind her, Agent Todd slumped in his ill-fitting overcoat, his expression sullen, appearing as if he'd rather be home on such a miserable night.

"Has the thief been caught?"

"Let's just say we're pursuing a strong lead." Agent Matthews's gaze flicked into the apartment and spotted Elizabeth. "Sorry for the interruption." She was anything but. A cat playing with a mouse. "May we come in?"

They were wasting their time. Until the statue arrived in America, they had no reason to arrest him. The theft had taken place in Rayas. That crime was for the authorities in Rayas to prosecute. However, trafficking in stolen merchandise would interest the FBI. Good thing he didn't do that sort of thing.

"Have you spoken to Dalton Rothschild?" Roark asked, still blocking the agents from entering the loft. "If someone stole the Gold Heart, he would be my lead suspect."

"Funny," Special Agent Matthews said. "That's exactly what he said about you."

"We'd like you to come in and tell us where and how you came by the statue Waverly's is planning to auction." Special Agent Todd didn't sound anywhere near as cordial as his words. They wanted answers and fast.

"I can't do that." The statement had more bite than he intended. Usually he was happy to cooperate with the FBI, but they'd interrupted a very promising interlude and reinforced the wall of distrust between him and Elizabeth. Roark exhaled and forced down his irritation. "I've signed a confidentiality agreement."

"How convenient," Agent Matthews drawled. "Let's go see if we can find something you can discuss."

"I'm not telling you anything."

Agent Matthews gaze moved past him. "Perhaps your fiancée knows something. Shall we bring her in and see?"

Roark ground his teeth. He didn't want Elizabeth involved in this mess. "I'll get my coat."

Triumph flashed in Agent Matthew's eyes. "You do that."

Although Elizabeth had remained in the kitchen, he had no doubt that she'd heard the entire exchange. The way she wouldn't meet his gaze as he neared spoke volumes.

"I should head home."

"Stay," he cajoled, cupping her face. "I'll explain everything when I get back."

"You don't owe me any explanations," she murmured, but the way she clutched the dish towel in her hands made Roark wonder if it was his neck she wanted to wring.

"Stay," he repeated. "I won't be long."

Her muscles softened minutely as he kissed her gently on the corner of her lips.

"Okay."

Satisfied, he returned to the agents.

"She seemed to need a lot of convincing to stick around," Special Agent Matthews remarked as they headed down the hall. "Doesn't she trust you?"

"She trusts me," he said as the elevator doors closed, trapping him in the small space with the two FBI agents. "It's you she doesn't trust."

"Really?" Matthews laughed. "And why is that?"

"She seems to think your pursuit is overzealous. Like maybe you've got the hots for me and this case is just an excuse to spend time alone with me."

Agent Matthews laughed, but there was no mirth in it. "She has no need to worry on that score."

"You're right about that. I'm a one-woman man and she's the one woman for me."

"From what I've heard, everyone is surprised by your engagement." Agent Matthews met Roark's impassive stare with her laser-sharp gaze. "Why keep Ms. Minerva such a secret if you two were so in love?"

"I wouldn't have pegged you as a fan of gossip, Agent Matthews." He accompanied his mocking words with a bland smile. "Do you have a pile of glossy magazines hidden away in your desk drawer?"

"I don't gossip, Mr. Black. I interview people for facts."

"And yet you're suspicious over the fact that I didn't flaunt my relationship with Elizabeth for the amusement of the New Yorkers that read Page Six."

While Agent Todd headed for the driver's side, Agent Matthews opened the back of the black cruiser and gestured Roark inside. "I'm suspicious over the timing of your engagement. It certainly has taken the focus off the Gold Heart statue."

Roark paused with his hand on the door and offered a sardonic grin. "What a cynic you are, Agent Matthews. Don't you realize that love finds you when you least expect it?"

Five

With Roark gone, the loft felt cold and cavernous. The man certainly filled a space with his charisma and sex appeal. She shivered.

What new information could the FBI have that would prompt them to drag Roark out of his apartment at nine o'clock at night? She regretted doubting him about the authenticity of the Gold Heart statue in his possession, but could he be protecting the true criminal out of a sense of loyalty to his old teacher? Had Darius stolen Rayas's statue?

Turned to ice by her thoughts, Elizabeth scooped a throw off the back of one of the couches and wrapped herself in it. The fat snowflakes drifting past the floor-to-ceiling windows drew her to the view of Manhattan.

Rampant longing continued to pulse in her loins. It shocked her how much she wanted Roark's hands on her, his mouth coasting over her skin. Her body ached with unfulfilled desires as she stared at the street seven stories below. If not for the FBI agent's interruption, she would have slept with Roark. What a mistake that would have been.

But even as the thought formed, the sentiment behind it was hollow. Elizabeth floundered in confusion. Either she was as misguided as ever when it came to romance, or Roark wasn't the bad boy he appeared to be.

Elizabeth turned away from the window. When had she stopped relying on logic and looked to her instincts for answers? His reputation, the trouble with the Gold Heart statue and the suspicions of the FBI should have given her more than enough reason to keep him at arm's length.

Instead, here she was, basing her decision to trust him on gut reaction. Granted, unlike other men she'd dated, not once had Roark acted in a way that undermined her confidence or made her feel insecure. But was she right to believe that he'd been truthful with her when his business dealings were questionable?

Emotions churning, she prowled across the living room's gleaming wood floors and trespassed into Roark's private domain. The last time she'd been in the loft, she'd been too busy with preparations for their "engagement" party to investigate the home of the man she was supposed to know everything about.

In fact, except for what she'd read in the papers and the little Roark had told her about his childhood, she had no idea about his interests outside treasure hunting and rock climbing. She knew he spent his days at Waverly's, meeting with Vance and Ann about the current crisis and the auction house's future.

The loft had four bedrooms in total. Elizabeth skipped the room she'd used to change the night of their engagement party and headed straight for Roark's master bedroom. No surprises here. White walls. A gorgeous oriental rug covering the hardwood floor. An enormous king-size bed. Dresser and nightstands in some dark wood. More floating shelves held vestiges of Roark's travels.

The lack of personal items and photos confirmed Elizabeth's concern that Roark was a man who wanted no ties, had no family celebrations to remember. He liked his freedom to take off whenever the next adventure called. And she was someone who had her days planned down to the minute months in advance.

Retreating back into the hall, she pushed open the door to the room opposite Roark's and stared in dumbfounded surprise. Here was the heart of Roark's house. A cozy, cluttered space filled with wall-to-wall bookshelves, a chunky wood desk piled high with books and papers. Opposite her, an overstuffed chair sat beside an ornate fireplace.

She located the light switch and the lamp behind the chair snapped on, illuminating the spill of photos covering the ottoman. Curiosity pulled her into the room. She glanced at the books on the shelves she passed and noticed a predominance of history tomes. Most of these were ancient European volumes, many not written in English, and as she circled, she began to notice more and more on the Middle East. Then she noticed an open cabinet behind the desk filled with scrolls.

Without touching anything on the desk, she tried to see what Roark had been working on. Two of the three books that lay open were written in Arabic. Considering the amount of time Roark spent hunting down artifacts in the Middle East, Elizabeth wasn't surprised that he could read Arabic, but the fact that his notes were a mixture of English and Arabic intrigued her. It was almost as if he thought in both languages interchangeably.

Diagrams and doodles also filled the pages strewn across the desk. Roark was searching for another treasure. How long before his research ended and he was off on another adventure?

The depth of her disappointment drove Elizabeth away

from the desk. So what if Roark left New York? She'd known from the first that it was bound to happen. No one could cage him for long, certainly not her, a woman playing at being his fiancée. But that she was sad at the thought of his leaving told her she was already in too deep.

Elizabeth found the switch that activated the gas fireplace and sat down in the chair, knocking the ottoman in the process and disturbing the stack of photos sitting there. Half a dozen slid to the floor. She picked them up, scrutinizing each. The last photo was of a statue of a woman, her heart rendered in gold. She stood on a base of more gold, stamped with some sort of seal. The statue Roark was accused of stealing. A hard knot developed in her stomach at the accusations lodged against him.

Restoring order to the photos, Elizabeth kicked off her shoes and curled up in the chair. She arranged the throw so it covered her chin to toes and let her head fall back. Gaze on the flames flickering a few feet away, she forced her mind still. In the weeks following the death of her sister, brother-in-law and niece, Elizabeth had perfected the technique of not thinking. If she hadn't she might have gone mad dwelling on all the ways she was going to miss them.

With her mind quiet and her body warm and comfortable, it didn't take long for Elizabeth's eyes to close. Sleep tugged at her. The week had been physically exhausting and emotionally taxing.

In the last moment of wakefulness came the tiniest tug of excitement. Her demanding, eventful week had left her little time to ponder. Now, as her thoughts slowed, she remembered why she'd risked getting involved with Roark. Soon she could start her next round of fertility treatments. Visions of diapers and pacifiers danced in her head as she drifted off to sleep.

She was awakened by the gentlest of touches above her eyebrow. The soft caress drifted down to her cheek and slipped behind her ear. She opened her eyes and gazed at Roark's face.

"What happened with the FBI?" she asked, her dreamy haze fading.

He toyed with her fingers. "They asked me the same questions as before."

"Did Darius steal Rayas's Gold Heart statue?" The question burst out of her, startling him.

"No." The corner of his lips twitched.

"You're sure?" She scanned his expression, unsure if she could read him well enough to determine if he was lying to her. "You said he needed money and he has motive to hurt the Sheikh."

"He's not a thief." He lifted her right hand and brushed a kiss across her palm. "I'm glad you made yourself at home. But you would have been more comfortable in my bed."

Firelight played across his strong bone structure, creating interesting shadows. Flames flickered in his eyes, causing parts of her to burn for him. Her breath grew shallow as a vise seemed to have clamped around her chest.

"And make things easy for you?" Despite the warmth of the room, she tugged the throw higher around her. "I thought you were a man who liked challenges."

"Getting you into bed isn't a challenge."

"You sound awfully confident about that."

As well he should be. He'd already proven how easily he breached her defenses. She might as well drop the drawbridge and wave the flag of surrender.

"I mean that I don't perceive making love to you as something I'm doing because my ego demands it, but because if I don't have you soon, I'm not sure how much longer I'll survive."

Elizabeth didn't know whether to trust his earnest speech, but his words struck the final blow to her guards. They became dust.

"Roark." She managed only his name before her throat locked up. But she'd always believed that actions spoke louder than words.

Catching his face in her hands, she leaned forward and kissed him. Beneath hers, his lips curved. She felt the muscles of his face shift against her fingertips and knew he was smiling. Happiness bloomed in her chest, an emotion lacking since her family's death.

She felt glorious. Rich and full. Awakening to the joy life used to hold for her.

Roark's mouth opened over hers as the kiss deepened. Her head swam as sensation overwhelmed her. She burned. Warmed inside and out by her need for this man. She craved his strength, his weight covering her. The touch of his skin against hers.

As if her hunger communicated to Roark, he slipped his hands beneath her body and scooped her into his arms. She clung to his shoulders. The throw fell away as he carried her from the room.

"Wait." She pushed at his chest as the cooler air from his bedroom struck her overheated skin. "Put me down. Please."

He heaved an enormous sigh, but did as she asked. "If you've changed your mind, give me thirty seconds to change it back."

"Thirty seconds?" She laughed, her head clearing with a little space between them. "Does your ego ever deflate?"

His smug grin bloomed. "Not until we're both completely satisfied."

He reached for her, but she backed away. "Stop." She sucked in a couple unsteady breaths and told her heart to slow. "I want to do this." She took stock of Roark, appraising his raw masculinity. A groan slipped free. "I really do, but you have to give me a second to clear my head. I took an oath, no more bad decisions about men. So, if I'm going to break my promise, I want to do so with my faculties fully engaged."

Roark stopped looking like a hungry lion and crossed his arms over his chest. Eyes narrowed, he met her gaze. "What does that mean?"

"Just stand there and don't move until I tell you to." When his eyebrows rose at her edict, she huffed, "Can you do that?"

He let one brawny shoulder hit the doorjamb and leaned there, watching her in silence. Elizabeth released a breath. Was she really going to do this?

She turned her back on Roark and grasped the first button on her blouse. The room was so silent she could hear her heart pounding. The rhythmic throb soothed her. She was going to do this and it was the right decision. Slowly, moving with deliberate determination, she opened her blouse and let it slip to the floor.

Roark would have traded the Monet hanging in his mother's bedroom to know what was running through Elizabeth's mind as she shimmied out of her skirt. This striptease of hers lacked any hint of sensuality. She was merely a woman taking off her clothes. Each move deliberate, slow, burdened with meaning.

The fact that she couldn't face him spoke volumes. Yet with each item she loosened and let slip to the floor a little of her tension fell away.

He was mesmerized.

And more than a little turned on.

Muscles played across her shoulders as she reached behind her to unfasten her bra. When had he last taken the time to just enjoy the curve of the female back? To admire a tiny waist. The flare of hips.

She wore lavender bikini panties. The bra that dangled from her fingers, the same matching silk. For the moment she remained immobile, her head down, studying the pool of fabric around her feet. Roark imagined she was torn between the need to neatly fold her clothes and whatever shyness kept her facing away from him.

The room seemed to hold its breath as he waited to see what she'd do next. The bra hit the floor, quickly followed by her silk panties.

Roark's lungs forgot how to work as she raised her arms and removed a series of pins from her hair. The golden honey mass plummeted downward, obscuring her shoulders and the top of her back. She shook her head and the waves shimmered in the lamplight. Then she stepped toward his bed.

Never had a woman captivated him the way Elizabeth had. Beautiful and smart. Wounded and vulnerable. It was an intoxicating combination.

In the silent room, his breath rasped with the effort to hold completely still. As much as it was killing him, Roark was happy to wait for her to signal she was ready for him.

She fisted her hand in the comforter and inched it back to reveal his sheets. Where she'd been moving slowly and deliberately until now, she quickened her movements and slipped into bed. Seated in the middle of his mattress, the cream-colored sheet tucked beneath her chin, she gave a sharp nod.

"Your turn."

Her dictatorial tone amused him, but he did as she asked. His fingers felt thick and clumsy as they worked his shirt buttons free. Beneath her steady regard, his already throbbing erection grew even more insistent. The frenzied passion of a few moments earlier had changed into something deeper, more dangerous. By approaching this moment with purpose, Elizabeth couldn't claim later that she'd been overwhelmed by physical desire. There was more to it than that. And Roark was eager to explore exactly what that was.

Removing his shirt, pants and socks, he paused to gather up her clothes and fold them neatly onto a chair before advancing toward the bed. She looked startled that he'd taken the time when his body so obviously reflected his acute desire for her.

Stopping beside the bed, he slid his underwear down his thighs, enjoying the play of emotions on her face as she got her first glimpse of what he had in store for her. "Ready?" he asked, gathering a handful of the sheet.

Her eyes were the deep blue of twilight as she stared at him. Her throat worked, lips parting, but nothing came out.

"Yes," she whispered at last.

Before the word was half out, he snapped his arm and tore the sheet from her grasp. A startled noise escaped her as he prowled onto the bed and bore her backward onto the waiting mattress.

"Oh, Roark." The cry broke from her lips as he gathered her hips in his hands and pulled her snug against him.

He sank into her mouth before she could speak again and ravaged her with long, sensual kisses. Teeth, tongue, lips all came into play as he learned exactly what pleased her. She gave him everything, held nothing in reserve. And her complete surrender unleashed something in him. Before he knew what had happened, he was devouring her in reckless, wild abandon, feeling her match his passion.

Panting, he released her mouth and drew his tongue down her neck. Her large round breasts filled his hands, tight nipples burning his palms. She moaned in breathless delight when his tongue flicked across one sensitive bud. The sound heated the blood speeding through Roark's veins.

Filling his nostrils with her scent, he savored the taste of her skin and let his fingers skim down her body. Her thighs parted as he skimmed over her mound and gently dipped into her hot flesh. Moisture spilled over his fingers. She was ready for him.

"I need you, Roark," she said, her fingers clutching his bare shoulders. Her eyes burned with fever as she bent her knees and opened still farther for him. "Don't make me wait any longer."

"Patience."

Stroking with more purpose, he circled her sensitive nub and watched her pupils dilate. Her breath seized, body jerking as he grazed her lightly before moving on. He wanted to know every inch of her before claiming her.

"Roark." Her desperation echoed his own driving need, but he continued to let his senses take her in.

"You are beautiful," he murmured, spanning her waist with his hands to hold her still while he deposited kisses on her abdomen. As he dipped his tongue into her navel and registered her startled gasp, he paused to reflect how one day soon she would have a baby growing inside her. With surprise he realized he'd like to see her belly swell with her pregnancy.

"Stop stalling and make love to me," she growled, squirming beneath him until he lay between her parted thighs. "I can't take much more of this. I need you."

"And I need you." Never one to deny a willing woman her pleasure, Roark kissed his way back up her body, pausing to drag his teeth across her nipples and further inflame her impatience.

Only when her hand closed around his erection did he appreciate the serious nature of her frustration. Fireworks exploded in his mind as her clever fingers stroked him. He shuddered at the enormous pleasure of her touch and shifted until he was poised at her entrance.

"Wait." He gasped as she shifted her hips upward and took him partway inside her. Sliding into her moist heat was the most incredible thing he'd ever experienced. She was so tight. It was acute torture to have to stop himself from driving all the way in. "You're not protected," he gasped, his lungs malfunctioning.

"I haven't been able to get pregnant with a doctor's help." Sorrow shadowed her expression for a moment. "There's no need for you to worry." And with that she lifted her hips and took him in fully.

As they merged he kissed her with something close to desperation. Breaking free of her lips, he buried his face in her neck and began to move inside her.

She matched his rhythm as if they'd been intimate for years. As her body shifted to take him still deeper, he struggled to slow the building pressure. He'd never expected her to be like this. Unrestrained. Demanding. Her hunger a match for his. Nothing had ever felt so perfect before. He wanted to hold on to the moment, but already his body was racing toward its completion.

"I'm sorry," he said, refusing to finish until he'd satisfied her. "I wanted this to take longer, but you feel so amazing." He slid his hand between them and touched her most sensitive spot.

Immediately she cried out. Her body bowed. She scored his back with her nails, the small pain pushing him over the edge. As her orgasm claimed her, Roark surrendered to his own climax. It hit him harder than he'd expected, searing his nerve endings, knocking him off balance.

He lowered his weight onto her, becoming aware that she'd wrapped her thighs around his hips and appeared to have no intention of letting go. He cradled her cheek in his hand and kissed her tenderly.

"Are you okay?"

"Terrific." She hadn't yet opened her eyes, but her lips bore a satisfied curve. She dragged the tips of her fingers up and down his spine. "You?"

"Never better."

Reluctant to disrupt their comfortable intimacy, he rolled them both onto their sides so she was no longer bearing his weight. She snuggled against him, boneless and relaxed, as if she had no intention of moving ever again.

Which is why her next words came as such a shock.

"It's late," she murmured, her soft sigh whispering over his skin. "I should probably get going."

Six

In the glowing aftermath of their charged lovemaking, Elizabeth and Roark were using very little of his king-size mattress. Clasped in his powerful arms, her legs entwined with his muscular ones, Elizabeth wasn't sure where her heartbeat stopped and his began.

"It's late," he said, his tone brooking no argument. "Stay."

His lips moved against her temple in a contented fashion, mirroring her profound satisfaction. It was going to be torture to leave this moment of pure bliss. But to linger would open her up to hopes better left unexplored.

"Look, this was nice." So very nice. "But I think it's better if I go."

Elizabeth heard the reluctance in her voice and winced. He was going to get the idea that she didn't want to leave. And that would lead him to suspect other things. Like the fact that every second she spent in his company she fell a little further beneath his spell.

"If you insist on leaving, I'll take you home." With a fond hug he released her and shifted toward the edge of the bed.

She shivered at the loss of his warm skin. "You don't need to do that."

"If you think I'm going to let you wander around the city alone at this time of night, you're crazy."

Her heart did a silly little flip at his chivalry. Not one of the men she'd dated previously would have left a warm bed to escort her home. "I wasn't going to wander around. I was going to take a cab back to my apartment."

"At 4:00 a.m."

"You say that as if I haven't done it before."

His eyes narrowed. "You make a habit out of heading home at this hour?"

She could see where his mind had gone. He was trying to ascertain how often she'd spent half the night with a man and then headed home in the quiet hours before dawn. Her chin nudged upward.

"I am an event planner. That means I stay for hours after a party winds down. New York is the city that never sleeps. Sometimes that means I don't either."

"I'm starving." He tossed the covers to the foot of the bed, exposing both of them. "Let's get out of here."

His abrupt change of subject was almost as startling as the rush of chilly air across Elizabeth's warm skin. She squawked in protest, but Roark was already off the mattress and striding toward his discarded clothes.

She forgot all about being cold, and about her own nudity at the sight of all those amazing naked muscles that rippled beneath his skin. A purr rose in her throat. The man was a work of art.

He glanced back and caught her staring at him. "If you don't stop looking at me like that, I'm not going to let you out of bed for a week."

Heat rose in her cheeks as he perused her naked body.

She slid off the bed and walked toward him. He'd already donned pants and shirt, but looked open to removing both if she insisted.

The purr rumbling in her chest intensified as she slid her arms around his midsection and hugged him. The move seemed to shock him because it took a couple heartbeats before his arms circled her.

With her cheek resting against his broad chest, she relaxed into the steady thump of his heart. "I really enjoyed myself tonight. Thank you."

She felt as much as heard his sigh. He tightened his arms.

"The night's not quite over." But he made no move toward the bed. The moment wasn't about sex. He seemed to get that. None of the other men she'd dated would have. With a gusty sigh he dropped a kiss on her head and pushed her to arm's length. "Let's go get some breakfast."

In ten minutes they were settled into a cab and heading uptown. Roark had his arm around her shoulders. Elizabeth snuggled into his side, delighted that he was sharing his heat with her. The temperature had dropped. Last night's slush had become rock-hard ice, uneven and treacherous beneath her four-inch heels.

Fifteen minutes later, the taxi stopped on Fifth Avenue in front of an elegant building. The entire block was residential.

Elizabeth scanned the area. "What are we doing here?"

"Breakfast." He tapped her on the nose, eyes dancing at her confusion.

"I don't see a restaurant."

"That's because there isn't one."

Roark paid the driver and stepped out of the cab. Elizabeth shrank from the hand he offered her.

He regarded her wryly. "Don't you trust me?"

Elizabeth pondered the loaded question even as she took his hand and let him pull her to her feet. "I think you enjoy keeping everyone guessing."

"Perhaps I do."

With a gusty sigh, she resigned herself to being surprised by whatever he had in mind. Her curiosity increased as he nodded at the doorman and escorted her into the building without being announced.

They disembarked from the elevator on the top floor and he strode into the penthouse as if he owned it. At this hour, the lights were off, and the space had a vacant vibe.

"Who lives here?" she whispered, reluctant to disturb whatever ghosts lingered about.

"Mrs. Myott, she takes care of the place."

Roark flipped a light switch and illuminated the foyer. The gleaming wood floor of a long, wide gallery led the way into the apartment. A large fortune in artwork kept watch as Elizabeth let Roark usher her forward.

"And is this Mrs. Myott going to call the police when she notices us prowling around?" She stopped short in front of a painting. "That's a Monet."

"Yes." Roark's hand applied pressure on the small of her back, urging her on. "The kitchen's this way."

Elizabeth put her weight into her heels and refused to budge. "I'm not taking another step until you tell me whose apartment this is."

Roark shot her a mischievous grin. "Where's your sense of adventure?"

She let her raised eyebrows provide the answer.

"It's mine."

Another piece of the puzzle that was Roark Black snapped into place, but the picture wasn't any clearer.

"Yours?" This time Elizabeth was too shocked to resist when he nudged her into motion. "But you live in Soho."

"This is where I grew up."

"It's wonderful." The apartment's red damask wallpaper, antique furnishings and ornate marble fireplace might be the polar opposite of the white walls and contemporary furniture of Roark's loft, but the marble lions flanking the entry into the living room revealed where he'd come by his love of history and antiquities. "Why don't you live here?"

It was just a tiny flinch, little more than a twitch near his left eye, but Elizabeth noticed and realized that hidden beneath Roark's good-humored facade lay a thin layer of anxiety.

"Because I like my loft better."

"Why don't you sell it?"

"Want a tour?"

Once again he'd avoided a direct answer to her question. From the grin curving his lips as he imparted a tale about his boyhood antics, she could tell he was fond of the apartment. Good memories had been made here. But during one brief glance he shot her way, she spied melancholy deep in his eyes.

She could relate to the sadness. Her happy memories of her sister were intertwined with the aching reality that she'd never see Stephanie's face again or hear her laugh. They'd never stay up late talking about Elizabeth's job or the latest antics of Stephanie's book club members.

"And this was my bedroom."

Lost in thought, Elizabeth realized she'd missed a chunk of the tour. "Nice." She followed her comment with a grin. "Has it always looked like this?"

The large room, wallpapered in rich brown, was not exactly how she'd decorate a boy's room. A bed, canopied in heavy gold curtains dominated the wall opposite three large windows. The ceiling had been painted a dark turquoise, the color picked up in the two wing chairs flanking the heavy marble fireplace.

"I think it has looked like this since my grandfather bought the place."

Elizabeth rolled her lips in to contain a smile. "Not exactly your taste, is it?"

"No, but the bed's comfortable." And before she caught

his intent, he swept her up in his arms and dropped her in the middle of the mattress. "When I was a teenager, I spent a lot of time imagining what it'd be like to have a girl in this bed."

Her thoughts melted into puddles of incoherence as he eased himself down on her and captured her mouth in a sweet, sexy kiss. Sliding her fingers into his hair, she lost herself in the feint and retreat of his tongue as it tangled with hers.

Despite the long hours they'd spent together, her desire for him rekindled, but he seemed perfectly content to take his time exploring her mouth in slow, tender kisses that awakened more of a tumult in her heart than in her loins. Last night she'd decided she could handle keeping their relationship purely physical. This affectionate intimacy was way more dangerous.

In the past few days she'd learned he liked her as well as desired her. It's why she'd decided to stop fighting the attraction between them. Trouble was, she was damned close to really liking him back. And therein lay trouble.

A throat cleared behind them.

"Welcome home, Roark."

A woman's wry voice cut through the romantic tension rising in Elizabeth. She put her hand on Roark's shoulder to push him back, but he'd already released her lips and set his forehead against hers. His chest pumped as he sucked air into his lungs.

From her position pinned beneath Roark, Elizabeth couldn't see the woman who stood in the doorway, but apparently Roark knew exactly who'd interrupted them.

"Hello, Mrs. Myott."

"I hear you are engaged." The caretaker's tone was so casual she might have been asking what he wanted in his coffee. "Is this the lucky lady?"

"Yes." Roark grinned down at Elizabeth. "Elizabeth, I'd like you to meet Mrs. Myott. Mrs. Myott, my fiancée, Elizabeth. I was giving her a tour of the apartment."

"And you decided to start with your bedroom. Is she impressed?"

Despite their compromising pose, Elizabeth was beginning to catch Roark's amusement.

"You'll have to ask her."

Cheeks on fire, Elizabeth cleared her throat. "It's very nice."

"Hopefully you'll approve of the rest of the house, as well."

Elizabeth poked Roark hard in the ribs, but although he grunted, he didn't move. "I'm sure it's lovely."

"Should I start breakfast?"

"Give us an hour," Roark answered.

"Very well."

The slap of slippers against the parquet floor faded as the caretaker headed off down the hall.

He didn't seriously intend to return to kissing her while Mrs. Myott started the coffee, did he? When his lips swooped towards hers once more, Elizabeth realized that's exactly what he had in mind.

"Stop it," she whispered, wedging her arms between them. "We can't keep doing this. She knows we're here."

"She won't come back if that's what you're worried about."

"I'm not."

"Then what's the problem?"

And that's when Elizabeth shoved him aside and sat up. Roark rolled onto his back and grinned at her. The wicked light dancing in his eyes informed Elizabeth that he was teasing her. Well, it wasn't funny.

And yet, he looked so damned appealing with his crooked grin and his hair all mussed from her roving fingers, she almost leaned down and kissed him.

"A cup of coffee sounds really good right now," she said, ignoring Roark's smug expression. "Do you think Mrs. Myott has started some?"

Since she'd already tossed casual and unaffected out the

window, Elizabeth scrambled off the bed in an ungainly assortment of legs and arms. With her feet on the floor, she smoothed her rumpled hair and tugged to straighten her disheveled clothes.

Roark came up behind her. Wrapping his arms around her waist, he nuzzled her ear. "No need to get all presentable on my account. I rather like you rumpled and out of sorts."

"I'm not doing it for you." She pulled out of his arms and headed for the door.

"You're doing it for Mrs. Myott."

"I'm doing it…"

"To make a good impression."

Damn him for being right.

"You don't need to worry," he murmured, taking her hand to lead the way when Elizabeth stalled in the hallway, unsure which way led to the kitchen. "She's going to love you."

"It doesn't matter if she loves me or not. We're not getting married."

"Then why do you care?"

"I…" She had an answer to his question, just not one she was willing to give him. So, she stole from his playbook. "Is that your mother?"

They were passing the library. His mother's favorite room in the house. Large and windowless, shelves lined every inch of wall space except for the large fireplace and the life-size portrait of Guinevere Black hanging over it.

"Yes."

Even though he knew it was little more than a trick of his subconscious, Roark had never been able to shake the sensation that her eyes followed him wherever he went in the room. He'd first noticed the phenomenon when he turned seven and spent long hours studying math, language, geography and history with his tutor. Despite her being elsewhere in the apartment, Roark always felt as if she watched over his lessons.

"She's beautiful." Elizabeth glanced his way. "You have her eyes."

"And her love of books." To his relief, the scent of coffee reached his nose. "Come on, Mrs. Myott has started breakfast."

"Why would she do that when you gave her the impression we'd be a while?"

He was growing rather fond of the way Elizabeth's cheeks turned pink and wondered what accounted for his change of taste. The women he usually dated didn't blush at the slightest hint of impropriety. When had he lost interest in audacious, free spirits? He appreciated their independent natures. Never worried that they'd grow too attached.

"She knows me." He wrapped his arm around Elizabeth's waist and guided her down the hall.

In the eighteen years he'd lived in the apartment, the kitchen had been a big, serviceable room meant to be a functional space with little aesthetic appeal. White subway tile on the walls. Gray tile on the floors. Stainless countertops.

Five years ago when he'd toyed with selling the place, he'd had the room renovated. Now, granite and slate in warm, earthy tones made the gourmet kitchen an elegant space to cook and entertain.

He guided Elizabeth onto a bar stool on the opposite side of the enormous center island from where Mrs. Myott cooked bacon on the six-burner stove and headed for the coffeepot. As he passed the diminutive woman with short, curly brown hair and keen blue eyes, he leaned over her shoulder and peered at the batter resting beside the heating waffle iron.

"Is there any of your famous strawberry preserves?"

"I put up a dozen jars this summer, all for you."

"That's my girl."

Mrs. Myott shot him a dry look. "I think you already have your hands full with the girl you've got."

"You have no idea," he murmured, fetching two cups of

coffee and returning to Elizabeth. "I hope you like waffles. Mrs. Myott makes the best in New York City. And wait until you taste her preserves."

"Is there anything I can do to help?" Elizabeth asked.

"Not one thing. I made this boy breakfast for eighteen years until he ran off to serve his country."

"She was my nanny," Roark explained.

"Came to work for Ms. Black two days after this one was born."

Her husband had been killed during the invasion of Grenada in 1983. Roark remembered photos of her husband in his uniform, and the stories she'd told of the missions he'd gone on. It's probably where the first seed had been planted that led him to join the marines.

"And she stayed because by the time I no longer needed a nanny, she'd become part of the family."

"Your mother was a dear."

Elizabeth's expression was intent as she followed the exchange. "So, you have lots of stories from when Roark was growing up?"

"I do."

"That's not why I brought you here." His pulse hitched at Elizabeth's mischievous smile.

He reined in the urge to kiss all thought of teasing him right out of her mind. It seemed every time he turned around, he came up with another excuse to take her hand, touch her back, slide his arm around her waist and kiss her soft lips. She had bewitched him.

"No?" She sipped her coffee, eyes sparkling at him over the rim. "You could have taken me to any restaurant in Manhattan, but instead you brought me here. I think you want me to know every little detail about you."

Damned if she wasn't right. And here was the funny part. She had no idea that she'd just hit a bull's-eye. She thought she was poking fun at him when in fact, he'd just presented her with a tour guide to his past.

"No restaurant can compare to Mrs. Myott's waffles."

Lines appeared at the corners of the older woman's eyes as her expression softened. Nowhere near a real smile for the average person, but positively beaming for his former nanny.

While Mrs. Myott served up hot waffles and her delicious strawberry preserves, she filled Elizabeth in on some of the more entertaining stories from his childhood.

"Your poor tutor." The laughter in Elizabeth's velvet blue eyes belied her sympathetic tone. "What if he'd had a heart attack or something?"

"He was lying to my mother. I wouldn't care if he had." The exploding spring mechanism that Roark had placed beneath his tutor's coffee cup had dumped the hot contents into the man's lap. The way he'd gone after Roark had shown his true colors and not the polite face he presented to Roark's mom.

"You could have found a better way to convince your mother he was abusive."

"Yes, but none would have been as much fun."

The women exchanged a look. Their non-verbal communication was Roark's cue to get Elizabeth out of there. If they stayed much longer, there'd be no mystery left. And he needed to keep her intrigued with him. For a little while longer, anyway.

"I need to grab a couple books from Mom's library and then I'll take you home."

"Of course." Elizabeth smiled at Mrs. Myott. "Are you sure I can't help you with the dishes?"

"No need. This darling young man renovated a few years ago and I have top-of-the-line everything. It'll take me a second or two to clean up."

While Roark located the books he wanted, Elizabeth strolled up and down the hallway that ran from the gallery to the master bedroom. Seven feet wide and sixty feet long, the walls held some of the incredible artwork his mother had collected over the years.

"I could stare at these all day," she said when he rejoined her. "It's like living in a museum." She shook her head. "And yet, it's your home."

"My mother's home. I live in a loft in Soho, remember?"

"Why don't you move some of these there? Your walls could use some brightening."

"I'm not home enough. And your comment about a museum makes me think I should loan some of these out." Something he'd said had lost her. Roark felt her pull into herself. The camaraderie of these past few hours vanished as if it had never been.

"I imagine quite a few museums would be thrilled to display them."

Roark caught her arm as she turned to go and set his fingers beneath her chin to tip her face upward. "What's wrong?"

"Nothing." But she evaded his gaze. "I have an event tonight. I should get home and go over my preparations to make sure everything will run smoothly."

"Will you come over afterwards?"

She lifted her chin from his grasp. "It'll be late."

"I'll give you a key. You can wake me."

Her mouth dropped open. "A key to your loft? Why?"

"I should think it was obvious. We're engaged. You should feel free to come and go."

"Last night…" She stopped talking and rolled her lips inward. Her fingers knitted together in front of her. "I'm not sure I understand what's going on."

"Then let me make it perfectly clear. Last night was amazing. I think you felt it, too. We have incredible chemistry. I want to explore it a whole lot further."

"I don't know. When I agreed to help you out, it was supposed to be a simple charade. Uncomplicated by anything physical."

"There's nothing complicated about what happened between us last night."

She gave him a you-have-to-be-kidding look. "Maybe not for you, but I have a bad habit of getting in too deep with men like you."

"Men like me?" Her generalization ignited his irritation. "What sort of man am I?"

"The sort who likes to take off without warning and views commitment like one step up from death."

He had no way to refute her claim. "And you want stability."

"More than that, I need to feel connected. To have someone I can count on. A year ago I lost my sister, her husband and my niece. They were killed in a car accident. She was my best friend. We talked every day. It's like a piece of my heart was cut out. Being alone is so hard. I'm afraid I'll start to rely on you and soon you'll be gone."

The pain throbbing in her voice lanced through him. He remembered the day his CO had informed him a call had come in while he was on training maneuvers. A thousand miles away his mother had died, alone and miserable because her only son had abandoned her.

"Of course I understand." How could he not. He had his own issues with letting people get too close.

Which left him with a conundrum. Making love with Elizabeth had been fantastic. He wasn't ready to give her up just because they wanted different things.

"Of course, now that we've slept together," she continued, "I'm almost guaranteed to start wanting more. It would be less of a problem if I wasn't so attracted to you or if you'd sucked in bed."

His mood lightened at her admission. "Then what would you suggest?"

She grimaced. "Just give me a little space to sort everything out. Get my head on straight."

"How much space?" He wanted her again. Now. He thundered with the craving to snatch her into his arms and plunder her mouth, to strip her bare and sink into her warmth. Hearing her admit that she had little defense against the chemistry between them was a powerful aphrodisiac.

"A few days."

"We have the Children's Hospital benefit to attend tomorrow night."

"Oh, right." She eyed him solemnly. "Can I count on you to keep your displays of affection strictly PG?"

He grinned. "Only if you promise to do the same."

Seven

"And this one?" Elizabeth drew the tip of her finger along a three-inch scar that transected Roark's right rib cage.

"An alley in Cairo." For the past hour she'd been cataloging all the damage done to his body, most of it in pursuit of antiquities, and Roark had explained every wound in the same matter-of-fact tone. "I'd gone there to get some information from a guy and ran into a competitor of mine instead."

It was close to midnight. Roark lounged in the middle of her bed, hands behind his head, lips quirked in a wry grin, his naked body laid out for her perusal. At the Children's Hospital benefit this evening he'd been respectful of her space just as he promised. No breath-stealing kisses. No provocative flirting. Just routine public displays of affection. His hand around her waist. His lips grazing her cheek.

And every second she'd grown more jittery with yearning. She knew he was bad for her, but her body betrayed her with every heartbeat.

"Dangerous business you're in." Her voice grated like a

spoon caught in a garbage disposal. She couldn't match his nonchalance. She'd counted fifteen scars, nine from knives, five from bullets and one from a cigarette. "What happens when your luck runs out?"

"Who said anything about luck? I was trained by Master Li in Wing Chun and by the marines. I'm the Jackie Chan of treasure hunters."

She knew he was trying to lighten her mood, but now that she'd seen just how perilous his business could be, she was gripped by a familiar fear. *Let it go. He's not yours to worry about.*

"And if you're ambushed by ten burly men?"

"I'd run like hell to safety." Roark sat up and wrapped his arm around her waist. His free hand tangled in her hair, trapping her. His gray-green eyes had gone serious as he stared at her. "I'm smart enough to know when the odds are against me."

Her heart clenched. She wanted to kiss him hard and long, until the ache in her chest faded, but losing herself in passion would only stave off anxiety. It didn't solve anything. Hadn't she learned that?

She tried a laugh, but it sounded hollow. "I believe you think you're smart enough." She gasped as Roark's teeth grazed her neck. "I'm just not sure you know when to give up."

He tumbled her backward and let his weight push her into the mattress. Her fingers drilled into his hair. The texture was as soft and wonderful as she'd once imagined it would be and addictive as hell. So were his kisses. And the slide of his body into hers.

She moaned.

Her thighs parted, hips lifted and she found him hard and ready to drive her straight to the stars once more. An hour ago they'd come together in a frantic frenzy. Hands tearing at clothes, mouths fastened to each other as they'd circled and sidestepped the twelve-foot span from her front door to her bed.

It wasn't until he'd collapsed on her, chest heaving, that she'd thought to wonder if one of them had remembered to shut her front door. The thought of what a passing neighbor might have witnessed roused a giggle.

"Usually when a man is making love to you," Roark groused, his long fingers enclosing her breast. "It's polite not to laugh at him."

She opened her eyes and caught him scowling at her. "I was just…oh." He'd sucked her nipple into his mouth and the wet suction blazed a trail of sensation straight down. The place between her thighs grew heavy with anticipation. She smiled beneath its weight.

It was easy to surrender to the moment with Roark kissing his way down her body. Later, she could fuss about the consequences of her actions tonight. Repeating that she had no intention of letting the lines blur between their fake public relationship and all too real private one made little sense anymore.

She might just have to accept that she was hopelessly infatuated with Roark and maybe even on the verge of falling in love. If she simply enjoyed their time together without dwelling on the reality that he would soon no longer need her, the next few months would be a lot more fun.

And the heartache that followed?

She'd survive. After all, she had lots of practice.

"You're still not paying attention to me." His tongue dipped into her navel and provoked a shiver. "I'll just have to do better."

Before she grasped his intent, he'd slipped lower on the mattress, his broad shoulders nudging between her thighs. When his mouth settled on her, Elizabeth cried out. The pleasure was so intense she stopped breathing.

Gathering handfuls of the sheets, she held on for dear life

as Roark's clever tongue propelled her into a sensual storm. Her lungs seized. Her stomach clenched. The pressure built. Roark's fingers bit hard into her butt, holding her still as her hips began to writhe. And then she was flying, soaring upward like a roman candle. Exploding in the clean, cold air high above. Fragmenting into a million pieces that drifted back to earth on a peaceful, gentle breeze that cradled her.

"What was that?" she croaked, her throat raw from panting and screaming.

"That is what I'm going to do to you every time you aren't paying attention to me."

"I'll make sure I neglect you at least once a day."

Roark kissed his way back up her body. When he reached her mouth, he settled his lips over hers in a deep, penetrating kiss. As his tongue tangled with hers, he slipped inside her and groaned as his hips collided with hers.

"That feels amazing." He laced his fingers with hers and held perfectly still for a long moment.

Elizabeth set her feet on the mattress and shifted the angle of her hips to take him deeper. Roark obliged and then began a slow retreat. The friction revived her hunger for him and she began to move in time with his thrusts.

In the hours following the first time they'd made love, she told herself that sex with Roark had been so perfect because she'd been clear-headed when she'd made the decision to make love with him. She hadn't been seduced into it by smooth talk or her own insecurities.

But now she understood that what happened between them had a magical quality she'd never known before. It was as if they enjoyed perfect synchronicity. One body. One mind. One soul. She knew what he wanted without being told. He anticipated her needs as if he read her thoughts.

It might have terrified her if another orgasm wasn't approaching at the speed of light. Elizabeth dug her nails into his back and shuddered beneath the force of yet another massive climax.

"You okay?"

That he held off his own finish to worry about her made Elizabeth smile. "Perfect."

His face contorted with concentration as he pumped furiously and began to shudder with his release. She held tight while he spilled himself inside her, thrilled by the power of his orgasm.

In the aftermath, he snuggled his face into her neck and became a boneless heap. His absolute relaxation was at odds with the energy buzzing through her veins. Normally when she felt like this she cleaned her tiny studio, rearranged her closets or revisited her itinerary for the upcoming week.

Her muscles relaxed as Roark's arm settled across her midsection.

"Can I spend the night?"

She hadn't expected his request. Didn't know how to answer. And every second she hesitated, he shifted a little closer to unconsciousness. His breathing settled into a sleepy rhythm.

Elizabeth's gaze traced her ceiling. Contentment settled over her body, but her mind was a jumble of fragmented thoughts. Had her heart fallen into a familiar pattern? Was she closing her eyes to why she and Roark didn't work in order to savor how much she enjoyed being with him?

So what if Roark was wealthy. A scholar. Or that Elizabeth would never need to worry that he'd move in with her and then have sex with another woman while she was at work. That had been Philip. A struggling musician with a band named Puked Rabbits.

Tom was next. He'd caught her in a vulnerable place after she'd broken up with Philip and sweet-talked her right into bed. The day she asked him where their relationship was going was the last time she saw him.

Elizabeth shifted her head on the pillow and stared at Roark. She'd dated enough jerks to know that he didn't fall into that category. He might profess he didn't sell his mother's penthouse because of the memories it held, but she was certain he held on to it because it had been Mrs. Myott's home for almost thirty years.

Still, there was no question her taste ran to unavailable men. She'd long ago understood she was challenged by the idea of turning them into something better. She liked the idea of taking something anyone else would give up on and making it work. Like the loft venue for the wine auction party where she'd met Roark. Elizabeth had accepted the challenge after three other event planners had turned it down, intimidated by the magnitude of the transformation the loft required. It's why she'd gotten the job on such short notice. But she'd made it work. And brilliantly.

"You're going to have a hard time falling asleep if you don't shut your eyes," Roark's low masculine voice murmured close to her ear.

"I thought you were already asleep."

"I was dozing." His eyes opened and searched her face. "Your loud thinking woke me up."

"As if that could happen." But she couldn't make her expression match her lighthearted tone.

"What's wrong?"

"I was thinking about my sister. Wondering what she'd think about what we were doing."

"You don't think she'd approve." Once again, he'd read her like a professional poker player.

"Ever since we were kids she was my moral compass. Of course, back then I called her Little Miss Goody Two-shoes." Elizabeth swallowed the lump that had formed in her throat. "Everyone loved her. She never did anything wrong. Or at least she never got caught. That's what I was for. I got blamed for everything that happened."

"I could have used a little brother for that."

"Hard to believe she and I would grow up to be best friends."

"Would she have liked me?"

"Doesn't everyone?"

"I could put you to sleep counting all the enemies I have in the world."

She didn't like the reminder of the numerous healed wounds on his body. "Then, let me rephrase. Don't all the women you meet like you?"

"Pretty much. And you didn't answer my question."

"She would have liked you."

"You don't sound sure."

"She would have liked you," Elizabeth repeated with more conviction. "She just wouldn't have liked you for me."

Roark mulled over his reaction to Elizabeth's declaration as he let himself into the loft the following morning. Despite being fully absorbed in his thoughts, he immediately knew he wasn't alone in the loft. It was a disturbance in the air, a vibration that had saved his ass any number of times. Moving quietly, he plucked a sharp knife from a drawer in the kitchen and headed in search of his intruder.

His first destination was the study. Given the troubles over the Gold Heart statue, he expected whoever had entered the loft would start here. A regular thief would've walked off with the Matisse he'd brought over from the penthouse. It was his favorite of all the artwork and Elizabeth had been right to say the loft needed something on the walls.

The study was undisturbed. Roark frowned. He wasn't wrong about someone being in the loft, but if neither his research nor his artwork was what the intruder was after, was Roark's life in danger?

He crossed the hall and regarded his partially closed bedroom door. Did an assassin lurk behind it just out of sight?

Heart thumping in anticipation of the fight to come, Roark reached out to nudge the door open and heard a soft sleepy groan coming from the direction of the bed. In his experience, killers rarely fell asleep while waiting for their prey. Roark shoved the door fully open and growled.

Sabeen lay sprawled across his sheets, black hair falling in luxurious waves over her naked back. She'd obviously slipped in during the evening with the idea of surprising him. What would have happened if he hadn't accompanied Elizabeth home? If he'd been able to convince her to come here for a nightcap? Granted, they weren't truly engaged, but he had little doubt Elizabeth wouldn't take kindly to finding a naked woman in his bed.

He wasn't taking kindly to it, either.

"Sabeen, get up and get dressed."

The young woman had been in the early stages of waking and Roark's sharp, loud demand acted like a shrill alarm clock. She sat up and clutched a sheet to her small breasts, but not before giving Roark a good look at what she was offering. He scowled at her. Her sleepy mind took a second to catch up to what she was seeing. A second later, her eyes went wide and her mouth dropped open as she stared at the knife in his hand.

"Roark, where have you been?"

"Making love to my fiancée. You remember Elizabeth, don't you?" Contentment rolled through him as he recalled the last several hours with Elizabeth. "She's the only woman I want in my bed."

Color flooded Sabeen's cheeks at Roark's rebuke, but her confidence never wavered. "She's too dull for you. You need a woman with passion. Someone who can satisfy you."

"Elizabeth satisfies me. More than any woman I've ever known." Roark had no idea what prompted him to add the second sentence, but he spoke the truth.

"You've never known me." She let the sheet fall and reached up to run her fingers through her long hair.

Roark felt nothing. For all that he thought of her as a little sister, she was an incredibly beautiful woman. But her nudity and seductive pose aroused him no more than a marble statue.

Time for a little hard truth. "And I never will. You are a child, Sabeen. Elizabeth is a woman."

"You don't love her. The engagement isn't even real."

Any warm spot Roark may have once had for his mentor's precocious daughter turned to ice at her accusation. "You don't know what you're talking about."

"Don't I?" Sabeen slid off the bed and stalked him like a jungle cat. "You forget that I'm not one of your stupid society friends, ready to believe any story you concoct. I know where you've been this last year and what you've been doing. There's been no woman in your life."

Roark scooped her clothes off the chair where she'd left them and tossed them her way. "Get dressed."

"Tell me you love her." Sabeen wasn't going to let the issue of his engagement drop until she received some confirmation of its legitimacy.

Roark wasn't going to lie. "My relationship with Elizabeth is none of your business."

"You don't love her."

"And you're such an expert?" In her attempt to goad him, she'd unleashed his impatience. "What about the business between you and that fortune hunter? When you looked in his eyes, did you see love or dollar signs?"

Gasping, Sabeen turned her back on him. Her hunched shoulders told Roark his point had hit home. Not proud of his counterattack, he returned the knife to the kitchen and brewed a pot of coffee. As the dark brown liquid streamed into a glass pot, the blast of adrenaline receded. Weariness hit him. Roark rubbed his face and wondered how Elizabeth was doing. He wished he was snuggled beside her in that ridiculously tiny apartment she lived in.

They'd been hitting the social scene pretty hard these past ten days in an effort to establish the legitimacy of Roark's transformation from playboy into someone stable and responsible. Not that it was all for show. He might not want to tear up the town with a different woman every night, but that didn't mean the itch to embark on his next antiquity hunt was gone. Already the necessity to appear at parties and charity events chafed at him. He wasn't cut out to dress up and play nice. He'd rather be skulking through back alleys in Cairo or tracking down hidden caches in Kabul.

Only in the private moments he shared with Elizabeth did the restlessness leave him. Damn. He was on the verge of being domesticated.

"May I have a cup of coffee or are you planning on kicking me out as soon as possible?"

Roark poured a second cup and slid it across the counter toward her. Sabeen had dressed in black leggings and a short green skirt. A long black and maroon scarf, wound several times around her neck, almost obscured the black lace blouse she wore. Intricate gold earrings, Middle Eastern in design, played peekaboo with her black hair.

She wasn't dressed to seduce. Her appearance in his bed had been an act of opportunity rather than premeditation.

"Give me the key." He looked at her purse. "Your brother has access to the loft so he can assist me when I'm overseas and need him to research something. You are not to come here without my permission."

She sulked as she fetched the key. "I came because I'm worried about Darius."

"So worried that you crawled naked into my bed?"

His point struck right where he wanted. She wouldn't look at him.

"The wedding is just around the corner. He's going to do something stupid—I just know it."

Concern buzzed. "The only stupid thing he could do is to help Fadira escape her father's plans for her."

And Sabeen's expression told him that's exactly what her brother intended to do. Cursing, Roark pulled out his phone and dialed Darius's number. It rolled to voice mail and Roark left him a terse message.

This is what love did to you. It made you stupid and foolhardy. Darius was going to risk his freedom, possibly his life, and for what? A pretty face. Some fleeting passion? Darius was twenty. Too young to have settled on one woman for the rest of his life.

Roark closed his eyes and imagined throttling the impulsive youth. Then, he refocused on the problem at hand and scrolled through the list of contacts on his phone.

"When did he leave?"

"Yesterday morning, I think."

Twenty-four hours. Darius could be in deep trouble already. "I'll make some calls."

"Thank you."

"I'm not doing this for you. I'm doing it for your father. I promised him that I would look out for you two." And the responsibility was like being trapped in a newly discovered Egyptian tomb. "I just had no idea it was going to become a full-time job."

Eight

The pre-sale exhibit at Waverly's had attracted a very se-
lect crowd. Elizabeth tried not to gawk at the who's who of
New York society as she circled the room on Roark's arm.
Although she'd protested against his purchasing the emer-
ald gown she wore, Elizabeth appreciated that she'd lost this
particular battle.

As she surveyed the collection of artwork, furniture
and formal china that would be auctioned off the following week, the emerald-and-diamond earrings on loan from
Roark's mother's collection tapped her neck. He'd refused
to disclose their price or the value of the matching bracelet
that she touched every few minutes to reassure herself it remained on her wrist, but she had the sneaking suspicion that
what she wore cost upwards of a hundred thousand dollars.

Elizabeth glanced Roark's way. The man might be physically present, but his mind was a thousand miles away. He'd
been distracted for the past two days, only abandoning whatever bothered him to make her body sing over and over. A

tremor clutched her knees as she pictured the things he'd done to her in the hours leading up to the party.

Roark's phone rang, disturbing her sultry memories. He frowned at the screen and sent her an apologetic glance.

"Take it," she said, hoping the call would clear up whatever had been distracting him. "I'm going to get myself a glass of champagne and a plate of shrimp."

That he hadn't shared his troubles with her was yet another reminder that they were only playing at being engaged. It helped to slow the slide into falling in love with him. Or at least she was better able to brace for the eventual pain when she landed hard in reality. She pushed aside her concern and gave him an encouraging smile.

He answered the phone with a tight nod. "This is Roark."

The rest of the conversation was lost in the hum of voices around her as Roark strode toward the exit. This whole fake engagement was starting to mess with her head. Each time she behaved as if Roark owed her explanations, she drew closer to the moment when her expectations would lead to disappointment.

And she'd only have herself to blame.

"Elizabeth, how wonderful you look."

Elizabeth turned in the direction of the voice and smiled at Charlotte Waverly, the wife of Vance Waverly, Roark's half brother.

The woman was radiant in a white, strapless gown with an empire waist banded in silver sequins and a feather skirt that made the most of her curvy figure. Her long blond hair trailed over one shoulder. Diamonds dangled from her ears.

"I love your dress," Elizabeth retorted. "You look like an angel."

"Thank you, and your jewelry is divine. A gift from Roark?"

"On loan from his mother's collection."

Charlotte grinned. "A loan today, but yours the day you two get married."

Elizabeth's stomach twisted. More and more, any mention of her upcoming marriage was like a knife thrust to her gut. The longer this pretend engagement went on, the deeper beneath Roark's spell she slipped. Her worst fears were coming to light. Losing Roark from her life would leave a hole in her heart as big as the state of Texas.

"Vance and I were hoping you'd join us for Thanksgiving dinner."

"Me?" Elizabeth's thoughts rushed to catch up with what Charlie was saying.

Charlie laughed. "Of course. You'll be family soon, and Roark mentioned that you have too many events that weekend to be able to get out of town to spend Thanksgiving with your parents."

Being swamped with work was what helped Elizabeth from crumbling beneath the weight of grief. Thanksgiving Day would mark a year since her sister and her family had died. Guilt stabbed at her. If Elizabeth hadn't been too busy with work to leave the city, Stephanie and her family wouldn't have been driving in to spend the holiday and they wouldn't have been killed on the road.

"That's awfully kind of you." Elizabeth groped for a way to refuse, but her throat closed, preventing any excuses from escaping.

"We'll have dinner around four. I'm so glad you can join us. From what Vance has told me, it's rare that Roark is in town, much less around for the holidays. Vance is looking forward to being surrounded by family this year."

A familiar arm circled her waist. "Mind if I steal my fiancée away? I have someone she must meet."

"Of course."

"You looked like you needed rescuing," Roark murmured. "What was she saying to you?"

"She invited me to Thanksgiving dinner." Elizabeth kept her expression smooth, but her insides were cramping. "Did you know about this?"

"Vance mentioned something about dinner, but it slipped my mind."

"I hate this."

"Hate what?"

Yes, what? The lies? The pretense that she was unaffected by being included in a Thanksgiving dinner with his family? The fact that they weren't truly engaged and so she couldn't be the happy future bride with a wedding to plan? What a self-delusional idiot she was to claim that she was okay with never getting married, when it was why she'd always tried so hard in relationships even though it was obvious that the men she'd chosen didn't want the same things.

Elizabeth bit her lip hard to bring her wayward emotions back under control. The pain helped distract her from the ache in her chest.

"This time of year." She let out a ragged sigh. "My sister and her family died last Thanksgiving. They were driving down to the city to spend the weekend with me."

"Elizabeth, I'm so sorry."

His fingers covered hers. He understood about loss. And guilt.

"They wouldn't have died if I had taken the days off to drive up to Albany. But I put my career first and booked events all four days. Stephanie was determined I wasn't going to spend Thanksgiving by myself." Elizabeth gave a bitter laugh. "And now I'm always alone for the holidays."

"What about your parents?"

"Their life is in Oregon. They moved there seven years ago and have only been back once, when Trina was born." Elizabeth stared at the bracelet on her right wrist. "I suppose you think I'm being overly dramatic. From what you've said, you're almost never in New York for the holidays."

"They're just another day for me."

For a second she felt sorry for him. His mother had been his whole life. Growing up without brothers, sisters, cousins or grandparents left him without a support network to rely on. His old nanny was as close to family as he knew. But now there was Vance and Charlotte and her son. Only Roark didn't want to acknowledge his importance in their lives and theirs in his.

"Are you going to Vance's for Thanksgiving?"

"Do you want to go?"

He was giving her the choice?

"I know this fake engagement has been difficult for you," he continued. "If you don't want to spend the day with Vance and Charlie, I'll understand."

"I knew it." Sabeen came around the corner like a vengeful spirit. Attired in gold from head to toe, dazzling earrings, sparkling sequined dress, metallic sandals, she shimmered as she stalked toward them, her expression intent and malicious. "I was right that you didn't love her."

Roark met her halfway and seized her arm. The way Sabeen flinched, his grip must have been punishing. He halted her five feet from Elizabeth.

"You were eavesdropping?"

"I followed you to see if you'd heard anything from Darius." Her dark eyes flashed with malicious glee. "And I hear that you're not really engaged."

Roark gave her a rough shake. "This is for the good of Waverly's. You will say nothing."

Sabeen was one of those women who had a pretty pout. "Why didn't you pretend with me?"

"Because you would have seen it as something more than it is."

And he was counting that Elizabeth would not. She held her ground when everything inside her longed to flee the truth. She was in love with Roark. Despite her determination to stay strong, she'd tumbled head over heels.

"You and I belong together." Sabeen set her hand against Roark's cheek and stared up at him. "My father knew that. It's why he asked you to watch over me. He believed once I was old enough you would see me as your perfect mate."

Roark seized both her wrists and held her away from him. "Your father entrusted me with your fortune and your welfare. He expected nothing more than that I do right by you and your brother. This fantasy of yours needs to stop. I am not meant for you or anyone. Elizabeth is pretending to be engaged to me because Rothschild is trying to take over Waverly's and I need the board to be confident that Ann, Vance and I are the perfect choice for the future of Waverly's." He gave her a little shake. "Do you understand?"

"No." Sabeen tore free. "I love you. Why can't you give us a chance?"

Roark set his hands on his hips. "Sabeen…"

Before he could say more she backed away. "This isn't over."

Elizabeth began to breathe again as the brunette vanished the way she'd come. "Do you think she'll tell someone?"

"Who is she going to tell?"

Elizabeth pictured the roomful of New York society a few steps away. "I can think of a couple hundred people out there."

Roark's arm came around her. He lifted her chin and kissed her passionately. Elizabeth responded as if the past ten minutes had never happened. It was easy to forget everything in Roark's strong embrace. His lips transported her to another universe, a whole new dimension where her senses were in control and passion ruled.

"Don't worry about Sabeen," he murmured. His lips swept across her cheek and lingered near her ear. "She's just worried about her brother. Once she calms down, she'll forget all about what she heard tonight."

Elizabeth longed for even a fraction of Roark's confidence. The best she could do was press her cheek against his powerful chest and gather strength from the arms that circled her. He had more to lose if their masquerade became public knowledge.

"You might be underestimating what your rejection might drive her to do." Elizabeth pushed out of Roark's arms. She had no more claim to him than Sabeen and it was time she remembered that. "She's an emotional young woman with strong feelings for you."

"She's a girl who should be focused on finishing school and tormenting boys her own age."

Roark's words made Elizabeth shake her head. He might not have encouraged Sabeen, but he didn't understand how intoxicating his charisma was in large doses. And Elizabeth had been absorbing the stuff for two weeks now. She was hooked. No doubt the young Egyptian girl had become addicted in a similar fashion.

Roark had been put in charge of her welfare by the girl's father. He'd rescued her brother from the Amazon jungle. It made perfect sense that hero worship had become infatuation.

"And if we stick to our story," Roark continued, squeezing her hand. "Stick together, it's the word of a hotheaded girl against the two of us."

Elizabeth forced away her anxiety. Over the next week, she was in charge of six different events, two of them last minute parties she'd scored thanks to the connections she'd made while on Roark's arm. All that meant she had enough to worry without loading up on Sabeen's drama.

"Is her brother really in danger?"

"He is unless I find and stop him."

"Is that why you've been so preoccupied these last few days?"

Roark cocked an eyebrow. "Have I neglected your needs?"

"No." She felt her cheeks heat beneath his loaded question. "It's just that you've been carrying your phone more as if you're waiting for someone to call."

All expression dropped from Roark's features. Worry shadowed his eyes. "The boy is a fool. He has gone to Cairo to steal Fadira away before her wedding. If he's caught, he could face imprisonment, maybe worse."

"Can you stop him?"

"If I can find him. I have friends looking for him now." Roark sounded annoyed and Elizabeth almost felt sorry for Darius. "And from what I discovered earlier today," he continued. "I'm not sure she'll go with him if he gets to her."

"Why not?"

"Her family is in trouble. It's why her father is forcing her to marry."

"Financial trouble?" Elizabeth recalled the reason Darius had gone looking for the temple in the Amazon.

"More like blackmail. He's trying to locate the documents that will exonerate her father and free her."

Elizabeth could see Roark was itching to join the action. "Are you going to help him look?"

"For now, I need to be here."

But she had to wonder how much longer before he took off on another adventure? Would he last much past Thanksgiving? Elizabeth scrutinized his frown and tense body language. She'd better prepare herself to say goodbye.

Roark was hanging by his fingertips thirty feet off the gym floor when his cell phone began to ring. This better be the call he'd been waiting for. Swinging his leg up, he slipped his toe into a hold and freed his right hand to tap the Bluetooth headset.

"Roark."

"I found someone who can help us find Mas."

Not the call he was waiting for, but just as good. "Where?"

"Cairo."

Not only was Roark searching for any word on Darius, he was tracking the thief who'd stolen the Gold Heart statue documents. "How long ago?"

"Two hours. Keeps a girlfriend in Agouza."

"Keep an eye on him, I'll be there in twelve hours."

Roark disconnected the call as soon as his feet hit the ground. He'd rappelled down the rock wall during the brief conversation and gathered up his duffel as soon as he'd packed away his gear.

On the street he hailed a taxi and dialed Vance. "I have some business in Cairo to take care of. Can you and Charlie escort Elizabeth to the gala tonight?" This evening's function benefited the local food pantry.

"Charlie and I will take care of your fiancée, but are you sure that leaving town is a good idea right now?"

"It's the perfect time. With all the suspicion surrounding the Gold Heart statue, I have to retrieve the documents that prove it's authentic and not the one missing from Rayas."

"And Elizabeth will be okay that you're not going to spend Thanksgiving with her?"

Roark shied away from the true answer. "This isn't a real engagement, remember?" The words didn't reflect well on his character, Roark decided. On this anniversary of her family's tragic accident, Elizabeth was counting on him to be there for her. She hadn't come right out and said so, but he'd noticed how much comfort she took in his presence. And wasn't that exactly what he'd hoped to avoid when he'd chosen Elizabeth to become his pretend fiancée?

"I remember," Vance said. "It's just that after seeing you two together I thought…"

"You thought what?" Roark interrupted, taking his bad mood out on his brother. "It's all an act."

"Well, it's a damned good one." Vance paused a second. "In fact, if I didn't know better, I'd say you had real feelings for Elizabeth."

"You don't know better. This is all for Waverly's. As soon as Rothschild's takeover threat is dealt with, I'm heading back to Dubai and Elizabeth will get on with her life."

Vance's words ate at Roark as he went to his loft to grab the bag he always kept packed for just such quick escapes before heading to a downtown Manhattan heliport. He'd already contacted a man who owed him a favor. To avoid being stopped by the FBI, he was hitching a ride on the businessman's Gulfstream to Amsterdam. From there he'd hop a commercial flight to Cairo.

Traffic slowed the taxi. Roark made use of the time to dial Elizabeth's cell. It went straight to voice mail. She didn't deserve to hear about his trip in a message. He disconnected the call. She was probably meeting with her boss. When she'd left his loft this morning, her mind had been far from her perfunctory goodbye kiss. Already they were behaving like a couple that had been together for years, taking each other for granted.

Yet, they'd only known each other three weeks.

Guilt nudged him, but he shoved it aside. Elizabeth knew what she was getting into when she'd agreed to help him out. He wasn't the sort who stayed put and enjoyed being domesticated. He craved the thrill of the chase. Wanted no one and nothing to pin him down.

Sure, this elaborate hoax to save Waverly's was a little unusual for him. But he wasn't doing it because he intended to stick around and get involved with the day-to-day running of Waverly's. That was Ann's responsibility.

Roark slipped his phone into a side pocket of his duffel and headed to the waiting helicopter that would take him to Long Island MacArthur Airport. The chopper ride would be too noisy for another try at calling Elizabeth. He would just have to wait.

The private plane was taxiing toward the runway when he finally made contact.

"That was a long meeting with Josie," he said. "How'd it go?"

"Much as I expected. She's determined the only way she'll make me a partner is if I convince Sonya Fremont to let us plan her event. What if I can't do that?"

"You could quit. Start your own business."

A long pause greeted his words. "Starting from scratch would take more time and money than I have."

"You have thirteen thousand dollars."

"You know what I'm going to use that money for."

They'd been around and around on the subject of her up-coming motherhood. In Roark's opinion she was too young to tie herself down with a child. "I'm sure there's at least one investor in Manhattan that believes in you and would be happy to lend you some start-up capital."

"I'm not taking any more of your money. Besides, I'm going to start the in vitro treatments as soon as Thanksgiving is over. I want to be a mom more than I want to be an entrepreneur. What I need is the security I will get from be-coming Josie's partner." A thread of frustration ran through her voice. "But enough about my unproductive morning. Are you calling to tell me what time you'll pick me up tonight?"

"I'm calling to let you know that I'm not going to make it to the gala tonight, but I want you to go. I've already spoken with Vance. He will escort you."

"I'm not going if you can't."

"If you don't go you'll miss the chance to meet Sonya and speak with her about her gala." Over the past sev-eral days, she'd grown more melancholy as the anniversary of her sister's death approached. Leaving her alone on the holi-day ate at him, but he needed to get those documents back.

"Very well. Why aren't you able to make it tonight?"

"I have a lead on the thief that stole the Gold Heart docu-ments."

"You're leaving town?" Her voice cracked.

"I'm on a plane right now."

Silence greeted him.

"Elizabeth, you know I have to get the provenance paperwork back or the statue's only worth will be the gold it's composed of."

"Of course, I understand. When will you be back?"

"A few days. No more than a week."

"You'll miss Thanksgiving dinner tomorrow."

"I know. I'm sorry."

"It's fine."

But it wasn't. Roark heard a whiff of disappointment. They both knew it didn't belong there. Which is why she'd worked so hard to sound neutral.

"I hope you still intend to celebrate with Vance and Charlie."

"I'll make some excuse."

"They will be expecting you."

"They're expecting you and your fiancée." She let her point sink in for a second before saying, "Looks like there's an emergency with the Chapwell party. Stay safe."

She disconnected the call before he could reply. The jet raced down the runway, the momentum pushing him deep into his seat. They took to the air and Roark's stomach gave a familiar lurch. Land fell away as the plane climbed.

Unable to shake the sensation that what he was leaving behind was as important as what he intended to retrieve, he shut his eyes, but what played through his mind wasn't the mission ahead, but the night before. Elizabeth naked above him, her full breasts offered up for his possession as she rode him into a storm of pleasure so acute it had shaken him to his core.

With a silent curse he jerked his attention back to the present.

"Can I get you something?" A twentysomething brunette dressed in a crisp white blouse and black skirt smiled at him.

What he wanted was whiskey to burn away whatever this

emotion was that ate at him, but eleven o'clock in the morning was too early for alcohol.

"Coffee. Black."

Might as well be fully awake to appreciate the waves of guilt rolling over him. For the second time in his life, he'd run from the most important woman in his life to pursue his own agenda. He hoped this time it wouldn't end as badly as the last.

Nine

The Waldorf-Astoria Starlight Roof accommodated six hundred and the room was half full when Elizabeth arrived on Vance's left arm, feeling distinctly like the third wheel she was. As kind as Charlie and Vance had been to her in Roark's absence, they were so obviously a newlywed couple that it was almost painful for her to be in their company.

After collecting their table assignments in the foyer, the trio posed for a photo. Elizabeth stepped aside, insisting that Vance and his wife should take one without her, and headed into the venue eager to gather ideas for future events of her own. Although she'd been expecting to be impressed, the room's eighteen-foot ceilings and tall windows draped in black and ivory gave her a momentary pang of envy. What would it be like to plan an event for a room like this?

Fifty tables of eight had been arranged in the long, narrow room. At the center of each table a thirty-inch pedestal arrangement of red roses and white delphinium offered a splash of color in the otherwise monochrome surroundings.

Elizabeth scouted where she'd be sitting before approaching the open bar at the far end of the room. She ordered a white wine and stood in relative privacy away from the guests streaming into the center of the room. The table where she and the Waverly's would be sitting was near the podium. The food pantry was one of Ann Richardson's favorite charities and her work was being honored tonight.

Her heart began to pound as she spied Sonya Fremont enter the room. The woman had been in possession of Elizabeth's proposal for over ten days. As far as she knew no decision had been made on an event planner. Her future hinged on her ability to convince Sonya that she was the perfect person to handle the event.

Setting the wine down, Elizabeth started across the room in Sonya's direction. When she drew within ten feet, doubts closed in. What was she doing? Her only credibility at these sorts of functions came from standing beside Roark. Without him she might as well be invisible.

"Mrs. Fremont?" Where she found the courage to follow through on her initial impulse, Elizabeth would never know. "My name is Elizabeth Minerva. I'm—"

"Roark Black's fiancée." A dimple appeared beside Sonya's mouth as the petite blonde woman extended her hand. "The clever girl who tamed the city's most intriguing adventurer."

"I wouldn't go so far as to say tame." Elizabeth warmed beneath the woman's approval and relaxed. "I'm here and he's on a plane, heading to…" Had Roark told her where he was headed? She'd been so damned mad when he'd announced that he wasn't going to make it tonight, she couldn't recall if he'd said. She certainly hadn't asked. "Actually I have no idea where he's off to."

Sonya laughed. "Oh, dear, you've lost track of him already?" She linked her arm through Elizabeth's and turned toward the bar. "Not to worry. Roark is the sort of man who needs a long leash."

The notion of Roark putting up with any sort of leash amused Elizabeth to no end. "You sound like you know him pretty well."

"My husband has followed his career for some time. I think he secretly wishes he'd run off on his own adventures when he was young instead of becoming an investment banker."

While Sonya flirted with the attractive bartender, Elizabeth retrieved her white wine and wondered how to broach the subject of the proposal. The room was three-quarters full and before too much longer everyone would begin to make their way to their tables. Her window would be lost.

"I suppose you're wondering if I've chosen the event planner for the gala."

Instead of groaning, Elizabeth applied a rueful smile to her lips. "Was I so obvious?"

"I figured it was high on your list when you approached me."

"That's a nice way of putting it."

Sonya flashed her a wicked grin. "I'm rarely nice. But I'm sure you know that. How is my old friend, Josie?" The very deliberate slur on the word "friend" took a sledgehammer to Elizabeth's optimism.

"She's fine."

"Still the same manipulative bitch she always was?"

"I…" Elizabeth felt the event slipping through her fingers with each question. She stood with one foot on either side of an ever-widening crevasse. "She hasn't changed much in the three years I've worked for her."

Sonya's laugh rang out. "You, my dear, should have been a diplomat. I like you very much. If you weren't working for my worst enemy I would hire you in a second."

"Please reconsider. I would do an incredible job for you."

"Did my old friend tell you what happened between us?"

Elizabeth's heart sank. There was bad blood between her boss and one of New York's most influential socialites? "No."

"Twenty years ago we were best friends. Two weeks before my wedding, she slept with my fiancé."

Elizabeth sucked in a shocked breath. Now she understood. Her boss had set her up to fail and since that was the case, Elizabeth had nothing to lose. "Please don't believe for a second that I'm unsympathetic to how much that hurt you, but keep in mind that for the last twelve years she has been supporting an unpublished writer who has yet to propose to her while you are obviously very happy with a husband who adores you and can afford to keep you in Alexander McQueen and Dolce & Gabbana."

Sonya sipped her wine and regarded Elizabeth over the rim. "Are you always this straight-speaking?"

"Some clients like hearing the truth."

"Do they now?"

Neither the socialite's neutral tone nor her intent expression gave Elizabeth any idea how her bluntness had been received. "Others need their hand held and their reality sugar-coated."

"And you think I'm the former."

"I do."

"If I hire you can I expect more such truth from you?"

Elizabeth's head swam. She was so close to her goal that it was hard to hold her breath and talk at the same time. "I'm afraid so."

"Never be afraid of who you are." Sonya's head canted to the side as she studied Elizabeth. "I like you. I'd like to hire you, but I've sworn never to put a single coin in that woman's pocket."

"I understand." This is why Josie had made Sonya's event the basis for her partnership. It was never going to happen. She'd been destined to fail from the start.

"Call me if you ever wise up and leave Josie's employ. I think we could make beautiful parties together."

"You'll be the first to know."

Leaving Sonya to work the room, Elizabeth pulled out her

phone and typed a quick text. It wasn't until she'd sent the
message that she realized her first impulse had been to share
the results of the encounter with Roark.

With her mood further dampened, Elizabeth made her way
back to the Waverly table. She was the last to arrive.

Ann Richardson broke off her conversation as Elizabeth
approached. "Where's Roark?"

Six pairs of eyes awaited her answer. Only two pairs held
any sympathy: Vance and Charlie. The weight of her fake
engagement sat heavily on Elizabeth's shoulders. Irritation
fired. How dare Roark abandon her at such a crucial time.
What was she supposed to tell people when she had no idea
what had prompted him to take off the way he had?

"He had an errand to run." The excuse sounded lame.

Ann narrowed her eyes. "What sort of an errand?"

"Hello, sorry I'm late." Wearing a bright smile, Sabeen appeared at Elizabeth's side in a strapless gown of cobalt-blue.
"Roark called and told me to be your date tonight."

Given the tenor of their last conversation, Elizabeth wasn't
sure whether or not to believe Sabeen. Roark had to know
that having the young woman at her side during the dinner
would increase Elizabeth's discomfort rather than ease it.
But if Roark hadn't mentioned the gala, why else would Sabeen show up?

"That was thoughtful of him," Elizabeth murmured.

"And where is Roark?" Ann Richardson wasn't going to
be satisfied until she had answers.

The look Sabeen shot Elizabeth was filled with triumph.
"Didn't Elizabeth tell you? He's heading to Cairo."

Was that true? Roark hadn't shared his destination during their brief phone call. Of course, she hadn't asked any
questions.

"He left the country?" Angry color flared in Ann's cheeks.
"Without telling anyone? When is he coming back?"

"I believe a week," Elizabeth said.

Sabeen's lips curved in a feline smile. "He told me he planned to be back by Sunday."

Violent impulses stirred in Elizabeth as Vance and Charlie shared a sympathetic look. She neither needed nor deserved their pity. She and Roark weren't engaged, it was all a pretense. They'd known each other less than a month. It made perfect sense that he'd share more with Sabeen, a woman he'd known for ten years.

So, why did she feel so betrayed?

"And did he also tell you why he was in Cairo?" Ann gave Sabeen her full attention, dismissing Elizabeth in a way that made her grind her teeth.

All the problems with the Gold Heart statue had created tension between Ann and Roark. Elizabeth's resentment of Roark's abandonment grew as she took the backlash on her chin. More than anything she wanted to run away from this party and consume a quart of ice cream in her apartment, but she'd lose even more face if she did. Instead, she took her seat beside Vance and composed her features.

Roark's brother leaned over and muttered, "Roark didn't invite Sabeen to this party."

"You don't know that."

"He would never have done that to you. She took it upon herself to humiliate you like this."

Vance's words boosted Elizabeth's confidence out of the basement.

"Thank you."

Sabeen wore a triumphant expression as she took Roark's seat. Elizabeth let her have the battle. The younger woman waged a pointless war. As soon as the takeover of Waverly's was no longer a threat, Elizabeth and Roark would part ways, and he would return to his adventures. She wasn't Sabeen's competition. The world of antiquities procurement was.

While Sabeen drank glass after glass of wine and bubbled about a gallery opening she'd attended and a cat fight she'd glimpsed between two well-known socialites, Elizabeth nibbled at her salmon and willed the evening to be over.

The waiter was clearing her untouched dessert when she tuned back into what Sabeen was saying.

"And when he explained to me why he and Elizabeth had gotten engaged after knowing each other about a day, of course I forgave him."

Elizabeth's blood crystalized in her veins as Sabeen's words sunk in. The rest of the table seemed equally stunned as they stared her way.

"What exactly did he say?" Ann directed the question at Sabeen, but it was Elizabeth who took the brunt of her displeasure.

"That they'd gotten engaged because of the Waverly's takeover threat. One of your board members promised his support against the sale if Roark could prove he'd settled down enough to be an asset to Waverly's instead of a liability."

"Is this true?" Ann demanded.

Elizabeth was saved from answering by the head of the food pantry stepping to the podium to introduce Ann. Grateful for the minor reprieve, Elizabeth joined the clapping as Ann stood. Elizabeth went cold at the way Ann was staring at her from the raised platform. "You had no right to break Roark's confidence," Elizabeth said.

Sabeen tossed her head like a spoiled child. "How was I supposed to know he hadn't told these people? What's the big deal, anyway? He's doing it for them."

"And what if others heard you?" As soon as the words were out, Elizabeth could tell there was no reasoning with Sabeen.

"No one heard. You're just mad because you can't pretend Roark loves you anymore."

"Do you honestly think I have any illusions about my relationship with Roark? I'm not some foolish child who imagines that I can manipulate him into loving me by destroying everything else in his life that matters to him."

The tightness in her chest made her heart work hard for each beat. Her chair was too close to the table. The crowd of six hundred attendees sucked the oxygen from the room. Sweat broke out on her skin.

Ann's strong voice became a roar in her ears as Elizabeth noticed a woman at the next table wasn't paying attention to the speech, but was staring her way. Had she overheard Sabeen?

Anxiety crawled across Elizabeth's skin. If Roark had been here they could have faced down the gossip together. He'd have kissed her passionately in front of everyone and shut down the rumors that they weren't really engaged. Alone, Elizabeth couldn't rally the conviction to deny Sabeen's claim. All she could do was sit and try to keep her panic from showing.

But that took all her energy and by the time Ann's speech concluded, Elizabeth was completely drained.

She turned to Vance. "I need to go." She pushed back from the table and stood.

Vance got to his feet as well and put a gentle hand on her arm. "Charlie and I will take you home."

"No." Elizabeth shook her head. "Please stay. I will be fine."

Without a word to Sabeen, she headed for the exit, weaving her way between the tables. Her hands shook as she reclaimed her coat and slipped into it. The cold November air bit deep into her bones as she stepped onto the sidewalk. On the way back to her apartment her shivers grew in intensity despite the heat blowing from the taxi's air vents. By the time she'd stripped off her finery and crawled between the sheets she was convinced she'd never feel warm again.

The harsh midday sun bounced off the pitted pavement and stabbed at Roark's tired, dry eyes. He'd chosen a small round table by the window. A cup of coffee sat untouched near his elbow. Roark swiped at the sweat gathering on his forehead and scanned the traffic passing the café's open door.

Worry rubbed Roark's already short temper into something nasty. Smith was late. That wouldn't happen unless something was wrong. The ex-military man had an uncanny sense of time. Halfway through their first tour together, Roark had labeled him a walking timepiece.

His phone vibrated in his pocket. Roark's first thought was that Elizabeth had responded to one of his texts. He'd sent her several since arriving in Cairo, asking how her evening had gone. Her reply had been nonexistent. A muscle ticked in his jaw.

At first he'd assumed Elizabeth was still mad at him for taking off so unexpectedly and at a time when she most needed his support, but then Vance had filled him in about what had happened at the gala with Sabeen.

His gut clenched. The first thing he intended to do after returning to New York was show Sabeen what happened to someone who crossed him. After that, he was going to apologize to Elizabeth and kiss her senseless. Providing of course, that she was willing to see him.

Slipping the cell out, he checked the message.

Outside

Cryptic bastard. The text was from Smith, not Elizabeth. Disappointment sliced razor sharp. He reminded himself that it was a little after noon in Cairo, 5:00 a.m. in New York. Elizabeth probably wouldn't be up for another couple of hours.

Shoving the phone back into his pocket, Roark headed for the exit. Had he really expected that she'd be quick to forgive him after facing the exposure of their masquerade all by herself? Granted, Sabeen had only told Roark's family and Ann Richardson. The story wouldn't spread beyond them, but Ann couldn't have taken the news well. And Elizabeth shouldn't have had to face everyone alone.

Roark stepped from the café and spotted Smith leaning against the passenger door of a rusty brown Toyota, enormous biceps crossed over a powerful chest.

The six-foot-four-inch former marine pushed away from the car as Roark neared. "Get in."

"Where are we going?"

"Somewhere quiet."

Another thing about Smith was his brevity. The man rarely strung more than four words together at a time. While Smith negotiated the Cairo traffic, Roark sent Elizabeth another text.

"Trouble?" Smith inquired.

Roark put the phone away. "Yeah."

"What kind?"

"Female."

Smith grunted. "Not like you."

"This one's different."

Smith let one raised eyebrow speak for him.

"She's doing me a favor and it landed her in some hot water."

"Sleeping with her?"

This time it was Roark who let his expression do the talking.

Smith's thin lips twitched. "Idiot."

"Shut up."

And that was last the two men spoke until Smith popped the car trunk. "Got Masler's fence."

They were alone in an empty warehouse on the outskirts of Old Cairo. The building was practically falling down around them, but for whatever Smith had in mind, this was the perfect location.

"Does he know where Masler is?"

"Let's find out."

The two men pulled the terrified Egyptian out of the trunk and set him on his feet, keeping a hold on his arms as he swayed unsteadily. Beneath his olive complexion, the man was green. Roark understood why. Smith's driving through Cairo involved short bursts of acceleration, followed by hard braking and frequent lane changes. The fence had probably gotten pretty scrambled. Roark only hoped the guy retained enough of his faculties to assist them.

"I'm not telling you anything," the fence declared after Smith shoved him into a chair.

Roark had just finished securing their captive's legs and arms when a plain black car entered the warehouse. Adrenaline spiking, Roark cursed the intrusion, but Smith's only reaction was to shoot the vehicle a look of disgust. Vigilance easing, Roark slid the hunting knife with its six-inch blade back into its sheath inside his boot.

"You're late," Smith said to the man approaching them.

He was about a head shorter than Smith and wore a navy windbreaker emblazoned with an Interpol emblem. "You said one o'clock. It's five after."

Smith grunted a reply and handed a camera to Roark, and a beer to the Interpol agent. Before the fence knew what they were about, the Interpol agent goosed him in the ribs, producing a somewhat lively expression and Roark caught the two men in a celebratory moment. After a quick check to make sure he'd gotten the shot they needed, he handed the camera off to Smith who uploaded the photo on to his laptop.

"Nice," Smith remarked and tossed a fat envelope toward the agent. "Thanks."

Without checking its contents, the man from Interpol pocketed the envelope. "Call me when you track down Masler."

"Will do."

Roark stared at the fence while Smith clicked away on the computer. It took a lot of willpower not to grin at the terrified Egyptian. "My friend here is uploading that photo of you and an Interpol agent even as we speak." He glanced toward Smith. "Where are you posting it?"

"His Facebook page."

The man's dark eyes showed white all around. "I don't have a Facebook page."

"You do now. I'm sure Masler is going to be very unhappy to see you being so chummy with your new Interpol buddy. Not to mention how the rest of your clients will react."

"It will ruin me."

"It will get you killed."

"Or worse," Smith added as Roark watched the man's composure fragment.

"Yes, killed." The fence nodded vigorously, a bead of sweat sliding down his temple. "They will kill me. You cannot do this."

"Maybe you should tweet about it while you're at it. Hashtag snitch." Keeping his gaze glued on the fence, Roark tossed the suggestion over his shoulder. "I've heard Masler follows Interpol."

Obviously it never occurred to the panicky fence that someone in Masler's business stayed miles away from any sort of social networking. His gaze bounced between Smith and Roark, agitation growing by the second.

"Stop," the fence cried, clearly at the end of his rope. "I'll tell you how to find Masler."

Smith stopped typing and stared at the man in the chair, his finger hovering over the laptop. "Speak."

An hour later, Smith and Roark dumped the man a mile from his home and then drove to Roark's hotel.

Inside the hotel room, Roark asked over a passable single malt, "Think he'll warn Masler we're on to him?"

Smith tossed his back in one swallow and poured a second. "Doubtful."

That meant he could set a trap for Masler and bait it with something the thief would find irresistible like the second leopard statue. Smith finished his second shot with the same efficiency as the first and headed toward the door.

"Thanks for your help on this," Roark called after him. "And let me know when you locate Darius."

"Will do." Smith paused halfway out the door and turned back. "This girl, she good for you?"

Smith's question caught Roark off guard. His first impulse was to toss off a careless answer, but after what his buddy had done for him both today and in the past, Roark decided he owed him better than that.

"Very good."

"Love her?"

"Don't know."

Smith shook his head. "Idiot."

"Yeah." Roark sighed as the door closed on his friend. "Damn straight."

Ten

Elizabeth's hand hovered over the pint of ice cream in her freezer. At seven in the morning, it was too early for her to get started, but today's Page Six article gave her a solid excuse to indulge in Cherry Garcia.

Her first phone call this morning had come from Allison, warning her that Sabeen's indiscretion last night had indeed been overheard. That call had been followed by one from Charlotte and three from Josie. Elizabeth had let those calls go to voice mail. After speaking to Allison, she'd been unable to face anyone else.

Shutting the freezer door before she surrendered to self-destructive eating, she took her phone back to bed. Curled beneath the warm comforter, she scanned through the dozen texts Roark had sent her the previous night. As low as she felt at the moment, reading the messages gave her mood a minor boost. In his autocratic way, Roark did appear somewhat remorseful that he'd abandoned her to the wolves. But this was his fight to wage, not hers, and just because he was conveniently missing in action didn't mean she had to be the one to clean up his mess.

An hour later she grew tired of moping and decided to bake the pumpkin pie she'd intended to bring to Thanksgiving dinner at Vance and Charlie's home. After reading the Page Six article, there was no way she was leaving her apartment, but no reason why she couldn't celebrate the holiday.

She was rolling out the pie dough when her doorbell rang. Dusting flour from her hands, she headed to the front door. Josie stood in the hall.

"I suppose you thought to make a fool of me by pretending to be engaged to Roark Black," her boss began without even a hello. "Well, I'm here to tell you that not only am I never going to make you a partner, but you're fired, as well."

On the heels of everything else that had happened in the last twenty-four hours, Elizabeth saw Josie's pinched mouth and accusatory, close-set eyes through a glaze of red. "Fine. Then I guess I'll be opening my own event planning company. And my first client will be Sonya Fremont. She's agreed to let me plan her gala."

The sheer insanity of the boast shocked Elizabeth out of her fury. She had no idea if Sonya would even agree to take her call once she read the Page Six story. For that matter, Elizabeth had no idea if any of the society women who'd hired her would let her continue working on their projects.

Josie's mouth opened and closed. She looked thunderstruck. "Sonya agreed to hire us?"

"She agreed to hire *me,*" Elizabeth corrected, emphasizing the last word. Or she prayed that Sonya's offer still stood. "She refuses to have anything to do with you."

Having an important client like Sonya Fremont would make it easy enough for Elizabeth to find a job with another event planner.

"I can't believe you'd turn on me like this," Josie said. "After everything I did for you."

"You fired me." Granted, Elizabeth hadn't gotten a full night's sleep, but was she hearing things or had her boss fired her thirty seconds earlier. "How have I turned on you?"

"You said terrible things to Sonya about me, didn't you? That's why she won't work with me."

"I didn't say anything to Sonya about you." What the hell had she been thinking to continue working for someone as crazy as Josie?

"What about your events this weekend? Are you planning on abandoning all of those, as well?"

"I guess you should have thought about that before you fired me."

As she shut the door in her boss's face, Josie's last words struck her. "I'm going to make sure that no other event planners will dare touch you," Josie yelled, her voice carrying loud and clear through the door. "You're going to rue the day you messed with me."

Rue the day?

Between her former boss's poison and the outing of her pretend engagement to Roark, what if Elizabeth couldn't find another job? Earlier in the week she'd gone to the fertility clinic to have blood work done in the hopes that she could start the process towards another in vitro attempt. The third round had to be the charm. But if she had no job, it wouldn't matter if Roark's money helped her get pregnant—she wouldn't be able to support a child on unemployment.

Covering her mouth with both hands, Elizabeth set her back against the door as her knees gave way. She slid down the door. When her butt hit the floor she collapsed in a fit of giggles. It wasn't until she was gasping for breath that she realized she was crying. Yep, it was official, she'd hit rock bottom.

On the one-year anniversary of the worst day of her life, she'd celebrated by becoming a social pariah and slamming the door in her boss's face instead of begging for her job back. It was perfect.

From her nightstand came the sound of her cell phone. Elizabeth wiped tears from her cheeks with the back of her hands and pushed off the floor. On the television, Garfield the cat floated into Times Square. Elizabeth had surrounded herself with all her favorite Thanksgiving traditions, but no cheer filled the hollow in her chest.

She didn't get to the phone before it rolled to voice mail. It was Roark.

"Elizabeth, Vance called and told me we hit Page Six. I'm sorry I'm not there to handle this, but I'm catching the first plane home. In the meantime, it would be best if you don't speak to any reporters or talk to anyone. That might make things worse. I'll deal with everything when I get back."

His voice sounded brisk and authoritative, an employer gearing up for damage control. Yet another reminder that they weren't in this as a couple, but as coconspirators. Still, it would be nice to feel his arms around her. To be able to lean on him.

Elizabeth shook off her unrealistic longing and went back to her pie. By the time it went into the oven, her kitchen was covered in a thin layer of flour and her sink was piled with dishes.

For the second time that morning her doorbell rang. She couldn't remember ever being this popular. With Roark's warning ringing in her ear, she checked the peephole before she opened the door in case an ambitious reporter had tracked her down. Vance Waverly stood in her hallway.

She opened the door.

"Hel-l-o." Both his tone and his eyebrows rose as he took in her appearance.

Too late, Elizabeth realized if the kitchen was covered in flour, she probably was, as well. "What are you doing here?"

"Roark called me after you didn't pick up. He's worried about you."

"I'm fine."

"I can see that." He looked past her. "Doing a little baking?"

"A pumpkin pie."

"Then you're still planning on coming for Thanksgiving dinner?"

Was it that late already? She'd been so busy worrying about her sudden unemployment she had forgotten all about calling to cancel. "I really don't know if that's such a great idea. Sabeen was right. Roark and I aren't really engaged. You have to know he was only thinking of Waverly's."

"And you? What were you thinking about?" Vance set his hand on the door frame and leaned in. "Why would a beautiful woman risk so much to help out a man she barely knew?"

"He's helping me." She waited for shock and outrage, but glimpsed only amusement. "What's so funny?"

"Roark could have had almost any woman in New York City, but he chose you. Have you asked yourself why?"

"No."

"You might want to."

The timer dinged on her stove, indicating that the pie was done and saving Elizabeth from having to reply. "Can I offer you some coffee?"

"Why don't I pour myself a cup while you get ready."

The words that would send him on his way hovered on her lips, but went unsaid. She really didn't want to be alone today.

"I have a lot of flour to wash off. It'll probably take me half an hour."

"The coffeepot looks full. I can wait."

"Afraid if you leave, I won't show up?"

"Of course not."

Elizabeth didn't believe him. Nor did she blame him for not trusting her. Facing even a small number of people today held little appeal.

An hour later, they arrived at Vance's palatial home in Forest Hills. Charlie's face reflected her relief as her husband escorted Elizabeth into the grand two-story foyer.

Despite the large scale of the rooms, Charlotte had managed to make the traditional styling welcoming and cozy. As Elizabeth slipped out of her coat, she couldn't help but compare the warm, elegantly decorated space to Roark's starkly appointed loft that, thanks to the odds and ends he'd collected on his travels, looked more like a Moroccan flea market than a home. The two living spaces were as different as the men who occupied them.

Vance, a wealthy businessman with a rock-solid personal life. Sophisticated and settled. His home, polished and perfect.

Roark, a scholar and an adventurer with a study crammed with books and a packed bag in his closet ready so he could be ready to leave town on a moment's notice. And then there was the penthouse on Fifth Avenue. Roark was a man holding on to his past because guilt kept him from confronting his mistakes and forgiving himself.

Envy ate at Elizabeth as she watched Vance kiss his wife and toss the toddler into the air. The room rang with the child's delighted cries and Elizabeth looked away. Not wishing to burden anyone with her melancholy, she moved apart and sat where she could gaze at the gardens behind the house.

She wanted what Charlie had. Wanted it so bad she couldn't breathe.

The strong, stable husband. The adorable toddler. The security of being loved and respected.

Instead, she'd fallen for yet another man who couldn't give her those things.

Would she ever learn?

Roark's flight from Cairo landed at JFK a little before four on Friday afternoon. He cleared customs without any trouble.

Brushing past the crowd shuffling toward baggage claim,

he stretched his long legs and headed for the taxi area. He hoped the line wasn't long. Now that he'd landed in New York City, the need to see Elizabeth had gone from prickly urgency to gnawing compulsion.

A short, Middle Eastern man in a black suit caught up to him as he stepped into the icy November afternoon. "Mr. Black, I'm your driver."

Who'd sent a car for him? Vance knew his travel plans, but he'd never send a car.

"No, thanks. I'd rather catch a cab." To Roark's relief, only a handful of people stood in line ahead of him.

"But I have a car waiting."

After everything that transpired in Cairo, he was more cautious than ever about getting into a car with a stranger. If Masler had any idea that Roark was setting a trap for him, he would have sprung one of his own.

"Who sent you?" Roark demanded.

"I have instructions to bring you to Waverly's."

Not Masler then. It was probably Ann.

"No, thanks," Roark repeated. He had a driving need to see Elizabeth.

"But…"

Roark slammed the taxi door on the man's protests and gave the driver an address. His head fell back against the seat. His eyelids became heavy and he let them droop. He'd barely catnapped during the twelve-hour flight from Cairo. Normally he was able to sleep anywhere he considered safe. And what could be more secure than a plane flying at thirty-thousand feet? Today, however, he'd been pestered by regrets. Haunted by what Elizabeth had not said when he called to tell her he was heading out of town.

As exhausted as he was, Roark couldn't quite step across the threshold of sleep. He'd disappointed Elizabeth by running off on such short notice. She might not have asked, but she'd needed him to be there for her on Thanksgiving. He remembered how hard it had been to be alone with the news about his mother's death. Growing up, he'd never spent much time with kids his own age. Learning about friendship was something it had taken him years to figure out.

Even now, he could count on one hand the people he considered friends and most of those were buddies like Smith that he counted on when he needed help, not confidants he shared his aspirations and fears with.

In fact, until Elizabeth had entered his life, Vance was the only person Roark had confided in. And he'd never brought his half brother to his mother's apartment. Elizabeth alone had seen it and Roark remained baffled that he'd given her that glimpse into his psyche.

Gray and tan buildings swept past the taxi's window in a hypnotic blur as they neared the restaurant where Elizabeth was organizing a birthday party for one of her clients. She was in charge of setup. The restaurant would take care of the rest. Before he'd left for Cairo, the plan had been for him to pick her up at seven and take her out to dinner. He was here to make sure those plans hadn't changed.

Roark held the front door for two men carrying in an enormous cake decorated with realistic-looking women's shoes. Inside, the restaurant's urban edge had been softened with black tulle, strings of white lights and sprays of white ostrich feathers. Four-tops had been pushed together to make long rows and arranged in a horseshoe along the walls of the narrow restaurant. Down the center of the tables tall crystal candleholders alternated with crystal vases containing sprigs of greenery and white orchids. Roark saw Elizabeth in every detail.

A woman in her mid-thirties was showing two young women how the place settings needed to be set up. Elizabeth was nowhere in sight. He approached the trio.

"I'm looking for Elizabeth."

The woman in charge spoke. "You're Roark Black. I recognize your photo from Page Six." Her smile carried more than a trace of malice. "Elizabeth is no longer in charge of this event. Or any event for Josie Summers's Event Planning. She was fired." Her delight in Elizabeth's downfall was so obvious that Roark turned away without responding.

Without question, this had been his fault. Elizabeth was on her way to becoming Josie Summers's partner before he'd entered her life. Now, because Sabeen had behaved badly, Elizabeth had been terminated.

Flagging down another taxi, he headed for her apartment. She answered the door as if she'd been expecting his arrival. Her expression was neither surprised nor delighted and he half expected her to slam the door in his face. Instead, she stepped back, but made no welcoming gesture.

"Sabeen said you weren't returning to New York until Sunday." Her rebuke came through loud and clear.

Roark entered her apartment and dropped his duffel near the door. "Sabeen doesn't know my business."

"Neither does anyone else, apparently."

The black turtleneck she wore emphasized her skin's paleness. She'd fastened her long blond hair into a lackluster ponytail. She stood with her arms crossed over her chest, her shoulders hunched. This was not the vibrant woman he'd made love to on Wednesday morning.

"I went to the restaurant, but some woman said you'd been fired."

"Josie didn't think having one of her employees embroiled in a Page Six scandal was good for her business."

"We can fix this."

Instead of answering she retreated to her small dining table and picked up an envelope. "Here."

"What is this?"

"The money I took from you. It's all there."

He left his hands at his sides, letting her know he wasn't

going to take the envelope. "I gave you the money in exchange for your help."

"What help? Thanks to Sabeen, everyone knows our engagement was fake. Your reputation is worse than before."

"It's her word against ours."

"It's more than that." She waggled the envelope to catch his attention. "I can't pretend anymore."

Her dejection wrenched at him. When she'd needed him to be at her side, he disappointed her. He didn't blame her for cutting her losses.

"Keep the money. This fiasco was my fault, not yours."

"I don't feel right taking it."

"How are you planning on paying for your next round of in vitro without it?"

She shoved her chin to a belligerent angle. "I'll manage."

"Don't be stubborn." He might have accepted her decision, if not for the dark circles beneath her eyes. It was his fault that she wasn't sleeping. That she'd lost her job. If he'd postponed his trip for a few days they could have confronted Sabeen's accusation together. She wouldn't have had to face the anniversary of her family's death alone. "Have you forgotten that you're out of a job?"

"Not likely."

Frustration rushed at him like a speeding bullet. "Why can't you just let me help you?"

"Because I don't feel right taking anything from you."

"Why not? I thought we were friends." Even as he said the words, he realized he thought of her as a lot more than that.

"Friends." She repeated the word too softly for Roark to catch any inflection that hinted at her thoughts.

Oh, who was he kidding? What he felt for her went way past friendship. But how far did it go? He instinctively shied away from the word *love*. He'd never shown a propensity for the commitment and responsibility to another required for that emotion.

And what could he expect from Elizabeth when he had no idea what he intended to offer her?

Bypassing the envelope she continued to hold out to him like some sort of shield, Roark stepped into her space and slid his fingers into the hair at the back of her head, undoing the ponytail. While her hair cascaded around her shoulders, he lowered his head and stole her surprised gasp.

After only a moment's hesitation, her lips moved beneath his, answering his passion with a hunger that sent his libido into overdrive. He crushed her body in his arms, plundered her mouth and drank from her moans.

When he'd planned how to get her to forgive him, storming her defenses with long, drugging kisses had been pretty far down his list. Her fingers burrowed beneath his shirt, finding skin. Any ability to think rationally vanished in a haze of desire so strong he tore buttons loose getting the shirt off. The shirt landed atop his leather jacket at his feet. A second later, he'd swept her into his arms and carried her the blessedly short distance to her bed.

With the mattress against her back she stiffened. "Wait."

Roark had already been waiting for days. His patience was long gone. Kissing his way down her neck, he traced his fingertip around the nipple that had hardened to a tight bud beneath the black silk camisole she wore. Her turtleneck lay on the floor beside his discarded clothes.

She arched her back, offering her body for his pleasure, but her next words blunted his desire. "Roark, stop. I'm angry with you."

He drifted his lips along the skin just above the camisole's lace edge, tantalizing her with kisses, but ventured no lower. If he wanted to make love to her, he could seduce her into forgetting everything that was wrong between them. But as the glow from their passionate reunion faded, the same issues would resurface. He'd abandoned her when she'd needed him. She wasn't going to forgive that easily.

"I'm sorry I took off the way I did."

"You're sorry?" She shoved at his chest until he rolled off her. Sitting up, she ran her fingers through her hair and glared at him. "Do you have any idea what I've been through in the last three days?"

"I have an idea."

"Sabeen humiliated me in front of your friends. Then my name was plastered all over Page Six in a career-ruining scandal. You asked why I gave you back your money. It's because I can't afford to have a child right now."

"I did this. Let me help you until you're back on your feet."

She scrambled off the mattress. "I can't do this."

"Do what?"

"This." She waved her hand to indicate them both. "I never should have let you in today."

"Why did you?" Roark came to stand before her. He set his hands on her hips, slid his palm over the jut of her hipbone. Momentum carried him to the swell of her bottom.

"It's over between us," she said, ignoring his question.

He eased her against the thunderous ache in his groin, dropped his cheek to her soft golden hair. "It doesn't have to be."

"So I'm just supposed to be grateful you're going to stick around for the near future?" The edge in her tone told him the opposite would be true. "And then you go your way and I go mine?"

Silk sighed against his palm as he drew his hand up her spine. In seconds he could whisk the fabric over her head and bare her gorgeous breasts. The trembling in her limbs told him she was fighting what her body craved. Already the fists she'd made were loosening. The anger was ebbing out of her and with it, her determination to fight him.

"Can I borrow your shower?"

"I guess." The confusion in her bright blue eyes dominated the sensual fullness of her parted lips. She hadn't expected him to back off so easily and stood lost between battle and surrender.

"Thank you. It was a long flight from Cairo." He kissed her nose and headed for the bathroom.

She called after him. "Why aren't you showering at the loft?"

"Because your place is closer."

"Is that why you came over? To use my shower?"

Roark grinned as he turned on the water. The disappointment in Elizabeth's voice gave him hope. Naked, he stepped into the doorway and gave her an eyeful of what she'd just passed on.

"No, I came by to see you. I couldn't stop thinking about you the entire time I was gone."

Even if he lived an infinite number of lifetimes, he'd never stop enjoying the way she was staring at him at the moment. The stark lust in her eyes as her gaze drifted from his chest to his groin. The dreamy expression that told him she liked what she saw. And the way she bit down on her lower lip as if holding back was the most difficult thing she'd ever done.

"How was Cairo?" As if it took a great amount of will, she looked away. "Were you able to find Darius?"

"He was gone before I got there."

"What about the other thing you were looking for?"

"I got a lead."

He'd said the wrong thing.

"A lead." Her chest rose with the deep breath she sucked in. "When are you leaving again?"

"In a week or so." He stepped into the shower. She preferred a berry-scented body wash and shampoo. If he used it he would probably spend the rest of the day half aroused at the memory of her.

"What you're doing is dangerous, isn't it?" She'd stepped into the bathroom to pursue their conversation.

"There's an element of danger, but I take every precaution."

"This isn't what I signed up for." Her voice was closer. The door to the shower slid open. "Everything in my life was exactly the way I wanted it before you came along."

He snagged her wrist and drew her into the shower with him. She didn't protest. Not even when the water drenched her clothes.

"And it will get back to being that way again," he assured her, stripping the sodden fabric off her body.

"After you're gone?" She reached up on tiptoe and cupped his face in her hands. Her eyes were bottomless pools of angst as he gathered her in his arms.

"As soon as you take me up on my offer to start you in your own business and use the money I paid you to get pregnant."

"Thank you for reminding me what's most important in my life." And then she was kissing him, her tongue plunging into his mouth as passion ignited between them once again.

Eleven

Elizabeth shredded lettuce and watched Roark talk on the phone. It was 7:00 p.m. The lasagna she'd made earlier that day was due to come out of the oven in ten minutes. From the tone of Roark's voice and the annoyance pinching his mouth, she doubted he'd get a chance to sample her culinary skills.

"Can't this wait until Monday?" he demanded. From his duffel bag he'd pulled fresh clothes and a small bag containing toiletries. "I don't really give a damn what Ann wants." The rest of his side of the conversation was distorted when he headed into her bathroom.

Getting into that shower with him had been a mistake. The water might not have ruined her brand-new camisole, but she'd ruined any chance at a clean break with Roark. Despite spending the past two hours romping with him, hunger tugged at her loins. The lure of the man was her Achilles' heel.

"I've been summoned to Waverly's for a meeting with Ann Richardson. Supposedly there's some huge crisis that can't wait until Monday morning." He wrapped his arms around her waist and kissed her cheek. "I can be back in an hour."

"I don't think you should come back." The words took all her courage to say.

"What's wrong? I thought we straightened everything out."

"I know. I'm sorry if my behavior was misleading." She kept her cheek pressed tight to his chest. If she looked into his eyes, she would never get the words out. "I can't keep seeing you. Every time you walk away I wonder if it's the last time we'll be together. Living on the edge of the unknown is what makes you happy. It's tearing me apart."

"Elizabeth."

The throb in his voice put a lump in her throat the size of a golf ball. Talking was impossible so she whispered. "Please understand how hard this is for me."

"It doesn't have to be hard. You've become important to me."

This was a powerful admission coming from Roark. Elizabeth listened to his steady heartbeat and fought to stay strong. "You've become important to me, too. That's why I need to stop seeing you. Before it hurts too much."

That was a lie. It already hurt too much. She'd been blindsided when she'd heard that her sister and her family were dead. The pain had been instant and devastating. Losing Roark was like slowly being smothered beneath a pile of stones. The ache was crushing the life from her with each second that ticked by.

"I don't want to lose you." Roark took her face in his hands and searched her eyes.

She scrutinized him in return, but he'd closed off all emotion. "Please don't ask me to be your friend." She tried to smile, but couldn't compel her facial muscles to produce an emotion she wasn't feeling. "There'd always be this sexual energy between us that I'd give in to. We'd hook up. In a day or a week, you'd disappear and I'd be left resenting you because you'll never be happy settling down in New York."

"You've got it all figured out, don't you?"

"I know my pattern. It's why I'd decided to have a baby on my own. I'm always falling for the wrong sort of guy."

"Like me."

"Like you."

Roark would never be domesticated. He had no interest in being part of a traditional family. As a child he'd spent too much time alone. He'd learned about independence, not what it meant to rely on someone. While his brother was content to be a husband and a father, Roark craved adventure. It wasn't fair to be frustrated with him because she expected too much. But she didn't have to bang her head against a wall either.

"So, if I really care about you, I should leave you alone."

No. If you really care about me, you should stay in New York and spend the rest of your life making me the happiest woman on earth.

"Yes, you should leave me alone."

Heart breaking, she continued, "The reason for us being together no longer exists."

"Then I'll stay away." He grazed her forehead with his lips, picked up his jacket and duffel and headed toward her front door.

Was she making a mistake? He said he didn't want to lose her, but she'd not given him a chance to tell her where he wanted to take their relationship. She just assumed it wasn't where she wanted to go. And yet by abandoning her at Thanksgiving when he knew how devastating the holiday would be for her, he'd demonstrated exactly where his priorities lay.

The guessing game tore at her confidence and reminded her how many times she'd played this same game with herself.

"Roark…"

He'd reached the hallway and turned when she spoke his

name. His face was granite, but behind in his eyes intense emotions burned. "I would only end up hurting you. I never wanted that. You have to do what's right for you. Goodbye, Elizabeth."

She should be grateful that he was sympathetic to her plight and strong enough to follow through when she would have called him back and repeated her mistakes. But she couldn't feel happy or even relieved that their relationship had ended cleanly. After such a short time together, her heart should be barely bruised.

So, why did her chest ache and her eyes burn with unshed tears?

Because she'd fallen in love him despite all her determination to be smarter this time. And that made her a first-class idiot because his actions had demonstrated that she would always come a distant second to his adventures.

Roark caught a taxi in front of Elizabeth's apartment and directed it to Waverly's. This wasn't how he'd expected his day to end. The lasagna cooking in Elizabeth's oven made his mouth water and he realized it had been over twelve hours since he'd eaten anything. Food hadn't seemed important while he was gorging himself on sensual delicacies. With Elizabeth in his arms, nothing else mattered.

So, why had he let her push him away? His instincts demanded that he stay and fight for her. Walking out her door had been one of the hardest things he'd ever done. If not for his decision he'd made after his mother's death to avoid all romantic entanglements, he might have…

What?

She wanted something from him he couldn't commit to. A family. Security. He wasn't cut out to settle down and be someone's everything. Hadn't he failed his mother? Wasn't his leaving what had made her heart give out? He swore he'd never get close enough to hurt anyone like that again.

The taxi let Roark out in front of Waverly's. This late on a Friday, all of the building's seven floors were dark except the top one where Waverly's executives ran the business. He paused before approaching the building. When Vance had first brought him into the Waverly's fold, Roark had been adamant in his refusal to be tied to an office and a day-to-day routine. But after spending three months in the Amazon, eluding thugs with machine guns, and the troubles over the Gold Heart statue, he no longer perceived Waverly's as a straightjacket he needed to avoid.

Kendra Darling pushed open the front door as he neared. She reminded him of Elizabeth. A career woman hiding her femininity behind tortoise-shell glasses, unglamorous pantsuits and professionalism.

"You're working late," he remarked, passing from the chilly November night into the impressive foyer.

An enormous crystal chandelier cast a soft glow over the classical artwork adorning polished-wood paneling. During the day Waverly's clients strode along the gold carpet or sat on one of the couches upholstered in rich fabrics that dotted the large space. Tonight, the empty space had a haunted quality.

"I'm supposed to escort you up as soon as you arrive." As Ann's longtime assistant, Kendra was used to dealing with all sorts of tough situations, from unhappy clients to nosy reporters.

"Ann doesn't think I can find my own way?"

"After you refused the car I sent to pick you up, she insisted I make sure you weren't sidetracked."

"Lead the way."

Ann wasn't behind her desk when Kendra gestured him into the CEO's office. Roark could tell by Ann's agitated pacing as she wore a path from one tall, narrow window to the next that something was seriously wrong.

"Where have you been?"

Great. She was on fire. "Cairo."

"How dare you take off without telling me."

"I had something I needed to take care of."

"Do you know what's happened?"

"Fill me in."

"His Highness Raif Khouri called. His uncle, Mallik, was left at the altar by his young royal bride."

At first relief blasted through him that Darius had succeeded in freeing the woman he loved from her intended's villainous plot. Annoyance arrived a moment later. If Roark's connection to this event came to light, it might prove the final nail in the coffin for Waverly's.

"What does that have to do with me?"

"He's blaming all the trouble on the curse that has befallen his family because the Gold Heart statue is missing from the palace."

"His uncle's troubles have nothing to do with their missing statue."

"I know that, but Raif is adamant that we produce our statue. He's convinced it is the one stolen from the palace."

"It isn't."

"Then produce it so we can prove that."

"I can't."

"Why not?"

"Because the Gold Heart statue's provenance documents are missing and until I can get them back from the man who stole them, the prince could claim that it's his and we'd have no proof it wasn't."

Ann gasped. "He'd never do that."

"Maybe not, but I'm the one the FBI believes stole the statue."

"The reputation of Waverly's is resting on that statue." Ann's voice throbbed with anger and worry.

"You don't think I know that?"

"I need that statue. I'm flying to Rayas next Thursday to

meet with His Highness and he's expecting me to produce the statue. Without it we'll be ruined."

"I'm working on getting the documents back, but it's not going to happen by next Thursday."

Leaving Ann seething with annoyance, Roark passed by Vance's office on his way back to the elevator and wasn't surprised to find it dark. Since Charlie had come into his life, Vance's priorities had shifted. He now put family before business and seemed happy with the new arrangement.

Was it really that simple?

Roark jabbed the down button on the elevator. He rolled his shoulders to ease the tension, but relief wasn't in his future. Too much was wrong in his life at the moment.

Unless he retrieved the missing provenance documents, he had no way of proving that the Gold Heart statue owned by Sheikh Rashid bin Mansour was not the one missing from Rayas's palace.

Then there was Darius, who'd stolen a royal bride from Mallik Khouri and was on the run.

And worst of all, he'd lost the one bright spot in this whole misadventure. Elizabeth. She'd sent him packing, and he had no idea how to change her mind. Nor was he sure he should even try. She deserved to be happy and if being with him made her miserable, he should put her feelings first and let her be. Unfortunately, every fiber of his being rejected that as the worst idea he'd ever had.

As he was leaving Waverly's, his phone rang. It was Smith.

"Got them," the former marine said.

Relief rushed through Roark. "They okay?"

"Fine." Behind Smith were the sounds of laughter and conversation. "We'll be in New York by tomorrow."

"Bring them to the loft. They can stay here until we can make sure Fadira is safe from her father and Khouri."

Roark caught a cab and headed to the apartment Darius and Sabeen shared. She would be anxious for word about her brother and Roark wanted to talk to her about what she'd done to Elizabeth.

"Your brother and Fadira are safe and heading to New York," Roark said when Sabeen opened the door.

With a cry she hugged him. "I've been so worried."

And Roark could see that she had been. All at once she was the happy young girl she'd been before her father's death.

"Let's have a drink and celebrate." She caught Roark's hand and led him toward the couch.

"I can't stay."

"One drink," she cajoled.

Roark twisted free of her grip and crossed his arms over his chest.

She pouted. "What's wrong?"

"You ask that, after what you did to Elizabeth at the gala?"

Defiance flared in her eyes. "You're angry because everyone knows you aren't engaged?"

"I asked you to keep quiet about what you knew, not broadcast my business to the media. Elizabeth has lost her job. Waverly's is in more trouble than ever. What were you thinking?"

"That if she was out of your life you would see that I'm all the woman you'll ever need."

"That's your excuse? You were jealous of a woman I was pretending to be engaged to?" He downplayed his deeper feelings for Elizabeth to give his reprimand more punch.

"She might be pretending, but you are not." Sabeen rushed at the desk and placed both palms on its surface. "I see how you look at her. You're in love with her, and she doesn't feel the same way."

Sabeen's accusation smacked into his diaphragm. "You don't know what you're talking about," he told her.

"You don't think I know when a woman's in love? She feels it here." With a dramatic flourish, Sabeen covered her heart with her right hand. "And it shows here." She gestured to her eyes.

Pain bloomed in Roark's head. Was Sabeen right about Elizabeth? If she loved him wouldn't she want him in her life? His thoughts retreated to his afternoon with Elizabeth. He'd glimpsed something in her gaze as he'd made love to her, but had he mistaken passion for love?

And what did it matter anyway? She'd made her feelings clear. Their relationship was over. She would have her baby. He would return to hunting antiquities. They'd enjoyed a few delightful weeks. Made memories he could reflect on the next time he got stuck in the jungle for months on end.

"Look in my eyes," Sabeen continued. She cupped his head and met his gaze. "See how I burn for you."

Roark did look, but all he saw was insecurity. Sabeen had latched on to him as a lifeline after her father's death. At the time she'd been young and frightened by the loss of a second parent in six years. Today, she was no longer a child, but a capable woman with the ability to take care of herself. Time she discovered that.

"I'm taking away your allowance until you prove to me you're ready to accept responsibility for your inheritance. This week's stunt demonstrates that you are a child in a woman's body. Everything has come easily for you and you've not matured because of it."

She obviously wasn't expecting this. Her nostrils flared. "I am a woman. A woman who loves you."

"A child who loves me. Like an older brother." Clarity startled him with its sudden appearance. "That's it, isn't it? Darius has won his princess and plans to marry her. You're afraid that Elizabeth will take me away from you. That's why you sabotaged her. You're afraid to be alone."

A fat tear rolled down Sabeen's cheek, but her eyes remained confrontational. "I hate you." She pushed away from his chair and raced out of the room.

Feeling much older than his twenty-seven years, Roark

left the apartment, but didn't feel much like heading back to his empty loft.

Forty minutes later he let himself into his mother's apartment. He'd called ahead to let Mrs. Myott know he was coming. She had leftover pot roast waiting for him. Seated at the center island, he wolfed down the meal. She'd slow-cooked the meat and it practically melted in his mouth.

Mrs. Myott drank coffee and watched him over the rim of her cup. "When did you last eat?"

"On the plane. It's been a hectic few hours since I landed."

"Here's the envelope that came for you today." She slid a plain manila envelope toward him.

Roark set down his fork and picked up the envelope. It bore his name and nothing more. Curious, he slit open the flap with his knife and pulled out a smaller envelope bearing his mother's bold handwriting.

She'd addressed the envelope to Edward Waverly.

"Who sent this?"

"I don't know. I received a call from the doorman that he'd received an envelope addressed to you."

"Did he say which courier service dropped it off?"

"It never occurred to me to ask." Mrs. Myott had also recognized the familiar handwriting. Sadness darkened her eyes. "Why would someone send you a letter your mother wrote to Edward Waverly?"

"I have no idea." Roark suspected she told Edward she was pregnant and never received a reply. If he'd wanted nothing to do with an illegitimate son, why then had he written a letter to Vance telling him about his half brother so many years later?

Hoping for a clue as to who sent his mother's letter, Roark peered into the envelope and spied a sheet of paper. He pulled it out. An unfamiliar hand had penned a short note.

Your mother wrote this letter to Edward Waverly. You are as much a Waverly as Vance.

Vance was the only person Roark could imagine having

access to Edward Waverly's personal correspondence, but he knew Vance's handwriting and this wasn't it. Mystified, he handed Mrs. Myott the note and then carefully pulled a sheet of yellowed paper from the envelope.

To My Love,

I have kept a secret from you all these years and done you a terrible wrong. You have a son. Roark turned eighteen yesterday and enlisted in the marines. I have never been so proud of him, nor so filled with regret. I know now that by holding him too tight all these years, I instead drove him away.

I'm sorry I didn't tell you the truth sooner. When you left me I was devastated. It took months for me to accept that I mustn't blame you for moving forward with your life. I could never have been the wife you needed. The world outside these walls is too big and too terrifying for me to face. In the end, my fears were stronger than my love for you.

Many nights I paced the floor, debating whether or not to tell you about Roark. In the end, I was afraid that if you knew you had a son you would take him into the world and away from me. I couldn't bear to lose both of the men that I loved. Please don't take your anger with me out on Roark. From a stubborn and clever boy he has grown into a determined and intelligent man. You will be proud to claim him as your son.

Forever yours,

Guinevere

Here was the admission from his mother Roark had been waiting all his life for. He stared at his mother's letter. Strange how he felt no different now than he had a moment ago. No lights came on in his mind. Nothing snapped into place. The words left him numb.

He didn't even care that Edward Waverly had never sought him out after discovering the truth. What good would it do to resent a man who'd been dead almost five years? His parents' relationship was complicated and colored by bitterness. It was their difficulties that had kept them apart his entire life.

Nothing at all to do with him. And in a strange way, Roark was glad he and Vance had been able to begin their relationship free of their father's baggage.

Then, slowly he became aware that one change had happened. Reading his mother's letter had dispelled the restlessness that drove him to spend his days seeking his place in the world. He knew where he belonged. Who he was. The hazy doubts he'd always carried in the back of his mind about being Vance's half brother were a thing of the past. He was a Waverly. In blood if not name. Waverly's wasn't a straightjacket to be avoided at all costs, but his family's legacy and he was going to do whatever it took to save it from the likes of Dalton Rothschild.

"Roark, are you all right?" Mrs. Myott had come to stand beside him. Her hand covered his.

He blinked and reoriented himself in the penthouse. The hum of the refrigerator. The lingering scent of the pot roast. The comforting sight of Mrs. Myott's face. "I'm fine. Just need to make a phone call."

Even though he wasn't sure if she'd pick up, Roark dialed Elizabeth's number. To his relief, she answered.

"Roark?"

"Someone delivered a ten-year-old letter to the penthouse from my mother to Edward Waverly telling him about me."

"Who?"

"It was delivered by messenger. I have no idea where it came from."

"Vance?"

"Not his handwriting and definitely not his style."

"How odd." Her voice took on a thoughtful note. "And after all this time. Do you think it was recently discovered?"

"Edward has been dead five years. Vance went through all his papers. That's where he found the letter telling him about me. I know if he'd found this letter he would have given it to me immediately."

"So why has it surfaced now?"

"Because Waverly's is in more trouble than ever. The note that accompanied the letter states that I'm as much a Waverly as Vance. The auction house is as much my responsibility to save as Vance's."

"So, what are you going to do?"

"Fight."

"How? With George Cromwell stepping down, there's no one to stop Rothschild from securing the votes he needs from the Waverly's board."

"It might help if I had someone by my side to help me."

"You have Vance and Ann."

"I was thinking about you."

"Me?" Her tone sharpened. "I can't help you, Roark. Even if we could somehow make the world believe our engagement wasn't a lie, you aren't going to stick around as long as it's going to take to save Waverly's. It's not in your nature."

"What if my nature has changed?"

"I don't believe it can any more than I believe you want it to." She spoke so softly it was hard to hear her words. "Maybe it's time to give up on Waverly's. Let Rothschild have it. Ann's brilliant, she'll land on her feet. Vance has numerous businesses to occupy him."

"And the hundreds of people Waverly's employs? What of them?"

Elizabeth didn't speak for a long time. Roark tamped down his frustration. Had he really expected her to come running just because he'd received a letter confirming he was a Waverly? She'd never truly believed he was committed to saving Waverly's. And he'd further damaged her trust when he'd run off to Egypt the day before Thanksgiving.

"I'm sorry, I can't help you, Roark. I really do hope you can save Waverly's. It sounds like you're fully committed to the task."

"I appreciate your faith in me. Good night, Elizabeth."

"Goodbye, Roark."

He didn't miss the finality of her words as the phone went dead in his hand.

Twelve

The Monday after Thanksgiving dawned with clear skies and temperatures in the forties. All dressed up, but with no place she had to be, Elizabeth headed to the coffee shop on the corner. She had to get out of her apartment and at least pretend she was making progress. After spending Sunday updating her résumé and assembling a digital portfolio of her best work, she'd emailed all of Josie's competitors, praying one of them would give her a shot. The holiday season took its toll on event planners. Surely someone could use an extra set of hands.

For an hour she sipped coffee and stared out the window. On her laptop awaited the phone numbers she would dial. Nerves kept the coffee from sitting well in her stomach. What if she couldn't find a job doing what she was good at? How was she supposed to start over?

Five phone calls later, anxiety had turned to dread. A stone had lodged itself in her throat making talking difficult. It wasn't just that no one had an opening or was unimpressed

with her work. Three of the five event planners warned her
that Josie planned to wage war on anyone who hired her.

She was sunk.

Her phone rang. Elizabeth checked the unfamiliar number against the companies she'd sent résumés to. It matched
none of them. She hit Talk.

"Elizabeth Minerva?"

"Yes."

"Please hold for Mrs. Fremont."

Her heart thumped against her ribs like a loose shutter in
a hurricane. Sonya Fremont was calling her?

"Elizabeth. You were supposed to call me if ever you got
free of that employer of yours."

"I know. I just assumed that with the Page Six article…"
She let her words trail off. What if Sonya didn't read the gossip page? Had Elizabeth just blown any chance of working
with the woman? And what if she got the job and was later
fired because Sonya found out about the whole fake engagement with Roark?

"Oh, for heaven's sakes, Elizabeth. This is New York City.
You're already yesterday's news."

"I am?"

Sonya laughed. "I've never heard anybody sound so glad
to have their fifteen minutes of fame behind them."

Elizabeth's confidence was returning with each second. "I
think you'll find I'm happier behind the scenes."

"And that's what I'd like to talk to you about. Now that
you're no longer employed by that woman, I'd like to hire you
to plan the gala. Your proposal was original and inspiring.
Can you come by tomorrow to discuss a few minor changes
I'd like to make?"

"Of course."

Did this mean she was going into business for herself?
Josie's decision to blackball her from working with other

event planners had backed Elizabeth into a corner. Hope floated through her, erasing most of her doubts.

After she hung up with Sonya, Elizabeth tackled a list of things she'd need to go into business for herself. The money she'd tried to return to Roark would have to be diverted from her fertility treatments to rent, food and other basic survival needs. Was it enough to last until she could find other clients?

Elizabeth dialed the fertility clinic. She needed to cancel her upcoming appointments. She'd already come to terms with the reality that motherhood would have to wait until she could afford it. The switchboard connected her to Bridget Sullivan, her doctor's nurse. In the eight months Elizabeth had been trying to get pregnant, Bridget had been so kind to her. She deserved an explanation why Elizabeth couldn't move forward at the moment.

"I just wanted to let you know that I've cancelled my upcoming appointments."

"Of course you have," Bridget crowed. "Congratulations."

This was so far from the sympathetic response she'd braced for that Elizabeth wondered if Bridget knew who was on the phone. "Bridget, this is Elizabeth Minerva."

"What timing. I have your file in front of me. I was about to give you a call."

"But you said congratulations."

Now it was Bridget's turn to be confused. "I thought you'd be thrilled. You're pregnant. Isn't that what you've been hoping for all these months?"

"Pregnant? How is that possible?"

Bridget laughed. "Since I'm confident you haven't been cheating on us with another fertility clinic, I'm guessing that fiancé of yours has the right stuff. You must be over the moon. A baby on the way and a wedding to plan. You're one lucky lady."

"Lucky." It wasn't the first word that she'd use to describe her current situation. She was pregnant? The room tilted as she tried to absorb what she'd just heard. "But two rounds of in vitro failed. Dr. Abbot told me it would be impossible for me to get pregnant without help."

"I don't know how to explain it other than sometimes miracles happen. A couple that has struggled with fertility for years adopts a child and suddenly the wife is pregnant. Maybe you just needed to find the right guy."

But Roark wasn't the right guy for her. He was an amazing man. A terrific lover. Wonderful friend. Loyal to the core, but he wasn't interested in making a commitment to her or anyone.

"Do you need us to recommend an obstetrician? I can email you a list."

"That would be great." Her thoughts were like cotton in her head. Thanking Bridget, she disconnected the call and stared at the list of event planners on her laptop screen.

In the space of ten minutes she'd become an entrepreneur and learned she was pregnant. What if she wasn't ready to tackle both at the same time?

And Roark. How angry would he be when she told him he was going to be a father? This was all her fault. She'd told him she couldn't get pregnant. He would think she'd tricked him.

Elizabeth caught a cab and gave the driver the address for Roark's loft. In the back of her mind, she knew it would be prudent to call ahead and warn him she was coming, but after breaking things off, what was she supposed to give him as an excuse for needing to see him? Telling him that she was pregnant with his child was not a conversation she wanted to have on the phone.

She rapped on Roark's door. The sound barely drowned out the thunder of her heart as she anticipated the scene to come. Conversation openers spun through her head while she waited, making her dizzy. Her nerve was fading by the second. She'd actually started backing down the hall when

Roark's door opened. A beautiful young woman with disheveled dark hair peered out. She wore a sleepy expression and a gorgeous turquoise silk nightgown that hinted at the flawless figure beneath.

"Hello?" She spoke in accented English. "Can I help you?"

This was yet another development Elizabeth hadn't foreseen. Her first impulse was to make an excuse and race away, but she'd never been one to run from her problems. "I'm looking for Roark."

"He's not here." Her dark brown eyes smiled. "Are you a friend?"

"Yes." Elizabeth's head bobbed. "Elizabeth Minerva."

"I am Fadira. How wonderful to meet you."

This was the woman Darius had raced halfway around the world to save. Elizabeth understood his fascination. Fadira was breathtaking.

"Do you know where Roark might have gone?"

"I do not, but he may have called while I was sleeping. Please come in." The woman opened the door wide and turned to address someone inside the loft. "Darling, have you heard from Roark this morning?"

Darius appeared beside the slim Middle Eastern woman and put his arm around her waist. She leaned into his embrace and slid her hand onto his bare chest.

"Hello, Elizabeth. I see you have met my fiancée."

Tears sprang to her eyes. "Congratulations."

"She is looking for Roark," Fadira explained.

"I thought he might be here." Renewed anxiety displaced her momentary relief. "I'm sorry to intrude. I should have called before coming over."

"Roark didn't tell you that he gave us the apartment for a few days?" Darius asked. "I have not heard from him since he left Saturday night. Are you worried about him?"

"Nothing like that. I had something I wanted to discuss with him. Do you know where he might have gone?"

"No. I'm sorry."

Which meant her news would have to wait a little while longer.

Roark sat at the desk in his mother's bedroom and for the first time, read the entries she'd made after he'd left for the marines. It had taken him two days of wandering like a ghost through the penthouse before he been able to face his mother's heartache.

He'd spent those days reliving memories of her. How he'd done his homework at this desk, while she'd sat in her favorite chair by the fireplace and read. If he'd gotten stuck on a math problem or wanted to discuss a social studies assignment, she was always close, ready to offer what help she could. Sometimes he pretended he didn't understand just so she'd lean over his shoulder. Her light, floral scent would fill his nostrils while her musical voice would explain the complexities of iambic pentameter or point out where he'd gone wrong with a formula.

To his surprise, his mother hadn't been devastated by his departure. She'd been proud that he'd chosen to serve his country, and she'd understood that he needed to make his mark on the world.

If he'd had the courage to say goodbye, he wouldn't have been burdened by guilt all these years. He could have left knowing that his mother wished nothing but the best for him.

Instead he'd acted like a fool and his mother had suffered. He'd hurt her like he'd hurt Elizabeth. All because he believed that love was a trap he had to avoid at all costs. An obligation that interfered with his freedom.

Well, Elizabeth hadn't tried to hold on to him and these past few days without her had been some of the most miserable hours of his life.

"Roark?" Elizabeth's soft voice came from the doorway. "I hope it's okay that Mrs. Myott let me in."

Dressed in a dark gray wool coat, her cheeks pink from the cold, she stood just outside the room as if afraid of her welcome.

His heart soared at the sight of her. "It's fine." More than fine. It was fantastic. Since she'd turned him down a second time on Friday night, he'd been moldering in a stew of recrimination. Unable to contain his relief, he crossed the room and hauled her into his arms, whirling her off her feet. "How'd you know to find me here?"

For two complete spins she melted into his embrace and he savored the peace he always felt in her company. The second her toes met the floor once again, she pushed out of his arms.

"I stopped by the loft." She moved out of reach. "Darius said he hadn't heard from you since Saturday. I couldn't think of anyplace else you might have gone." She gazed around the room, not meeting his eyes. "I met Fadira. I'm so glad they're able to be together."

"They blamed the canceled wedding on the missing statue," Roark said. "Which of course means that the Rayas royal family is more determined than ever to get their hands on the Gold Heart statue Waverly's is going to auction. Ann needs me to give her the statue I found, but I still haven't located the missing documentation."

"What are you going to do?"

"Stall Ann and get the documents back. I've got a lead on them. The man who stole them has business in the Bahamas in a week. I plan on heading down there to get them back."

"How do you know he'll have them?"

"I had a chat with an acquaintance of his in Cairo."

"What sort of a chat?"

"The sort that gets information."

"And after you get the documents back, what then?"

"Waverly's reputation is saved. The Gold Heart statue is brought up for auction. We fight off whatever Dalton Rothschild has in store for us next."

She seemed to have run out of questions. That was fine. He had a few of his own.

"Would you come with me?"

"Where?"

"For starters to the Bahamas. You no longer have work as an excuse to stay in New York."

"I can't just go."

"Why not? You have nothing keeping you here."

"It's my home."

"I'm not asking you to move across the world, just to spend a couple weeks seeing new places, meeting new people."

"What happens when a couple weeks becomes a month, then six months? What if I get to a point where I never want to leave you?"

"Then don't." He snatched her back into his arms and tasted her surprise as his mouth settled on hers. She met the searching plunge of his tongue with a joyful moan and slid her fingers into his hair.

In an instant everything that had been dull in his world burst into vivid color. Kissing her was like the return of spring after a long cold winter. She was sunshine and warming earth, lilacs and hyacinth. Nothing in the world compared to having her in his arms.

"Roark." Her breath came in soft pants. "I have something I need to tell you."

He'd surrendered her mouth so that he could nibble his way down her neck. She arched her back, pressing her breasts into his chest. Her coat was on the floor at her feet. In a few minutes he intended for her black suit to join it.

His fingers plucked her white blouse free of her pants. "I'm all ears."

"No, you're not," she gasped, grabbing for his hands a second too late. He'd released the clasp on her bra and swallowed one breast in his palm. "You're all hands."

"And lips." His mouth covered hers.

Slow and deep, he kissed her until all resistance vanished. He scooped her up and sat down in his mother's favorite chair with Elizabeth cradled in his lap.

"You're going to want to stop once you hear what I have to say," she warned him, her fingers fanned across his cheek. She brushed his lower lip with her thumb.

"Nothing you could say would ever make me want to stop making love to you," he told her.

Here in his mother's bedroom, surrounded by her things, he'd discovered something. He was no longer the boy who'd run away to join the marines because he needed adventure. He was the man who had found the adventure of a lifetime in the woman he held in his arms.

"Oh, I think this one will." She drew her finger between his brows, exploring the frown her words had produced. "What's the one thing you dread more than anything else in the world?"

"Until four days ago, I would have said being tied down to a place and responsible for another person's happiness."

She nodded sagely. "I'm pregnant."

Joy hit him square in the chest. "Congratulations."

"Congratulations?" She gaped at him, so obviously expecting him to be horrified because she was pregnant with his child.

"Well, yes." He cocked his head and searched her expression. "Isn't that what you wanted?"

The heel of her hand collided with his chest and she levered herself off his lap. "It's what *I* wanted. Not what *you* wanted."

"I want you to be happy." And all he'd done lately was upset her. "You are happy, aren't you?"

"How can an intelligent man like you be so dense?"

Easily, the blood had evacuated his brain and settled in his groin. Even now with her indigo eyes flashing danger signals at him and her unconfined breasts moving with distracting enticement beneath her blouse, his craving for her increased.

"Come sit down." He patted his thighs. "And I'll explain it to you."

Her eyes widened as her gaze trailed up his thighs and found him fully aroused. Her cheek color deepened, but when he held out his hand to her, she backed up.

"You aren't listening." She pointed at her stomach. "You're going to be a father."

His entire life he'd dreaded those six words. And now that he'd heard them? Now that the six words had turned his world upside down? The freedom he cherished: in jeopardy. The career he lived for: too dangerous. The woman he loved: bound to him forever. Life had never been more perfect.

She hadn't moved far enough away to escape his reach. All Roark had to do was lean forward and catch her wrist. Before the gasp passed her lips she was back on his lap, imprisoned by his arms.

Roark eyed her solemnly. "Are you okay about this?"

"Am I okay?" She stared at him as if he'd lost his mind. "Are you okay?"

"Very okay."

Before he could demonstrate exactly how okay he was, she stopped his lips from reaching hers by turning her head. "You have to know I don't expect anything from you."

"Oh, surely you have some expectations." He seized her earlobe between his teeth to distract her from the fact that he was steadily unbuttoning her blouse.

She shook her head. "I planned from the start to be a single mom. Nothing has changed."

"You have no job." The last button gave way. Pushing the edges of her blouse aside, he spanned her flat stomach with his hand and marveled at the life growing beneath. "No money."

"Sonya Fremont offered me the gala." She covered his hand with hers. "Other projects will come up."

"And how will you live in the meantime?"

"I'll do kids' birthday parties." She grimaced. "Weddings if I have to. Whatever it takes."

"And run yourself ragged in the process. You have more than yourself to worry about now. There's the baby to consider."

She scowled at him. "You don't think I know that?"

"Have you thought about what's going to happen after the baby's born? Are you going to take time off? Your apartment is barely big enough for you. What happens when the baby comes along?"

"Everything will work out fine." Her eyes glinted with confidence. "I'm not worried."

"Well, I am. For the last two days I've been sitting in this empty apartment, thinking about your situation and remembering how it once was filled with laughter and love. It's a waste of real estate, don't you think?"

"I guess." She caught her lip between her teeth and eyed him from beneath her long lashes. "Are you thinking it's time to sell?"

"I promised Mrs. Myott I wouldn't do that."

"So, what are you going to do with it?"

"I thought maybe you'd like to live here."

Her jaw dropped. "I couldn't. This place is too much. You don't even live here."

"Maybe that's something else that needs to change."

"You said you could never live here. That all the memories of your mother reminded you why she died."

"Maybe it's time some new memories were made here. Memories that wouldn't replace the ones I have of my mother, but that would blunt the guilt I feel for how I left."

She threw her arms around his neck and hugged him hard. "I think that's a wonderful idea."

Had she figured out what he'd just offered her? Roark hadn't meant to present his proposal in such a roundabout fashion, but teasing Elizabeth was something he enjoyed.

"Then you'll live here with me?"

"With you?" She leaned back and gazed at him in confusion. "But you're not staying in New York."

"As soon as I've cleaned up the situation with the Gold Heart statue, that's exactly what I intend to do."

She narrowed her eyes. "For how long?"

"For however long you want me."

"Do you mean that?" She sounded breathless. Unsure.

"When I headed to Cairo on Wednesday, it was the first time I didn't want to leave New York. And the entire time I was gone, I was miserable. All because of you."

"You missed me?" Hope sparked in her eyes. Roark was glad to be the one who put it there.

"Terribly."

"I'm really glad you want to be a part of your child's life."

"More than just a part of it." Roark watched her smile fade as his statement sank in. "Marry me and I swear I'll be there for you and our children as long as I live."

"Oh, Roark. That's the most perfect thing anyone has ever said to me." She hugged him hard and kissed him softly. Her tears dampened his cheeks. "But I can't ask you to do that. You're an adventurer. Seeking artifacts, finding treasure no one has seen for hundreds of years, that's your passion. It's what makes you happy."

"You make me happy. The rest is stuff I did while waiting for you to come into my life and make me complete."

"I love you," she told him, her voice fierce. Her joy was the most beautiful thing he'd ever seen. "I didn't realize how empty my life was until you came along. I guess what I needed was a little adventure." She kissed him sweetly on the lips. "Are you sure you won't miss all the excitement of chasing artifacts and tangling with bad guys?"

Roark chuckled as he recalled those three miserable months he'd spent in the Amazon. "Lately I've discovered that living on the edge has lost its appeal. I will continue to do the research and let others take all the risks." It was time to tackle a whole new set of challenges. "From now on, you and our baby are all the excitement I need."

Thirteen

Elizabeth leaned against the veranda railing, her attention riveted on the gorgeous male emerging from the azure water. Morning sunlight sparkled off his wet torso, highlighting the chiseled perfection of his abs and dazzling her already overstimulated hormones. This was their third morning on the island. The third time she'd enjoyed the spectacle of her magnificent husband returning to her from the sea.

"The water is wonderful," he announced, mounting the steps to the porch that surrounded their quaint beach cottage. "Why don't you join me?"

"And miss the view?"

"It's better close up." He hooked his arm around her waist and pulled her against his wet body.

Heedless of the damage the saltwater was doing to her silk nightgown, Elizabeth lifted on tiptoe and brushed her lips against his. "So it is."

Being married to Roark had far exceeded her expectations. From the second he'd found out she was carrying his child, the walls he'd erected around his heart had tumbled down. No shadows darkened his gray-green eyes. His smiles had become broader, less lopsided. He made love to her with the same single-minded passion, but the reverence in his caresses brought tears to her eyes.

Following the pattern of the past three mornings, Elizabeth joined Roark in the shower. As her hands stroked over his soap-slick body, she reveled in the joy of her fortune. What if her moratorium against bad boys had led her to refuse to act as Roark's fiancée? She never would have had the chance to discover that there was so much more to him than he let the world see.

With Roark sated by their second passionate encounter of the morning, Elizabeth knew this was the best time to approach him about yesterday's unsettled argument. While he lay sprawled on his back in the middle of the bed, she lifted his phone off the nightstand and rolled back toward him. His eyes were closed, but the corners of his lips drifted upward as her breasts made contact with his chest.

"You've got to call Ann and tell her what you're up to."

His palm coasted over her naked butt and up her spine in a possessive caress. "I really don't think she'll want to hear how I've spent my last three days."

Elizabeth ignored the delight tickling over her skin and forced herself to be firm. "Call her back. She's left three messages."

Roark opened one eye. "How do you know that?"

"I might have spoken with Kendra about the pre-auction exhibit for the Gold Heart collection."

He exhaled harshly. "We both agreed no Waverly's trouble, Gold Heart statue, or event planning emergencies while we're on our honeymoon."

"I know what I promised, but I haven't been unavailable for more than five hours in the last three years."

"Very well, I'll listen to the messages, but unless it's life or death, I'm not calling her back."

Elizabeth had to be content with that. She kissed him on the cheek and curled up beside him as they both listened to the messages on Roark's phone. Several offered congratulations. Roark had given Vance a heads-up on their plans as they'd headed to the airport. Vance must have passed the word along to Roark's friends.

Roark cut off one message from a deep-voiced man named Smith. Elizabeth figured that was the man who was helping Roark with his elusive thief. Ann Richardson's messages progressed from irritation to acute displeasure. Elizabeth winced as Roark deleted the third one.

Ann was heading to Rayas and was pretty upset with Roark for taking off without giving her the statue. She was worried that the negative publicity coming out of Rayas about the missing Gold Heart statue would cause the board to vote to sell the company to Dalton Rothschild. Or worse, with the way the company's stock was plummeting, he might be able to acquire enough stock for a hostile takeover.

The final message had been sent only a few minutes earlier.

"I was at the airport waiting for my flight to Rayas this morning when Interpol stopped me from getting on the plane. They detained me for questioning because your mysterious sheikh's shipment arrived and the Gold Heart statue wasn't part of the cargo. I explained to them that because of all the controversy he'd decided not to sell the statue, but they wouldn't let me leave the country until I produce some sort of proof that his statue isn't the one missing from Rayas. Somehow a reporter caught wind that I was being questioned by Interpol and wrote an article speculating about our recent troubles. Waverly's stock has dropped even further. I need you back in New York and I need that statue. Call me."

Roark's features were set in grim lines as he deleted the message.

"What are you going to do?" Elizabeth asked.

"The same thing I was going to do before her call. I have to get the documents back from Masler before he can give them to Rothschild. It's the only way Rashid will let anyone see his statue and the only way to prove once and for all that it's not the one missing from Rayas's palace."

He tossed the phone onto a nearby chair and rolled Elizabeth onto her back. He threaded his fingers through her damp hair and dusted kisses over her nose, cheeks and eyes.

"But first," he murmured. "I'm going to make love to my wife."

With a heart bursting with love and a broad smile, Elizabeth teased, "I'll bet you never thought you'd hear yourself say those words."

"I think I knew the moment I set eyes on you."

"Really?" Seeing he meant every word, she snuggled closer. "I think I've loved you since the moment you took my hand and asked me if I like to play with new ideas."

He turned her palm up and traced her love line. "The way this curves means you're romantic and passionate."

She chuckled. "Don't you mean foolish when it comes to love?"

"Not at all. See how your head line and your life line start at the same point but separate right away? That means a decisive and determined personality. Someone who can handle adventurous and erratic situations."

"Meaning marriage to you?"

"I promise you'll never be bored."

As Roark's hands skimmed down her sides, Elizabeth reached up to pull his lips to hers. "I never doubted that for a second."

* * * * *

A BEAUTY FOR THE BILLIONAIRE

ELIZABETH BEVARLY

Prologue

There was nothing Hogan Dempsey loved more than the metallic smell and clink-clank sounds of his father's garage. Well, okay, *his* garage, as of the old man's death three years ago, but he still thought of it as his father's garage and probably would even after he passed it on to someone else. Not that he was planning on that happening anytime soon, since he was only thirty-three and had one to leave the place to—his mother had been gone even longer than his father, and there hadn't been a woman in his life he'd consider starting a family with since…ever. Dempsey's Parts & Service was just a great garage, that was all. The best one in Queens, for sure, and probably the whole state of New York. People brought their cars here to be worked on from as far away as Buffalo.

It was under one of those Buffalo cars he was working at the moment, a sleek, black '76 Trans Am—a gorgeous piece of American workmanship if ever there was one. If Hogan spent the rest of his life in his grease-stained coveralls, his hands and arms streaked with engine guts, lying under cars like this, he would die a happy man.

"Mr. Dempsey?" he heard from somewhere above the car.

It was a man's voice, but not one he recognized. He looked to his right and saw a pair of legs to go with it, the kind that were covered in pinstripes and ended in a pair of dress shoes that probably cost more than Hogan made in a month.

"That's me," he said as he continued to work.

"My name is Gus Fiver," the pinstripes said. "I'm an attorney with Tarrant, Fiver and Twigg. Is there someplace we could speak in private?"

Attorney? Hogan wondered. What did an attorney need with him? All of his affairs were in order, and he ran an honest shop. "We can talk here," he said. "Pull up a creeper."

To his surprise, Gus Fiver of Tarrant, Fiver and Twigg did just that. Most people wouldn't even know what a creeper was, but the guy toed the one nearest him—a skateboard-type bit of genius that mechanics used to get under a car chassis—and lay down on it, pinstripes and all. Then he wheeled himself under the car beside Hogan. From the neck up, he didn't look like the pinstripe type. He looked like a guy you'd grab a beer with on Astoria Boulevard after work. Blonder and better-looking than most, but he still had that working-class vibe about him that was impossible to hide completely.

And Hogan should know. He'd spent the better part of a year when he was a teenager trying to keep his blue collar under wraps, only to be reminded more than once that there was no way to escape his roots.

"Sweet ride," Fiver said. "Four hundred and fifty-five CUs. V-8 engine. The seventy-six Trans Am was the best pony car Pontiac ever made."

"Except for the sixty-four GTO," Hogan said.

"Yeah, okay, I'll give you that."

The two men observed a moment of silence for the holy land of Detroit, then Fiver said, "Mr. Dempsey, are you familiar with the name Philip Amherst?"

Hogan went back to work on the car. "It's Hogan. And nope. Should I be?"

"It's the name of your grandfather," Fiver said matter-of-factly.

Okay, obviously, Gus Fiver had the wrong Hogan Dempsey. He could barely remember any of his grandparents since cancer had been rampant on both sides of his family, but neither of his grandfathers had been named Philip Amherst. Fortunately for Hogan, he didn't share his family's medical histories because he'd been adopted as a newborn, and—

His brain halted there. Like any adopted kid, he'd been curious about the two people whose combined DNA had created him. But Bobby and Carol Dempsey had been the best parents he could have asked for, and the thought of someone else in that role had always felt wrong. He'd just never had a desire to locate any blood relations, even after losing what family he had. There wasn't anyone else in the world who could ever be family to him like that.

He gazed at the attorney in silence. Philip Amherst

must be one of his biological grandfathers. And if Gus Fiver was here looking for Hogan, it could only be because that grandfather wanted to find him. Hogan wasn't sure how he felt about that. He needed a minute to—

"I'm afraid he passed away recently," Fiver continued. "His wife, Irene, and his daughter, Susan, who was his only child and your biological mother, both preceded him in death. Susan never married or had any additional children, so he had no other direct heirs. After his daughter's death in a boating accident last year, he changed his will so that his entire estate would pass to you."

Not even a minute. Not even a minute for Hogan to consider a second family he might have come to know, because they were all gone, too. How else was Gus Fiver going to blindside him today?

He had his answer immediately. "Mr. Amherst's estate is quite large," Fiver said. "Normally, this is where I tell an inheritor to sit down, but under the circumstances, you might want to stand up?"

Fiver didn't have to ask him twice. Hogan's blood was surging like a geyser. With a single heave, he pushed himself out from under the car and began to pace. *Quite large.* That was what Fiver had called his grandfather's estate. But *quite large* was one of those phrases that could mean a lot of different things. *Quite large* could be a hundred thousand dollars. Or, holy crap, even a million dollars.

Fiver had risen, too, and was opening a briefcase to withdraw a handful of documents. "Your grandfather was a banker and financier who invested very wisely. He left the world with no debt and scores of assets. His main residence was here in New York on the Upper East Side, but he also owned homes in Santa Fe, Palm Beach and Paris."

Hogan was reeling. Although Fiver's words were making it into his brain, it was like they immediately got lost and went wandering off in different directions.

"Please tell me you mean Paris, Texas," he said.

Fiver grinned. "No. Paris, France. The *Trocadéro*, to be precise, in the sixteenth *arrondissement*."

"I don't know what that means." Hell, Hogan didn't know what any of this meant.

"It means your grandfather was a very rich man, Mr. Dempsey. And now, by both bequest and blood-line, so are you."

Then he quoted an amount of money so big, it actually made Hogan take a step backward, as if doing that might somehow ward it off. No one could have that much money. Especially not someone like Hogan Dempsey.

Except that Hogan did have that much money. Over the course of the next thirty minutes, Gus Fiver made that clear. And as they were winding down what the attorney told him was only the first of a number of meetings they would have over the next few weeks, he said, "Mr. Dempsey, I'm sure you've heard stories about people who won the lottery, only to have their lives fall apart because they didn't know how to han-dle the responsibility that comes with having a lot of money. I'd advise you to take some time to think about all this before you make any major decisions and that you proceed slowly."

"I will," Hogan assured him. "Weird thing is I've already given a lot of thought to what I'd do if I ever won the lottery. Because I've been playing it religiously since I was in high school."

Fiver looked surprised. "You don't seem like the lottery type to me."

"I have my reasons."

"So what did you always say you'd buy if you won the lottery?"

"Three things, ever since I was eighteen." Hogan held up his left hand, index finger extended. "Number one, a 1965 Shelby Daytona Cobra." His middle finger joined the first. "Number two, a house in Ocean City, New Jersey." He added his ring finger—damned significant, now that he thought about it—to the others. "And number three..." He smiled. "Number three, Anabel Carlisle. Of the Park Avenue Carlisles."

One

"You're my new chef?"

Hogan eyed the young woman in his kitchen—his massive, white-enamel-and-blue-Italian-tile kitchen that would have taken up two full bays in his garage—with much suspicion. Chloe Merlin didn't look like she was big enough to use blunt-tip scissors, let alone wield a butcher knife. She couldn't be more than five-four in her plastic red clogs—Hogan knew this, because she stood nearly a foot shorter than him—and she was swallowed by her oversize white chef's jacket and the baggy pants splattered with red chili peppers.

It was her gigantic glasses, he decided. Black-rimmed and obviously a men's style, they overwhelmed her features, making her green eyes appear huge. Or maybe it was the way her white-blond hair was piled haphazardly on top of her head as if she'd just grabbed it in two fists and tied it there without even looking to see what she was doing. Or it could be the red lipstick. It was the only makeup she wore, as if she'd filched it from her mother's purse to experiment with. She just looked so…so damned…

Ah, hell. Adorable. She looked adorable. And Hogan hated even thinking that word in his head.

Chloe Merlin was supposed to be his secret weapon in the winning of Anabel Carlisle of the Park Avenue Carlisles. But seeing her now, he wondered if she could even help him win bingo night at the Queensboro Elks Lodge. She had one hand wrapped around the handle of a duffel bag and the other steadying what looked like a battered leather bedroll under her arm—except it was too skinny to be a bedroll. Sitting beside her on the kitchen island was a gigantic wooden box filled with plants of varying shapes and sizes that he was going to go out on a limb and guess were herbs or something. All of the items in question were completely out of proportion to the rest of her. She just seemed…off. As if she'd been dragged here from another dimension and was still trying to adjust to some new laws of physics.

"How old are you?" he asked before he could stop himself.

"Why do you want to know?" she shot back. "It's against the law for you to consider my age as a prerequisite of employment. I could report you to the EEOC. Not the best way to start my first day of work."

He was about to tell her it could be her last day of work, too, if she was going to be like that, but she must have realized what he was thinking and intercepted.

"If you fire me now, after asking me a question

like that, I could sue you. You wouldn't have a legal leg to stand on."

Wow. Big chip for such a little shoulder.

"I'm curious," he said. Which he realized was true. There was just something about her that made a person feel curious.

Her enormous glasses had slipped down on her nose, so she pushed them up again with the back of her hand. "I'm twenty-eight," she said. "Not that it's any of your business."

Chloe Merlin must be a hell of a cook. 'Cause there was no way she'd become the most sought-after personal chef on Park Avenue as a result of her charming personality. But to Hogan's new social circle, she was its latest, and most exclusive, status symbol.

After he'd told Gus Fiver his reasons for wanting to "buy" Anabel that first day in his garage—man, had that been three weeks ago?—the attorney had given him some helpful information. Gus was acquainted with the Carlisles and knew Anabel was the current employer of one Chloe Merlin, personal chef to the rich and famous. In fact, she was such a great chef that, ever since her arrival on the New York scene five years ago, she'd been constantly hired away from one wealthy employer to another, always getting a substantial pay increase in the bargain. Poaching Chloe from whoever employed her was a favorite pastime of the Park Avenue crowd, Gus had said, and Anabel Carlisle was, as of five months prior, the most recent victor in the game. If Hogan was in the market for someone to cook for him—and hey, who wasn't?—then hiring Chloe away from Anabel would get the latter's attention and give him a legitimate reason to reenter her life.

Looking at the chef now, however, Hogan was beginning to wonder if maybe Park Avenue's real favorite pastime was yanking the chain of the new guy, and Gus Fiver was the current victor in that game. It had cost him a fortune to hire Chloe, and some of her conditions of employment were ridiculous. Not to mention she looked a little…quirky. Hogan hated quirky.

"If you want to eat tonight, you should show me my room," she told him in that same cool, shoulder-chip voice. "Your kitchen will be adequate for my needs, but I need to get to work. *Croque monsieur* won't make itself, you know."

Croque monsieur, Hogan repeated to himself. Though not with the flawless French accent she'd used. What the hell was *croque monsieur*? Was he going to be paying her a boatload of money to cook him things he didn't even like? Because he'd be fine with a ham and cheese sandwich.

Then the other part of her statement registered. The kitchen was *adequate*? Was she serious? She could feed Liechtenstein in this kitchen. Hell, Liechtenstein could eat off the floor of this kitchen. She could bake Liechtenstein a soufflé the size of Switzerland in one oven while she broiled them an entire swordfish in the other. Hogan had barely been able to find her in here after Mrs. Hennessey, his inherited housekeeper, told him his new chef was waiting for him.

Adequate. Right.

"Your room is, uh… It's, um…"

He halted. His grandfather's Lenox Hill town house was big enough to qualify for statehood, and he'd just moved himself into it yesterday. He barely knew where his own room was. Mrs. Hennessey went home at the end of the workday, but she'd assured him there were "suitable quarters" for an employee here. She'd even shown him the room, and he'd thought it was pretty damned suitable. But he couldn't remember now if it was on the fourth floor or the fifth. Depended on whether his room was on the third floor or the fourth.

"Your room is upstairs," he finally said, sidestepping the problem for a few minutes. He'd recognize the floor when he got there. Probably. "Follow me."

Surprisingly, she did without hesitation, leaving behind her leather bedroll-looking thing and her gigantic box of plants—that last probably to arrange later under the trio of huge windows on the far side of the room. They strode out of the second-floor kitchen and into a gallery overflowing with photos and paintings of people Hogan figured must be blood relations. Beyond the gallery was the formal dining room, which he had yet to enter.

He led Chloe up a wide, semicircular staircase that landed on each floor—there was an elevator in the house, too, but the stairs were less trouble—until they reached the third level, then the fourth, where he was pretty sure his room was. Yep. Fourth floor was his. He recognized the massive, mahogany-paneled den. Then up another flight to the fifth, and top, floor, which housed a wide sitting area flanked by two more bedrooms that each had connecting bathrooms bigger than the living room of his old apartment over the garage.

Like he said, pretty damned suitable.

"This is your room," he told Chloe. He gestured

toward the one on the right after remembering that was the one Mrs. Hennessey had shown him, telling him it was the bigger of the two and had a fireplace.

He made his way in that direction, opened the door and entered far enough to give Chloe access. The room was decorated in dark blue and gold, with cherry furniture, some innocuous oil landscapes and few personal touches. Hogan supposed it was meant to be a gender-neutral guest room, but it weighed solidly on the masculine side in his opinion. Even so, it somehow suited Chloe Merlin. Small, adorable and quirky she might be, with clothes and glasses that consumed her, but there was still something about her that was sturdy, efficient and impersonal.

"There's a bath en suite?" she asked from outside the door.

"If that means an adjoining bathroom, then yes," Hogan said. He pointed at a door on the wall nearest him. "It's through there." *I think*, he added to himself. That might have actually been a closet.

"And the door locks with a dead bolt?" she added.

He guessed women had to be careful about these things, but it would have been nice if she hadn't asked the question in the same tone of voice she might have used to accuse someone of a felony.

"Yes," he said. "The locksmith just left, and the only key is in the top dresser drawer. You can bolt it from the inside. Just like you said you would need in your contract."

Once that was settled, she walked into the room, barely noticing it, lifted her duffel onto the bed and began to unzip it. Without looking at Hogan, she said, "The room is acceptable. I'll unpack and report to the kitchen to inventory, then I'll shop this afternoon. Dinner tonight will be at seven thirty. Dinner every night will be at seven thirty. Breakfast will be at seven. If you'll be home for lunch, I can prepare a light midday meal, as well, and leave it in the refrigerator for you, but I generally spend late morning and early afternoon planning menus and buying groceries. I shop every day to ensure I have the freshest ingredients I can find, all organic farm-to-table. I have Sundays and Mondays off unless you need me for a special occasion, in which case I'll be paid double-time for those days and—"

"And have an additional day off the following week," he finished for her. "I know. I read and signed your contract, remember? You have Christmas Eve, Christmas Day and Thanksgiving off, with full pay, no exceptions," he quoted from it. "Along with three weeks in August, also with full pay."

"If I'm still here then," she said. "That's ten months away, after all." She said it without a trace of smugness, too, to her credit. Obviously Chloe Merlin knew about the Park Avenue chef-poaching game.

"Oh, you'll still be here," he told her. Because, by August, if Hogan played his cards right—and he was great at cards—Anabel would be living here with him, and his wedding present to her would be a lifetime contract for her favorite chef, Chloe Merlin.

Chloe, however, didn't look convinced.

Didn't matter. Hogan was convinced. He didn't care how many demands Chloe made—from the separate kitchen account into which he would deposit a specific amount of money each week and for which she alone would have a card, to her having complete dominion over the menus, thanks to his having no dietary restrictions. He was paying her a lot of money to cook whatever she wanted five days a week and letting her live rent-free in one of New York's toniest neighborhoods. In exchange, he'd created a situation where Anabel Carlisle had no choice but to pay attention to him. Actually not a bad trade, since, if history repeated—and there was no reason to think it wouldn't—once he had Anabel's attention, they'd be an item in no time. Besides, he didn't know what else he would do with all the money his grandfather had left him. It was enough to, well, feed Liechtenstein.

Hogan just hoped he liked…what had she called it? *Croque monsieur.* Whatever the hell that was.

Chloe Merlin studied her new employer in silence, wishing that, for once, she hadn't been driven by her desire to make money. Hogan Dempsey was nothing like the people who normally employed her. They were all pleasant enough, but they were generally frivolous and shallow and easy to dismiss, something that made it possible for her to focus solely on the only thing that mattered—cooking. Even having just met him, she found Hogan Dempsey earthy and astute, and something told her he would never stand for being dismissed.

As if she could dismiss him. She'd never met anyone with a more commanding presence. Although he had to be standing at least five feet away from her, she felt as if he were right on top of her, breathing down her chef's whites, leaving her skin hot to the touch. He was easily a foot taller than she was in her Super Birkis, and his shoulders had fairly filled the doorway when he entered the room. His hair was the color of good semolina, and his eyes were as dark as coffee beans. Chloe had always had a major thing for brown-eyed blonds, and this man could have been their king. Add that he was dressed in well-worn jeans, battered work boots and an oatmeal-colored sweater that had definitely seen better days—a far cry from the fresh-from-the-couturier cookie-cutter togs of other society denizens—and he was just way too gorgeous for his own good. Or hers.

She lifted her hand to the top button of her jacket and twisted it, a gesture that served to remind her of things she normally didn't need reminding of. But it did no good. Hogan was still commanding. Still earthy. Still gorgeous. Her glasses had begun to droop again, so she pushed them up with the back of her hand. It was a nervous gesture she'd had since child-hood, but it was worse these days. And not just be-cause her big black frames were a size larger than they should be.

"So…how's Anabel doing?" he asked.

Of all the questions she might have expected, that one wasn't even in the top ten. Although he didn't strike her as a foodie, and although he'd already filled out a questionnaire she prepared for her employers about his culinary expectations and customs, she would have thought he would want to talk more about her position here. She'd already gathered from Ana-bel that her former employer and her new employer shared some kind of history—Anabel had tried to talk Chloe out of taking this position, citing Hogan's past behavior as evidence of his unsophisticated palate. But Chloe neither cared nor was curious about what that history might be. She only wanted to cook. Cooking was what she did. Cooking was what she was. Cooking was all that mattered on any given day. On every given day. Chloe didn't do well if she couldn't keep every last scrap of her attention on cooking.

"Anabel is fine," she said.

"I mean since her divorce," Hogan clarified. "I understand you came to work for her about the same time her husband left her for one of her best friends."

"That was none of my business," Chloe told him. "It's none of yours, either. I don't engage in gossip, Mr. Dempsey."

"Hogan," he immediately corrected her. "And I'm not asking you to gossip. I just…"

He lifted one shoulder and let it drop in a way that was kind of endearing, then expelled his breath in a way that was almost poignant. Damn him. Chloe didn't have time for endearing and poignant. Especially when it was coming from the king of the brown-eyed blonds.

"I just want to know she's doing okay," he said. "She and I used to be…friends. A long time ago. I haven't seen her in a while. Divorce can be tough on a person. I just want to know she's doing okay," he repeated.

Oh, God. He was pining for her. It was the way he'd said the word *friends*. Pining for Anabel Carlisle, a woman who was a nice enough human being, and a decent enough employer, but who was about as deep as an onion skin.

"I suppose she's doing well enough in light of her… change of circumstances," Chloe said.

More to put Hogan out of his misery than anything else. Chloe actually didn't know Anabel that well, in spite of having been in her employ for nearly six months, which was longer than she'd worked for anyone else. Now that she thought about it, though, Anabel was doing better than *well enough*. Chloe had never seen anyone happier to be divorced.

"Really?" Hogan asked with all the hopeful earnestness of a seventh-grader. *Gah. Stop being so charming!*

"Really," she said.

"Is she seeing anyone?"

Next he would be asking her to pass Anabel a note during study hall. "I don't know," she said. But because she was certain he would ask anyway, she added, "I never cooked for anyone but her at her home."

That seemed to hearten him. Yay.

"Now if you'll excuse me…" She started to call him *Mr. Dempsey* again, remembered he'd told her to call him *Hogan*, so decided to call him nothing at all. Strange, since she'd never had trouble before addressing her employers by their first names, even if she didn't prefer to. "I have a strict schedule I adhere to, and I need to get to work."

She needed to get to work. Not wanted. Needed. Big difference. As much as Chloe liked to cook, and as much as she wanted to cook, she needed it even more. She hoped she conveyed that to Hogan Dempsey without putting too fine a point on it.

"Okay," he said with clear reluctance. He probably wanted to pump her for more information about Anabel, but unless his questions were along the lines of how much Anabel liked Chloe's pistachio *financiers*, she'd given him all she planned to give.

And, wow, she really wished she'd thought of another way to put that than *He probably wanted to pump her*.

"If you need anything else," he said, "or have any questions or anything, I'll be in my, uh…"

For the first time, he appeared to be unsure of himself. For just the merest of moments, he actually seemed kind of lost. And damned if Chloe didn't have to stop herself from taking a step forward to physically reach out to him. She knew how it felt to be lost. She hated the thought of anyone feeling that way. But knowing it was Hogan Dempsey who did somehow seemed even worse.

Oh, this was not good.

"House," he finally finished. "I'll be in my house."

She nodded, not trusting herself to say anything. Or do anything, for that matter. Not until he was gone, and she could reboot herself back into the cooking machine she was. The cooking machine she had to be. The one driven only by her senses of taste and smell. Because the ones that dealt with hearing and seeing and, worst of all, feeling—were simply not allowed.

A ham and cheese sandwich.

Hogan had suspected the dinner Chloe set in front of him before disappearing back into the kitchen without a word was a sandwich, because he was pretty sure there were two slices of bread under the crusty stuff on top that was probably more cheese. But his first bite had cinched it. She'd made him a ham and cheese sandwich. No, maybe the ham wasn't the Oscar Mayer he'd always bought before he became filthy, stinking rich, and the cheese wasn't the kind that came in plastic-wrapped individual slices, but *croque monsieur* was obviously French for *ham and cheese sandwich*.

Still, it was a damned good ham and cheese sandwich.

For side dishes, there was something that was kind of like French fries—but not really—and something else that was kind of like coleslaw—but not really. Even so, both were also damned good. Actually, they were better than damned good. The dinner Chloe made him was easily the best not-really ham and cheese sandwich, not-really French fries and not-really coleslaw he'd ever eaten. Ah, hell. They were better than all those spot-on things, too. Maybe hiring her would pay off in more ways than just winning back the love of his life. Or, at least, the love of his teens.

Chloe had paired his dinner with a beer that was also surprisingly good, even though he was pretty sure it hadn't been brewed in Milwaukee. He would have thought her expertise in that area would be more in wine—and it probably was—but it was good to know she had a well-rounded concept of what constituted dinner. Then again, for what he was paying her, he wouldn't be surprised if she had a well-rounded concept of astrophysics and existentialism, too. She'd even chosen music to go with his meal, and although he'd never really thought jazz was his thing, the mellow strains of sax and piano had been the perfect go-with.

It was a big difference from the way he'd enjoyed dinner before—food that came out of a bag or the microwave, beer that came out of a longneck and some sport on TV. If someone had told Hogan a month ago that he'd be having dinner in a massive dining room at a table for twelve with a view of trees and town houses out his window instead of the neon sign for Taco Taberna across the street, he would have told that person to see a doctor about their hallucinations. He still couldn't believe this was his life now. He wasn't sure he ever would.

The moment he laid his fork on his plate, Chloe appeared to remove both from the table and set a cup of coffee in their place. Before she could escape again—somehow it always seemed to Hogan like she was trying to run from him—he stopped her.

"That was delicious," he said. "Thank you."

When she turned to face him, she looked surprised by his admission. "Of course it was delicious. It's my life's work to make it delicious." Seemingly as an afterthought, she added, "You're welcome."

When she started to turn away, Hogan stopped her again.

"So I realize now that *croque monsieur* is a ham and cheese sandwich, but what do you call those potatoes?"

When she turned around this time, her expression relayed nothing of what she might be thinking. She only gazed at him in silence for a minute—a minute where he was surprised to discover he was dying to know what she was thinking. Finally she said, "*Pommes frites.* The potatoes are called *pommes frites.*"

"And the green stuff? What was that?"

"*Salade de chou.*"

"Fancy," he said. "But wasn't it really just a ham and cheese sandwich, French fries and coleslaw?"

Her lips, freshly stained with her red lipstick, thinned a little. "To you? Yes. Now if you'll excuse me, your dessert—"

"Can wait a minute," he finished. "Sit down. We need to talk."

She didn't turn to leave again. But she didn't sit down, either. Mostly, she just stared at him through slitted eyes over the top of her glasses before pushing them into place again with the back of her hand. He remembered her doing that a couple of times earlier in the day. Maybe with what he was paying her now, she could afford to buy a pair of glasses that fit. Or, you know, eight hundred pairs of glasses that fit. He was paying her an awful lot.

He tried to gentle his tone. "Come on. Sit down. Please," he added.

"Was there a problem with your dinner?" she asked.

He shook his head. "It was a damned tasty ham and cheese sandwich."

He thought she would be offended that he relegated her creation—three times now—to something normally bought in a corner deli and wrapped in wax paper. Instead, she replied, "I wanted to break you in slowly. Tomorrow I'm making you *pot au feu*."

"Which is?"

"To you? Beef stew."

"You don't think much of me or my palate, do you?"

"I have no opinion of either, Mr. Dempsey."

"Hogan," he corrected her. Again.

She continued as if he hadn't spoken. "I just happened to learn a few things about my new employer before starting work for him, and it's helped me plan menus that would appeal to him. Which was handy since the questionnaire I asked this particular employer to fill out was, shall we say, a bit lean on helpful information in that regard."

"Shouldn't I be the one doing that?" he asked. "Researching my potential employee before even offering the position?"

"Did you?" she asked.

He probably should have. But Gus Fiver's recommendation had been enough for him. Well, that and the fact that stealing her from Anabel would get the latter's attention.

"Uh…" he said eloquently.

She exhaled a resigned sigh then approached the table and pulled out a chair to fold herself into it, setting his empty plate before her for the time being. "I know you grew up in a working-class neighborhood in Astoria," she said, "and that you're so new money, with so much of it, the Secret Service should be crawling into your shorts to make sure you're not printing the bills yourself. I know you've never traveled farther north than New Bedford, Massachusetts, to visit your grandparents or farther south than Ocean City, New Jersey, where you and your parents spent a week every summer at the Coral Sands Motel. I know you excelled at both hockey and football in high school and that you missed out on scholarships for both by *this much*, so you never went to college. I also know your favorite food is—" at this, she bit back a grimace "—taco meatloaf and that the only alcohol you imbibe is domestic beer. News flash. I will *not* be making taco meatloaf for you at any time."

The hell she wouldn't. Taco meatloaf was awesome. All he said, though, was, "How do you know all that? I mean, yeah, some of that stuff is probably on the internet, but not the stuff about my grandparents and the Coral Sands Motel."

"I would never pry into anyone's personal information on the internet or anywhere else," Chloe said, sounding genuinely stung that he would think otherwise.

"Then how—"

"Anabel told me all that about you after I gave her my two weeks' notice. I didn't ask," she hastened to clarify. "But when she found out it was you who hired me, and when she realized she couldn't afford to pay me more than you offered me, she became a little... perturbed."

Hogan grinned. He remembered Anabel *perturbed.* She never liked it much when she didn't get her way. "And she thought she could talk you out of coming to work for me by telling you what a mook I am, right?" he asked.

Chloe looked confused. "Mook?"

He chuckled. "Never mind."

Instead of being offended by what Anabel had told Chloe, Hogan was actually heartened by it, because it meant she remembered him well. It didn't surprise him she had said what she did. Anabel had never made a secret of her opinion that social divisions existed for a reason and should never be crossed—even if she had crossed them dozens of times to be with him when they were young. It was what she had been raised to believe and was as ingrained a part of her as Hogan's love for muscle cars was ingrained in him. Her parents, especially her father, had been adamant she would marry a man who was her social and financial equal, to the point that they'd sworn to cut her off socially and financially if she didn't. The Carlisle money was just that old and sacred. It was the *only* thing that could come between Hogan and Anabel. She'd made that clear, too. And when she went off to college and started dating a senator's son, well... Hogan had known it was over between them without her even having to tell him.

Except that she never actually told him it was over between them, and they'd still enjoyed the occasional hookup when she was home from school, in spite of the senator's son. Over the next few years, though, they finally did drift apart.

But Anabel never told him it was over.

That was why, even after she'd married the senator's son, Hogan had never stopped hoping that someday things would be different for them. And now his hope had paid off. Literally. The senator's son was gone, and there was no social or financial divide between him and Anabel anymore. The blood he was born with was just as blue as hers, and the money he'd inherited was just as old and moldy. Maybe he was still feeling his way in a world that was new to him, but he wasn't on the outside looking in anymore. Hell, he'd just drunk beer from a glass instead of a longneck. That was a major development for him. It wouldn't be long before he—

"Hang on," he said. "How does Anabel know I only drink domestic beer? I wasn't old enough to drink when I was with her."

"That part I figured out myself," Chloe said.

"There are some damned fine domestic beers being brewed these days, you know."

"There are. But what you had tonight was Belgian. Nice, wasn't it?"

Yeah, okay, it was. He would still be bringing home

his Sam Adams on the weekends. *So there, Chloe Merlin.*

"Is everything you cook French?" he asked. He wasn't sure why he was prolonging a conversation neither of them seemed to want to have.

"Still angling for that taco meatloaf, are we?" she asked.

"I like pizza, too."

She flinched, but said nothing.

"And chicken pot pie," he threw in for good measure.

She expelled another one of those impatient sighs. "Fine. I can alter my menus. Some," she added meaningfully.

Hogan smiled. Upper hand. He had it. He wondered how long he could keep it.

"But yes, all of what I cook is French." She looked like she would add more to the comment, but she didn't.

So he tried a new tack. "Are you a native New Yorker?" Then he remembered she couldn't be a native New Yorker. She didn't know what a mook was.

"I was born and raised in New Albany, Indiana," she told him. Then, because she must have realized he was going to press her for more, she added, with clear reluctance, "I was raised by my grandmother because my parents…um…weren't able to raise me themselves. Mémée came here as a war bride after World War Two—her parents owned a bistro in Cherbourg—and she was the one who taught me to cook. I got my degree in Culinary Arts from Sullivan University in Louisville, which is a cool city, but the restaurant scene there is hugely competitive, and I wanted to open my own place."

"So you came to New York, where there's no competition for that kind of thing at all, huh?" He smiled, but Chloe didn't smile back.

He waited for her to explain how she had ended up in New York cooking for the One Percent instead of opening her own restaurant, but she must have thought she had come to the end of her story, because she didn't say anything else. For Hogan, though, her conclusion only jump-started a bunch of new questions in his brain. "So you wanted to open your own place, but you've been cooking for one person at a time for... how long?"

She met his gaze levelly. "For five years," she said.

He wondered if that was why she charged so much for her services and insisted on living on-site. Because she was saving up to open her own restaurant.

"Why no restaurant of your own by now?" he asked.

She hesitated for a short, but telling, moment. "I changed my mind." She stood and picked up his plate. "I need to see to your dessert."

He wanted to ask her more about herself, but her posture made clear she was finished sharing. So instead, he asked, "What am I having?"

"*Glissade.*"

"Which is? To me?" he added before she could.

"Chocolate pudding."

And then she was gone. He turned in his chair to watch her leave and saw her crossing the gallery to the kitchen, her red plastic shoes whispering over the marble floor. He waited to see if she would look back, or even to one side. But she kept her gaze trained on the kitchen door, her step never slowing or faltering.

She was a focused one, Chloe Merlin. He wondered why. And he found himself wondering, too, if there was anything else—or anyone else—in her life besides cooking.

Two

The day after she began working for Hogan Dempsey, Chloe returned from her early-afternoon grocery shopping to find him in the gallery between the kitchen and dining room. He was dressed in a different pair of battered jeans from the day before, and a different sweater, this one the color of a ripe avocado. He must not have heard her as she topped the last stair because he was gazing intently at one photograph in particular. It was possible that if she continued to not make a sound, he wouldn't see her as she slipped into the kitchen. Because she'd really appreciate it if Hogan didn't see her as she slipped into the kitchen.

In fact, she'd really appreciate it if Hogan never noticed her again.

She still didn't know what had possessed her to reveal so much about herself last night. She never told anyone about being raised by a grandmother instead of by parents, and she certainly never talked about the desire she'd once had to open a restaurant. That was a dream she abandoned a long time ago, and she would never revisit it again. Never. Yet within hours of meeting Hogan, she was telling him those things and more. It was completely unprofessional, and Chloe was, if nothing else, utterly devoted to her profession.

She gripped the tote bags in her hands more fiercely and stole a few more steps toward the kitchen. She was confident she didn't make a sound, but Hogan must have sensed her presence anyway and called out to her. Maybe she could pretend she didn't hear him. It couldn't be more than five or six more steps to the kitchen door. She might be able to make it.

"Chloe?" he said again.

Damn. Missed it by that much.

She turned to face him. "Yes, Mr. Dempsey?"

"Hogan," he told her again. "I don't like being called 'Mr. Dempsey.' It makes me uncomfortable. It's Hogan, okay?"

"All right," she agreed reluctantly. "What is it you need?"

When he'd called out to her, he'd sounded like he genuinely had something to ask her. Now, though, he only gazed at her in silence, looking much the way he had yesterday when he'd seemed so lost. And just as she had yesterday, Chloe had to battle the urge to go to him, to touch him, and to tell him not to worry, that everything would be all right. Not that she would ever tell him that. There were some things that could never be all right again. No one knew that better than Chloe did.

Thankfully, he quickly regrouped, pointing at the photo he'd been studying. "It's my mother," he said. "My biological mother," he quickly added. "I think I resemble her a little. What do you think?"

What Chloe thought was that she needed to start cooking. Immediately. Instead, she set her bags on the floor and made her way across the gallery toward him and the photo.

His mother didn't resemble him *a little*, she saw. His mother resembled him a lot. In fact, looking at her was like looking at a female Hogan Dempsey.

"Her name was Susan Amherst," he said. "She was barely sixteen when she had me."

Even though Chloe truly didn't engage in gossip, she hadn't been able to avoid hearing the story of Susan Amherst over the last several weeks. It was all the Park Avenue crowd had talked about since the particulars of Philip Amherst's estate were made public, from the tearooms where society matriarchs congregated to the kitchens where their staff toiled. How Susan Amherst, a prominent young society deb in the early '80s, suddenly decided not to attend Wellesley after her graduation from high school a year early, and instead took a year off to "volunteer overseas." There had been talk at the time that she was pregnant and that her ultra-conservative, extremely image-conscious parents wanted to hide her condition. Rumors swirled that they sent her to live with relatives upstate and had the baby adopted immediately after its birth. But the talk about young Susan died down as soon as another scandal came along, and life went on. Even for the Amhersts. Susan returned to her rightful place in her parents' home the following spring and started college the next year. For all anyone knew, she really had spent months "volunteering overseas."

Until Hogan showed up three decades later and stirred up the talk again.

"You and she resemble each other very much," Chloe said. And because Susan's parents were in the photograph, as well, she added, "You resemble your grandfather, too." She stopped herself before adding that Philip Amherst had been a very handsome man.

"My grandfather's attorney gave me a letter my grandfather wrote when he changed his will to leave his estate to me." Hogan's voice revealed nothing of what he might be feeling, even though there must be a tsunami of feeling in a statement like that. "The adoption was a private one at a time when sealed records stayed sealed, so he couldn't find me before he died.

"Not that I got the impression from his letter that he actually *wanted* to find me before he died," he hastened to add. Oh, yes. Definitely a tsunami of feeling. "It took a bunch of legal proceedings to get the records opened so the estate could pass to me. Anyway, in his letter, he said Susan didn't want to put me up for adoption. That she wanted to raise me herself. She even named me. Travis. Travis Amherst." He chuckled, but there wasn't an ounce of humor in the sound. "I mean, can you see me as a Travis Amherst?"

Actually, Chloe could. Hogan Dempsey struck her as a man who could take any form and name he wanted. Travis Amherst of the Upper East Side would have been every bit as dynamic and compelling as Hogan Dempsey of Queens. He just would have been doing it in a different arena.

"Not that it matters," he continued. "My grandparents talked Susan out of keeping me because she was so young—she was only fifteen when she got pregnant. They convinced her it was what was best for her and me both."

He looked at the photo again. In it, Susan Amherst looked to be in her thirties. She was wearing a black cocktail dress and was flanked by her parents on one side and a former, famously colorful, mayor of New York on the other. In the background were scores of people on a dance floor and, behind them, an orchestra. Whatever the event was, it seemed to be festive. Susan, however, wasn't smiling. She obviously didn't feel very festive.

"My mother never told anyone who my father was," Hogan continued. "But my grandfather said he thought he was one of the servants' kids that Susan used to sneak out with. From some of the other stuff he said, I think he was more worried about that than he was my mother's age." He paused. "Not that that matters now, either."

Chloe felt his gaze fall on her again. When she looked at him, his eyes were dark with a melancholy sort of longing.

"Of course it matters," she said softly. "Your entire life would have been different if you had grown up Travis Amherst instead of Hogan Dempsey." And because she couldn't quite stop herself, she added, "It's…difficult…when life throws something at you that you never could have seen coming. Especially when you realize it's going to change *every*thing. Whatever you're feeling, Hogan, they're legitimate feelings, and they deserve to be acknowledged. You don't have to pretend it doesn't matter. It matters," she repeated adamantly. "It matters a lot."

Too late, she realized she had called him Hogan. Too late, she realized she had spilled something out of herself onto him again and made an even bigger mess than she had last night. Too late, she realized she couldn't take any of it back.

But Hogan didn't seem to think she'd made a mess. He seemed to be grateful for what she'd said. "Thanks," he told her.

And because she couldn't think of anything else to say, she replied automatically, "You're welcome."

She was about to return to the kitchen—she really, really, really did need to get cooking—but he started talking again, his voice wistful, his expression sober.

"I can't imagine what my life would have been like growing up as Travis Amherst. I would have had to go to some private school where I probably would have played soccer and lacrosse instead of football and hockey. I would have gone to college. I probably would have majored in business or finance and done one of those study-abroads in Europe. By now Travis Amherst would be saddled with some office job, wearing pinstripes by a designer whose name Hogan Dempsey wouldn't even recognize." He shook his head, clearly baffled by what might have been. "The thought of having to work at a job like that instead of working at the garage is…" He inhaled deeply and released the breath slowly. "It's just… A job like that would suffocate me. But Travis Amherst probably would have loved it."

"Possibly," Chloe said. "But maybe not. Travis

might have liked working with his hands, too. It's impossible to know for sure."

"And pointless to play 'what if,' I know," Hogan agreed. "What's done is done. And the idea that I would have never known my mom and dad or have the friends I've had all my life… The thought of all the memories that live in my head being completely different…"

Chloe winced inwardly at the irony of their situation. They both grieved for the unknown. But with him, it was a past that hadn't happened, and for her, it was a future that would never be.

"I need to cook," she told him. She pushed her glasses into place with the back of her hand and took a step backward. "I'm sorry, but…" She took another step back. "I need to cook. If you'll excuse me…"

"Sure," he said. "No problem." He didn't sound like there wasn't a problem, though. He sounded really confused.

That made two of them.

When Chloe turned to head back to the kitchen, she saw Mrs. Hennessey topping the last stair. Hogan's housekeeper reminded her of her grandmother in a lot of ways. She wore the same boxy house dresses in the same muted colors and always kept her fine white hair twisted into a flawless chignon at her nape. She was no-nonsense and professional, the way Chloe was. At least, the way Chloe was before she came to work for Hogan. The way she knew she had to be again if she wanted to keep working here.

And she did want to keep working here. For some reason. A reason she wasn't ready to explore. It was sure to be good, whatever it was.

Mrs. Hennessey announced to the room at large, "There's an Anabel Carlisle downstairs to see you. I showed her to the salon."

That seemed to snap Hogan out of his preoccupation with what might have been and pull him firmly into the here and now. "Anabel is here? Tell her I'll be right down."

"No, Mr. Dempsey, she's here to see Ms. Merlin."

Hogan's jaw dropped a little at that. But all he said was, "Hogan, Mrs. Hennessey. Please call me Hogan." Then he looked at Chloe. "Guess she refigured her budget and wants to hire you back."

Chloe should have been delighted by the idea. Not only did it mean more money coming in, but it also meant she would be free of Hogan Dempsey and his damnable heartache-filled eyes. She should be flying down the stairs to tell Anabel that she'd love to come back to work for her and would pack her bags this instant. Instead, for some reason, she couldn't move. "Tell Anabel we'll be right down," Hogan told Mrs. Hennessey.

The housekeeper nodded and went back down the stairs. Chloe stood still. Hogan gazed at her curiously.

"Don't you want to hear what she has to say?"

Chloe nodded. She did. She did want to hear what Anabel had to say. But she really needed to cook. Cooking was something she could control. Cooking filled her head with flavors and fragrances, with methods and measurements. Cooking restored balance to the universe. And Chloe could really use some balance right now.

"Well then, let's go find out," Hogan said.

Chloe looked at him again. And was immediately

sorry. Because now he looked happy and eager and excited. And a happy Hogan was far more overwhelming, and far more troubling, than a conflicted one. A happy Hogan reminded her of times and places—and people—that had made her happy, too. And those thoughts, more than anything, were the very reason she needed to cook.

Hogan couldn't understand why Chloe looked so unhappy at the thought of seeing Anabel. Then again, Chloe hadn't really looked happy about anything since he met her. He'd never encountered anyone so serious. Even cooking, which she constantly said she wanted to do, didn't really seem to bring her any joy.

Then he remembered she'd never actually said she *wanted* to cook. She always said she *needed* to. For most people, that was probably a minor distinction. He was beginning to suspect that, for Chloe, there was nothing minor about it at all.

"C'mon," he told her. "Let's go see what Anabel wants." And then, because she was standing close enough for him to do it, he leaned over and nudged her shoulder gently with his.

He might as well have jabbed her with a red-hot poker, the way she lurched away from him at the contact. She even let out a soft cry of protest and lifted a hand to her shoulder, as if he'd struck her there.

"I'm sorry," he immediately apologized, even though he had no idea what he needed to apologize for. "I didn't mean to…"

What? Touch her? Of course he meant to touch her. The same way he would have touched any one of his friends, male or female, in an effort to coax them out of their funk. People always nudged each other's shoulders. Most people wouldn't have even noticed the gesture. Chloe looked as if she'd been shot.

"It's okay," she said, still rubbing her shoulder, not looking like it was okay at all.

Not knowing what else he could say, he extended his arm toward the stairs to indicate she should precede him down. With one last, distressed look at him, she did. He kept his distance as he followed her because she seemed to need it, but also because it gave him a few more seconds to prepare for Anabel. He'd known he would run into her at some point—hell, he'd planned on it—but he'd figured it would be at some social function where there would be a lot of people around, and he'd have plenty of time to plan. He hadn't thought she would come to his house, even if it was to see someone other than him.

What Mrs. Hennessey called a "salon," Hogan thought of as a big-ass living room. The walls were paneled in maple, and a massive Oriental rug covered most of the green marble floor. A fireplace on one wall had a mantel that was dotted with wooden model ships, and it was flanked by brown leather chairs—a matching sofa was pushed against the wall opposite.

Three floor-to-ceiling arched windows looked out onto a courtyard in back of the house, and it was through one of those that Anabel Carlisle stood looking, with her back to them. Either she hadn't heard them come in, or she, too, was giving herself a few extra seconds to prepare. All Hogan could tell was that the black hair that used to hang in straight shafts to the middle of her back was short now, cut nearly to her chin.

And her wardrobe choices were a lot different, too. He remembered her trying to look like a secondhand gypsy, even though she'd probably spent hundreds of dollars in Fifth Avenue boutiques on everything she wore. Today's outfit had likely set her back even more, despite merely consisting of sedate gray pants and sweater. But both showcased lush curves she hadn't had as a teenager, so maybe they were worth the extra expense.

As if he'd spoken his appraisal out loud, Anabel suddenly spun around. Although she looked first at Chloe, she didn't seem to be surprised by Hogan's presence. But whether the smile on her face was for him or his chef, he couldn't have said. "Hogan," she said in the same throaty voice he remembered. God, he'd always loved her voice. "Good to see you."

"You, too, Anabel. How have you been?"

She began to walk toward where he and Chloe stood in the doorway. She still moved the way she used to, all grace and elegance and style. He'd always loved watching her move. She was just as gorgeous now as she'd been when they were kids. Even more, really, because she'd ditched the heavy eye makeup and dark lipstick she used to wear, so her natural beauty shone through. Strangely, the lack of makeup only made her blue eyes seem even bluer than he remembered them and her mouth even fuller and lusher.

He waited for the splash of heat that had always rocked his midsection whenever he saw her, and for the hitch of breath that had always gotten caught in his chest. But neither materialized. He guessed he'd outgrown reactions like that.

"I imagine you've already heard most of the high-

lights about how I've been," she said as she drew
nearer. "My divorce was the talk of the town until
you showed up." She smiled again, but there was only
good humor and maybe a little nostalgia in the gesture. "I should actually probably thank you for that."

"You're welcome," he said, smiling back.

It really was good to see her. She really did look
great. So what if his heart wasn't pumping like the
V-8 in a Challenger Hellcat, the way he would have
thought it would be. People grew up. Hormones settled down.

With one last look at Hogan she turned her attention to Chloe.

"I want you to come back to work for me," she said,
straight to the point. "I can pay you three percent more
than Hogan offered you."

Hogan looked at Chloe. She still seemed shell-
shocked from whatever the hell had happened between
them in the gallery. She glanced at Hogan, then back
at Anabel, but said nothing.

Cagey, he thought. She was probably thinking if
Anabel was offering three percent, she could get more
from Hogan. Fine. Whatever it took to keep Chloe on,
Hogan would pay it. Especially if it meant Anabel
might come around again.

"I'll raise your salary five percent," he told her.

Anabel looked at him, her lips parted in surprise.
Or something. Then she looked back at Chloe. "I can
go six percent," she said coolly. "And you can have
the entire month of August off, with pay."

Again, Chloe looked at Hogan, then back at Anabel. Again, she remained silent.

"Eight percent," Hogan countered.

Now Anabel narrowed her eyes at him in a way he remembered well. It was her *I'll-get-what-I-want-or-else* look. She always wore it right before he agreed to spring for tickets for whatever band happened to be her favorite at the time, or whatever restaurant was her favorite, or whatever whatever was her favorite. Then again, she'd always thanked him with hours and hours of hot *I-love-you-so-much* sex. Well, okay, maybe not hours and hours. He hadn't been the most controlled lover back in the day. But it had for sure been hot.

Anabel didn't up her salary offer this time, but she told Chloe, "And I'll give you the suite of rooms that face the park."

Chloe opened her mouth to reply, but Hogan stopped her with another counteroffer. "I'll raise your pay ten percent," he said. He didn't add anything about a better room or more time off. Not just because she already had a damned suitable room and more time off than the average person could ever hope to have, but because something told him money was way more important to Chloe than anything else.

What she needed the money for, Hogan couldn't imagine. But it was her salary that had been the most important part of her contract, her salary that lured her from one employer to another. Chloe Merlin wanted money. Lots of it.

For a third time she looked at Hogan, then at Anabel. "I'm sorry, Anabel," she said. "Unless you can offer to pay me more than Mr...." She threw another glance Hogan's way, this one looking even more edgy than the others. Then she turned so that her entire body was facing Anabel. "Unless you can offer me more than...that... I'm afraid I'll have to remain here."

There was a brief expectant pause, and when Anabel only shook her head, Chloe made her way to the doorway. "I'll draw up a rider for my contract and have it for you this evening," she said to Hogan as she started back up the stairs.

And then she was gone, without saying goodbye to either of them.

"She is such an odd duck," Anabel said when Chloe was safely out of earshot.

There was nothing derogatory in her tone, just a matter-of-factness that had been there even when they were teenagers. She wasn't condemning Chloe, just stating the truth. His chef was pretty unique.

"But worth every penny," she added with a sigh. She smiled again. "More pennies than I can afford to pay her. Obviously, she's working for someone who's out of my league."

Hogan shook his head. "Other way around, Anabel. You were always out of my league. You said so yourself. More than once, if I remember."

She winced at the comment, even though he hadn't meant it maliciously. He'd learned to be matter-of-fact from her. "I was a dumb kid when we dated, Hogan," she told him. "I was so full of myself back then. I said a lot of things I shouldn't have."

"Nah," he told her. "You never said anything I wasn't thinking myself. You were right. We came from two different worlds."

"Even so, that didn't give me the right to be such an elitist. My parents just taught me their philosophy well. It took me years to figure out I was wrong."

Now there was a loaded statement. Wrong about what? Wrong about the prejudice her parents taught her? Wrong about some of the comments she'd made? Wrong about their social circles never mixing? Wrong about leaving him for the senator's son?

Probably better not to ask for clarification. Not yet anyway. He and Anabel had rushed headlong into their relationship when they were kids. The first time they'd had sex was within days of meeting, and they'd almost never met without having sex. He'd sometimes wondered if maybe they'd gone slower, things would have worked out differently. This time he wasn't going to hurry it. This time he wanted to do it right.

"So how have you been?" she asked him. "How are your folks? I still think about your mom's Toll House cookies from time to time."

"My folks are gone," he told her. "Mom passed five years ago. Dad went two years later. Cancer. Both of them."

She looked stricken by the news. She lifted a hand to his shoulder and gave it a gentle squeeze. "Oh, Hogan, I am so sorry. I had no idea."

He covered her hand with his. "You couldn't have known. And thanks."

For a moment neither of them said anything, then Anabel dropped her hand. She crossed her arms over her midsection and looked at the door. Hogan told himself to ask her something about herself, but he didn't want to bring up her divorce, even if she didn't seem to be any the worse for wear from it. Her folks, he figured, were probably the same as always. Maybe a little more likely to invite him into their home than they were fifteen years ago, but then again, maybe not.

But for the life of him, he couldn't think of a single thing to say.

"I should probably get going," she said. "I have a thing tonight. My aunt and uncle are in town. We're meeting at the Rainbow Room." She expelled a sound that was a mixture of affection and irritation. "They always want to meet at the Rainbow Room. Which is great, but really, I wish they'd expand their repertoire a bit. Try Per Se or Morimoto sometime. Or Le Turtle. I love that place."

Okay, she'd just given Hogan the perfect opening. Three different restaurants she obviously loved. All he had to do was say, *What a coincidence, Anabel, I've been wanting to expand my repertoire, too. Why don't you and I have dinner at one of those places? You pick.* And they'd be off. For some reason, though, he just couldn't get the words to move out of his brain and into his mouth.

Not that Anabel had seemed to be angling for an invitation, because she didn't miss a beat when she continued, "Ah, well. Old habits die hard, I guess."

Which was another statement that could have been interpreted in more ways than one. Was she talking about her aunt and uncle now, and their dining habits? Or was she talking about her and Hogan, and how she still maybe had a thing for him? It didn't used to be this hard to read her. And why the hell didn't he just ask her out to see how she responded?

"It was good to see you again, Hogan," she said as she took a step in retreat. "I'm glad Philip Amherst's attorneys found you," she continued as she took another. "Maybe our paths will cross again before long."

"Maybe so," he said, finding his voice.

She lifted a hand in farewell then turned and made her way toward the exit. Just as she was about to disappear into the hallway, Hogan thought of something to ask her.

"Hey, Anabel."

She halted and turned back around, but said nothing.

"If I'd grown up an Amherst…" Hogan began. "I mean, if you'd met me as, say, a guy named Travis Amherst from the Upper East Side who went to some private school and played lacrosse and was planning to go to Harvard after graduation, instead of meeting me as Hogan Dempsey, grease monkey…"

She smiled again, this one definitely nostalgic. "Travis Amherst wouldn't have been you, Hogan. He would have been like a million other guys I knew. If I'd met you as Travis Amherst, I never would have bothered with you."

"You bothered with the senator's son," he reminded her. "And he had to have been like those million other guys."

"Yeah, he was. And look how that turned out."

Good point.

"You take care, Hogan."

"You, too, Anabel."

She threw him one last smile, lifted a hand in goodbye then turned around again and made her way down the hall. He heard her footsteps gradually fade away, then heard Mrs. Hennessey open and close the front door for her. Then, as quickly as she'd shown up in his life again, Anabel was gone.

And as the front door clicked shut behind her, it occurred to Hogan that, just like last time, she never actually told him goodbye.

Three

Although Chloe had Sundays and Mondays off, she rarely used them to relax. She generally went out in the morning and often didn't return until nearly dark—or even after—but the hours in between were almost always devoted to things related to cooking. Sometimes she explored new shops or revisited old favorites to familiarize herself with what they had in stock or to pick up a few essentials. Sometimes she sat in on lectures or classes that addressed new methods or trends in cooking. Sometimes she checked out intriguing restaurants to see what was on their menus that she might adapt for her own. Sometimes she attended tastings of cheeses, charcuterie, beers or wines.

It was to one of the last that she was headed out late Monday afternoon when she ran into Hogan, who was coming in the back door. She'd been exceptionally good at avoiding him since last week when Anabel had tried to hire her back—the same afternoon she'd shared those odd few moments with Hogan in the gallery that had ended with her completely overreacting when he nudged her shoulder with his.

She still wanted to slap herself for recoiling from him the way she had. There had been nothing inappropriate in his gesture. On the contrary, he'd obviously been trying to be friendly. There was a time when Chloe loved having her shoulder nudged in exactly that same way by…friends. It had just been so unexpected, that was all. Especially coming from someone who wasn't…a friend.

And, okay, it had also been a long time since someone had touched her with anything resembling friendship. It had been a long time since anyone had touched her at all. She went out of her way to avoid physical contact these days. With everyone. It just wasn't professional. Among other things.

It was those *among other things* that especially came into play with Hogan. Because even an innocent touch like a nudge to the shoulder felt… Well. Not innocent. Not on her end anyway. Not since it had been so long since anyone had touched her with anything resembling friendship. Or something.

Which was why she had been super careful not to let it happen again. Since that afternoon, dinner every night had been nothing but serving, identifying and describing Hogan's food. No more sitting down at his table. No more spilling her guts. And certainly no more touching. She was his chef. He was her employer. Period. Thankfully, he finally got the message, because after three or four nights of her sidestepping every question he asked about her by replying with something about the food instead, he'd finally stopped asking.

At least, that was what she'd thought until she saw him today. Because the minute he stepped inside he smiled that damnably charming smile of his and said, with much friendliness, "Chloe, hi. Where you going?"

It was the kind of question, spoken with the kind of expression that was almost always followed by *Can I come, too*? He just looked so earnest and appealing and sweet, and something inside Chloe that had been cold and hard and discordant for a very long time began to grow warm and soft and agreeable.

Stop that, she told that part of herself. *Stop it right now*.

But that part wouldn't listen, because it just kept feeling better. So she did her best to ignore it.

"Must be someplace really nice," he added. "'Cause you look really nice."

Had she thought that part of her was only growing warm? Well, now it was spontaneously combusting. The man's smile just had that effect. As did the fact that he was wearing garage-issue coveralls streaked with machine oil, an outfit that should have been unappealing—and on anyone else in her social sphere, it probably would have been—but only served to make Hogan look even more handsome.

She'd always found the working-class hero too damnably attractive. Men who worked with their hands *and* their brains could, at the end of the day, point to something concrete that was actually useful to society and say *Hey, I did that with my bare hands*. Inevitably, that always made her think about what else a man like that could do with his bare hands—especially at the end of the day. And, inevitably, she always remembered. Men like that could make a woman feel wonderful.

She pushed her glasses up with the back of her hand—it was a nervous gesture, she knew, but dammit, she was nervous—and, without thinking, told him, "You look really nice, too."

Only when he chuckled did she realize what she had said and immediately wished she could take back the words.

But Hogan shrugged off the comment. "No, I look like I've spent the better part of the afternoon under a 1957 Mercedes-Benz Three Hundred SL Gullwing that belonged to my grandfather. Which I have been. *You* look really nice. So where you going?"

It was nice of him to say so, but Chloe was the epitome of plain in a black pencil skirt, white shirt, claret-colored cardigan and black flats—all of which she had owned since college—with her hair piled on top of her head, the way it always was.

"Thank you," she made herself say, even though she was uncomfortable with the compliment. "I'm going to a wine-tasting."

She thought the announcement would put an end to any idea he might have about joining her. She was still serving him beer with his dinner—though he had certainly expanded his horizons there—and was hoping to find a few wines at this tasting today that might break him in easily.

"Sounds like fun," he said. Even though he didn't sound like he thought it was fun. In spite of that, he added, "Want some company?"

Of course she didn't want company. Chloe hadn't wanted company for years. Six years, in fact. Six years and eight months, to be precise. Six years, eight months, two weeks and three days, to be even more precise.

"I mean, knowing about wine," Hogan continued, "that could help me in the Anabel department, right? I need to know this stuff if I'm going to be moving in her circles. Make a good impression and all that."

He wasn't wrong, Chloe thought. She knew for a fact that Anabel Carlisle knew and enjoyed her wines. She could invite Hogan to come along, if for no other reason than that. And what other reason could there be?

Even so, she hedged, "Actually, I—"

But Hogan cut her off. "Great. Gimme ten minutes to clean up and change clothes. Be right back."

She was so stunned by his response that it took her a minute to react. She spun around and said, "But—"

But she knew he wouldn't hear her, because he was already pounding up the stairs.

She told herself to leave before he got back and explain her disappearance later by saying she'd assumed he was joking so went her merry way. She really didn't want company today. Or any day. So why didn't she slip out the door and make her way up 67th Street to Madison Avenue, where she could lose herself in both the crowd and the sunny October afternoon? Why did her feet seem to be nailed to the floor? More to the point, why did a part of her actually kind of like the prospect of spending the rest of the afternoon with Hogan?

She was still contemplating those questions and a

host of others when he reappeared ten minutes later. The man was nothing if not punctual. And also incredibly handsome. So far she'd seen him in nothing but jeans and sweaters and greasy coveralls, but, having clearly taken a cue from her own outfit, he now wore a pair of khaki trousers, a pinstriped oxford and a chocolate-colored blazer. And in place of his usual battered work boots were a pair of plain leather mocs—not quite as well-worn as the boots, but still obviously, ah…of a certain age. Just like everything else he had on.

How could a man have inherited as much money as Hogan had and not have spent at least some of it on new shoes and clothes? Then again, who was she to judge? The last time Chloe bought a new article of clothing for herself, it had been for… Well, it wasn't important what she'd bought the dress for. It had been six years since she'd worn it. Six years, eight months, two weeks and six days, to be precise. And she'd gotten rid of it soon after.

As Hogan began to walk toward her, heat bloomed in her midsection again, only this time it was joined by a funny sort of shimmying that only made it more enjoyable.

No! she immediately told herself. *Not enjoyable.* What she was feeling was…something else. Something that had nothing to do with enjoyment.

As he drew nearer, she noticed he hadn't managed quite as well with his grooming as he had his clothing. There was a tiny streak of oil over his eyebrow that he'd missed.

"All set," he said when he stopped in front of her.

"Not quite," she told him.

His expression fell. "I've never been to a wine-tasting. Should I change my clothes?"

She shook her head. "No, your outfit is fine. It's a casual event. It's just that…"

He was within touching distance now, and she had to battle the urge to lift a hand to his face and wipe away the oil herself. The gesture would have been no more inappropriate than his nudging of her shoulder had been last week. For some reason, though, the thought of touching him in such a way felt no less innocent than that one had.

So instead, she pointed at his eyebrow and said, "You missed a spot of grease there. Over your left eyebrow."

He swiped the side of his hand over the place she indicated…and missed the streak by millimeters.

"It's still there," she said.

He tried again, this time with the heel of his palm. But again, he missed it by *that much*.

"Still there," she said again.

He uttered an impatient sound. "Do you mind getting it for me?"

He might as well have asked her if she minded picking him up and heaving him out the window. Did he really not understand that physical contact was a physical impossibility for her after the way she'd overreacted to being touched by him last week? Were they going to have to endure another awkward moment to make that clear?

Strangely, though, the thought of touching Hogan now was slightly less…difficult…than it should have been. Resigning herself, she reached toward his face. Hogan's gaze hitched with hers, making it impossible for her to untether herself. Those brown, brown eyes, richer than truffles and sweeter than muscovado, made her pulse leap wildly, and her mouth go dry. Finally, finally, her hand made contact with his face, the pad of her index finger skimming lightly over his brow.

Her first attempt to wipe away the smudge was as fruitless as his had been—not surprising, since she was barely touching him. She tried again, drawing her thumb over his skin this time—his warm, soft skin—and that was a bit more successful. But still, the stain lingered. So she dragged her thumb across it again, once, twice, three times, until at last, the spot disappeared.

She didn't realize until that moment how her breathing had escalated while she was touching him, or how hot her entire body had become. Her face, she knew, was flushed, because she could feel the heat in her cheeks, and her hand felt as if it had caught fire. Worse, her fingers were still stroking Hogan's forehead, lightly and idly, clearly not to clean up a speck of oil, but simply because she enjoyed the feel of a man's skin under her fingertips and didn't want to stop touching him yet. It had been so long since Chloe had touched a man this way. So long since she had felt the simple pleasure of warmth and strength and vitality against her skin. Even a fingertip.

Worst of all, Hogan seemed to realize exactly what she was feeling. His face was a little flushed, too, and his pupils had expanded to nearly eclipse the dark brown of his irises. Seemingly without thinking, he covered her hand with his and gently removed it. But instead of letting it go after maneuvering it between them, which she had thought he would do—which he really should do—he held on to it, stroking his thumb lightly over her palm.

The warmth in her midsection went supernova at that, rushing heat to her every extremity. So acute was the sensation that she actually cried out—softly enough that she hoped he might not have heard her… except she knew right off he did. She knew because he finally severed his gaze from hers…only to let it fall to her mouth instead.

For one insane moment she thought he was going to kiss her. She even turned her head in a way that would keep her glasses from being a hindrance, the way she used to when— The way a person did when they knew something like that was about to happen. That was just how far she had allowed her desire to go. No, not desire, she immediately corrected herself. Appetite. Instinct. Drive. It had been too long since she'd enjoyed the sexual release every human being craved. Hogan was a very attractive man. Of course her body would respond to him the way it did. It was a matter of hormones and chemistry. There was nothing more to it than that.

Not that that wasn't more than enough.

He still hadn't released her hand, so, with much reluctance, she disengaged it herself and took a giant step backward. Then she took a breath, releasing it slowly to ease her pulse back to its normal rhythm and return her brain to its normal thoughts.

"There," she said softly. "All better."

She hoped he would think she was only talking about the removal of the oil streak from his face. But *all better* referred to herself, too. Her physical self, anyway. The emotional parts of her, though…

Well. Chloe knew she would never be *all* better. Not with so much of herself missing. But she was better now than she had been a few minutes ago, when touching Hogan had made so much of her feel so alive. That feeling was just a cruel ruse. She knew she would never feel alive again.

"All better," she tried again, forcefully enough this time that she sounded as if she actually believed it. "We should get going," she added. "We don't want to be late."

Hogan watched Chloe escape through the back door, his hand still hanging in the air between them. And he wondered, *What the hell just happened?* One minute he was asking her to wipe away a smudge of grease—an action that should have taken less than a second and been about as consequential as opening a jar of peanut butter—and the next, they were staring at each other, breathing as hard as they would have been if they'd just had sex. Really good sex, too.

His hand was even trembling, he noted as he forced himself to move it back to his side. And his whole body was hot, as if she'd run her fingers over every inch of him, instead of just his forehead. What the hell was up with that? The only person who was supposed to be making his hands shake and his skin hot was Anabel. Certainly not a near-stranger with a chip on her shoulder the size of the Brooklyn Bridge.

He gave his head a good shake to clear it. Then he made his feet move forward to follow Chloe, who had already gone through the back door. Outside on 67th Street, she was standing near a tree with her back to him, her face in profile as she gazed toward Madison Avenue—though she didn't look as if she was in any hurry to get anywhere. In fact, her expression was kind of distant and dreamy, as if it wasn't tasting wine she was thinking about, but tasting…uh… something else instead.

Hogan shoved the thought away. He had to be imagining things. Chloe Merlin had made it clear that she wanted to keep her distance from him, physically, mentally, emotionally, spiritually and every other-*ly* there was. Ever since that day last week when she'd reeled away from him in the gallery, she'd been professional to a fault. Every effort he'd made to get to know her better—because he always wanted to know a person better who was working for him, the same way he knew the guys who worked for him at the garage— had fallen flat.

Then again, he'd never met anyone like Chloe, so maybe it was just because of that.

By the time he drew alongside her on the street, she was back to her regular cool composure. When she looked at him now, it was with the same sort of detachment she always did. Her red-lipsticked mouth was flat, and she straightened her glasses with her fingers this time, instead of the back of her hand, a much less anxious gesture than usual. But he still couldn't quite forget that erotic little sound of surrender that had escaped her when he dragged his thumb along the inside of her palm. It would be a long time before he forgot about that.

"We're going to a new restaurant on Madison Avenue, just around the corner from sixty-seventh," she told him. "*L'Artichaut.* They don't actually open until next week, so it will be nice to have a little sneak peek in addition to the wine-tasting."

It suddenly occurred to Hogan that there might be a charge for him to participate. "Is it okay if you show up with someone? I mean, I have my wallet, but I don't have a lot of cash on me."

It was something he might have said in the past, when not having cash on him was a fairly regular occurrence. Saying something like that now, in light of his new financial situation, made him think he sounded like he was expecting Chloe to pick up the tab for him.

"There's no charge," she said. "It's by invitation. And mine included a plus-one. I just didn't, um, have a plus-one to invite."

Wow. She really was a Park Avenue sensation if she got invited to stuff like this. Then the second part of her statement registered. And made him a lot happier than it should have.

"I hope you don't mind having one now," he said.

"It's fine," she told him. But she still didn't sound like it was.

"Now that all the legalities of inheriting my grandfather's estate have been settled, it's kind of hard for me to keep busy, you know? I mean, I don't really have to work anymore, and, as much as I liked working in the garage, I thought I'd like not working more. Isn't that what everyone wants? Even people who like their jobs? To not have to get up every day and go to work?"

"I don't know," she said. "Is that what everyone wants?"

Well, everyone except, apparently, Chloe Merlin. Then again, she'd never said she liked her work. She said she needed it. He still wanted to know what the difference was. "*I* always thought it was," he said. "I started working for a paycheck in my dad's garage when I was fourteen, cleaning up and manning the cash register and running errands until I was old enough to work on the cars. When I was in high school, I worked another job, too, at a market up the street from us, delivering groceries."

Because it had taken the income from two jobs to keep Anabel in the style to which she was accustomed. Not that Hogan regretted a bit of it. She'd been worth every extra minute on his time cards.

The point was that he'd been working hard for more than two-thirds of his life. When Gus Fiver told him how much money he had now, Hogan had realized he could sleep late every morning and stay up late every night and enjoy a million different pursuits. Problem was, he wasn't much of a night owl—he liked getting up early. And he didn't really have any pursuits. Not yet. He hadn't even been away from his job for two weeks, and already, he was restless.

"I don't understand how the idle rich handle being idle," he said. "It feels weird to have all this money I didn't work for. I don't want to be one of those people who gets everything handed to them, you know? I need to figure out a way to earn my place in the world."

"Some wealthy people who don't work keep themselves busy by finding causes to support and raising money to help them. You could become a philanthropist."

He shook his head. "I'd rather just have someone tell me who needs something and write them a check."

Which was something he'd actually started doing already. "There's nothing wrong with charity work," he hurried to add. "It's just not my thing. I'm not comfortable asking people for money, even if the money's not for me."

"But you are comfortable giving it away."

"Well, yeah. It's not like I need it. Just the income I get from my grandfather's investments has me set for life. Not only do I have that incredible house," he added, jabbing a thumb over his shoulder toward the place they'd just left, "but he left me three other houses to boot. The guy had four houses. Who needs that many?" Before she could answer—not that the question had really required an answer—he added, "And he collected cars. There are four parked under the town house and another eight in a storage facility in New Jersey. Not to mention another ten at his other houses. Twenty-two cars. Hell, even I think that's too many, and I've always wondered what it would be like to collect cars."

She almost smiled at that. Almost. It didn't quite make it into her eyes, though. Still, he guessed hearing some mook complain about having too many houses and cars was pretty funny. Her reaction made him feel better. Maybe they could get back on solid, if weird, ground again.

"So that was what you were doing this afternoon?" she asked. "Looking at the ones parked at the house?"

He nodded. "Yeah. They're in incredible condition. Maybe Philip Amherst wasn't a huge success in the father and grandfather departments, but the guy knew wheels. In addition to the Merc Gullwing, there's a 1961 Ferrari Spyder, a 1956 Maserati Berlinetta, and, just when I thought the guy was going to be one of those European snobs, I pull the cover off this incredible 1970 Chevy Chevelle SS 427 in absolute mint condition that's—"

He stopped midsentence, because Chloe was looking at him now with an actual, honest-to-God smile on her face, one that had reached her eyes this time, and the sight nearly knocked the breath out of his lungs. He'd been thinking all this time that she was cute. Quirky, but cute. But when she smiled the way she was smiling now, she was… She was a… She was an absolute… Wow. Really, really…wow.

But all he could manage to say was, "What's so funny?"

She looked ahead again. "I think you've found your purpose."

"What? Collecting cars?" he asked. "No, that's too much. I'm already having trouble justifying keeping them all."

"Then maybe you could do something else with cars," she suggested. "Start designing your own line."

He shook his head. "I don't have that kind of talent."

"Then invest in someone who does."

He started to shoot down that idea, too, but stopped. That actually wasn't a bad idea. He even already knew somebody he could put some money behind. The daughter of one of the guys who worked at the garage. She was still in high school, but the kid knew cars inside and out, and had some great ideas for what to do with them. No way could her parents afford to send her to college. But Hogan could. And there were probably dozens of kids like her in New York…

But he still needed to figure out what to do with

himself. Investing in the future generation was great and all that, but Hogan needed a purpose, too. He'd worked with his hands all his life. He just couldn't see himself never working with them again.

Chloe halted, and Hogan realized they were standing in front of their destination. Looked like, for now, at least, what he would be doing was spending a few hours in a French restaurant tasting wine he knew nothing about. A couple of months ago the idea of doing something like that would have made him want to stick needles in his eyes. Today, though, it felt like a good way to spend the time.

He looked at Chloe again, at how the afternoon sun brought out sparks of silver in her white-blond hair and how the breeze had tugged one strand loose to dance it around one cheek. He saw how the smile had left her lips, but hadn't quite fled from her eyes.

Yeah, tasting wine with Chloe Merlin didn't seem like a bad way to spend an afternoon at all.

Four

Since she began working as a personal chef five years earlier, Chloe had lived in some seriously beautiful homes, from her first job cooking for Lourdes and Alejandro Chavez in their charming Tribeca brownstone to Jack and Martin Ionesco's Fifth Avenue mansion a few years later to Anabel Carlisle's Park Avenue penthouse just weeks ago. All had been breathtaking in their own ways, and all of her employers had generously made clear she had the run of their homes in her off-time, be it their dens or their balconies or—in the case of the Ionescos—their home cinema. Hogan, too, had assured her she was welcome in any part of his house at any time.

But Chloe had never ventured out of her room in any of her previous postings unless it was to cook in her employers' kitchens or to explore the culinary aspects of their various neighborhoods. She'd always been perfectly content to stay in her room reading books, watching movies or searching the internet for articles—but always something about cooking. She'd just never had the desire to involve herself any further in the homes or lives of her employers beyond cooking for them.

So why did she feel so restless in her room at Hogan's house? she wondered a few nights after their excursion to the wine-tasting—which had ended up being surprisingly enjoyable. And not just because Hogan had been such an agreeable companion, either. He'd also proved to have a fairly sophisticated palate, something that had astonished him as much as it had Chloe, and he had discovered some wines he actually enjoyed, all of them labels she would have chosen for him. She would have put his until then unknown oenophilia down to his Amherst genes, but somehow she suspected that whatever made Hogan Hogan was the result of Hogan alone. In any event, Chloe had actually almost had fun that day. She couldn't remember the last time she'd almost had fun.

Which was maybe why she suddenly felt so restless in her room. A part of her was itching to get out and almost have fun again. And no matter how sternly she told that part of herself to stop feeling that way, that part of herself refused to listen.

She looked at the clock on the nightstand. It was nearly midnight. Hogan, she knew, always turned in before eleven. She knew this because she often went to the kitchen to make a cup of *Mariage Frères* tea about that time before turning in herself, and the house was always locked up tight—dark and silent save a small lamp in the kitchen she required be kept on so that she could make late-night forages for things like *Mariage Frères* tea. She was confident enough he was in his own room by now that she didn't worry about having already donned her pajamas. Or what passed for pajamas for her—a pair of plaid flannel pajama pants and a T-shirt for François and the Atlas Mountains, her latest favorite band.

Even so, she padded as silently as she could in her sock feet down the stairs to the third floor—slowing only long enough at the fourth to ensure that, yes, Hogan's bedroom door was closed, and all the lights were off—where there was a library teeming with books, even though she was fairly sure they would be about things besides cooking. There might be a novel or two in the mix somewhere, and that would be acceptable.

The only light in the library was what spilled through the trio of arched floor-to-ceiling windows from a streetlamp outside—enough to tell her where the largest pieces of furniture lay, but not enough to distinguish any titles on book spines. So she switched on the first lamp she found, bathing the room in a pale, buttery glow.

She went to the set of shelves nearest her, pushing her glasses up on her nose so she could read the books' spines. All the titles there seemed to have something to do with maritime history. The next grouping was mostly atlases. After that came biographies, predominantly featuring robber barons, autocrats and politicians. So much for fun.

She went to the other side of the room and began working her way backward. Toward the middle, she finally came across novels. Lots of them. To her surprise, she found a number of historicals by Anya Seton, whom her grandmother had adored. She plucked out a title from the mix she recognized as one of Mémée's favorites, opened it to the first page, read a few lines and was immediately hooked. So hooked that she didn't look where she was going when she turned around and stepped away from the shelf, so she inadvertently toppled a floor lamp.

It fell to the ground, hitting the marble with what seemed like a deafening crash in the otherwise silent room. Hastily, she stooped to right it. No harm done, she decided when it was upright again with its shade back in place. Just to make sure, she flicked it on to see if the bulb still worked—it did—then turned it off again. After that the room—and the house—were silent once more.

She opened the book and went back to her reading, making her way slowly across the library as she did, skirting the furniture until she arrived back at the lamp she had turned on when she first entered. She stood there and continued to read until she finished a few more paragraphs, then absently turned off the light, closed the book and began picking her way through the darkness toward the wide library entrance—which, since she wasn't yet accustomed to the darkness, she had to struggle to make out, so her steps slowed even more. The moment she made her way through it and into the adjoining study, however, someone surged up behind her, wrapping an iron-hard arm around her waist to pull her back against himself—hard.

Chloe screamed at the top of her lungs and, simultaneously, elbowed him viciously in the gut and stomped down as hard as she could on his foot. When his grip on her loosened in response, she lurched away from him so fiercely that her glasses fell from her face and onto the floor. She barely noticed, though, because all of her attention went to hurling the heavy hardback as viciously as she could in the direction of her assailant—and hitting him square in the face with it if the expletive he yelled in response was any indication.

She was opening her mouth to scream again and about to race for the stairs when her attacker cried out, "Whoa, Chloe! I'm sorry! I didn't know it was you!"

Immediately, she closed her mouth. Hogan. Of course it was Hogan. Who else would it be? The house, she'd learned her first day on the job, had more security than Fort Knox, something she and Hogan both appeared to have forgotten. Realizing that now, however, did little to halt the flow of adrenaline to every cell in her body. Her heart was hammering, her breathing was ragged, her thoughts were scrambled and her body was trembling all over.

"I thought you were an intruder," he said.

He, too, sounded more than a little rattled—she could hear him breathing as heavily as she was. But his eyes must have been better adjusted to the dark, because he made his way effortlessly across the study to switch on a desktop lamp that threw the room into the same kind of soft, golden light the library had enjoyed only moments ago. In fact, the study was pretty much a smaller version of the room she'd just left.

Hogan, too, was bathed in soft, golden light, something that made him seem softer and more golden himself. His nightwear wasn't much different from hers, except that he was wearing sweatpants, and his T-shirt read "Vinnie's House of Hubcaps." And where her shirt hung loosely on her frame, Hogan's was stretched taut across his, so that it hugged every bump and groove of muscle and sinew on his torso. And there was a lot of muscle and sinew on his torso. And on his arms, too. Holy cow. His shirtsleeves strained against salient biceps that tapered into a camber of muscles in his forearms in a way that made her mouth go dry.

The moment Chloe realized she was staring, she drove her gaze back up to his face. But that didn't help at all, because his hair was adorably disheveled, his cheeks were shadowed by a day's growth of beard and his bittersweet-chocolate eyes were darker and more compelling than ever. Something exploded in her belly and sent heat to every extremity, but not before much of it pooled deep in her chest and womb.

Why did he have to be so handsome? So magnetic? So damnably sexy? And why couldn't she ignore all of that? She encountered handsome, magnetic, sexy men all the time, and she never gave any of them a second thought. What was it about Hogan that made that impossible to do?

He was gripping a baseball bat about a third of the way up, but he loosened his hold and let it slip to the knob as he lowered it to his side. With his free hand, he rubbed a spot on his forehead that was already turning red—the place where the book had hit him.

"I am so sorry," she said. "I thought you were an intruder, too."

He looked at his fingers, probably to check for blood, and when he saw that they were clean, hooked that hand on his hip. "Don't apologize for defending yourself. It was a nice shot."

She tried to smile at that, but she was so rusty at smiling these days, she wasn't sure she succeeded. "Thanks."

"I heard a loud noise," he said. "I thought someone had broken in."

"That was me. I knocked over a lamp in the library. I came down to look for a book, and then I got so caught up in my reading that I didn't look where I was going. I didn't realize it was that loud. I mean, it sounded loud when it went down, but I thought that was just because the room was so quiet. I mean this house must have walls like a mausoleum, and—"

And she made herself shut up before she started to sound like an idiot, even though it was probably too late for that.

"No worries," he told her. "It's fine."

Oh, sure. Easy for him to say. He wasn't staring at some luscious blond wondering what he looked like under that T-shirt. And those sweatpants. And socks. And anything else he might be wearing. Or not wearing.

Oh, she really wished she hadn't thought that.

They stood there for another moment in silence, their gazes locked, their breathing still a little broken. Though hers was doubtless more a result of her thoughts than any lingering fear for her safety. Her physical safety anyway. Her mental and emotional safety were another matter at the moment.

Finally, Hogan said, "I think I need a drink." One more look at her, and he added, "You look like you could use one, too."

She told herself to say no. Then said, "I wouldn't say no."

He nodded once, leaned the bat against a wide, heavy desk then crossed to a cabinet on the opposite side of the study, opening it to reveal a fairly substantial bar. Without even having to look through the options, he pulled down a bottle of very nice bourbon, along with a cut-crystal tumbler—obviously, he'd spent some time in this room—then turned around to look at Chloe.

"What's your poison?" he asked. "This is all bourbon. Something else my grandfather collected, I've discovered. If you'd rather have a glass of wine, I can go down to the cellar for some."

But she'd already recognized a familiar favorite on the shelf and shook her head. "I'll have a couple of fingers of the Angel's Envy," she told him.

His eyebrows shot up at that. "I never would have pegged you for a bourbon drinker."

"We're even, then," she said. "I wouldn't have guessed you'd be one, either." She'd been surprised enough at how quickly he'd taken to wine.

"I wasn't before," he admitted. "But after exploring my grandfather's study and discovering the bar, I realized cars weren't his only passion. I wanted to see if maybe we had this—" he gestured toward the spirits behind him "—in common, too." He grinned. "Turns out we do."

He withdrew her chosen label and a second tumbler for her and splashed a generous portion from each bottle into their respective glasses. Then he made his way back to her and handed her her drink, which she accepted gratefully.

He lifted his glass in a toast. "Here's to nonexistent intruders."

She lifted hers in response. "I'll drink to that."

They clinked their glasses and did so with enthusiasm, but after one taste, both seemed to lose track of where the conversation should go next. Chloe tried to focus on the heat of the bourbon as it warmed her stomach, but the heat in Hogan's eyes kept distracting her. He was looking at her differently from what she was used to, as if he were seeing something in her face that wasn't there before.

She realized what that was when he said, "You're not wearing your glasses. Or any lipstick. You're cute in them, but without them…"

It was only his mention of her glasses that made her remember she'd lost them in the scuffle. She really didn't need them that badly—only for up-close work—and mostly wore them because they were another way to keep distance between herself and others.

"I lost them when you, uh…when you, um…" *When you pulled me back against your rock-hard abs and made me want to crawl under your shirt to see them for myself* was the thought that tumbled through her mind, but she was pretty sure it wasn't a good idea to say that out loud. Especially since, at the time, what she'd really been thinking was that she needed to run for her life.

Then again, maybe the two thoughts had something in common after all.

He must have realized what she was trying to say—and thankfully not what she was actually thinking—because he glanced over toward the door where the two of them had been embraced a few minutes ago. Uh, she meant *embattled*, not *embraced*. Of course that was what she meant. Then he strode to the entryway, looked around on the floor and found them with little trouble. He picked up the book on his way back to Chloe and brought them both to her.

"Thanks," she said as she took her glasses from him. She started to put them back on then instead settled them on top of her head. She told herself it was only because she was sure they needed cleaning after what they'd just been through. It wasn't to get rid of any distance that might linger between Hogan and herself.

He looked at the spine of the book before handing it to her, eyeing her thoughtfully when he saw the unmistakably romantic title.

"It was Mémée's favorite," she said. Then, when she realized he would have no idea who Mémée was, clarified, "My grandmother. Anya Seton was her favorite author, and when I saw all the books in the library by her, it made me think of Mémée, and I just—"

She'd just felt kind of lonely, she remembered, when she saw all the books that reminded her of the grandmother who passed away when she was in college. She thought about Mémée often—nearly every time she cooked—but somehow, seeing all those novels had roused feelings Chloe hadn't felt for a very long time. Or maybe it was something else that had done that. Since coming to work for Hogan, nothing in her life had felt normal.

"I thought reading it might make me feel closer to her," she said halfheartedly. Then, because she couldn't quite stop herself, she added, "I just miss her."

Hogan nodded. "I lost my folks young, too," he said. "How old were you when your grandmother died?"

"Nineteen."

"Which means you were even younger when you lost your parents."

"I never actually knew my parents," Chloe said, again without thinking. Wondering why she offered the information to Hogan when it was something she never discussed with anyone. She really must be frazzled by the whole intruder thing. Because even though she told her brain to stop talking, her mouth just kept it up. "My father was never in the picture—I'm not even sure my mother knew who he was—and not long after my mother had me, she sort of…disappeared."

Which was something Chloe *really* never talked about. Only one other person besides her grandmother knew about her origins. And that person was gone, too. What was possessing her to say all this to Hogan?

Whatever it was, it had such a hold on her that she continued, "My mother was troubled. Mémée did her best, but you can only do so much for a person who refuses to get help."

Hogan said nothing for a moment, then, softly, he told her, "I'm sorry." Probably because he didn't know what else to say. Not that Chloe blamed him. She wasn't sure what to say about her origins, either. Other than that they had made her what she was, so she couldn't—wouldn't—regret them.

"It's okay," she said. "Mémée was a wonderful parent. I had a nice childhood, thanks to her. I loved her very much, and she loved me."

Hogan gazed down into his drink. "So I guess you and I have something in common with the biological mother, what-if-things-had-been-different, kind of stuff, huh?"

Chloe started to deny it, started to tell him that her own upbringing would have been virtually the same if her mother had been healthy, then realized there was no way she could know that was true. Maybe her upbringing would have been better, maybe not. Who knew? But her mother would have been the one to mold her, not Mémée, and there was no way of even speculating about what shape Chloe would have taken. Would she have ever discovered her love of cooking under her mother's care? Or would she be passionate about something else now? Had her childhood been different, she might never have come to New York. She might never have met Hogan. Or anyone else.

"Maybe," she finally said. "But things happen to people every day that change their lives, many of them events that are out of their hands. Or by the smallest choices they make. Even opting to cross the street in one place instead of another could have devastating results if you get hit by a bus."

He smiled at that. "Yeah, well, I was thinking more in terms of our quality of life."

"You don't think you had quality of life growing up in Queens?"

"I had great quality of life growing up in Queens. The best. I'm kind of getting the impression that growing up here with the Amhersts would have left me at a disadvantage."

His response puzzled her. "Growing up in a breathtaking, multimillion-dollar home with unlimited funds at your disposal would have left you at a disadvantage?"

This time he nodded. "Sure. If no one here loved me."

Her heart turned over at the matter-of-fact way he said it. As if it was a given that he wouldn't have been loved here in this world of excess.

"You don't think your mother would have loved you?" she asked.

He expelled an errant breath and moved to sit in one of the leather chairs. Chloe followed, seating herself in the one next to it. She wasn't sure why—she really should be going back to her room and making the effort to get into bed—but something in his demeanor prohibited her from abandoning him just yet.

"I don't know," he said. "She was awfully young when she had me. She might have started looking at me as a liability who kept her from living the kind of life her friends did. She might have started resenting me. But I know my grandfather wouldn't have cared for me. His letter to me was—" he inhaled deeply and released the breath slowly "—not the warmest thing in the world. I mean, he wasn't mean or anything, but it was pretty clear he was only leaving his estate to me because the Amhersts dating all the way back to the time of knights and castles considered bloodline to be more important than anything else. He obviously wasn't happy about doing it."

He looked at something above the door. Chloe followed his gaze and saw an ornate coat of arms hanging there.

"The Amherst crest," he said. "There's one of those hanging in nearly every room in this house. Have you noticed?"

In truth, she hadn't. But when it came to physical surroundings, Chloe deliberately wasn't the most observant person in the world.

"No," she told him. "I suppose if there are that many, then bloodlines did indeed mean a lot to him."

"In his letter, he even asked that I consider legally changing my last name to Amherst so the direct line to the family name wouldn't die out with him. I guess he always figured Susan would forget about me and go on with her life. Get married and have other kids whose names she could hyphenate or something. Kids he could proudly call his progeny. His legacy. Instead of some grease monkey whose blue collar was stained with sweat."

"I'm sure Susan never forgot you, Hogan," Chloe said with absolute conviction. "And I'm sure she loved you very much. In a way, you were probably her first love. No one ever forgets or stops loving their first love."

He gave her another one of those thoughtful looks, the kind where the workings of his brain fairly shone in his eyes. His dark, beautiful, expressive eyes. "You sound like you're talking from experience."

She said nothing in response to that. She'd said too much already.

But her response must have shown on her face, too, because Hogan grinned a melancholy grin. "So there's some guy back there in your past you're still pining for, huh? The same way I've been pining for Anabel all these years? Is that something else you and I have in common?"

Maybe it was the bourbon. Maybe it was the pale, otherworldly light. Maybe it was the last lingering traces of mind-scrambling adrenaline. Maybe it was just the way Hogan was looking at her. Whatever it was, Chloe couldn't resist it.

"I'm not pining for him," she said. "I'll never get him back. He's gone."

Hogan's grin fell. He met her gaze levelly, and whatever he saw in her eyes made his eyebrows arrow downward and his jaw clench tight. "Gone," he repeated. "Gone like…he moved to another country?"

Chloe shook her head. It wasn't the bourbon. It wasn't the light. It wasn't the adrenaline. It was definitely Hogan this time and the way he was looking at her that made her say the rest.

"Samuel was my husband. He was a chef, too. We were going to open our own restaurant. We were going to have kids and teach them to cook, too. We were going to have a long life together, full of family and food. We were going to retire fat and happy in Lyon, and we were going to have our ashes scattered together in the Pyrenees. Instead, his ashes were scattered in Brown County State Park, where he and I had our first date when we were in ninth grade."

Hogan was looking kind of horrified now, confirming what Chloe already suspected—she had made her biggest mess yet. So she gripped her glass and downed what was left of its contents. Then she rose and carried it back to the cabinet from which Hogan had taken it. She started to leave it there for him to take to the kitchen with his own glass when he was ready. Instead, she picked up the bottle of bourbon that was still sitting on the bar and left with both it and the glass. It was definitely time to go back to her room and make the effort to get into bed. Somehow, though, she knew it was going to be a while before she actually made it to sleep.

Five

Hogan didn't expect to see Chloe the morning after she bared the depths of her soul to him. Not just because a person as private as she was would obviously be embarrassed about having revealed what she had last night, but because he knew firsthand what too much bourbon—even good bourbon—could do to a person. She'd looked pretty serious about making a dent in the bottle she'd taken back to her room.

So it surprised him when he went into the kitchen Friday morning to make himself breakfast and found her in there cooking. She was wearing one of her gigantic chef's jackets and gaudy pants—these decorated with silhouettes of pigs and the word "oink"—and had her hair gathered at the top of her head the way she always did. Her glasses were back in place, her red lipstick was perfect and she looked none the worse for wear for having been up late drinking and grieving for a man she would have loved for the rest of her life if he hadn't died far too soon.

He still couldn't believe she was a widow at twenty-eight. Had been a widow since twenty-three or younger, considering she'd been in New York cooking for people for the past five years. Though her revelation last night went a long way toward explaining why she was the way she was, cool and aloof and serious to a fault. Had Hogan experienced what she had, had he, say, married Anabel and then lost her so young, he would have been putting his fist through something every chance he got. And there wouldn't have been enough bourbon in the world to keep him numb.

Then he remembered that Chloe wasn't cool or aloof or serious to a fault. There had been moments since he'd met her when her veneer had cracked enough for him to see through to the other side. That day in the gallery when she told him his feelings of confusion about his place in the world were valid. That afternoon of the wine-tasting when she uttered that erotic little sound at the touch of his thumb. Last night when she fought like a tiger for her safety. Chloe Merlin had a sensitive, passionate, fiery soul, one that clawed its way out of wherever she buried it whenever her guard was down. Though, now that he knew more about her, he understood her guardedness. He just wished she didn't feel like she had to be so wary around him.

"Good morning," he said as he headed for the coffeemaker.

She jumped at the sound of his voice and spun

around, but her expression offered nothing of what she might be feeling.

"Your breakfast will be ready in ten minutes," she said in reply.

"Great," he told her. "But you know, after last night, you didn't have to—"

"Your breakfast will be ready in ten minutes," she repeated before he could finish, in exactly the same way.

"But—"

"Your breakfast will be ready in ten minutes," she said a third time, more adamantly. Then, to drive that point home, she added, "Have a seat in your dining room, and I'll bring it out to you."

Ah. Okay. So they were just going to ignore what happened last night and go back to the way things were. Pretend she never said all the things she said—and pretend he never saw her looking all soft and vulnerable and pretty.

Which should have been fine. They had separate lives that didn't need to intersect except for mealtimes or if he happened to run into her in the house at some point.

Like he had last night.

He guessed that was beside the point—Chloe's point anyway. And it was a good point. For some reason, though, Hogan didn't want to take it. He didn't want to forget last night happened. He didn't want to forget what she said. He didn't want to forget how she looked. And he didn't want to go back to their old routine and roles.

Chloe obviously did, though. So, without saying anything more, he poured himself a cup of coffee—

ignoring her frown, since, as far as she was concerned, that was her job—then went to the dining room to wait for his breakfast.

But when he sat down at the table—the same way he'd sat down at the table every morning for a few weeks now—he didn't feel any more comfortable than he had on any of the other mornings waiting for his breakfast. Maybe a legal document had made this place his house, but it still didn't feel like home. Maybe he never had to work another day in his life, but his life right now didn't have any purpose. Maybe he was eating better than he ever had before, but he didn't like eating by the clock and by himself. Hell, at least he'd had the Mets and the Knicks to keep him company before.

Hogan's point was that he didn't like having someone else fixing and bringing him his breakfast. Even if hiring Chloe to do just that had been—and still was—the best way to bring Anabel back into his life. Which was something he needed to be focusing his attention on. And he would. ASAP. Just as soon as he figured out a way to do it that would keep Anabel in his house for longer than the few minutes she'd been here last time.

For now, though, he'd just have to keep putting up with breakfast Chloe's way instead of making his own, the way he'd been doing from the time he was a preschooler splashing more milk out of the cereal bowl than into it all the way up to grabbing a cruller from Alpha Donuts on his way to work. That was breakfast for normal people. Breakfast wasn't—

Chloe arrived at his side and set a plate in front of him. Beside a couple of slices of melon settled into what he'd come to recognize as chard was a wedge of something layered with… Ah, hell. He was too tired to try to identify what all the layers were.

So he asked, "What's that?"

"*Tartiflette avec les lardons, le reblochon et les truffes noires.*"

"Which is?"

"Potato casserole with bacon, cheese and mushrooms."

Hogan sighed. Breakfast wasn't *tarti*-whatever. It wasn't even potato casserole with bacon, cheese and mushrooms. He started to tell Chloe he'd have breakfast out this morning. He could take the train to Queens and stop by Alpha Donuts to treat himself to a baker's dozen. He could visit the garage while he was in the neighborhood, maybe go back to his old apartment for a few things he hadn't thought he'd need here. And then he could grab lunch at Taco Taberna across the street before he came ho— Before he came back to Lenox Hill.

He glanced at Chloe. Up close, she didn't look as put together as he first thought. In fact, up close, he could see smudges of purple beneath red-rimmed eyes and a minuscule smudge of lipstick at the corner of her usually flawlessly painted mouth. Not to mention an expression on her face that was a clear mix of *I'm-the-fiercest-human-being-in-the-world* and *I'm-barely-holding-it-together*. She'd gotten up early on a morning when she probably felt like crap because she had to do her job. She'd dressed and hauled herself into work, even though she probably felt uncomfortable facing her boss. Hogan would be the biggest mook in New York if he left now.

"It looks delicious," he told her. "Thank you."

She looked surprised by his gratitude. This after he'd thanked her every time she brought him a meal. But she replied, as she always did, "You're welcome." Then she spun on her heel to return to the kitchen.

As he often did, Hogan turned around to watch her retreat. Usually, she headed straight for her sanctuary, head held high, her step never faltering. This morning, though, she moved sluggishly, her head dipping down. She even lifted her hand to her face at one point, and he was pretty sure she was wiping something out of her eyes.

He turned back around and looked at his breakfast. Even if it wasn't what he usually ate, it was, like everything else she'd cooked, very…artful. In fact, it was, like everything else she'd cooked, almost too artful to eat.

He suddenly wondered what chefs fed themselves. Did Chloe prepare her own breakfast as painstakingly as she made his? Or was she in the kitchen right now, jamming a Pop-Tart into her mouth without even bothering to toast it first? Would her lunch be a slice of reheated pizza? With maybe some Sara Lee pound cake for dessert? Hogan really liked Sara Lee pound cake. He missed Sara Lee pound cake. And, while he was at it, when did Chloe eat dinner anyway? Before or after she made his? Did she fix a double batch of everything? One for him and one for her? Or did she just throw together a ham and cheese sandwich to eat while she was waiting for him to finish? A real ham and cheese sandwich. Not a French one.

He was still wondering about all that as he picked up his fork and dug in to the potato whatever. And he wondered about something else, too: How did he convince his chef there was more to life than timetables and fancy potato casseroles?

By the time Chloe left for her grocery shopping Friday afternoon, she felt almost human again. A mid-morning nap—which she took completely by accident in Hogan's wine cellar when she lay down to look at the bottles on the very bottom shelf—had helped. What helped more was Hogan's acceptance that they pretend last night never happened. But what helped most of all was losing herself in the sounds and sights and smells of Greenmarket, scouring the farmers' stalls for what seasonal finds this early November day had to offer. She needed shallots for the *confit de canard* she would be making for dinner, Brussels sprouts and mesclun to go with, and pears for the *clafoutis* she planned for dessert.

She took her time as she wandered through the market, stopping at a stall whenever she saw a particularly delectable-looking piece of produce to wonder what she could make with it. The apples always smelled so luscious this time of year. And there was a vendor with maple syrup. Had to have some of that. Oh, and fennel! She hadn't made anything with fennel for a long time. Fennel was delicious in vichyssoise. Had to have some of that, too. And this would be the last of the tomatoes until next year. She should probably pick up a few and use them for something, too. Maybe a nice *tartine*…

By the time Chloe returned from Greenmarket, she had two canvas totes teeming with vegetables and fruits and other goodies, more than enough to get her through Friday and Saturday both. Enough, really, so that Hogan could have leftovers on Sunday if he wanted to fix something for himself while she was out doing something. Something that wasn't staying in Hogan's house. Something that kept her mind busy with thoughts that had nothing to do with Hogan. Or the way Hogan looked last night after she told him about Samuel. Or thoughts about Samuel, for that matter. Or anything other than food and its preparation. Its wonderful, methodical, intricate preparation that could keep even the most prone-to-wandering-to-places-it-really-shouldn't-wander mind focused on the task at hand.

She couldn't wait to get started on dinner.

She had just finished putting everything away—save what she would be using tonight—and was about to head to her room to change from her khaki cargo pants and baggy pomegranate-colored sweater into her chef's duds, when Hogan entered the kitchen carrying two white plastic bags decorated with the red logo of a local grocery chain.

"I'm cooking tonight," he said without preamble when he saw her. Before she could object, he hurried on, "I was in my old neighborhood today to stop by my old place, and I dropped in at the market where I used to shop, and—"

"Why did you have to go to the market there?" Chloe interrupted.

She didn't mean to be rude. She was just so surprised and flustered by his appearance in the kitchen again—save this morning, he hadn't ventured into the room once since that first day when he greeted her here—that she didn't know what else to say. And that could also be the only explanation for why she sounded not just rude, but also a tad jealous, when she said what she did.

Hogan must have heard the accusatory tone in her voice, too, because he suddenly looked a little guilty. All he said, though, was, "I needed a few things."

"What kind of things?"

His guilty look compounded. "Uh…things. You know. Personal things. Things I needed to get. That are personal."

"And you had to go all the way to Queens? Does Manhattan not have these personal things you needed?"

And could she just stop talking? Chloe demanded of herself. She sounded like a suspicious wife. Where Hogan went, what he bought, why he went there and bought it was none of her business. *For God's sake, shut* up, *Chloe.*

"Sure, I could have gotten them here," he said. "But C-Town is right up the street from the garage, and it was on the way to the train, so I went in there. For some things. And while I was there, I picked up some stuff for dinner. I thought I could give you a break."

A break? she echoed incredulously to herself. She hadn't even been working for him for a month, and already he was tired of her cooking? No one got tired of Chloe's cooking. Not only was it the best in New York, they also paid her too much to get tired of her cooking.

"Dinner is my job," she reminded him. "It's what you pay me to do. I don't need a break."

"I know, but I thought—"

"Am I not performing to your standards?" she asked.

Now he looked surprised. "What? Of course you are. I just—"

"Have I not cooked you acceptable meals?"

"Yes, Chloe, everything you've cooked has been great, but—"

"Then why do you suddenly want to cook for yourself?"

And why did she still sound like a possessive spouse? Bad enough she was grilling him about things she had no business grilling him about. She was only making it worse sounding like she thought she was entitled to do it. Even if she did have some bizarre desire to actually be Hogan's spouse—which she of course did *not*—it was Anabel Carlisle he wanted to cast in that role. Chloe was his *chef.* So why wasn't she acting like one?

Hogan didn't seem to be offended by her outburst, though. In fact, he suddenly looked kind of relieved. He even smiled. "No, Chloe, you don't understand. I'm not cooking for myself. I'm cooking for us."

Okay, now she was really confused. As weird as it was for her to be behaving like a scorned lover, it was even weirder for Hogan to be acting like a cheerful suitor. Especially one who could cook.

Before she could say anything else, though, he was emptying the contents of the bags onto the kitchen island. A pound of ground chuck, a couple of white onions, a bag of shredded, store brand "Mexican blend" cheese, a bag of tortilla chips and a jar of salsa—both of those were store brand, too—a packet of mass-produced taco seasoning, a bottle of mass-produced taco sauce and a half dozen generic white eggs.

She hastily added up the ingredients in her chef's brain and blanched when she calculated the sum. "Oh, my God. You're going to make taco meatloaf, aren't you?"

He was fairly beaming as he withdrew a burned and battered loaf pan.

"Yep," he said proudly. "In the sacred Dempsey meatloaf pan, which is the mother of all meatloaf pans. On account of it was my mother's. And it gets even better."

He spoke as if that were a paean.

What he withdrew from the second sack was a bag of frozen "crinkle cut" carrots, which he said would be divine with a glaze of butter and Sucanat—except he really said they would taste great stirred up in a pan with some margarine and brown sugar, both of which he was sure Chloe had on hand—then came a tube of prefab biscuits whose label proudly proclaimed, "With flaky layers!" And then—*then*—to her absolute horror, he withdrew the single most offensive affront to gastronomy any chef could possibly conceive: a box of—Chloe could scarcely believe her eyes—macaroni and cheese.

"But wait, that's still not the best part," he told her.

Well, of course it wasn't the best part. There was no *best part* of anything sitting on the counter. He could pull a rabid badger out of the bag, and it would still be better than anything he'd removed so far. But it wasn't a rabid badger he pulled out of the bag. It was far, far worse. A ready-made pound cake wrapped in tinfoil that looked dense enough to, if there were a few thousand more of them, build a garage, followed by a gigantic plastic tub of something called Fros-Tee

Whip, which self-identified as a "non-dairy whipped topping." Chloe couldn't help but recoil.

"I know, right?" Hogan said, evidently mistaking her flinch of repugnance for a tremor of excitement. "It's the greatest dessert ever invented by humankind."

This was going to be news to the creators of *crème brûlée, crêpes Suzette* and *soufflé au chocolat*.

"Look, I know you're not big on the processed foods," he said when he saw her looking at the assortment of, um, groceries. "But you're going to love all this. And I got the good kind of mac and cheese. The kind with the liquid cheese in the pouch, not the powdered stuff in the envelope."

Oh, well, in *that* case…

When she looked at him again, he was grinning in a way that let her know he was perfectly aware that the meal he was proposing was the complete antithesis of epicurean. But he clearly intended to prepare it anyway.

"Hogan, do you realize how much sodium there is in that pile of…of…?" she asked.

"I think 'food products' is the phrase you're looking for," he supplied helpfully.

Actually, she had been thinking of another word entirely. Even so, the *products* part of his suggestion, she would concede. It was the *food* part she found debatable. So she only reiterated, "Hogan, do you realize how much sodium there is in that pile?"

He grinned. "Chloe, I don't care how much sodium there is in that pile. No one cares how much sodium comes out of their grocery bags."

"People who want to live to see their first gray hair do."

"This—" he pointed at his purchases on the island "—is a lot closer to the typical American diet than that is." Now he pointed at the items from her shopping trip she'd left on the counter. "Not to mention the typical American diet is a lot easier to prepare."

"Ease does not equate to edible. Or enjoyable."

"It does when it's taco meatloaf."

"If this—" now Chloe was the one to point to the… groceries…he'd bought "—is the sort of thing you want to eat, then why did you hire me to cook for you in the first place?"

She knew the answer to that question, of course. He was using her to get Anabel Carlisle's attention. Chloe knew that because Hogan himself had said so and, hey, it hadn't made any difference to her. It was irrelevant. She worked for whoever paid her the most. That was rule number one when it came to choosing her employers. For some reason, though, it suddenly kind of bothered her to be used as a means to an end. Especially that end in particular.

Hogan's reply, however, had nothing to do with Anabel. In fact, it wasn't a reply at all. At least not to the question she'd asked.

"Come on. Let me cook dinner tonight," he cajoled. "Have you even eaten taco meatloaf?"

She gave him one of those *What do you think?* looks and said nothing.

"Then how do you know you won't like it?" he asked.

"Two words. Butylated hydroxyanisole."

"Gesundheit." He grinned again.

And damn that grin anyway, because every time she saw it, something in Chloe's chest grew warmer.

At this point, it was also spreading into body parts that really shouldn't be feeling warm in mixed company.

"I guarantee you'll love it," he told her. "If you don't, I promise I'll never invade your kitchen again."

She started to remind him that the room they were standing in was actually *his* kitchen, but hesitated. For some reason she did feel a little proprietary when it came to Hogan's kitchen. Certainly more than she had any other kitchen where she'd worked. She told herself it was because it was less sterile than most with its tile the color of the French Riviera and its creamy enamel appliances and its gleaming copper pots that dangled like amaranth from the ceiling and its gigantic windows that spilled more sunshine in one morning than she'd seen working for months in most places. From the moment she'd set foot in here, she'd coveted this kitchen. In the weeks that followed, she'd come to feel as if she never wanted to leave.

Though, if she were honest with herself, there were days, she supposed, when she wasn't sure that was entirely because of the kitchen.

"Fine," she conceded reluctantly. "You can cook dinner tonight."

"For us," he clarified.

Although she wasn't sure why he needed or wanted that concession—and although she wasn't sure it was a good idea for her to make it—Chloe echoed, "For us."

When Hogan had gotten the bright idea to cook taco meatloaf for Chloe, he'd been wanting something for dinner that was a taste of home—his real home, not his adopted one. He'd been lying under the chassis of a Dodge Charger at the time—one Eddie Deflorio was thinking of buying, to give it a once-over and make sure Eddie wasn't about to get shafted—when Eddie said something about Hogan's mom's taco meatloaf. And just like that, Hogan had been jonesing for it more than he had in years. And not just the taco meatloaf, but also the carrots and biscuits and mac and cheese his mom always made to go with it. And—it went without saying—some Sara Lee pound cake for dessert.

It had just felt so good to be back in the garage, surrounded by familiar sounds and smells and people, talking about familiar stuff—not to mention *doing* something—that Hogan had just wanted the day to go on for as long as it could. And he'd wanted to keep *doing* something. Even if it was making taco meatloaf. If he was going to do that, then he had to go up to his old apartment to get his mom's meatloaf pan. Then, once he was back in his apartment…

He'd just felt better than he had in weeks. He'd felt like he was home. Then he'd realized he wanted to share that feeling with someone. And the person that popped into his head was Chloe Merlin. She had shared something of herself with him last night and obviously wished she hadn't. Now he wanted to share something with her so she wouldn't feel like she had to hide her emotions. From him or anyone else.

What better way to share a piece of his neighborhood home with her than to bring a taste of Queens into a kitchen of Lenox Hill?

Thankfully, Chloe had hung around while he was putting together the meatloaf to tell him where everything was, even if he sometimes had to walk clear across the room to find what he needed. Mostly, she had sat on a stool sipping a glass of red wine, throwing out words like *monosodium glutamate* and *propyl gallate* and *potassium bromate*. But she'd at least poured him a glass of wine, too, and turned on some halfway decent music to cook by, even if he didn't understand a word of what was being sung.

He had managed to combine all the ingredients of the dish and make a fairly serviceable loaf out of it—even if it was a little bigger on one end than the other, something that, now that he thought about it, actually made it more authentic—and was ready to put in the oven, when he realized he forgot to turn on the oven to preheat it. Which, now that he thought about that, too, also made the experience more authentic. What didn't make it authentic was that he had no idea how to work the damned stove, because it was three times the size of a normal stove and had roughly a billion knobs on it.

"How do you turn this thing on?" he asked Chloe.

She had finally ended her indictment of the processed food industry and was now reading a book about somebody named Auguste Escoffier—in French. She looked up at the question, studying Hogan over the tops of her glasses for a moment. Then she pushed them into place with the back of her hand, set her book down on the counter and rose to cross to the stove.

"What temperature do you need?" she asked.

"Three-fifty," he told her.

She flipped one of the knobs, and the oven emitted a soft, satisfying hiss. "Give it a minute."

She looked at the meatloaf, still sitting on the kitchen island in its pan, surrounded by stray bits of onion and cheese, splatters of salsa and a fine dusting of taco seasoning. Okay, and also a little puddle of wine, the result of Hogan having an accident during a momentary wild idea to add some red wine to the meatloaf, thinking maybe that would make Chloe like it better. Fortunately, he came to his senses before doing it, mostly to keep his mother from spinning in her grave, but also because he wasn't sure he was ready to wing it in the kitchen just yet. Chloe looked back at him, took off her glasses and met his gaze levelly. *"Ce travail, c'est pas de la tarte, n'est-ce pas?"*

He had no idea what she said, but he was pretty sure by her expression that she was commiserating with him. He was also pretty sure that the reason he was suddenly getting kind of aroused was because she just spoke French. And call him crazy, but arousal probably wasn't a good idea in the middle of a kitchen when the meatloaf wasn't even in the oven yet. Which was *not* a euphemism for *any*thing sexual.

"Uh…" he began eloquently.

She emitted a soft sigh, folded her glasses and set them on the counter, then gave him another one of those almost-smiles he'd seen from her once or twice. And liked. A lot.

"Cooking isn't for the fainthearted," she told him. "It's harder than people think."

Yeah, and he was only using like five ingredients, most of which came out of boxes and bags. He couldn't imagine how much trouble Chloe went to whenever she prepared a meal.

"Thanks for your help," he said.

"I didn't do anything."

"You told me where to find the scissors. That was major."

She almost smiled again.

"And you poured me a glass of wine. That was really major."

"It was the least I could do."

"Thanks again."

They stood staring at each other for another minute, Hogan trying not to notice how beautiful her green eyes were, or how great she looked wearing something besides her giant chef clothes, or how her hair was longer than he first thought, falling past her shoulders in a rush of near-white silk. Those weren't things he should be noticing about his chef. They were things he should be noticing about Anabel. Things he doubtless *would* notice about Anabel, once the two of them got together again. Just as soon as he called her up and invited her to, um, do something. Which he would totally figure out. Soon.

"The stove is ready," Chloe said.

Stove? he wondered. What stove? Oh, right. The one they were standing right next to. That must be the reason he was suddenly feeling so hot.

"Isn't there a beeper or something that's supposed to go off to tell us that?" he asked.

She shook her head. And kept looking at him as intently as he was looking at her. "Not on a stove like this."

"Then how do you know it's ready?"

"I just know."

Of course she did.

"So I guess I should put the meatloaf in the oven,

then," he said. Not thinking about any kind of sexual euphemisms *at all*.

"I guess you should."

Hogan nodded. Chloe nodded. But neither of them did anything. Finally, she took the initiative and picked up the pan. Then she opened the oven and pushed in the meatloaf. Really deep. Pretty much as far as it would go. Hogan tried not to notice. He did. Honest.

"There," she said, straightening as she closed the oven door. "How long does it need to go?"

Oh, it needed to go for a very long time, he wanted to say. Hours and hours and hours. Maybe all night. What he said, though, was, "Sixty minutes ought to do it."

Chloe nodded. Hogan nodded. And he wondered how the hell he ever could have thought it would be a good idea to cook dinner for Chloe in a hot kitchen with an even hotter oven.

"I should probably clean up my mess," he said.

But there weren't enough cleaners in the world to take care of the mess he'd made today. He was supposed to be focused on winning back Anabel. But lately, he was hardly ever even thinking about Anabel. Because, lately, his head was too full of Chloe.

Yeah, Chloe. A woman who had pledged her life to a man she'd lost much too young. And who was still grieving for him five years later. And who would probably never want anyone else again.

Six

"So? Come on. What did you think?"

Chloe looked at Hogan from her seat on his right at his gigantic dinner table. He was beaming like a kid who'd just presented for show-and-tell a salamander he fished out of the creek all by himself.

"You liked it, didn't you?" he asked. "I can tell, because you cleaned your plate. Welcome to the clean plate club, Chloe Merlin."

"It was…acceptable," she conceded reluctantly.

He chuckled. "Acceptable. Right. You had second helpings of everything, and you still cleaned your plate."

"I just wanted to be sure I ate enough for an accurate barometer of the taste combinations, that's all."

"And the taste combinations were really good, weren't they?"

All right, fine. Taco meatloaf had a certain *je ne sais quoi* that was surprisingly appealing. So did the carrots. And even the biscuits. Chloe had never eaten anything like them in her life. Mémée had never allowed anything frozen or processed in the house when Chloe was growing up. Her grandmother had kept a small greenhouse and vegetable garden in the backyard, and what she hadn't grown herself, she'd bought at the weekly visits she and Chloe made to the farmers' markets or, in the coldest months, at the supermarket—but organic only.

Chloe had just never felt the urge to succumb to the temptation of processed food, even if it was more convenient. She *enjoyed* prepping and cooking meals. She *enjoyed* buying the ingredients fresh. The thought of scooping food out of bags and jars and boxes was as alien to her as having six limbs. It wasn't that she was a snob about food or cooking, it was just that...

Okay, she was kind of a snob about food and cooking. Clearly, her beliefs could use some tweaking.

"You know," she told Hogan, "I could make some taco seasoning myself for you to use next time, from my own spice collection. It would have a lot less sodium in it."

He grinned. "That would be great. Thanks."

"And salsa is easy to make. I could make some of that fresh, the next time you want to cook this."

"I'd love that."

"Even the biscuits could be made—"

"I have to stop you there," he interjected. "I'm sorry, but the biscuits have to be that specific kind. They're what my mom always made. It's tradition."

And it was a taste of his childhood. Chloe got that. She felt the same way about *gratin Dauphinois*.

"Okay," she conceded. "But maybe fresh carrots next time, instead of frozen?"

He thought about that for a minute. "Okay. I mean, we already changed those anyway, since that stuff you call brown sugar is actually beige sugar, and you didn't have any margarine. By the way, what kind of person doesn't have margarine in their kitchen?"

Before, Chloe would have answered a question like that with some retort about hexane and free radicals. Instead, she said, "Butter is better for you."

She managed to stop herself before adding, *And you need to stay healthy, Hogan.* Because what she would have added after that was *I need you to be healthy, Hogan.*

She refused to think any further than that. Such as *why* she needed Hogan to be healthy. She told herself it was for the same reason she wanted anyone to be healthy. Everyone deserved to live a long, happy life. No one knew that better than Chloe, who had seen one of the kindest, most decent human beings she'd ever known have his life jerked out from under him. She didn't want the same thing to happen to Hogan. Not that it would. The man looked as hearty as a long-shoreman. But Samuel had looked perfectly healthy, too, the day he left for work in the morning and never came home again.

She pushed the thought away and stood. "Since you cooked, I'll clean up. It's only fair."

Hogan looked a little startled by her abrupt an-nouncement, but stood, too. "You helped cook. I'll help clean up."

She started to object but he was already picking up his plate and loading it with his flatware. So she did likewise and followed him to the kitchen. Together they loaded the dishwasher. Together they packed the leftovers in containers. Together they put them in the fridge.

And together they decided to open another bottle of wine.

But it was Hogan's suggestion that they take it up to the roof garden. Although he'd told her on her first day at work the house had one, and that she should feel free to use it whenever she wanted, especially since he probably never would, Chloe hadn't yet made her way up there. She really did prefer to stay in her room when she wasn't working or out and about. Save that single excursion to the library—and look how that had turned out. When they made it up onto the roof, however, she began to think maybe she should reconsider. New York City was lovely at night.

So was Hogan's rooftop garden. The living section—which was nearly all of it—was a patchwork of wooden flooring and was lit by crisscrossing strings of tiny white lights woven through an overhead trellis. Terra-cotta pots lined the balustrade, filled with asters and camellias and chrysanthemums, all flaming with autumn colors from saffron to cinnamon to cayenne. Beyond it, Manhattan twinkled like tidy stacks of gemstones against the night sky.

Knowing the evening would be cool, Chloe had grabbed a wrap on her way up, a black wool shawl that had belonged to her grandmother, embroidered with tiny red flowers. She hugged it tightly to herself as she sat on a cushioned sofa pushed against a brick access bulkhead and set her wine on a table next to it. Hogan sat beside her, setting his wine on a table at his end. For a long moment neither spoke. They only gazed out at the glittering cityscape in silence.

Finally, Chloe said, "I still have trouble sometimes believing I live in New York. I kind of fell in love with the city when I was a kid, reading about it and seeing so many movies filmed here. I never actually thought I'd be living here. Especially in a neighborhood like this."

"Yeah, well, I grew up in New York," Hogan said, "but this part of the city is as foreign to me as the top of the Himalayas would be. I still can't believe I live here, either. I never came into Manhattan when I was a kid. Especially someplace like Park Avenue. I never felt the need to."

"Then how did you meet Anabel?" Chloe asked. "She doesn't seem like the type to ever leave Park Avenue."

He grinned that damnably sexy grin again. He'd done that a lot tonight. And every time he did, Chloe felt a crack open in the armor she'd worn so well for so long, and a little chink of it tumbled away. At this point, there were bits of it strewn all over his house, every piece marking a place where Hogan had made her feel something after years of promising herself she would never feel anything again. What she ought to be feeling was invaded, overrun and offended. Instead, she felt...

Well. Things she had promised herself she would never feel again—had sworn she was incapable of ever feeling again. Things that might very well get her into trouble.

"How I met Anabel is actually kind of a funny story," Hogan said. "She and a couple of her friends were going to a concert at Shea Stadium, but they pissed off their cab driver so bad on the way, he stopped the car in the middle of the street in front of my dad's garage and made them get out. She and the guy got into a shouting match in the middle of Jamaica Avenue, and a bunch of us working in the garage went out to watch." He chuckled. "I remember her standing there looking like a bohemian princess and cursing like a sailor, telling the cabbie she knew the mayor personally and would see to it that he never drove a cab in the tristate area again."

Chloe smiled at the picture. She couldn't imagine Anabel Carlisle, even a teenaged one, behaving that way. Her former employer had always been the perfect society wife when Chloe worked for her.

"Anyway, after the cabbie drove off without them, all us guys started applauding and whistling. Anabel spun around, and I thought she was going to give us a second helping of what she'd just dished out, but she looked at me and…" He shook his head. "I don't know. It was like how you see someone, and there's just something there. The next thing I knew, me and a couple of the guys are walking up the street with her and her friends, and we're all going for pancakes. After that she came into Queens pretty often. She even had dinner at my house with me and my folks a few times. But she never invited me home to meet hers."

There was no bitterness in his voice when he said that last sentence. There was simply a matter-of-factness that indicated he understood why she hadn't wanted to include him in her uptown life. That was gentlemanly of him, even if Chloe couldn't understand Anabel's behavior. She imagined Hogan had been just as nice back then as he was now. Anabel must have realized that if she'd become involved with him. Who cared what neighborhood he called home?

"It was her parents," he said, as if he'd read her mind. "Her dad especially didn't want her dating outside her social circle. She would have gotten into a lot of trouble if they found out about me. I understood why she couldn't let anyone know she was involved with me."

"If you understood," Chloe said, "then how come you're still unattached after all this time? Why have you waited for her?"

She thought maybe she'd overstepped the bounds—again—by asking him something so personal. But Hogan didn't seem to take offense.

"I didn't sit around for fifteen years waiting for her," he said. "I dated other girls. Other women. I just never met anyone who made me feel the way Anabel did, you know? There was never that spark of lightning with anyone else like there was that night on Jamaica Avenue."

Chloe didn't understand that, either. Love wasn't lightning. She did, however, understand seeing a person and just knowing there was something there. That had happened to her, too. With Samuel. The day he walked into English class in the middle of freshman year, she'd looked up from *The Catcher in the Rye* and into the sweetest blue eyes she'd ever seen, and she'd known at once that there was something between them. Something. Not love. Love came later. Because love was something so momentous, so stupendous, so enormous, that it had to happen over time. At least it did for Chloe. For Hogan, evidently, it took only a sudden jolt of electricity.

"And now Anabel is free," she said, nudging aside thoughts of the past in an effort to get back to the present. "You must feel as if you're being tasered within an inch of your life these days."

Even if he hadn't done much in the way of trying to regain the affections of his former love, she couldn't help thinking. She wondered why he hadn't.

He looked thoughtful for a moment. "I think maybe I've outgrown the fireworks part," he said cryptically. "But yeah. I really need to call her and set something up."

"Why don't you have a dinner party and invite her?" Chloe suggested. Wondering why her voice sounded so flat. She loved preparing meals for dinner parties. It was great fun putting together the menus. "You could ask her and a few other couples. Maybe she's still friends with some of the girls who were with her the night you met her," she added, trying to get into the spirit. And not getting into the spirit at all. "Other people would offer a nice buffer for the two of you to get reacquainted."

By the time she finished speaking, there was the oddest bitterness in Chloe's mouth. Maybe the wine had turned. Just to make sure, she took another sip. No, actually, the pinot noir tasted quite good.

"Maybe," Hogan said.

"No, definitely," she insisted. Because…

Well, just because. That was why. And it was an excellent reason. Hogan clearly needed a nudge in Anabel's direction, since he wasn't heading that way himself. He'd made clear since Chloe's first day of employment that he was still pining for the woman he'd loved since he was a teenager. He needed a dinner party. And Chloe needed a dinner party, too. Something to focus on that would keep her mind off things it shouldn't be on.

"Look, Chloe," he said, "I appreciate your wanting to help, but—"

"It will be perfect," she interrupted him. "Just a small party of, say, six or eight people."

"But—"

"I can get it all organized by next weekend, provided everyone is available."

"But—"

"Don't worry about a thing. I'll take care of all the details. It will be your perfect entrée into society, which, for some reason, you haven't made yet."

"Yeah, because—"

"A week from tomorrow. If you'll supply the names, I'll make the calls to invite everyone."

"Chloe—"

"Just leave it to me."

He opened his mouth to protest again, but seemed to have run out of objections. In fact, he kind of looked like the proverbial deer in the headlights. Okay, proverbial stag in the headlights.

Then he surprised her by totally changing the subject. "So what was it like growing up in… Where did you say you're from? Someplace in Indiana."

"New Albany," she replied automatically. "It's in the southern part of the state, on the Ohio River."

"I'm going to go out on a limb and say it probably

wasn't much like Manhattan," he guessed. "Or even Queens."

"No, not at all. It's quiet. Kind of quirky. Nice. It was a good place to grow up." She couldn't quite stop herself from drifting back into memories again. "Not a whole lot to do when you're a kid, but still nice. And Louisville was right across the river, so if we wanted the urban experience, we could go over there. Not that it was as urban as here, of course. But there were nights when we were teenagers when Samuel and I would ride our bikes down to the river and stare at Louisville on the other side. Back then it seemed like such a big place, all bright lights and bridges. Compared to New York, though…"

When she didn't finish, Hogan said, "You and your husband met young, huh?"

And only then did Chloe realize just how much she had revealed. She hadn't meant to bring up Samuel again. Truly, she hadn't. But it was impossible to think about home without thinking of him, too. Strangely, though, somehow, thinking about him now wasn't quite as painful as it had been before.

"In high school," she heard herself say. "Freshman year. We married our sophomore year in college. I know that sounds like we were too young," she said, reading his mind this time—because everyone had thought marrying at twenty was too young. Everyone still thought that. For Chloe and Samuel, it had felt like the most natural thing in the world.

"How did he…?" Hogan began. "I mean…if you don't mind my asking… What happened?"

She expelled a soft sigh. Of course, she should have realized it would come to this sooner or later with

Hogan. It was her own fault. She was the one who'd brought up her late husband. She couldn't imagine why. She never talked about Samuel with anyone. Ever. So why was she not minding talking about him to Hogan?

"Asymptomatic coronary heart disease," she said. "That's what happened. He had a bad heart. That no one knew about. Until, at twenty-two years of age, he had a massive heart attack that killed him while he was performing the physically stressful act of slicing peppers for *tastira*. It's a Tunisian dish. His specialty was Mediterranean cooking," she added for some reason. "We would have been an unstoppable team culinarily speaking, once we opened our restaurant."

Hogan was silent for a moment, then, very softly, he said, "Those are his chef's jackets you wear, aren't they?"

Chloe nodded. "After he was… After we sprinkled his ashes in Brown County, I realized I didn't have anything of him to keep with me physically. We didn't exchange rings when we married, and we weren't big on gift-giving." She smiled sadly. "Symbols of affection just never seemed necessary to either of us. So, after he was gone, I started wearing his jackets when I was cooking."

She had thought wearing Samuel's jackets would make her feel closer to him. But it hadn't. It wasn't his clothing that helped her remember him. If she'd needed physical reminders for that, she never would have left Indiana. But she'd been wearing them for so long now, it almost felt wrong to stop.

She reached for her wine and enjoyed a healthy taste of it. It warmed her mouth and throat as she swallowed, but it did nothing to combat the chill that suddenly enveloped her. So she put the glass down and wrapped her shawl more tightly around herself.

"I'm sorry, Chloe," Hogan said, his voice a soft caress in the darkness. "I shouldn't have asked for details."

"It's okay," she told him, even though it really wasn't okay. "It was a long time ago. I've learned to…cope with it. The money I make as a chef goes into a fund I started in Samuel's name that makes testing for the condition in kids less expensive, more common and more easily accessible. Knowing that someone else—maybe even a lot of someone elses—might live longer lives with their loved ones by catching their condition early and treating it helps me deal."

Hogan was being quiet again, so Chloe looked over to see how he was handling everything she'd said. He didn't look uncomfortable, though. Mostly, he looked sympathetic. He'd lost people he loved at a young age, too, so maybe he really did understand.

"I lied when I said the reason I came to New York was to open my own restaurant," she told him. "There's no way I could do that now, without Samuel. It was our dream together. I really came to New York because I thought it would be a good place to lose myself after he died. It's so big here, and there are so many people. I thought it would be easier than staying in a place where I was constantly reminded of him. And it's worked pretty well. As long as I'm able to focus on cooking, I don't have to think about what happened. At least I didn't until—"

She halted abruptly. Because she had been *this close* to telling Hogan it had worked pretty well until

she met him. Meeting him had stirred up all sorts
of feelings she hadn't experienced in years. Feelings
she'd only ever had for one other human being. Feelings she'd promised herself she would never, ever, feel
again. She'd barely survived losing Samuel. There
was no way she could risk—no way she *would* risk—
going through that again. No way she would ever allow
someone to mean that much to her again. Not even—

"At least you did until I asked about it." Hogan finished her sentence for her. Erroneously, at that. "Wow.
I really am a mook."

"No, Hogan, that's not what I was going to say."
Before he could ask for clarification, however, she
quickly concluded, "Anyway, that's what happened."

The temperature on the roof seemed to have plummeted since they first came outside, and a brisk wind
riffled the potted flowers and rippled the lights overhead. Again, Chloe wrapped herself more snugly
in her shawl. But the garment helped little. So she
brought her knees up on the sofa and wrapped her
arms around her legs, curling herself into as tight a
ball as she could.

"You know how people say it's better to have loved
and lost than to never have loved at all?" she asked.

"Yeah," Hogan replied softly.

"And you know how people say it's better to feel
bad than to feel nothing at all?"

"Yeah."

"People are full of crap."

He paused before asking even more softly than before, "Do you really think that?"

She answered immediately. "Yes."

Hogan waited a moment before moving closer,

dropping an arm across her shoulders and pulling her to him, tucking the crown of her head beneath his chin. Automatically, Chloe leaned into him, pressing her cheek to his shoulder, opening one hand over his chest. There was nothing inappropriate in his gesture or in her reaction to it. Nothing suggestive, nothing flirtatious, nothing carnal. Only one human being offering comfort to another. It had been a long time since anyone had held Chloe, even innocently. A long time since anyone had comforted her. And now here was Hogan, his heat enveloping her, his scent surrounding her, his heart thrumming softly beneath her palm. And for the first time in years—six years, nine months, one week and one day, to be precise—Chloe felt herself responding.

But there, too, lay problems. After Samuel's death, she'd lost herself for a while, seeking comfort from the sort of men who offered nothing but a physical release for the body and no comfort for the soul. The behavior had been reminiscent of her mother's—erratic and self-destructive—and when Chloe finally realized that, she'd reined herself in and shut herself up tight. Until tonight.

Suddenly, with Hogan, she did want holding. And she wanted comforting. And anything else he might have to offer. She reminded herself that his heart and his future were with someone else. He was planning a life with Anabel. But Chloe didn't want a future or a life with him. She'd planned a life once, and the person she'd planned it with was taken from her. She would never make plans like that again. But a night with Hogan? At the moment a night with him held a lot of appeal.

She tilted her head back to look at his face. His brown eyes were as dark as the night beyond, and the breeze ruffled his sandy hair, nudging a strand down over his forehead. Without thinking, Chloe lifted a hand to brush it back, skimming her fingers lightly along his temple after she did. Then she dragged them lower, tracing the line of his jaw. Then lower still, to graze the column of his throat. His pupils expanded as she touched him, and his lips parted.

Still not sure what was driving her—and, honestly, not really caring—she moved her head closer to his. Hogan met her halfway, brushing her lips lightly with his once, twice, three times, four, before covering her mouth completely. For a long time he only kissed her, and she kissed him back, neither of them shifting their position, as if each wanted to give the other the option of putting a stop to things before they went any further.

But neither did.

So Chloe threaded her fingers through his hair, cupped the back of his head in her palm and gave herself more fully to the kiss. At the same time, Hogan dropped his other hand to her hip, curving his fingers over her to pull her closer still. She grew ravenous then, opening her mouth against his, tasting him more deeply. When he pulled her into his lap, wrapping both arms around her waist, she looped hers around his neck and held on for dear life.

She had no idea how long they were entwined that way—it could have been moments, it could have been millennia. Chloe drove her hands over every inch of him she could reach, finally pushing her hand under the hem of his sweater. The skin of his torso was hot and hard and smooth beneath her fingertips, like silk-covered steel. She had almost forgotten how a man's body felt, so different from her own, and she took her time rediscovering. Hogan, too, went exploring, moving his hand from her hip to her waist to her breast. She cried out when he cupped his hand over her, even with the barrier of her sweater between them. It had just been so long since a man touched her that way.

He stilled his hand at her exclamation, but he didn't move it. He only looked at her with an unmistakable question in his eyes, as if waiting for her to make the next move. She told herself they should put a stop to things now. She even went so far as to say, "Hogan, we probably shouldn't..." But she was unable—or maybe unwilling—to say the rest. Instead, she told him, "We probably shouldn't be doing this out here in the open."

He hesitated. "So then...you think we should do this inside?"

Chloe hesitated a moment, too. But only a moment. "Yes."

He lowered his head to hers one last time, pressing his palm flat against her breast for a moment before dragging it back down to her waist. Then he was taking her hand in his, standing to pull her up alongside him. He kissed her again, long and hard and deep, then, his fingers still woven with hers, led her to the roof access door. Once inside the stairwell, they embraced again, Hogan pressing her back against the wall to crowd his body against hers, their kisses deepening until their mouths were both open wide. She drove her hands under his sweater again to splay them open against the hot skin of his back, and he dropped a hand between her legs, petting her over the fabric of her pants until she was pushing her hips harder into his touch.

Somehow they made it down the stairs to Hogan's bedroom. Somehow they made it through the door. Somehow they managed to get each other's clothes off. Then Chloe was naked on her back in his bed, and Hogan was naked atop her. As he kissed her, he dropped his hand between her legs again, growling his approval when he realized how damp and ready for him she already was. He took a moment to make her damper, threading his fingers through her wet flesh until she was gasping for breath, then he drew his hand back up her torso to her breast. He thumbed the ripe peak of one as he filled his mouth with the other, laving her with the flat of his tongue and teasing her with its tip. In response, Chloe wove her fingers together at his nape and hooked her legs around his waist as if she intended to hold him there forever.

Hogan had other plans, though. With one final, gentle tug of her nipple with his teeth, he began dragging openmouthed kisses back down along her torso. He paused long enough to taste the indentation of her navel then scooted lower still, until his mouth hovered over the heated heart of her. Then he pressed a palm against each of her thighs and pushed them open, wide enough that he could duck his head between them and taste the part of her he'd fingered long moments ago.

The press of his tongue against her there was almost more than Chloe could bear. She tangled her fingers in his hair in a blind effort to move him away, but he drove his hands beneath her fanny and pushed her closer to his mouth. Again and again, he darted his tongue against her, then he treated her to longer, more leisurely strokes. Something wild and wanton coiled tighter inside her with every movement, finally bursting in a white-hot rush of sensation that shook her entire body. Before the tremors could ebb, he was back at her breast, wreaking havoc there again.

After that Chloe could only feel and react. There were no thoughts. No cares. No worries. There was only Hogan and all the things he made her feel. Hogan and all the things she wanted to do to him, too. When he finally lifted his head from her breast, she pulled him up to cover his mouth with hers, reaching down to cover the head of his shaft with her hand when she did. He was slick and hard, as ready for her as she was for him. But she took her time, too, to arouse him even more, palming him, wrapping her fingers around him, driving her hand slowly up and down the hard, hot length of him.

When he rolled onto his back to facilitate her movements, Chloe bent over him, taking as much of him into her mouth as she could. Over and over she savored him, marveling at how he swelled to even greater life. When she knew he was close to coming, she levered her body over his to straddle him, easing herself down over his long shaft then rising slowly up again. Hogan cupped his hands over her hips, guiding her leisurely up and down atop himself. But just as they were both on the verge of shattering, he reversed their bodies so that Chloe was on her back again. He grinned as he circled each of her ankles in strong fists, then he knelt before her and opened her legs wide. And then—oh, *then*—he was plunging himself into her as deep as he could go, thrusting his hips against hers again and again and again.

Never had she felt fuller or more complete than she did during those moments that he was buried inside her. Every time he withdrew, she jerked her hips upward to stop him, only to have him come crashing into her again. They came as one, both crying out in the euphoria that accompanied climax. Then Hogan collapsed, turning their bodies again until he was on his back and she was lying atop him. Her skin was slick and hot. Her brain was dazed and shaken. And her heart...

Chloe closed her eyes, refusing to complete the thought. There would be no completion of thought tonight. There would be completion only for the body. And although her body felt more complete than it had in a very long time, she already found herself wanting more.

Her body wanted more, she corrected herself. Only her body. Not her. But as she closed her eyes against the fatigue that rocked her, she felt Hogan press a kiss against the crown of her head. And all she could think was that, of everything he'd done to her tonight, that small kiss brought her the most satisfaction.

Seven

Chloe awoke slowly to darkness. She hated waking up before the alarm went off at five, because she could never get back to sleep for that last little bit of much needed slumber. Invariably her brain began racing over the list of things she had to do that day, not stopping until she rose to get those things done. Strangely, though, this morning, her brain seemed to be sleepier than she was, because it wasn't racing at all. There were no thoughts bouncing around about the intricacies of the asparagus-brie soufflé she planned for this morning's breakfast. No reminders ricocheting here and there that her savory and marjoram plants were looking a little peaked, so she needed to feed them. No, there were only idle thoughts about—

Hogan. Oh, my God, she'd had sex with Hogan last night. Worse, she had woken up in his bed instead of her own. Now she would have to sneak out under cover of darkness before he woke up so she could get ready for work and make his breakfast, then figure out how to pretend like there was nothing different about this morning than any of the mornings that had preceded it and *Just have a seat in the dining room, Hogan, and I'll bring you your breakfast the way I always do, as if the two of us weren't just a few hours ago joined in the most intimate way two people can be joined.*

Oh, sure. *Now* her brain started working at light speed.

Thankfully, Mrs. Hennessey had weekends off, so Chloe didn't have to worry about explaining herself to the housekeeper. Even if Mrs. Hennessey did remind her of her grandmother, who Chloe could just imagine looking at her right now and saying with much disappointment, *"Mon petit doigt me dit..."* which was the French equivalent of "A little bird told me," a phrase Mémée never had to finish because as soon as she started to say it, Chloe would always break down in tears and confess whatever it was she'd done.

And now she'd *really* done it.

Panicked by all the new worries rioting in her head, Chloe turned over, hoping to not wake Hogan. But the other side of the bed was empty. She breathed a sigh of relief...for all of a nanosecond, because her gaze then fell on the illuminated numbers of the clock on the nightstand beyond.

It was almost nine thirty! She never slept until nine thirty! Even on her days off! Which today wasn't!

By now she should have already finished cleaning up breakfast and should be sipping a cup of rose and lavender tea while she made a list for her afternoon

shopping. She had completely missed Hogan's breakfast this morning. Never in her life had she missed
making a meal she was supposed to make for an employer. How could she have slept so late?

The answer to that question came immediately, of
course. She had slept so late because she was up so
late. And she was up so late because she and Hogan
had been... Well. Suffice it to say Hogan was a very
thorough lover. He'd been even more insatiable than
she.

Heat swept over her at some of the images that wandered into her brain. Hogan hadn't left an inch of her
body untouched or untasted. And that last time they'd
come together, when he'd turned her onto her knees
and pressed her shoulders to the mattress, when he'd
entered her more deeply than she'd ever felt entered
before, when he threaded his fingers through her damp
folds of flesh and curried them in time with the thrust
of his shaft, then spilled himself hotly inside her...

Oh, God. She got hot all over again just thinking
about it.

How could she have let this happen? She wished
she could blame the wine. Or Hogan's unrelenting
magnetism. Or the romance of New York at night.
Anything besides her own weakness. But she knew
she had only herself to blame. She had let her guard
down. She had opened herself up to Hogan. She had
allowed herself to feel. And she had lost another part
of herself as a result.

No, not lost, she realized. She had surrendered herself this time. She had given herself over to Hogan
willingly. And she would never be able to get that
part of herself back.

She'd barely been able to hold it together after Samuel died. She'd had to tie herself up tight, hide herself so well that nothing outside would ever get to her again. Because losing something—someone—again might very well be the end of her.

She tried looking at it a different way. Okay, so she and Hogan had sex. So what? She'd had sex before. It was just sex. She'd been physically attracted to Hogan since the minute she met him. He was a very attractive man. Last night she'd simply acted on that attraction. As had he. But it was just an attraction. Hogan was in love with Anabel. He'd been in love with Anabel for nearly half his life. And Chloe still loved her late husband. Just because she and Hogan had enjoyed a little—okay, a lot of—sex one night didn't mean either of them felt any differently about each other today. It was sex. Not love.

So why did everything seem different?

She had to get out of Hogan's room and back to her own so she could regroup and figure out what to do. She was fumbling for a lamp on the nightstand when the bedroom door opened, throwing a rectangle of light onto the floor and revealing Hogan standing before it. He was wearing jeans and nothing else, and his hair was still mussed from the previous night's activities. He was carrying a tray topped with a coffeepot and a plate whose contents she couldn't determine.

"You're awake," he said by way of a greeting, his voice soft and sweet and full of affection.

Chloe's stomach pitched to hear it. Affection wasn't allowed. Affection had no place in a physical reaction. No place in sex. No place in Chloe's life anywhere.

"Um, yeah," she said, pulling the covers up over

her still-naked body. "I'm sorry I overslept. I can have your breakfast ready in—"

"I made breakfast," he interrupted.

Well, that certainly wasn't going to look good on her résumé, Chloe thought. Mostly because she was afraid to think anything else. Like how nice it was of Hogan to make breakfast. Or how sweet and earnest he sounded when he told her he had. Or the warm, fuzzy sensation that swept through her midsection when he said it.

"I mean, it's not as good as what you would have made," he continued when she didn't respond. "But I didn't want to wake you. You were sleeping pretty soundly."

And still, she had no idea what to say.

Hogan made his way silently into the dim room. He strode first to the window and, balancing the tray in one hand, tugged open the curtains until a wide slice of sunlight spilled through. Then he smiled, scrambling Chloe's thoughts even more than they already were. When she didn't smile back—she couldn't, because she was still so confused by the turn of events—his smile fell. He rallied it again, but it wasn't quite the same.

When he set the tray at the foot of the bed, she saw that, in addition to the coffee, it held sugar and cream, along with a modest assortment of not-particularly-expertly-cut fruit, an array of not-quite-done to far-too-done slices of toast, some cheese left over from last night and a crockery pot of butter.

"I wasn't sure how you like your coffee," he said. "But I found cream in the fridge, so I brought that. And some sugar, just in case."

When Chloe still didn't reply, he climbed back into bed with her. But since it was a king-size, he was nearly as far away from her as he would have been in Queens. Even so, she tugged the covers up even higher, despite the fact that she had already pulled them as high as they would go without completely co-cooning herself. Hogan noticed the gesture and looked away, focusing on the breakfast he'd made for them.

"It's weird," he said. Which could have referred to a lot of things. Thankfully, he quickly clarified, "You know what I like for every meal, but I don't even know what you like to have for breakfast. I don't even know how you take your coffee."

"I don't drink coffee, actually," she finally said.

He looked back at her. "You don't?"

She shook her head.

"Then why is there cream in the fridge?"

"There's always cream in the fridge when you cook French."

"Oh. Well. Then what do you drink instead of cof-fee?"

"Tea."

"If you tell me where it is, I could fix you—"

"No, that's okay."

"If you're sure."

"I am."

"So…what kind of tea?"

"Dragon tea. From Paris."

"Ah."

"But you can get it at Dean and DeLuca."

"Gotcha."

"I don't put cream in it, either."

"Okay."

"Or sugar."

"Noted."

The conversation—such as it was—halted there. Chloe looked at Hogan. Hogan looked at Chloe. She fought the urge to tug up the sheet again. He mostly just sat there looking gorgeous and recently tumbled. She told herself to eat something, reminded herself that it was the height of rudeness to decline food someone had prepared for you. But her stomach was so tied in knots, she feared anything she tried to put in it would just come right back up again.

Before she knew what she was doing, she said, "Hogan, about last night…" Unfortunately, the cliché was as far as she got before she realized she didn't know what else to say. She tried again. "What happened last night was…" At that, at least, she couldn't prevent the smile that curled her lips. "Well, it was wonderful," she admitted.

"I thought so, too."

Oh, she really should have talked faster. She really didn't need to hear that he had enjoyed it, too. Not that she didn't already know he'd enjoyed it. Especially considering how eagerly he'd—

Um, never mind.

She made herself say the rest of what she had hoped to get in before he told her he'd enjoyed last night, too, in case he said more, especially something about how eagerly he'd—

"But it never should have happened," she made herself say.

This time Hogan was the one to not say anything in response. So Chloe made an effort to explain. "I was feeling a little raw last night, talking about Samuel and things I haven't talked about to anyone for a long time. Add to that the wine and the night and New York and…" She stopped herself before adding *and you* and hurried on, "Things just happened that shouldn't have happened. That wouldn't have happened under normal circumstances. That won't happen again. You're my employer, and I'm your employee. I think we can both agree that we should keep it at that."

When he continued to remain silent, she added, "I just want you to know that I'm not assuming anything will come of it. I don't want you to think I'm under the impression that this—" here, she gestured quickly between the two of them "—changes that. I know it doesn't."

And still, Hogan said nothing. He only studied her thoughtfully, as if he was trying to figure it all out the same way she was.

Good luck with that, Chloe thought. Then again, maybe he wasn't as confused as she was. Maybe he'd awoken this morning feeling perfectly philosophical about last night. Guys were able to do that better than girls were, right? To compartmentalize things into brain boxes that kept them neatly separate from other things? Sex in one box and love in another. The present moment in one box and future years in another. He probably wasn't expecting anything more to come of last night, either, and he'd just been sitting here waiting for her to reassure him that that was how she felt, too.

So she told him in no uncertain terms—guys liked it when girls talked to them in no uncertain terms, right?—to make it perfectly clear, "I just want you to know that I don't have any expectations from this. Or from you. I know what happened between us won't go any further and that it will never happen again. I know you still love Anabel."

"And you still love Samuel," he finally said.

"Yes. I do."

He nodded. But his expression revealed nothing of what he might actually be feeling. Not that she wanted him to feel anything. The same way she wasn't feeling anything. She wasn't.

"You're right," he agreed. "About all of it. What happened last night happened. But it was no big deal."

Well, she didn't say *that*. Jeez. Oh, wait. Yes, she did. At least, she'd been thinking it before Hogan came in with breakfast. Looking and sounding all sweet and earnest and being so gorgeous and recently tumbled. Okay, then. It was no big deal. They were both on the same page.

She looked at the breakfast he'd prepared. She had thought getting everything about last night out in the open the way they had would make her feel better. But her stomach was still a tumble of nerves.

Even so, she forced a smile and asked, "Could you pass the toast, please?"

Hogan smiled back, but his, too, looked forced. "Sure."

He pulled up the tray from the foot of the bed until it was between them, and Chloe leaned over to reach for the plate of toast. But the sheet began to slip the moment she did, so she quickly sat up again, jerking it back into place.

"I should let you get dressed," Hogan said, rising from bed.

"But aren't you going to have any breakfast?"

"I had some coffee while I was making it. That'll hold me for a while. You go ahead." He started to back toward the door. "I have some things I need to do today anyway."

"Okay."

"And, listen, I'm pretty sure I won't be here for dinner tonight, so don't go to any trouble for me."

"But I was going to make *blanquette de veau*. From my grandmother's recipe."

"Maybe another time."

Before she could say anything else—not that she had any idea what to say—he mumbled a quick "See ya," and was out the door, leaving Chloe alone.

Which was how she liked to be. She'd kept herself alone for six years now. Six years, nine months, one week and… And how many days? She had to think for a minute. Two. Six years, nine months, one week and two days, to be precise. Alone was the only way she could be if she hoped to maintain her sanity. Especially after losing her mind the way she had last night.

She was right. It shouldn't have happened.

As Hogan bent over the hood of Benny Choi's '72 Mustang convertible, he repeated Chloe's assertion in his head again. Maybe if he repeated it enough times, he'd start believing himself. Chloe had been spot-on when she said last night was a mistake. It had been a mistake. An incredibly erotic, unbelievably satisfying mistake, but a mistake all the same.

She was still in love with her husband. First love was a potent cocktail. Nothing could cure a hangover from that. Hell, Hogan knew that firsthand, since he was still punch-drunk in love with Anabel fifteen years after the fact. Right? Of course right. What happened between him and Chloe last night was just a byproduct of the feelings they had for other people, feelings they'd both had bottled up for too long. Chloe had been missing her husband last night. Hogan had been missing Anabel. So they'd turned to each other for comfort.

Stuff like that happened all the time. It really was no big deal. Now that they had it out of their systems, they could go back to being in love with the people they'd loved half their lives.

Except that Chloe couldn't go back to her husband. Not the way Hogan could go back to Anabel.

"Thanks for coming in to work, Hogan," Benny said when Hogan dropped the hood of his car into place. "Now that your dad's gone, you're the only guy I trust with my baby."

Benny and Hogan's father had been friends since grade school. With what was left of Hogan's mother's family living solidly in the Midwest, Benny was the closest thing to an uncle Hogan had here in town. He was thinning on top, thickening around the middle and wore the standard issue blue uniform of the New York transit worker, having just ended his shift.

"No problem, Benny," Hogan assured him. "Feels good to come in. I've been missing the work."

"Hah," the other man said. "If I came into the kind of money you did, I wouldn't even be in New York. I'd be cruising around the Caribbean. Then I'd be cruising around Mexico. Then Alaska. Then… I don't even know after that. But I sure as hell wouldn't have my head stuck under Benny Choi's Mach One, I can tell you that."

Hogan grinned. "To each his own."

They moved into Hogan's office so he could prepare Benny's bill. Which seemed kind of ridiculous since Hogan wasn't doing this for a living anymore, so there was no need to charge anyone for parts or labor. With the money he had, he could buy a whole fleet of Dempsey's Garages and still have money left over. He knew better than to tell Benny the work was on the house, though. Benny, like everyone else in Hogan's old neighborhood, always paid his way. Even so, he knocked off twenty percent and, when Benny noticed the discrepancy, called it his new "friends and family" rate.

Hogan sat in his office for a long time after Benny left, listening to the clamor of metal against metal as the other mechanics worked, inhaling the savory aroma of lubricant, remembering the heft of every tool. He couldn't give this up. A lot of people would think he was crazy for wanting to keep working in light of his financial windfall, but he didn't care. Hogan had been working in this garage for nearly two decades, most of it by his father's side. It was the only place he'd ever felt like himself. At least it had been until last night, when he and Chloe had—

A fleet of Dempsey's Garages, he thought again, pushing away thoughts of things that would never happen again. He actually kind of liked the sound of that. There were a lot of independent garages struggling in this economy. He could buy them up, put the money into them that they needed to be competitive, keep everyone employed who wanted to stay employed and give everything and everyone a new purpose. He could start here in the city and move outward into the state.

Then maybe into another state. Then another. And another. This place would be his flagship, the shop where he came in to work every day.

And it would be a lot of work, an enterprise that ambitious. But Hogan always thrived on work. Being away from it was why he'd been at such loose ends since moving uptown. Why he'd felt so dissatisfied. Why his life felt like something was missing.

And that was another thing. He didn't have to live uptown. He could sell his grandfather's house. It didn't feel like home anyway, and it was way too big for one person. Of course, Hogan wouldn't be one person for much longer. He'd have Anabel. And, with any luck, at some point, a few rug rats to keep tabs on. Still, the Lenox Hill town house was just too much. It didn't suit Hogan. He and Anabel could find something else that they both liked. She probably wouldn't want to move downtown, though. Still, they could compromise somewhere.

The more Hogan thought about his new plans, the more he liked them. Funny, though, how the ones for the garage gelled in his brain a lot faster and way better than the ones for Anabel did. But that was just because he was sitting here in the garage right now, surrounded by all the things he needed for making plans like that. Anabel was still out there, waiting for him to make contact. But he'd be seeing her next weekend, thanks to Chloe's dinner party plans. Yeah, Hogan was *this close* to having everything he'd ever wanted.

Thanks to Chloe.

Eight

A week later, Hogan stood in his living room, wondering why the hell he'd let Chloe arrange a dinner party for him. It was for Anabel, he reminded himself. This entire situation with Chloe had always been about winning back Anabel.

Despite his recent encounter with Chloe—which neither of them had spoken about again—that was still what he wanted. Wasn't it? Of course it was. He'd spent almost half his life wanting Anabel. She was his Holy Grail. His impossible dream. A dream that was now very possible. All Hogan had to do was play his cards right. Starting now, with the evening ahead. If he could just keep his mind off making love to Chloe—or, rather, having sex with Chloe—and focus on Anabel.

He still wasn't looking forward to the night ahead, but he was relieved there wasn't going to be a large group coming. Chloe had only invited Anabel and three other couples, two of whom were friends of Anabel's that Chloe had assured him it would be beneficial for him to know, and one of whom was Gus Fiver and his date.

Hogan realized he should have been the one to plan something, and he should have been the one who invited Anabel to whatever it was, and he should be in charge of it. He also realized it should just be him and Anabel, and not a bunch of other people, too.

So why hadn't he done that? He'd been living in his grandfather's house for a month now, plenty of time for him to figure out how things were done here and proceed accordingly where it came to pursuing the love of his life. But the only time he'd seen Anabel since ascending to his new social status had been the day she came over to try and lure Chloe back to work for her. He'd thought about asking her out a lot of times over the last few weeks. But he'd always hesitated. Because he wanted the occasion to be just right, he'd told himself, and he hadn't figured out yet what *just right* was with Anabel these days.

Back when they were teenagers, they'd had fun walking along the boardwalk on Rockaway Beach or bowling a few sets at Jib Lanes or downing a couple of egg creams at Pop's Diner. Nowadays, though… Call him crazy, but Hogan didn't see the Anabel of today doing any of those things. He just didn't know what the Anabel of today did like. And that was why he hadn't asked her out.

Tonight he would find out what she liked and he *would* ask her out. Just the two of them. By summer, he promised himself again, they would be engaged.

Then they would live happily ever after, just like in the books.

"You're not wearing that, are you?"

Hogan spun around to see Chloe standing in the doorway, dressed from head to toe in stark chef's whites. He'd barely seen her since last weekend. She'd sped in and out of the dining room so fast after serving him his meals that he'd hardly had a chance to say hello or thank her.

Tonight her jacket looked like it actually fit, and she'd traded her crazy printed pants for a pair of white ones that were as starched and pressed as the rest of her. Instead of the usual spray of hair erupting from the top of her head, she had it neatly twisted in two braids that fell over each shoulder. In place of bright red lipstick, she wore a shade of pink that was more subdued.

This must be what passed for formal attire for her. Even though she'd promised him the evening wasn't going to be formal. He looked down at his own clothes, standard issue blue jeans, white shirt and a pair of Toms he got on sale. Everything was as plain and inoffensive as clothing got, and he couldn't think of a single reason why Chloe would object to anything he had on.

"You said it was casual," he reminded her.

"I said it was *business* casual."

He shrugged. "Guys in business wear stuff like this all the time."

"Not for business casual, they don't."

"What's the difference?"

She eyed his outfit again. "Blue jeans, for one thing." Before he could object, she hurried on, "Okay, *maybe* blue jeans would be okay for some business casual functions, but only if they're dark wash, and only by certain designers."

"Levi Strauss has been designing jeans since the nineteenth century," Hogan pointed out.

Chloe crossed her arms over her midsection. "Yeah, and the ones you have on look like they were in his first collection."

"It took me years to get these broken in the way I like."

"You can't wear them tonight."

"Why not?"

"Because they're not appropriate for—"

"Then what is appropriate?" he interrupted. He was really beginning to hate being rich. There were way too many rules.

She expelled a much put-upon sigh. "What about the clothes you wore to the wine-tasting that day? Those were okay."

"That guy who bumped into me spilled some wine on my jacket, and it's still at the cleaner's."

"But that was weeks ago."

"I keep forgetting to pick it up. I never wear it."

"Well, what else do you have?"

He looked at his clothes again. "A lot of stuff like this, but in different colors."

"Show me."

Hogan opened his mouth to object again. People would be showing up soon, and, dammit, what he had on was fine. But he didn't want to argue with Chloe. These were the most words they'd exchanged in a week, and the air was already crackling with tension. So he made his way toward the stairs with her on his heels—at a safe distance. He told himself he was only changing his clothes because he wanted to look his best for Anabel, not like the kid from Queens she'd chosen someone else over. He wanted to look like a part of her tribe. Because he was a part of her tribe now. Why did he keep trying to fight it?

He took the stairs two at a time until he reached the fourth floor, not realizing until he got there how far behind Chloe was. He hadn't meant to abandon her. He was just feeling a little impatient for some reason. When she drew within a few stairs of him, he headed for his bedroom and threw open the closet that was as big as the dining room in the house where he grew up. It had four rods—two on each side—for hanging shirts and suits and whatever, a low shelf on each side beneath those for shoes, and an entire wall of drawers on the opposite end. Every stitch of clothing Hogan owned didn't even fill a quarter of it. The drawers were pretty much empty, too.

Mrs. Hennessey had started clearing out his grandfather's suits and shoes before Hogan moved in and was in the process of donating them to a place that outfitted homeless guys and ex-cons for job interviews—something that probably had his grandfather spinning in his grave, an idea Hogan had to admit brought him a lot of gratification. But the housekeeper had left a few things on one side she thought might be of use to Hogan because he and his grandfather were about the same size. Hogan hadn't even looked through them. He just couldn't see himself decked out in the regalia of Wall Street, no matter how high he climbed on the social ladder.

Chloe hesitated outside the bedroom door for some

reason, looking past Hogan at the room itself. The room that was furnished in Early Nineteenth Century Conspicuous Consumption, from the massive Oriental rug in shades of dark green, gold and rust to the leather sofa and chair in the sitting area, to the quartet of oil paintings of what looked like the same European village from four different angles, to the rows of model cars lining the fireplace mantel, to the mahogany bed and dressers more suited to a monarch than a mechanic.

Then he realized it wasn't so much the room she was looking at. It was the bed. The bed that, this time last week, they were only a few hours away from occupying together, doing things with and to each other that Hogan had barely ever even fantasized about. Things he'd thought about a lot since. Things, truth be told, he wouldn't mind doing again.

Except with Anabel next time, he quickly told himself. Weird, though, how whenever he thought about those things—usually when he was in bed on his back staring up at the ceiling—it was always Chloe, not Anabel, who was with him in his fantasies.

In an effort to take both their minds off that night, he said, "Yeah, I know, the room doesn't suit me very well, does it? Even the model cars are all antiques worth thousands of dollars—I Googled them—and not the plastic Revell kind I made when I was a kid. I didn't change anything, though, because I thought maybe I'd learn to like it. I haven't. Truth be told, I don't think I'll ever stop feeling like an outsider in this house."

He hated the rancor he heard in his voice. Talk about first world problems. Oh, boo-hoo-hoo, his house was too big and too luxurious for his liking. Oh, no, he had millions of dollars' worth of antiques and collectibles he didn't know what to do with. How would he ever be able to deal with problems like that? Even so, being rich was nothing like he'd thought it would be.

"Then redecorate," Chloe said tersely.

"Oh, sure," he shot back. "God knows I have great taste, what with working under cars on a street filled with neon and bodegas and cement. Hell, apparently, I can't even dress myself."

She winced at the charge. "I didn't mean it like that."

"Didn't you?"

"No. I—"

Instead of explaining herself, she made her way in Hogan's direction, giving him a wide berth as she entered the closet.

"My stuff is on the left," he told her. "The other side is what's left of my grandfather's things."

He hadn't been joking when he told her everything he had was like what he had on, only in different colors. He'd never been much of a clotheshorse, and he didn't follow trends. When his old clothes wore out, he bought new ones, and when he found something he liked, he just bought it in a few different colors. He hadn't altered his blue jeans choice since he first started wearing them, and when he'd started wearing them, he just bought what his old man wore. If it came down to a life-or-death situation, Hogan could probably name a fashion designer. Probably. He just didn't put much thought into clothes, that was all.

Something that Chloe was obviously discovering,

since she was pushing through his entire wardrobe at the speed of light and not finding a single thing to even hesitate over. When she reached the last shirt, she turned around and saw the drawers where he'd stowed his, um, drawers. Before he could stop her, she tugged open the one closest to her and thrust her hand inside, grabbing the first thing she came into contact with, which happened to be a pair of blue boxer-briefs. Not that Hogan cared if she saw his underwear, at least when he wasn't wearing it. And, yeah, okay, he wouldn't mind if she saw it while he was wearing it, either, which was something he probably shouldn't be thinking about when he was anticipating the arrival of his newly possible dream. So he only leaned against the closet door and crossed his arms over his midsection.

Chloe, however, once she realized what she was holding, blushed. Actually blushed. Hogan didn't think he'd ever seen a woman blush in his life. He'd never gone for the kind of woman who would blush. Especially over something like a guy's underwear that he wasn't even wearing.

"There are socks and T-shirts in the other drawers," he told her, hoping to spare her any more embarrassment. Not that there was anything that embarrassing about socks and T-shirts. Unless maybe it was the fact that he'd had some of them, probably, since high school. "But I'm thinking you probably wouldn't approve of a T-shirt for business casual, either."

She stuffed his underwear back where she found it and slammed the drawer shut. Then she looked at the clothes hanging opposite his. "Those belonged to your grandfather?"

"Yeah," Hogan told her. "Mrs. Hennessey is in the middle of donating all his stuff to charity."

Chloe made her way to the rows of shirts, pants and jackets lined up neatly opposite his own and began to give them the quick *whoosh-whoosh-whoosh* she'd given his. She was nearly to the end when she withdrew a vest and gave it a quick perusal.

"Here," she said, thrusting it at Hogan with one hand as she began to sift through a collection of neckties with the other.

He accepted it from her automatically, giving it more thorough consideration than she had. The front was made of a lightweight wool charcoal, and it had intricately carved black buttons he was going to go out on a limb and guess weren't plastic. The back was made out of what looked like a silk, gray-on-gray paisley. It was a nice enough vest, but he wasn't really the vest-wearing type.

In case she wasn't reading his mind, though, he said, "I'm not really the vest-wearing ty—"

"And put this on, too," she interrupted, extending a necktie toward him.

It, too, looked as if it was made of silk and was decorated with a sedate print in blues, greens and grays that complemented the vest well. It was nice enough, but Hogan wasn't really the tie-wearing type, either.

"I'm not really the tie-wearing ty—"

"You are tonight," Chloe assured him before he could even finish protesting.

As if wanting to prove that herself, she snatched the vest from its hanger, leaving the latter dangling from Hogan's fingers. Before he knew it, she was maneuvering one opening of the vest over both of those and up his arm then circling to his other side to bring the vest over his other arm. Then she flipped up the collar of his shirt, looped the tie around his neck and began to tie it.

She fumbled with the task at first, as if she couldn't remember how to tie a man's tie—that made two of them—but by her third effort, she seemed to be recovering. She was standing closer to him than she'd been in a week. Close enough that Hogan could see tiny flecks of blue in her green eyes and feel the heat of her body mingling with his. He could smell her distinctive scent, a mix of soap and fresh herbs and something else that was uniquely Chloe Merlin. He was close enough that, if he wanted to, he could dip his head to hers and kiss her.

Not surprisingly, Hogan realized he did want to kiss her. He wanted to do a lot more than kiss her, but he'd start there and see what developed.

"There," Chloe said, bringing his attention back to the matter at hand.

Which, Hogan reminded himself, was about getting ready for dinner with the woman he was supposed to be planning to make his wife. He shouldn't be trying to figure out his feelings for Chloe. He didn't have feelings for Chloe. Not the kind he had for Anabel.

Chloe gave the necktie one final pat then looked up at Hogan. Her eyes widened in surprise, and she took a giant step backward. "I need to get back to the kitchen," she said breathlessly.

Then she was speeding past him, out of the closet

and out of his room. But not, he realized as he watched her go, out of his thoughts. Which was where she should be heading fastest.

Hogan was surprised at how much fun he had entertaining near-strangers in his still-strange-to-him home. The wife of one couple who was friends of Anabel's had been in the cab with her the night Hogan met her, so they shared some history there. The other couple who knew her was affable and chatty. Gus Fiver and his date both shared Hogan's love of American-made muscle cars, so there was some lively conversation there. And Anabel...

Yeah. Anabel. Anabel was great. But the longer the night went on, the more Hogan realized neither of them were the people who met on Jamaica Avenue a decade and a half ago. She was still beautiful. Still smart. Still fierce. But she wasn't the seventeen-year-old girl who flipped off a cabbie in the middle of Queens any more than Hogan was the seventeen-year-old kid who'd fallen for her.

All he could conjure up was a fondness for a girl he knew at a time in his life when the world was its most romantic. And he was reasonably sure Anabel felt the same way about him. They talked like old friends. They joked like old friends. But there were no sparks arcing between them. No longing looks. No flirtation.

It was great to see her again. He wouldn't mind bumping into her from time to time in the future. But his fifteen-year-long fantasy of joining his life to hers forever evaporated before Chloe even brought in the second course. Which looked like some kind of soup.

"*Bisque des tomates et de la citrouille,*" she announced as she ladled the first helping into the bowl in front of Anabel.

"Ooo, Chloe, I love your tomato pumpkin bisque," Anabel said, leaning closer to inhale the aroma. "Thyme and basil for sure, but I swear she puts lavender in it, too." She looked at Chloe and feigned irritation. "She won't tell me, though. Damn her."

Chloe murmured her thanks but still didn't give Anabel the information she wanted. Then she circled the table with speed and grace, filling the bowls of everyone present before winding up at Hogan's spot. When she went to ladle up some soup for him, though, her grace and speed deserted her. Not only did she have trouble spooning up a decent amount, but when she finally did, she spilled a little on the tablecloth.

"I am so sorry," she said as she yanked a linen cloth from over her arm to dab at the stain.

"Don't worry about it," Hogan told her. "It'll wash out."

"That's not the point. I shouldn't have done it."

He was about to tell her it was fine, but noticed her hand was shaking as she tried to clean up what she'd done. When he looked at her face, he saw that her cheeks were flushed the same way they'd been in the closet, when she was handling his underwear. Must be hot in the kitchen, he decided.

"It's okay," he said again. Then, to his guests—because he wanted to take their attention off Chloe—he added, "Dig in."

Everyone did, but when Hogan looked at Anabel, she had a funny expression on her face. She wasn't looking at him, though. She wasn't even looking at the soup she professed to love. She was looking at Chloe. After a moment her gaze fell on Hogan.

"Your soup's going to get cold," he told her.

She smiled cryptically. "Not with the heat in this room, it won't."

Hogan narrowed his eyes. Funny, but he'd been thinking it was kind of cool in here.

The soup was, like everything Chloe made, delicious. As were the three courses that followed it. Everyone was stuffed by the time they were finished with dessert, a pile of pastries filled with cream and dripping with chocolate sauce that Anabel said was her most favorite thing Chloe made. In fact, every course that came out, Anabel had claimed was her most favorite thing Chloe made. Clearly, Chloe was doing her best to help Hogan woo the woman he had mistakenly thought was the love of his life. He wasn't sure how he was going to break it to her that all her hard work had been for nothing.

"We should have coffee on the roof," Anabel declared after the last of the dishes were cleared away.

Everyone agreed that they should take advantage of what the weather guys were saying would be the last of the pleasantly cool evenings for a while in the face of some inclement, more November-worthy weather to come. Hogan ducked into the kitchen long enough to tell Chloe their plans then led his guests up to the roof garden.

The view was the same as it was a week ago, but somehow the flowers looked duller, the white lights overhead seemed dimmer and the cityscape was less glittery. Must be smoggier tonight. He and his guests made their way to the sitting area just as Chloe appeared from downstairs. For a moment Hogan waited for her to join them in conversation, and only remembered she was working when she crossed to open the dumbwaiter. From it, she removed a tray with a coffeepot and cups, and little bowls filled with sugar, cream, chocolate shavings and some other stuff that looked like spices. Evidently, even after-dinner coffee was different when you were rich.

As Chloe brought the tray toward the group, Anabel drew alongside Hogan and hooked her arm through his affectionately. He smiled down at her when she did, because it was so like what she had done when they were kids. That was where the similarity in the gesture ended, however, because her smile in return wasn't one of the sly, flirtatious ones she'd always offered him when they were teenagers, but a mild, friendly one instead. Even so, she steered him away from his guests as Chloe began to pour the coffee, guiding him toward the part of the roof that was darkest, where the lights of the city could be viewed more easily. He didn't blame her. It was a really nice view. Once there, she leaned her hip against the balustrade and unlooped her arm from his. But she took both of his hands in hers and met his gaze intently.

"So how are you adjusting to Park Avenue life?" she asked, her voice low enough that it was clear she meant the question for him alone.

"I admit it's not what I thought it would be," he replied just as quietly. "But I guess I'll get used to it. Eventually."

He looked over at his other guests to make sure he wasn't being a neglectful host, but they were all engaged in conversation. Except for Chloe, who was busying herself getting everything set out on the table to her liking. And also sneaking peeks at Hogan and Anabel.

She was more concerned about the success of the evening than he'd been. He wished there was some way to signal her not to worry, that the evening had been a huge success, because he knew now the plans he'd made for the future weren't going to work out the way he'd imagined, and that was totally okay.

"I know it's a lot different from Queens," Anabel said, bringing his attention back to her. She was still holding his hands, but she dropped one to place her palm gently against his chest. "But Queens will always be here in your heart. No one says you have to leave it behind." She smiled. "In fact, I, for one, would be pretty mad at you if you did leave Queens behind. You wouldn't be Hogan anymore if you did."

"That will never happen," he assured her. "But it's still weird to think that, technically, this is the life I was born to."

She tipped her head to one side. "You have something on your cheek," she said.

Again? Hogan wanted to say. First the engine grease with Chloe, now part of his dinner with Anabel. Before he had a chance to swipe whatever it was away, Anabel lifted her other hand to cup it over his jaw, stroking her thumb softly over his cheekbone.

"Coffee?"

He and Anabel both jumped at the arrival of Chloe, who seemed to appear out of nowhere. Anabel looked guilty as she dropped her hand to her side, though Hogan had no idea what she had to feel guilty about. Chloe looked first at Hogan, then at Anabel, then at

Hogan again. When neither of them replied, she extended one cup toward Anabel.

"I made yours with cinnamon and chocolate," she said. Then she paraphrased the words Anabel had been saying all night. "I know it's your *most favorite*."

Hogan wasn't sure, but the way she emphasized those last two words sounded a little sarcastic.

"And, Hogan, yours is plain," Chloe continued. "Just the way I know *you* like it."

That, too, sounded a little sarcastic. Or maybe caustic. He wasn't sure. There was definitely something off about Chloe at the moment, though. In fact, there'd been something off about Chloe all night. Not just the soup-spilling when she'd ladled up his, but every course seemed to have had something go wrong, and always with Hogan's share of it. His *coq au vin* had been missing the *vin*, his *salade Niçoise* had been a nice salad, but there had hardly been any of it on his plate, his cheese course had looked like it was arranged by a five-year-old, and his cream puff dessert had been light on the cream, heavy on the puff.

He understood that, as the host, he was obligated to take whichever plates weren't up to standards, and he was fine with that. But that was just it—Chloe was *always* up to standards. She never put anything on the table that wasn't perfect. Until tonight.

Hogan and Anabel both took their coffee and murmured their thanks, but Chloe didn't move away. She only kept looking at them expectantly. So Hogan, at least, sipped from his cup and nodded.

"Tastes great," he said. "Thanks again."

Anabel, too, sampled hers, and smiled her approval. But Chloe still didn't leave.

So Hogan said, "Thanks, Chloe."

"You're welcome," Chloe replied. And still didn't leave.

Hogan looked at Anabel to see if maybe she knew why Chloe was still hanging around, but she only sipped her coffee and gazed at him with what he could only think were laughing eyes.

"So your coffee is all right?" Chloe asked Anabel.

"It's delicious," Anabel told her. "As you said. My *most favorite*. Somehow, tonight, it's even better than usual." She hesitated for the briefest moment then added, "Must be the company."

Even in the dim light, Hogan could see two bright spots of pink appear on Chloe's cheeks. Her lips thinned, her eyes narrowed and her entire body went ramrod straight.

"I'm so happy," she said in the same crisp voice. Then she looked at Hogan. "For both of you."

Then she spun on her heels and went back to his other guests. Once there, however, she turned again to study Hogan and Anabel. A lot.

"What the hell was that about?" Hogan asked Anabel.

She chuckled. "You really have no idea, do you?"

He shook his head. "No. Is it some woman thing?"

Now Anabel smiled. "Kind of."

"Should I be concerned?"

"Probably."

Oh, yeah. This was the Anabel Hogan remembered. Cagey and evasive and having fun at his expense. Now that he was starting to remember her without the rosy sheen of nostalgia, he guessed she really could be kind of obnoxious at times when they were teenagers. Not that he hadn't been kind of obnoxious himself. He guessed teenagers in general were just kind of annoying. Especially when their hormones were in overdrive.

He studied Anabel again, but she just sipped her coffee and looked amused. "You're not going to tell me what's going on with Chloe, are you?" he asked.

"No."

"Just tell me if whatever it is is permanent, or if she'll eventually come around and things can get back to normal."

She smiled again. "Hogan, I think I can safely say your life is never going to be normal again."

"I know, right? This money thing is always going to be ridiculous."

"I didn't mean the money part."

"Then what did you mean?"

She threw him another cryptic smile. "My work here is done." As if to punctuate the statement, she pushed herself up on tiptoe to kiss his cheek then told him, "Tonight was really lovely, Hogan. And illuminating."

Well, on that, at least, they could agree.

"Thank you for inviting me," she added. "But I should probably go."

"I'll walk you out."

"No, don't leave your guests. I can find my own way." She looked thoughtful for a moment before nodding. "In fact, I'm really looking forward to finding my own way in life for once."

She walked back toward the others. He heard her say her goodbyes and thank Chloe one last time, then she turned to wave to Hogan. As he lifted a hand in

return, she strode through the door to, well, find her
own way. Leaving Hogan to find his own way, too.

He just wished he knew where to go from here.

Nine

Tonight was a disaster.

Chloe was still berating herself about it even as she dropped the last utensil into the dishwasher. There was just no way to deny it. The evening had been an absolute, unmitigated disaster. And not just the dinner party, where every single course had seen some kind of problem. The other disaster had been even worse. Hogan's reunion with Anabel had been a huge success.

Chloe tossed a cleaning pod into the dishwasher, sealed the door and punched a button to turn it on. It whirred to quiet life, performing perfectly the function for which it had been designed. She wished she could seal herself up just as easily then flip a switch to make herself work the way she was supposed to. She used to be able to do that. She did that as efficiently and automatically as the dishwasher did for six years. Six years, nine months and…and…

She leaned back against the counter and dropped her head into her hands. Oh, God. She couldn't remember anymore how many weeks or days to add to the years and months since Samuel's death. What was wrong with her?

And why had it hurt so much to see Hogan and Anabel together tonight? Chloe had known since the day she started working for Hogan that his whole reason for hiring her had been to find a way back into Anabel's life. He'd never made secret the fact that he still wanted the girl of his dreams fifteen years after they broke up, nor the fact that he was planning a future with her.

For Pete's sake, Chloe was the one who had been so adamant about throwing the dinner party tonight so the two of them would finally be in the same room together. She'd deliberately chosen all of Anabel's favorite dishes. She'd helped Hogan make himself more presentable for the woman he'd loved half his life so he could make a good impression on her.

And she'd accomplished her goal beautifully, because the two of them had laughed more than Chloe had ever seen two people laugh, and they'd engaged in constant conversation. They'd even wandered off as the evening wound down to steal some alone time together on the roof. Alone time Anabel had used to make clear that her interest in Hogan was as alive as it had ever been.

Chloe didn't think she'd ever be able to rid her brain of the image of Anabel splaying one hand open on Hogan's chest while she caressed his face with the other, the same way Chloe had done a week ago when she and Hogan were on the roof themselves. She knew what it meant when a woman touched a man that way. It meant she was halfway in love with him.

No! She immediately corrected herself. That wasn't what it meant. At least not where Chloe was concerned.

She started wiping down the kitchen countertops, even though she'd already wiped them off twice. You could never be too careful. She wasn't in love with Hogan. Not even halfway. She would never be in love with anyone again. Loving someone opened you up to too many things that could cause pain. Terrible, terrible, *terrible* pain. Chloe never wanted to hurt like that again. Chloe never *would* hurt like that again. She just wouldn't.

She wasn't in love with Hogan. She would never fall in love again.

Anyway, it didn't matter, because Hogan and Anabel were back on the road to the destiny they'd started when they were teenagers. His hiring of Chloe had had exactly the outcome he'd intended. He'd won the woman of his dreams.

Before long Chloe would be cooking for two. She'd serve Hogan and Anabel their dinner every night, listening to their laughter and their fond conversation as they talked about their shared past and their plans for the future. And she'd bring in their breakfast every morning. Of course, Anabel liked to have breakfast in bed most days. She'd probably want that for her and Hogan both now. So Chloe would also be able to see them every morning all rumpled from sleep. And sex. More rumpled from sex than from sleep, no doubt, since Hogan's sexual appetites were so—

Well. She just wouldn't think about his sexual appetites anymore, would she? She wouldn't think about Hogan at all. Except in the capacity of him as her employer. Which was all he was. That was all he had ever been. It was all he would ever be. Chloe had reiterated that to him a week ago. All she had to do was keep remembering that. And forget about the way he—

She closed her eyes to shut out the images of her night with Hogan, images that had plagued her all week. But closing her eyes only brought them more fiercely into focus. Worse, they were accompanied by feelings. Again. Feelings she absolutely did not want to feel. Feelings she absolutely could not feel. Feelings she absolutely would not feel. Not if she wanted to stay sane.

She finished cleaning up the kitchen and poured what was left of an open bottle of wine into a glass to take upstairs with her. As she topped the step to the fifth and highest floor of Hogan's house, her gaze inevitably fell on the roof access door across from her. Unable to help herself, she tiptoed toward it and cracked it open to see if anyone was still up there. She'd been surprised that Anabel left first, until she remembered her former employer often turned in early on Saturday night because she rose early on Sunday to drive to a farm in Connecticut where she stabled her horses.

There were still a few voices coming from the roof—Chloe recognized not just Hogan's, but Mr. Fiver's and his date's, as well. She wondered briefly if she should go up and check on the coffee situation then decided against it. She'd sent up a fresh pot and its accoutrements before cleaning up the kitchen, and Hogan had assured her he wouldn't need anything else from her tonight.

Or any other night, she couldn't help thinking as she headed for her room. He had Anabel to take care of any nightly needs he'd have from now on. And every other need he would ever have again. Which was good. It was. Chloe was glad things had worked out between the two former lovers the way they had. She was. Hogan would be happy now. And Anabel was a nice person. She also deserved to be happy. Now Chloe could focus completely on her cooking, which would make her happy, too. It would.

Happiness was bursting out all over. They were all hip deep in happiness. Happy, happy, happy. Yay for happiness.

Thank God she had the next two days off.

Hogan had always loved Sundays. Sunday was the one day of the week Dempsey's Parts and Service was closed—unless there was an emergency. He loved Sunday mornings especially, because he could sleep late and rise when he felt like it, then take his time eating something for breakfast that he didn't have to wolf down on the run, the way he did during the work week.

At least, that had always been the case before he became filthy, stinking rich. Over the course of the past month, though, Sundays hadn't been like they used to be. He hadn't been working his regular shifts at the garage, so how could one day differ from any other? And he didn't have to eat on the run anymore, so a leisurely Sunday breakfast was no different from any other breakfasts during the no-longer-work-week. No, he hadn't been completely idle since leaving Queens, but he hadn't had a regular schedule to keep. He hadn't had places he *had* to be or things he *had* to get done.

Yeah, he was putting plans into place that would bring work and purpose back into his life, but there was no way his life—or his Sundays—would ever go back to being the way they were before.

The thing that had really made Sundays even less enjoyable than they were before, though, was that Chloe was never around on Sundays. She never stayed home on her days off, and the house felt even more alien and unwelcoming when she wasn't in it.

This morning was no different. Except that, somehow, it felt different. When Hogan stumbled into the kitchen in his usual jeans and sweater the way he did every Sunday morning to make coffee, the room seemed even more quiet and empty than usual. He busied himself making his usual bacon and eggs, but even eating that didn't pull him out of his funk.

Too little sleep, he decided. Gus Fiver and his date had hung around until the wee hours, so Hogan had logged half the amount of shut-eye he normally did. Of course, last weekend he'd woken having only logged a few hours of shut-eye, too, and he'd felt *great* that day. At least until Chloe had told him what a mistake the night before had been.

He stopped himself there. Chloe. What was he going to do about Chloe? The only reason he'd hired her was because he wanted to insinuate himself into Anabel's life. And the only reason he'd planned to keep her employed in the future was because she was Anabel's favorite chef. Not that he intended to fire her now—God, no—but her reason for being in his house had suddenly shifted. Hell, the whole dynamic of her place in his house seemed to have suddenly shifted. Hogan for sure still wanted Chloe around. But he didn't want her around because of Anabel anymore. He wanted Chloe around because of, well, Chloe.

He liked Chloe. He liked her a lot. Maybe more than liked her. All week he'd been thinking about Chloe, not Anabel. Even before he realized his thing for Anabel wasn't a thing anymore, it was Chloe, not Anabel, who had been living in his head. He'd had dozens of nights with Anabel in the past, and only one night with Chloe. But when he piled all those nights with Anabel into one place and set the single night with Chloe in another, that single night had a lot more weight than the dozens of others. He wanted to have more nights with Chloe. He wanted countless nights with Chloe. The problem was Chloe didn't want any more nights with him. She'd made that crystal clear.

And there was still the whole employer-employee thing. He didn't want Chloe as an employee anymore. He wanted her as…something else. He just wasn't sure what. Even by the time he finished his breakfast and was trying to decide what to do with his day—other than think about Chloe, since that would be a given— Hogan had no idea what to do about her. Even after cleaning up from his dinner that evening, he still didn't know what to do about her.

Chloe evidently did, though, because she came into the den Sunday night, where Hogan was putting together a preliminary plan for a state-wide chain of Dempsey's Garages, and handed him a long, white envelope.

"Here," she said as she extended it toward him.

She was dressed in street clothes, a pair of snug blue jeans and a voluminous yellow turtleneck, her hair in a ponytail, her glasses sliding down on her nose—which she pushed up with the back of her hand, so he knew she was feeling anxious about something.

"What is it?" he asked.

"My two weeks' notice."

He recoiled from the envelope as if she were handing him a rattlesnake. "What?"

"It's my two weeks' notice," she repeated. "Except that I'm taking advantage of article twelve, paragraph A, subheading one in my contract, and it's really my two days' notice."

Now Hogan stood. But he still didn't take the envelope from her. "Whoa, whoa, whoa. You can't do that."

"Yes, I can. That paragraph outlines my right to an immediate abdication of my current position in the event of force majeure."

His head was still spinning from her announcement, but he found the presence of mind to point out, "Force majeure only applies to things beyond our control like wars or strikes or natural disasters."

"Exactly," she said.

He waited for her to clarify whatever was beyond their control, but she didn't elaborate. So he asked, "Well, what's the force majeure that's making you give me your two weeks'—correction, two days'—notice?"

She hesitated, her gaze ricocheting from his to the shelves of books behind him. Finally, she said, "Impracticability."

Hogan narrowed his eyes. "Impracticability? What the hell does that mean?"

"It's a legitimate legal term. Look it up. Now, if you'll excuse me, I have a cab waiting."

"Wait, what? You're leaving right now? That's not two days' notice, that's two minutes' notice."

"Today isn't over yet, and tomorrow hasn't started," she said. "That's two days. And my new employers have a place ready for me, so there's no reason for me to delay starting."

She still wasn't looking at him. So he took a step to his left to put himself directly in her line of vision. As soon as he did, she dropped her gaze to the floor.

"You already have a new employer?" he asked.

"Yes."

Of course she already had a new employer. Since she'd come to work for him, Hogan had had to fend off a half dozen attempts from people besides Anabel to hire her away from him, upping her salary even more every time. He hadn't minded, though, especially now that he knew where the money went. He would have done anything to keep Chloe employed so he could keep himself on Anabel's radar. At least, that was what he'd been telling himself all those times. Now he knew there was another reason he'd wanted to keep Chloe on. He just still wasn't sure he knew how to put it in words.

"Who's your new employer?" he asked.

"I'm not required to tell you that," she replied, still looking at the floor.

"You might do it as a professional courtesy," he said, stalling. "Or even a personal one."

"It's no one you know."

"Chloe, if it's a matter of money, I can—"

"It isn't the money."

She still wasn't looking at him. So he tried a new tack.

"Haven't your working conditions here been up to standard?"

"My working conditions here have been—" She halted abruptly then hurried on, "My working conditions here have been fine."

"Well, if it isn't the money, and it isn't the working conditions, was it..." He hated to think it might be what he thought it was, but he had to know for sure. "Was it the taco meatloaf?"

She looked up at that, but she closed her eyes and shook her head.

Even though he'd assured her he wouldn't mention it again, he asked, "Then was it what happened after the taco meatloaf?"

Now she squeezed her eyes tight. "I have to go," she said again.

Hogan had no idea how to respond to that. She hadn't said specifically that it was their sexual encounter making her situation here "impracticable"— whatever the hell that was—but her physical reaction to the question was a pretty good indication that that was exactly what had brought this on. Why had she waited a week, though? If their hookup was what was bothering her, then why hadn't she given her notice last weekend, right after it happened?

He knew the answer immediately. Because of Anabel. Chloe had promised before they ended up in his bed that she would arrange a dinner party for him so he could spend time with Anabel and cinch their reconciliation. She'd stayed long enough to fulfill that obligation so Hogan would be able to reunite with the woman he'd professed to be in love with for half his life. Now she figured he and Anabel were on their way to their happily-ever-after, so there was no reason for her to hang around anymore. And, okay, he supposed it could get kind of awkward if Anabel reentered his life after he and Chloe had had sex. Maybe Chloe just wanted to avoid a scenario like that. His anxiety eased. If that was the case, it wasn't a problem anymore.

"Anabel and I aren't going to be seeing each other," he said.

At that, Chloe finally opened her eyes and met his gaze. This time she was the one to ask, "What do you mean?"

Hogan lifted his shoulders and let them drop. "I mean we're not going to be seeing each other. Not like dating anyway. We might still see each other as friends."

"I don't understand."

Yeah, that made two of them. Hogan tried to explain anyway. "Last night she and I both realized there's nothing between us now like there was when we were kids. No sparks. No fireworks. Whatever it was she and I had fifteen years ago, we've both outgrown it. Neither one of us wants to start it up again."

"But you've been pining for her for half your life."

This part, at least, Hogan had figured out. He told Chloe, "No, the seventeen-year-old kid in me was pining for her. I just didn't realize how much that kid has grown up in the years that have passed, and how much of his youthful impulses were, well, impulsive. The thirty-three-year-old me wants something else." He might as well just say the rest. He'd come this far. "The thirty-three-year-old me wants some*one* else."

Okay, so maybe that wasn't exactly saying the rest. He was feeling his way here, figuring it out as he went. Chloe, however, didn't seem to be following him. So

Hogan pushed the rest of the words out of his brain and into his mouth. And then he said them aloud.

"He wants you, Chloe. *I* want you."

He had thought the announcement would make her happy. Instead, she recoiled like he'd hit her.

But all she said was, "You can't."

Now Hogan was the one who felt like he'd been hit. Right in the gut. With a two-by-four. But he responded honestly, "Too late. I do."

Her brows arrowed downward, and she swallowed hard. "I can't get involved with you, Hogan."

"Why not?"

"I can't get involved with anyone."

"But last weekend—"

"Last weekend never should have happened," she interrupted.

"But it did happen, Chloe. And you'll never convince me it didn't have an effect on you, the same way it had an effect on me. A big one."

"Oh, it definitely had an effect on me," she assured him. Though her tone of voice indicated she didn't feel anywhere near as good about that effect as he did.

"Then why—"

"Because I can't go there, Hogan. Ever again. I was in love once, and it nearly destroyed me. I never want to love anyone like that again."

"Chloe—"

"You've experienced loss," she interrupted him. "With both of your parents. You know how much it hurts when someone you love isn't there for you anymore."

He nodded. "Yeah, but—"

"Now take that pain and multiply it by a hundred,"

she told him. "A thousand. As terrible as it is to lose a parent or a grandparent, it's even worse when you lose the person you were planning to spend the rest of your life with. Losing someone like that is so… It's…"

Tears filled her eyes, spilling freely as she continued. "Or even if you lose someone like that in old age, after the two of you have built a life together, you still have a lifetime worth of memories to get you through it, you know? You have your children to comfort you. Children who carry a part of that person inside them. Maybe they have their father's smile or his way of walking or his love of cardamom or something else that, every time you see it, it reminds you he's not really gone. Not completely. A part of him lives on in them. You walk through the house the two of you took years making your own, and you're reminded of dozens of Thanksgivings and Christmases and birthdays that were celebrated there. You have an *entire life* lived with that person to look back on. But when that person is taken from you before you even have a chance to build that life—"

She took off her glasses with one hand and swiped her eyes with the other. "It's a theft of your life before you even had a chance to live it," she said. "The children you planned to have with that person die, too. The plans you made, the experiences you should have shared, the memories you thought you'd make… All of that dies with him.

"A loss like that is overwhelming, Hogan. It brings with it a grief that goes so deep and is so relentless, you know it will never, ever, go away, and you know you can never, ever, grieve like that again. *I* can never grieve like that again. And the only way to avoid grieving like that again is to never love like that again. I have to go before I'm more—"

She halted abruptly, covering her eyes with both hands. Hogan had no idea how to respond to everything she'd said. As bad as it had been to lose his folks, he couldn't imagine losing someone he loved as much as Chloe had loved her husband. He hadn't loved anyone as much as she had loved her husband. Not yet anyway. But even after everything she'd just said—hell, because of everything she'd just said—he'd like to have the chance to find out what it *was* like to love someone that much. And if Chloe's last few words and the way she'd stopped short were any indication, maybe there was still a chance she might love that way again, too.

"I'm sorry, Chloe," he said. The sentiment was overused and of little comfort, but he didn't know what else to say. "Your husband's death was a terrible thing. But you can't stop living your life because something terrible happened. You have to do your best to move on and make a different life instead. You can't just shut yourself off from everything."

"Yes, I can."

He shook his head. "No. You can't. And you haven't."

She arrowed her brows down in confusion. "How do you know?"

He shrugged and smiled gently. "Because I think you pretty much just told me you love me."

"No, I didn't," she quickly denied. Maybe too quickly. "I don't love anyone. I'll never love anyone again. I can't."

"You mean you won't."

"Fine. I won't love anyone again."

"You think you can just make a choice like that? That by saying you won't love someone, it will keep you from loving them?"

"Yes."

"You really believe that?"

"I have to."

"Chloe, we need to talk more about this. A lot more."

"There's nothing to talk about," she assured him. Before he could object, she hurried on, "I'm sorry to leave you in the lurch. My letter includes a number of recommendations for personal chefs in the area who would be a good match for your culinary needs. Thank you for everything."

And then she added that knife-in-the-heart word that Anabel had never said to him when they were kids, the one word that would have let Hogan know it was over for good and never to contact her again, the word that, left unsaid the way it was then, had given him hope for years.

"Goodbye."

And wow, that word really did feel like a knife to the heart. So much so that he couldn't think of a single thing to say that would counter it, a single thing that would stop Chloe from leaving. All he could do was watch her rush out the door and head for the stairs. And all he could hear was her last word, with all its finality, echoing in his brain.

Ten

Chloe stood in the kitchen of Hugo and Lucie Fleury, marveling again—she'd made herself marvel about this every day for the last three weeks—at what a plumb position she had landed. Her new situation was perfect for her—something else she made herself acknowledge every day—because Hugo and Lucie had grown up in Paris and arrived in New York for his new job only a year ago, so they were about as Parisian as a couple could be outside the City of Light. They didn't question anything Chloe put on the table, so she never had to explain a dish to them, their Central Park West penthouse was decorated in a way that made her feel as if she were living at Versailles and she was using her second language of French every day, so there was no chance of her getting rusty. *Mais oui*, all Chloe could say about her new assignment was, *C'est magnifique!*

So why didn't she feel so *magnifique* after almost a month of working here? Why did she instead feel so blasé? More to the point, why hadn't a single meal she'd created for the Fleurys come out the way it was supposed to? Why had everything she put together been a little…off? And now she was about to undertake a dinner party for twelve, the kind of challenge to which she normally rose brilliantly, and all she could do was think about the last dinner party she'd put together, and how it had resulted in—

Not that the Fleurys had complained about her performance, she quickly backtracked. They'd praised everything she set in front of them, and tonight's menu was no exception. Not that they'd tasted any of it yet, but, as Lucie had told her this morning, *"Ne vous inquiétez pas, Chloe. J'ai foi en vous."* Don't worry, Chloe. I have faith in you.

Well, that made one of them.

Lucie and Hugo didn't seem to realize or care that they were paying her more than they should for a party they could have had catered for less by almost any bistro, brasserie or café in New York. But Chloe realized they were doing that. And in addition to making her feel guilty and inadequate, it was driving her crazy. She just hadn't been at her best since leaving Hogan's employ. And the whole reason she'd left Hogan's employ was because she'd feared losing her ability to be at her best.

Well, okay, maybe that wasn't really the reason she'd left Hogan. But she was beginning to wonder if she'd ever be at her best again.

He'd called her every day the first week after she left, but she'd never answered. So he'd left messages, asking her to meet him so they could talk, even if it meant someplace public, because even though he didn't understand her desire to not tell him where she was working now, he respected it, and *C'mon, Chloe, pick up the phone, just talk to me, we need to figure this out.* As much as she'd wanted to delete the messages without even listening to them, something had compelled her to listen…and then melt a little inside at the sound of his voice. But even after hearing his messages, she still couldn't bring herself to delete them. Deleting Hogan just felt horribly wrong. Even if she never intended to see him again.

I want you.

The words he said the night she left still rang in her ears. She wanted Hogan, too. It was why she couldn't stay with him. Because wanting led to loving. And loving led to needing. And needing someone opened you up to all kinds of dangers once that person was gone. Losing someone you needed was like losing air that you needed. Or water. Or food. Without those things, you shriveled up and died.

I think you pretty much just told me you love me.

Those words, too, wouldn't leave her alone. Because yes, as much as she'd tried to deny it, and as much as she'd tried to fight it, she knew she loved Hogan. But she didn't need him. She wouldn't need him. She couldn't need him. And the only way to make sure of that was to never see him again.

Unfortunately, the moment Chloe entered the Fleurys' salon in her best chef's whites with a tray of canapés, she saw that her determination to not see Hogan, like so many other things in life, was completely out of her control. The Fleurys had invited him to their dinner party.

Or maybe they'd invited Anabel, she thought when she saw her other former employer at Hogan's side, and he was her plus-one. Whatever the case, Chloe was suddenly in the same room with him again, and that room shrank to the size of a macaron the moment she saw him. He was wearing the same shirt with the same vest and tie she'd picked out for him the night of his own dinner party, but he'd replaced his battered Levi's with a pair of pristine dark wash jeans that didn't hug his form nearly as well.

As if he'd sensed her arrival the moment she noted his, he turned to look at her where she stood rooted in place. Then he smiled one of his toe-curling, heat-inducing smiles and lifted a hand in greeting. All Chloe wanted to do then was run back into the kitchen and climb into a cupboard and forget she ever saw him. Because seeing him only reminded her how much she loved him. How much she wanted him. How much— dammit—she needed him.

Instead, she forced her feet to move forward and into the crowd. Miraculously, she made it without tripping or sending a canapé down anyone's back. Even more astonishing, she was able to make eye contact with Hogan when she paused in front of him and Anabel. But it was Anabel who broke the silence that settled over them.

"Oh, yum. *Brie gougères.* Chloe, I absolutely love your *brie gougères.*" She scooped up two and smiled. "I love them so much, I need to take one over to Hillary Thornton. Talk amongst yourselves."

And then she was gone, leaving Chloe and Hogan

alone for the first time in almost a month. Alone in the middle of a crowd of people who were waiting to try her *brie gougères* and her *choux de Bruxelles citrons* and the half dozen other hors d'oeuvres she'd prepared for the evening. None of which had turned out quite right.

"Hi," he said softly.

"Hello," she replied.

"How've you been?"

"All right." The reply was automatic. Chloe had been anything but all right since she last saw him. The same way her food had been anything but all right. The same way life itself had been anything but all right.

They said nothing more for a moment, only stood in the middle of a room fit for a king, as nervous as a couple of teenagers on their first date.

Finally, Hogan said, "What are you doing after the party?"

Again, Chloe replied automatically. "Cleaning up the kitchen."

He grinned, and Chloe did her best not to have an orgasm on the spot. "What about after that?" he asked.

"I'll, um… I'll probably have a glass of wine."

"Want some company?"

She told herself to tell him no. That she hadn't wanted company for years. Lots of years. And lots of months and weeks and days—she just couldn't remember precisely how many. But she knew she was lying. She did want company. She'd wanted company for years. Lots of years and months and weeks and days. She just hadn't allowed herself to have it. Not until one glorious night three weeks, six days, twenty hours and fifty-two minutes ago, a night she would carry with her forever. Even so, she couldn't bring herself to say that to Hogan.

"Anabel is friends with the Fleurys," he said. "She told me the view from their roof is spectacular."

"It is," Chloe replied.

He looked surprised. "So you've been up there?"

She nodded. She'd gone up to the Fleurys' terrace a number of times since coming to work for the Fleurys. She didn't know why. The New York nights had turned cold and damp with winter setting in so solidly and hadn't been conducive to rooftop wanderings. But wander to the roof she had, over and over again. The view was indeed spectacular. She could see all of New York and Central Park, glittering like scattered diamonds on black velvet. But it had nothing on the view from Hogan's house. Probably because Hogan wasn't part of the view.

"Maybe you could show me?" he asked. "I mean, once you've finished with your party duties. Anabel said the Fleurys' parties tend to go pretty late, and she hates to be the first to leave."

"She was the first to leave at your party," Chloe said.

"That was because she was a woman on a mission that night."

"What mission?"

Hogan smiled again. But he didn't elaborate. "What time do you think you'll be finished?"

Chloe did some quick calculating in her head. "Maybe eleven?"

"Great. I'll meet you up on the roof at eleven."

She told herself to decline. Instead, she said, "Okay."

He looked at the tray. "What do you recommend?"

What a loaded question. All she said, though, was "Try the tapenade."

She remembered belatedly that he probably had no idea what tapenade was and was about to identify the proper selection, but he reached for exactly the right thing. Her surprise must have shown on her face, because he told her, "I've been doing some homework."

And then he was moving away, fading into the crowd, and Chloe was able to remember she had a job she should be doing. A job that would fall just short of success because, like the hors d'oeuvres and so much more, nothing she did was quite right anymore.

Instead, the party went off without a hitch, and every dish was perfect—if she did say so herself. Even the moments when she served Hogan, where she feared she would spill something or misarrange something or forget something, all went swimmingly. By the time she finished cleaning up the kitchen— which also went surprisingly well—she was starting to feel like her old self again. Like her old cooking self anyway. The other self, the one that wasn't so focused on cooking, still felt a little shaky.

She had just enough time to go to her room for a quick shower to wash off the remnants of *Moules à la crème Normande* and *carottes quatre epices*. Then she changed into blue jeans and a heavy black sweater and headed for the roof.

Hogan was already there waiting for her. He'd donned a jacket to ward off the chill and stood with his hands in his pockets, gazing at the New York skyline in the distance. The full moon hung like a bright silver dollar over his head, and she could just make out a handful of stars higher in the night sky. Her heart hammered hard as she studied him, sending her blood zinging through her body fast enough to make her light-headed. Or maybe it was the simple presence of Hogan doing that. How had she gone nearly a month without seeing him? Without hearing him? Without talking to him and feeling the way he made her feel? How had she survived without him?

Although she wouldn't have thought he could hear her over the sounds of the city, he spun around the moment she started to approach. The night was cold, but the closer she drew to him, the warmer she felt. But she stopped when a good foot still separated them, because she just didn't trust herself to not touch him if she got too close.

"Hi," he said again.

"Hello."

"It's good to see you."

"It's good to see you, too."

A moment passed where the two of them only gazed at each other in silence. Then Hogan said, "So I looked up impracticability."

She barely remembered using that as an excuse to cancel her contract with him. How could she have wanted to do that? How could she have thought the only way to survive was to separate herself from Hogan? She'd been dying a little inside every day since leaving him.

"Did you?" she asked.

"Yeah. I even used a legal dictionary, just to make sure I got the right definition. What it boiled down to is that one party of a contract can be relieved of their obligations if those obligations become too expensive, too difficult or too dangerous for them to perform."

"That about covers it, yes."

He nodded. "Okay. So I thought about it, and I figured it couldn't have become too expensive for you to perform your job, because I was paying for everything."

She said nothing in response to that, because, obviously, that wasn't the reason she'd had to leave.

"And it wasn't becoming too difficult for you to perform your job," he continued, "since you were excellent at it, and you made it look so easy and you seemed to love it."

"Thank you. And yes, I did love it. Do love it," she hastened to correct herself. Because she did still love to cook. She just didn't love cooking for the Fleurys as much as she'd loved cooking for Hogan. She hadn't loved cooking for anyone as much as she'd loved cooking for Hogan. Probably because it wasn't just cooking for Hogan she'd loved.

"So if you didn't think your job was too expensive or too difficult to perform," he said, "then you must have thought it was too dangerous."

Bingo. Because loving anything—or anyone— more than cooking was very dangerous indeed for Chloe. Loving anything—or anyone—more than cooking could very well be the end of her. At least that was what she'd thought since Samuel's death. Now she was beginning to think there were things much more harmful to her—and much more dangerous for her—than loving and wanting and needing. Like not loving. And not wanting. And not needing. She'd spent six years avoiding those things, and she'd told herself she was surviving, when, really, she'd been dying a little more inside every day. Losing more of herself every day. Until she'd become a shell of the woman she used to be. A woman who'd begun to emerge from that shell again the moment she met Hogan.

"Yes," she told him. But she didn't elaborate. She still didn't quite trust herself to say any of the things she wanted—needed—to say.

"So what was getting too dangerous?" he asked. "Were the knives too sharp? Because I can stock up on bandages, no problem."

At this, she almost smiled. But she still said nothing.

"Then maybe the stove was getting too hot?" he asked. "Because if that's the case, I can buy some fans for the kitchen. Maybe get a window unit for in there."

Chloe bit back another smile at the thought of a portable air conditioner jutting out of a window on the Upper East Side and dripping condensation onto the chicly dressed passersby below. She shook her head again. And still said nothing.

"Okay," he said. "I was hoping it wasn't this, but it's the only other thing I can think of. It was all that fresh, unprocessed whole food, wasn't it? I knew it. Someday scientists are going to tell us that stuff is poison and that boxed mac and cheese and tinned biscuits are the best things we can put in our bodies."

"Hogan, stop," she finally said. Because he was becoming more adorable with every word he spoke, and that was just going to make her fall in love with him all over again.

Then she realized that was ridiculous. She'd fallen

in love with Hogan a million times since meeting him. What difference would one more time make?

"Well, if it wasn't the sharp knives, and it wasn't the hot stove, and it wasn't the allegedly healthy food, then what was it that made working for me so dangerous?"

He was going to make her say it. But maybe she needed to say it. Admitting the problem was the first step, right? Now if she could just figure out the other eleven steps in the How-to-Fall-Out-of-Love-with-Someone program, she'd be all set. Of course, falling *out* of love with Hogan wasn't really the problem, was it? Then again, she was beginning to realize that falling *in* love with him wasn't so bad, either.

"It was you, Hogan," she said softly. "It was the possibility of falling in love with you." Then she made herself tell the truth. She closed her eyes to make it easier. "No, that's not it. It wasn't the possibility of falling in love with you. It was falling in love with you."

When he didn't reply, she opened first one eye, then the other. His smile now was completely different from the others. There was nothing teasing, nothing modest, nothing sweet. There was just love. Lots and lots of love.

"You can't fight it, Chloe," he said. "Trust me—I know. I've been trying to fight it for a month. Trying to give you the room you need to figure things out. Trying to figure things out myself. But the only thing I figured out was that I love you."

Heat swamped her midsection at hearing him say it so matter-of-factly. "Do you?"

"Yep. And I know you love me, too."

"Yes."

For a moment they only gazed at each other in silence, as if they needed a minute to let that sink in. But Chloe didn't need any extra time to realize how she felt about Hogan. She'd recognized it the night they made love. She'd just been trying to pretend otherwise since then.

Hogan took a step toward her, close enough now for her to touch him. "Do you think you'll ever stop loving me?" he asked.

She knew the answer to that immediately. "No. I know I won't."

"And I'm not going to stop loving you."

He lifted a hand to her face, cupping her jaw lightly, running the pad of his thumb over her cheek. Chloe's insides turned to pudding at his touch, and she tilted her head into his caress.

"So here's the thing," he said softly. "If we both love each other, and neither of us is going to stop, then why aren't we together?"

She knew the answer to that question, too. Because it would be too painful to lose him. But that was a stupid answer, because it was going to be painful to lose him whether they were together or not. Okay, then because she would live in fear of losing him for the rest of her life. But that didn't make any sense, either, because if she wasn't with him, then she'd already lost him. Okay, then because…because… There had to be a reason. She used to have a reason. If she could only remember what the reason was.

"It's too late for us, Chloe," he said when she didn't reply. "We love each other, and that's not going to change. Yeah, it's scary," he added, putting voice to her thoughts. "But don't you think the idea of life without each other is even scarier?"

Yes. It was. Being alone since Samuel's death had been awful. Although she could deny it all she wanted, Chloe hadn't liked being alone. She'd tolerated it because she hadn't thought there was any other way for her to live. But she hadn't liked it. The time she'd spent living with Hogan and being with Hogan was the best time she'd had in years. Some years and some months and some weeks and some days she didn't have to keep a tally of anymore. Because she wasn't alone anymore. Or, at least, she didn't have to be. Not unless she chose to.

Hogan was right. It was scary to fall in love. No, it was terrifying. But the prospect of living the rest of her life without him was far, far worse.

"I want to come back to work for you," she said.

He shook his head. "Just come back. We'll figure out the rest of it as we go."

Chloe finally smiled. A real smile. The kind of smile she hadn't smiled in a long time. Because she was happy for the first time in a long time. Truly, genuinely happy. "Okay," she said. "But I'm still not going to cook you taco meatloaf."

Hogan smiled back. "No worries. We can share the cooking. I need to introduce you to the joys of chicken pot pie, too."

Instead of wincing this time, Chloe laughed. Then she stood up on tiptoe, looped her arms around Hogan's neck and kissed him. Immediately, he roped his arms around her waist and pulled her close, covering her mouth with his and tasting her deeply as if she were the most delectable dish he'd ever had.

Chloe wasn't sure how they made it to her bedroom on the first floor without alerting the dinner guests still lingering in the Fleurys' salon, since she and Hogan nearly fell down every flight of the back stairs on their way, too reluctant to break their embrace and shedding clothes as they went. Somehow, though, they—and even their discarded clothing—did make it. He shoved the door closed behind them, then pressed her back against it, crowding his big body into hers as he kissed her and kissed her and kissed her.

By now, she was down to her bra, and the fly of her jeans was open, and he was down to his T-shirt, his belt loosened, his hard shaft pressing against her belly. She wedged her hand between their bodies enough to unfasten the button at his waist and tug down the zipper, then she tucked her hand into his briefs to press her palm against the naked length of him. He surged harder at her touch, and a feral growl escaped him before he intensified their kiss. He dropped his hands to her hips, shoving her jeans and panties down to her knees, then he thrust his hand between her legs to finger the damp folds of flesh he encountered.

This time Chloe was the one to purr with pleasure, nipping his lip lightly before touching the tip of her tongue to the corner of his mouth. Hogan rubbed his long index finger against her again, then inserted it inside her, caressing her with the others until she felt as if she would melt away. With his free hand, he slipped first one bra strap, then the other, from her shoulders, urging the garment to her waist to bare her breasts. Then he covered one with his entire hand, thumbing the sensitive nipple to quick arousal.

Her breath was coming in quick gasps now, and her

hand moved harder on his ripe shaft in response. He rocked his hips in time with her touches, until the two of them were *this close* to going off together. Just as the tightening circles of her orgasm threatened to spring free, he pulled their bodies away from the door and began a slow dance toward the bed. The moment they reached their destination, she yanked Hogan's shirt over his head, tossed it to the floor and pushed at his jeans to remove them, as well. Taking her cue, he went to work on removing what was left of her clothing, too.

When she turned to lower the bed's coverlet, he moved behind her, flattening his body against hers and covering her breasts with both hands. But when she bent forward to push away the sheets, he splayed his hand open at the middle of her back, gently bent her lower, and then, slow and deep, entered her from behind.

"Oh," she cried softly, curling her fingers tightly into the bedclothes. "Oh, Hogan…"

He moved both hands to her hips, gripping them tightly as he pushed himself deeper inside her. For long moments, he pumped her that way, the friction of his body inside hers turning Chloe into a hot, wanton thing. Finally, he withdrew, taking his time and caressing her fanny as he did, skimming his palms over her warm flesh before giving it a gentle squeeze. He tumbled them both into bed, lying on his back and pulling her atop him, straddling him. Instead of entering her again, though, he moved her body forward, until the hot feminine heart of her was poised for his taste.

His tongue flicking against her already sensitive flesh was her undoing. Barely a minute into his ministrations, Chloe felt the first wave of an orgasm wash over her. She moaned as it crested, waiting for the next swell. That one came and went, too, followed by another and another. But just when she thought she'd seen the last one, he turned her onto her back and positioned himself above her.

As he entered her again, another orgasm swept over her. But this time, Hogan went with her. He thrust inside her a dozen times, then emptied himself deep inside her. Only then did the two of them fall back to the bed, panting for breath and groping for coherent thought. Never had Chloe felt more satisfied than she did in that moment. Never had she felt so happy. So contented. So free of fear.

Loving wasn't scary, she realized then. Avoiding love—that was scary. Loving was easy. So love Hogan she would. For as long as she could. Because, *oh là là*, living without loving wasn't living at all.

It was a hot day in Brooklyn, the kind of summer day that cried out for something cold for dessert. So Chloe decided to add *tulipes de sorbet* to the daily menu of her new café, *La Fin des Haricots*. They would go nicely with the rest of the light French fare the little restaurant had become famous for in Williamsburg over the last year and a half, and it would make Hogan happy, since it was a reasonable compromise for the chocolate ice cream he preferred.

They'd compromised on a lot over the last eighteen months. He'd sold his grandfather's Lenox Hill town house, along with Philip Amherst's other properties—save the one in Paris, of course, where they planned to spend the month of August every year, starting with their honeymoon last summer. Then they purchased a funky brownstone they'd been renovating ever since, and in whose backyard Chloe had planted a small garden and built a small greenhouse. Hogan's chain of Dempsey's Garages was fast becoming reality—he was already operating three in the city and had acquired properties for a half dozen more. And *La Fin des Haricots* was fast becoming a neighborhood favorite. They worked hard every day and loved hard every night, and on Sundays…

Sundays were sacred, the one day they dedicated completely to each other. Usually by spending much of it in bed, either eating or talking or loafing or—their favorite—making love.

Hogan's other passion in life was the scholarship fund he'd set up in his parents' names for kids from both his old and his new neighborhoods. He'd also donated significantly to Samuel's fund. The losses of their pasts would help bring happiness into others' futures, and that made the two of them about as rich as a couple of people could be.

Life was good, Chloe thought as she finished up the menu and handed it off to her head waiter to record it on the ever-changing chalkboard at the door. Then she buttoned up her chef's jacket—one that fit, since she had packed Samuel's away and wore her own now—and headed back to the kitchen. Her kitchen. She might still be cooking for other people, but it was in her own space. A space where she was putting down roots, in a place she would live for a very long time, with a man she would love forever. It still scared her a little when she thought about how much she loved her husband. But it scared her more to think about not loving him.

He met her at the end of her workday as he always did, on this occasion arriving at the kitchen door in his grease-stained coveralls, since it was the end of his workday, too. They ate dinner together at the chef's table, then, hand in hand, they walked home. Together they opened a bottle of wine. Together they enjoyed it on their roof. Together they made plans for their trip to Paris in August. And then together they went to bed, so they could make love together, and wake up together and start another day in the morning together.

Because together was what they were. And together was what they would always be. No matter where they went. No matter what they did. No matter what happened.

And that, Chloe thought as she did every night when they turned off the light, was what was truly *magnifique*.

* * * * *

HIS BRIDE
BY DESIGN

TERESA HILL

If I had to list all the poor people who had to listen to me whine over the writing of this book – while also moving from a house we'd lived in for 18 years and sending our baby girl off to college – the list would probably be longer than the book.

But you all know who you are, and I thank you sincerely and say once again, I'm sorry, truly sorry. Couldn't have done it without you all.

Chapter One

Dreams did come true.

People had always told Chloe Allen that, but she hadn't quite believed it until the lights in the tent went down, the music rose and she had the world of New York fashion at her feet. If they loved her designs, Chloe would get absolutely everything she ever wanted.

"I think I'm going to throw up," she whispered to her cousin and first assistant, Robbie, who'd been hovering by her side the whole morning. Her business manager and accountant, Addie, who she claimed as a sister, was in the back somewhere, as was Robbie's twin, Connie, her second assistant. This was truly a family business.

"You can throw up later," Robbie said. "Right now, you have to do one last check of the models and start the show, before something happens."

"What do you mean, something happens? Something bad?"

Because Chloe felt it. Even standing in the dark, surrounded by the models in all her beautiful dresses ready to walk that runway, she felt like something bad was coming.

Robbie gave her a little shove to the spot by the entrance to the runway, thrusting her into the spotlight, and from there it was all a blur until it was time to send the last dress down the runway. Eloise, the snottiest model of all, stood before Chloe, pouting that usual model pout, except it always seemed extra-pouty when aimed at Chloe. She took off, doing that odd, abrupt model strut, the dress in ecru-colored silk charmeuse swishing and swaying beautifully as she walked down the runway.

The crowd was on its feet, cheering madly.

Chloe started to cry, couldn't help it.

She'd done it!

The models lined up and took one more turn around the runway, all together. Chloe fell into step behind Eloise and her pretend groom, who as Chloe understood it was actually Eloise's boyfriend of the moment.

They got to the spot where Chloe's fiancé, Bryce, a fashion photographer, stood covering the show, and their friends in the audience started calling for Bryce to join Chloe on the runway. He jumped up there, lean and fashionable in black jeans and a plain black T-shirt, smiling that dazzling Bryce smile, giving Chloe a kiss on the cheek. They stood at the end of the runway with Eloise and her model groom/boyfriend, cameras flashing from all directions.

Chloe finally started to breathe, to let it all sink in. The show had gone off without a hitch, the audience applauding wildly!

Then she felt Eloise fidgeting, heard a quiet hiss of sharp words. Chloe shot her a glance that said, *Surely this can wait until we're off the runway!* Eloise's boyfriend whispered back furiously, Bryce, too. People started to notice, falling silent and then whispering themselves.

Not now. Not now. Not now! Chloe chanted to herself.

"You bastard!" Eloise screamed, but not at her boyfriend. At Bryce? "You just couldn't keep your hands to yourself, could you?"

Chloe whimpered, all the breath going out of her in a rush.

Her fiancé was involved with her top model?

It was such a cliché, especially finding out while standing here at the end of the runway, like making it all the way down the aisle of a church to the altar only to find disaster. This was supposed to be Chloe's day. Didn't they understand? She was the real bride here!

Eloise shook a long, pointy finger in Bryce's face. "I told you to stay away. I told you I wouldn't stand for this anymore."

Bryce looked pale and defeated. Chloe's mind had gone foggy and sluggish. Eloise was telling Bryce to stay away? So, Bryce was like…annoying Eloise? Stalking her?

Laughter trickled in, getting louder and louder, and then the camera flashes became positively blinding. Chloe stood frozen in the midst of it.

Then she realized that Eloise didn't seem to be trying to keep Bryce away from her. She'd planted herself between Bryce and her model boyfriend/groom, shrieking, "He's mine!"

That couldn't be right.

Bryce was sexy as could be, and somehow he'd become Chloe's. He wanted her, despite spending his days photographing some of the most beautiful women in the world, unreal and yet gorgeous in that odd, perfect way of theirs.

Chloe caught a look passing not between Bryce and

Eloise, but Bryce and the male model. The ridiculously toned, tanned, good-looking male model.

An intimate, knowing, regretful look.

Which meant…

"Oh, no," Chloe whispered, fighting with all she had in her not to cry. Not here. Not now.

Chloe, wannabe wedding dress designer extraordinaire, part of the big machine that made little girls' wedding dreams come true, had a fiancé who was sleeping with another man!

James Elliott IV did not in any way keep up with fashion news.

His idea of fashion was—when he was feeling really daring—to forego his traditional white dress shirt in favor of one in pale yellow or perhaps blue.

But one fine September morning, as he walked from his apartment in Tribeca to his office in the financial district and stopped to buy his *Wall Street Journal* at his favorite newsstand, it was impossible to miss the fashion news. It was plastered across the front pages of the tabloids for all to see.

Some crazy model in a huge, billowing wedding dress jumping a guy on a runway, looking like she was about to claw his eyes out in the next instant.

Waiting for his turn to pay, James decided the model did indeed look crazy, but then most of them were, he suspected. Starvation made women mean and at least a little bit crazy. The photo showed that she had literally jumped on the guy, had her legs wrapped around his waist and her fingernails poised and ready to strike, the guy twisting to get out of the way.

In the background was a model in a tux, looking like he

wanted to jump in, but didn't have the balls to do it. And down at the bottom, in the foreground…it looked like…

"Chloe?"

She was his ex.

The ex, if he let himself admit it. The one who'd really gotten to him, endearing herself to him like no one else, infuriating him, baffling him, hurting him, until they'd finally gone their separate ways.

What the hell had happened to Chloe?

The headline on the tabloid read Taking Bridezilla to a Whole New Level: Bloodshed at Fashion Week as Eloise Goes on a Rampage!

Bridezilla?

And who was Eloise?

The next tabloid blared Wedding Dress Designer Chloe and Model Eloise's Man-on-Man Nightmare! Their Men Cheating… With Each Other!

James grimaced on Chloe's behalf.

And the third said Designer Chloe's Fashion Week Debut Every Woman's Wedding Nightmare: The Groom-to-Be Prefers Men!

Now James felt really bad.

There'd been a time right after their breakup when he'd been mad enough to want Chloe's heart broken, but this seemed unreasonably harsh. If it was even true. Most of the stuff in these rags wasn't, after all.

"Mr. Elliott?" The puzzled voice of the newspaper vendor, Vince, interrupted him. "You want one of those tabloids today?"

"What?" He looked at the man who'd been selling him financial news for years. Nothing but financial news. "Of course not. I was just…waiting to pay."

Vince shrugged like he didn't believe a word of it, then said, "Hot story this morning. We usually don't get anything good that normal people care about during Fashion Week. But a girl-on-girl brawl over two men…that's hot!"

"Chloe and that model got into it?"

"Who?"

"The wedding dress designer."

"Yeah." Vince nodded enthusiastically. "Right there on the runway, I heard. Hope somebody got video. I could get into that. You know that girl? Chloe?"

"Used to," he admitted. What the hell? It was Vince. They were morning newsstand buddies.

"She looks kind of mousy in most of the pictures," Vince said. "Like that Eloise chick could tear her apart if she wanted to."

James would never have said Chloe was mousy. She liked to pretend she was tough as nails and incredibly self-sufficient, especially when it came to her career. But when it came to her personal life, she could be sweet, gentle, vulnerable at times, fun, full of life, until she drove a man absolutely crazy. None of that equated to mousiness.

Although he had to admit, in the brawl photos, she looked tiny and sad standing there dejectedly on the sidelines. It looked like her show had been ruined, and she'd been working her whole life for a chance like that. She'd wanted it more than she'd wanted him, that was for sure. And it had just burned him up at the time.

"Sure you don't want one of those?" Vince asked, pointing at the tabloids. "They've got more pictures inside."

"No, thanks." No way he was going to buy that on the street. He'd swipe his assistant's copy.

Strolling into his office on the twenty-sixth floor, he greeted his secretary and his secretary's secretary and then asked Marcy, his assistant, to come into his office, a large, starkly bare room with a massive, gleaming wooden desk, big, cushy leather chairs and an expansive view all the way down to New York Harbor and Battery Park.

He believed in order, discipline, control, hard work and the power of his own mind. People called him a financial genius, and he just smiled and went on with his work. While the current times were challenging, they certainly hadn't caught him by surprise, and he was doing just fine while others around him floundered. Never believe the hype about anything—especially the economy—he always told people. The philosophy had served him well.

He wondered now if he'd hyped the whole idea of Chloe in his mind to an impossible level. He couldn't have been as happy with her as he remembered or as miserable without her, he told himself.

And he wasn't obsessing.

Just…curious.

"Mr. Elliott? Are you feeling all right?" Marcy asked.

"Of course," he claimed, then couldn't quite bring himself to ask for what he really wanted. He cleared his throat, adjusted his tie, frowned. "I just…I need…I want to see your copy of the *New York Mirror*."

Marcy sputtered. Her eyes got all big and round and then her cheeks turned red. "But I don't—"

"Oh, yes, you do. I know you have that thing, and I want it—"

"But why?"

"You know why. I'd bet a thousand dollars you know exactly why."

She looked truly flustered then, but didn't deny either having the damned thing or knowing why he wanted it. She'd come to work for him in the immediate post-Chloe era. He'd been in a truly ugly mood for weeks, and had ended up springing for unscheduled bonuses to her and a handful of other staff members forced to put up with him, as a way of saying he was sorry.

"Okay. I'll go get it," Marcy said, turning on her heel and heading out.

"And don't you dare tell anyone!" he yelled as she opened the door, his secretary and his secretary's secretary peering through, looking worried.

Great. Just great.

Marcy came back with the tabloid carefully rolled up tightly so no one could see what it was. At least she was embarrassed to have it. She scowled as she handed it to him, then reached over to type something into his computer.

"You'll want the tabloid for the photos, but the best written account is here." She pointed to a blog now up on his computer screen, then retreated from his office in an embarrassed huff.

James glanced through the tabloid photos, grimacing at what he saw, then turned to the blog.

The Bride Blog: News of all things bridal.

Bridal Brawl Breaks Out at NY Fashion Week!

Talk about a Bridal Nightmare!

Forget the bridesmaids! It's the other men modern-day brides have to worry about, as we saw in the amazing brawl that broke out at New York Fashion Week.

Wedding dress designer Chloe Allen, plucked from obscurity mere months ago when gorgeous pop star Jaden Lawrence got married in a Chloe gown, was having her first showing at Fashion Week when everything suddenly went horribly wrong.

It seems Chloe's fiancé, veteran fashion photographer Bryce Gorman, just couldn't keep his hands off the male model posing as the groom to model extraordinaire Eloise's bride at what was to be the climax of the show.

And what a climax it turned out to be!

One doesn't think of models like the beautiful Eloise as the kind to ever worry about losing a man to anyone, but lose him she did, and she clearly put the blame on Bryce Gorman.

Eloise jumped him—literally—designer wedding gown and all. She wrapped those incredibly long legs around his waist and held on tight, her long, pale pink fingernails clawing at his face, supposedly drawing blood.

Bryce swung around trying to dislodge her, as her long train and veil floated around them in an odd mélange of satin, lace and bridal horror that will not soon be forgotten.

So far the only video clips of the scene have been particularly unsatisfying. (A free bridal bouquet to the first person who sends a good video of the bridal brawl to this blog.)

Meanwhile, traumatized brides, especially the ones closest to their big day, have been writing to the Bride Blog like mad to say they're keeping a close eye on those groomsmen and any close friends of their grooms.

It seems that old nightmare of standing at the altar, surrounded by friends and family, and finding out at the last minute that the groom had a little fling with one of the bridesmaids has been replaced with the modern-day equivalent.

The groom doing another man!

* * *

Chloe woke from her post-apocalyptic haze the day after the show, praying it had all been a horrible nightmare and that she could do it all over again. Even for her—a woman who liked to think of herself as highly creative—the previous day had been outlandishly bad.

She looked up and there was Addie, whom Chloe claimed as a half sister, although no one had ever done the paternity tests to be sure. Chloe's father had slept with Addie's mother at about the right time, and that was enough for the two of them, who found each other much more reliable than their father.

"Tell me it didn't really happen," Chloe begged.

"Oh, honey. I wish I could." Addie sat down on the bed, her back against the headboard, offering Chloe a shoulder if she needed it.

Chloe leaned her head on Addie's shoulder and thought this had to be the absolute worst day of her life. Yesterday had been horrible, but her family had closed in around her, gotten her out of the tent and then poured drinks down her throat until everything became a blur.

Today, she didn't have the luxury of alcohol or denial. "I thought he was the one," she cried.

"I know, sweetie."

Addie, kindly, did not point out that Chloe always believed every new man in her life was *the one*. She wasn't stupid, just ever hopeful. At least that's what Chloe tried to tell herself. Although after being engaged three times and never making it to the altar, it was getting harder and harder to believe.

Her family loved weddings. They married over and over again. And the wedding was always the high point. All their relationships went downhill from there. Chloe thought she was breaking the pattern thus far by not marrying, but even that hadn't protected her from her own unique wedding curse.

There was Fiancé No. 1, her high school sweetheart. Chloe liked to think they'd merely been too young to know what they wanted, no giant failure there or any kind of sign.

Bryce, No. 3, was sexy, fun, confident and in the business, someone who understood exactly what it took to be a success. He had come along at the perfect time.

When Chloe was just getting over No. 2.

Addie said that timing was the only reason Chloe ever gave Bryce the time of day, but Chloe truly didn't think so. She wouldn't fall for one man to the point of becoming engaged to him—all just to get over another man, would she?

No. 2—although he would absolutely hate being thought of as second in anything—was James Elliott IV, one of the most eligible bachelors in New York, according to several magazine lists. Chloe didn't talk about No. 2.

"Wait a minute," Addie said, pouncing on her. "You're not even thinking about Bryce. You're thinking about… the other one!"

"Am not," Chloe claimed.

"You are so!"

"Well, now I am! Why did you have to say that?"

"Because you got that look. That look you only get when you're thinking about him! About—"

"Don't say it! Don't you dare say his name!"

"About good old No. 2," Addie said, looking quite smug about it.

"Haven't I been through enough humiliation already?" Chloe asked. "Without going into my long list of failures with men?"

"True," Addie agreed. "Sorry."

Chloe frowned. She hadn't even gotten out of bed yet, and already the day looked bleak. While her personal life might be truly disastrous, she'd always been so much better at managing her professional life. The fact that the two had now become entwined, her personal life mess spilling over into a huge career mess, was more than a little unsettling.

"Okay, how bad is it this morning?" Chloe asked. "Everyone saw…everything yesterday?"

"And got pictures, I'm afraid," Addie admitted.

Chloe groaned, seeing the explosion of camera flashes in her face once again.

"There are people who claim all publicity is good publicity," Addie tried.

"You've never been one of those people," Chloe reminded her.

"I could have been wrong about that all this time."

Not likely, but Chloe loved her for saying so.

"Okay, here it is." Addie spilled the ugly truth: "You're front-page news in all the tabloids today."

Chloe winced.

"A feat normally achieved only by celebrities and politicians in the midst of major sex scandals," she added.

"And here I never set that as one of my career goals."

"On the bright side, your name is out there once again."

"Except now I've designed a dress for a wedding nightmare—"

Addie looked horrified. "Don't say that! Don't you ever say that! Women get a little crazy about their weddings. A little…weird and controlling and fanatical and superstitious. You know that! They're all worried some disaster will strike."

"Exactly. And when they think of getting married in a Chloe original, they'll think disaster, guaranteed!"

"Chloe, I swear, never, ever say that again. Do you hear me? It's like tempting the Wedding Gremlins to attack."

"They already attacked! I mean, my fiancé was doing the groom. What else could possibly happen?"

"Oh, my God!" Addie crossed herself in horror. "Never, ever, ever, ever say that! The moment women start to believe your dresses are bad luck, you're dead as a wedding dress designer. We are happy people who sell wedding dreams. We believe in love, fairy tales, happily-ever-afters and all that crap."

"Okay!" Chloe said obediently. She could always count on Addie for a pep talk. "Sorry. I just had a bad moment, but I'm done now."

"Fine, but it can't go out of this room."

"Of course not," Chloe said, then had a flash of her sobbing, drinking and talking to someone. She had that same really icky feeling she'd had before the runway show, when she just knew something would go wrong.

Had she done something last night? Other than have a little too much to drink and cry a bit? She didn't think so, but she really couldn't remember.

Must have been a bad dream, she decided.

After all, her fiancé was sleeping with the groom.

What could possibly top that?

Addie left, and Chloe lay there in her bed a moment longer, working up the courage to face the day. Weariness weighed her down. She let her eyes drift shut and her mind float into that never-never land between real sleep and a groggy kind of wakefulness.

She was at the bar, last night but not really last night. She'd laughed, cried, gone over her entire, dreary history with men, and then, just when things seemed their bleakest, she'd looked to the end of the bar, and *he'd* been there.

Not Bryce.

James.

Chloe groaned, half in pain and half in longing, knowing she was crazy even for dreaming of him.

He looked so good. But then, James always had.

He could have been a model himself, although he hated to hear it. In fact, they'd met when Chloe had mistaken him for a model late for one of her shows. He had that rare quality of being an absolutely beautiful man, but still looking unmistakably masculine, as so few models did.

In the bar, he walked over to her, looking at her with the kind of understanding and concern that made her ache. Then he reached out with one of those perfect hands of his and wiped away her tears. And in the kindest move of all, put his beautiful body between her and the rest of the room, creating a tiny, safe space for her when she was so miserable she just wanted to curl up into a little ball and disappear.

He smelled so good, the way he always did. He'd admitted with a reluctance that bordered on pain that he still thought about her, that he missed her and that he just had to come see for himself that she was all right.

It was ridiculous.

Even in her dream, she realized that.

James Elliott was too proud, too stubborn and too independent to ever admit he missed anyone. But it was a lovely dream, bittersweet and achingly real.

Then she woke up once again, not twenty minutes later, in her bed, yet still very much inside her very own nightmare as fashion runway roadkill.

James fought the impulse all day, but nightfall found him standing on the corner across the street from the big, old Victorian near Prospect Park in Brooklyn that Chloe shared with her various relatives, who all worked for her in the first-floor showroom.

He stared up at the window of the small attic she'd turned into a tiny apartment for herself, where she had some measure of privacy. This after fighting with himself all day about coming anywhere near here.

It felt weirdly stalkerish to be there, just looking up at her window, and he was a man who did not stalk women. He just needed to know she was okay.

Which he couldn't tell from simply staring at her house.

Still, he felt a little better, just being this close to her.

He waited until the last light went out in her little attic, saw the slightest impression of her, he thought, ghostlike against the sheer curtains, as she walked across the room. He imagined her climbing into bed, her toes cold, letting her warm them on his, his hands hot against her cool, pale skin, tangling in her glorious hair.

So many nights they'd spent that way, together in that room.

He couldn't have her back, he told himself.

He'd made her crazy, and she'd done the same to him. He was as logical a man as there was on earth, and he knew without a doubt that no one needed to be hurt like that a second time.

So once the light was out, and he knew she was safe in her bed, at least for the night, he turned around and went home, swearing to himself that he wouldn't be back.

Chapter Two

The next morning, James faced the newsstand, hoping to see the usual mix of tabloid headlines screaming about drunken celebrities, corrupt politicians, alien sightings and baseball players on steroids.

No such luck.

That crazy model, Eloise, was back on the covers, in handcuffs, still wearing the wedding dress, her hair going every which way, mascara-streaked tears on her cheek, maybe a few drops of blood on the gown? The bridezilla label had been picked up by every tabloid he saw, now in this humongous font with letters the color of blood.

James winced as he stood there. *Bridezilla?* Had someone climbed a skyscraper in a bloody wedding gown and swatted at things? He didn't think so.

What about Chloe? He scanned the news. Supposedly in a fit of rage, she'd destroyed every gown in her showroom with a huge pair of scissors. No way James believed that.

She loved the clothes she made too much to ever destroy them, and Chloe didn't do *fits of rage.* She just didn't.

James got to the front of the line to hand over his money for his *Wall Street Journal,* and Vince said, "Your girl is back."

"Yeah, I see that."

"One of my customers just told me about this great video of the whole runway brawl," Vince confided. "YouTube, that thing the kids like on the computer? Type in 'Runway Brawl,' and it's supposed to come right up."

James nodded. He wouldn't be able to help himself. "I'll do that, Vince."

When he got to the office, he glared at Marcy, then gave a curt nod for her to follow him into his office. "People are online watching a video of the brawl at Chloe's show?"

"More than a hundred thousand people so far," Marcy said.

James grimaced. A hundred thousand? "Someone's keeping a count?"

"Of course. At the rate the video's being downloaded, it could go viral at any time."

Which would be bad for Chloe. "We need to stop that from happening."

"You can't stop it. It's already out there. It has a life of its own now."

"There has to be a way," he argued.

Marcy shrugged. "Maybe if Angelina Jolie actually left Brad Pitt or something equally earth-shattering."

James sighed. "I guess we can't make that happen."

"I can't. Unless you know how to find them, and you want to make a play for Angelina. I guess if you wanted me to do my best to seduce Brad…I mean, if you ordered me to, I'd have to do it for you."

James considered. "You're telling me you'd seduce Brad Pitt for me?"

"I'm a team player, sir," she claimed.

"Well, it's good to know you're willing, Marcy, if it ever comes to that."

"Yes, sir." Marcy made a face. "I'm afraid there's something else you need to know. Adam Landrey called. He said to tell you Chloe's company needs another infusion of cash."

James tried not to show anything in his face. "How much?"

"Six figures, at least." Marcy clearly disapproved. "You broke up with the woman, sold your interest to your friend, then guaranteed he wouldn't lose any money on the deal? You guaranteed his losses?"

"What if I did?" James argued.

"The two of you broke up!" Marcy repeated.

"I remember. Very well, thank you." He glared at her. "Your point?"

"Are you going to treat me this well if I leave you?" Marcy asked. "Because I've never had a guy be that nice to me after I left him."

"Leave me now, Marcy, or you might find out how badly I'll treat you."

She made a face, but left his office, closing the door behind her.

James went for the computer, found the video as easily as Vince said he would. It was like rubbernecking a particularly brutal car accident, except this accident involved someone he knew. Poor Chloe.

He picked up the phone to call Adam. When James and Chloe had broken up, she'd wanted him out, as an investor, immediately, and people weren't lining up to take a risk in the fashion industry. James felt bad about the way things ended between them. He felt guilty and couldn't bear to see her lose her design business, too. The only way he could get someone to take over his investment was to guarantee any losses the new investor might suffer.

Something Chloe would definitely not be happy about, even now, if she found out. It made James sound like some kind of controlling, overbearing, interfering man—all of which she'd accused him of being, when all he'd been trying to do was help. He was, after all, a brilliant businessman. What kind of a fiancé would he be if he didn't help her? Chloe was brilliant herself, but creatively, fashionably. She didn't have a businesslike bone in her body.

But all that was old news. Chloe should definitely be old news to him.

As long as nothing else really bad happened, she would be.

The Bride Blog: News of all things bridal.

Wedding Dress Designer Chloe's Shocking Video Confession: She Never Really Believed in Love.

After three failed engagements, did she put a secret curse on all her gowns? So that no one else gets a happily-ever-after, either?

The question on the minds of brides-to-be everywhere: How could anyone marry in a Chloe gown and ever think their love will last?

Word is that brides are storming Chloe's showroom in Brooklyn, demanding to return their dresses and to get their money back, much like the old-fashioned run on a failing bank.

How long can the House of Chloe hold out?

Time will tell, dear brides.

Time will tell.

Addie was scared to go downstairs that morning. They hadn't actually had *hordes* of angry brides demanding refunds so far, but they'd had enough to scare Addie. What would they find today, after the latest Bride Blog piece, and a new video of Chloe, drunk in the bar the night of the bridal brawl, talking about her diastrous three engagements and claiming she never believed in love? Chloe even described herself as "cursed in love" in the new video. So Addie was scared to even look outside.

She crept into the showroom without turning on any of the lights and peeked out between the window blinds in the corner farthest from the door, and there stood…one, two, three hysterical-looking brides already, bridal garment bags in hand, no doubt the much-feared, supposedly cursed wedding dresses inside, ready to be returned.

"Oh, my God!" Addie cried, then crept away from the window, for fear that they would see her.

They weren't even supposed to open the store until noon. This was the day they stayed open until 8:00 p.m., for brides-to-be who worked all day, and it was barely 9:00 a.m. now. They were about to be overrun, all because of that stupid Bride Blog woman!

James wasn't surprised later that morning to see Adam looking a little uncomfortable across the breakfast table, saying he was sorry, but he just couldn't put any more money into Chloe's business right now. Another friend had already clued James in to the fact that Adam himself was not in the best financial shape at the moment. Hardly anyone was.

"I'll take care of it." James held out a checkbook for his personal account.

"If that's what you want." Adam looked like he was dying to ask what James was doing, bailing out a woman who'd dumped him a year and a half ago.

Fair question, and not one James cared to answer for anyone, not even to himself. He shrugged, tried to play it off and said, "She's great in bed."

Adam looked like he didn't believe that reason at all, but volunteered, "I wouldn't know about that."

"Good," James said, ridiculously happy to hear it.

"I mean, she's adorable, funny, seems very sweet, obviously unusually talented and driven when it comes to her work."

James nodded. She was. What could he say? He hated the idea of her being hurt, of her losing her business, losing her dream. Other than that…he just didn't know.

As James handed his check to Adam, Marcy burst in, looking absolutely petrified. "There's a riot at Chloe's!"

James gaped at her. "Riot!"

Marcy nodded frantically. "That Bridal Blog lady? She said there's a riot breaking out at Chloe's store right now. Disgruntled brides storming the place, wanting their money back for the cursed dresses. It's all over Twitter. I thought you'd want to know right away."

He did. He'd ordered Marcy to keep him updated on the Chloe situation. But now that he knew this, he should probably run in the opposite direction. His life had gotten weird from the moment she came back into it. Not that she was truly in his life again. It just felt like it. From the distance of cyberspace, his favorite corner newsstand and that one night on the street corner across from her house, she was having her strange effect.

And he was afraid he liked it. He'd liked it the first time.

Life had been interesting, surprising, even felt a little…
fun. He could have that again. She was in trouble, and he
was going to help her. Crazy as it was, it was what he'd
wanted from the moment he'd looked up and seen her face
on those stupid tabloid covers.

"I'm going over there," he said, feeling better than he
had in ages.

Now that James had given in, he couldn't get to Chloe
fast enough.

"She makes me a little crazy," he confessed to Adam,
who'd gotten into the taxi with James, probably to see just
how crazy James was. Over a woman.

"Chloe's a very interesting person," Adam said carefully.

"She is. I just need to make sure she's okay," James
claimed, which was so obviously a lie. He was acting like
a madman over her.

"Hey, I like Chloe. She's great," Adam began.

"You swear you never slept with her?" James just
couldn't help but ask.

"I swear. My life is screwed up enough—"

He broke off as James scowled at him.

"I mean, complicated. My life is really complicated.
The last thing I need is to get involved with any woman.
Even one as interesting and cute as Chloe."

"Okay," James said, satisfied for the moment on that
count.

After about twenty minutes, he looked out the car window, and there, a block away, was Chloe's shop, that huge,
old Victorian where she lived with her two cousins and
Addie. He saw some kind of commotion out front and two,
no, three camera crews and some of those big, tall lights
the TV people used when they filmed things.

James charged into the mass of crazy, garment-bag-wielding brides, just as one of them drew back to take a swing at Chloe, who looked like a waif in her pajama bottoms and one of those stretchy little spaghetti-strap tops she liked to sleep in.

He thought those were the sexiest things he'd ever seen.

Especially when she wore one of those tops and nothing else except a little scrap of lacy panties. Chloe at her softest, most inviting, rumpled best.

God, he'd missed her!

Just then, another bride took a swing at her with her garment bag. The blow sent her stumbling backward. James stepped in and caught her hard against him, feeling a huge surge of relief, just having his arms around her. She went limp like she suddenly didn't have any bones and looked absolutely stunned, either from the blow or seeing him, he couldn't be sure. He lifted her up into his arms, glaring at the garment-bag-slinging woman, daring her or anyone else to come close to Chloe now that he had her.

Chloe reached out a hand to ever so lightly touch the side of his face, like she needed to know he was real. "James?"

"It's okay," he said, tucking her face against his chest, trying to reassure himself that she was truly okay. "I've got you."

When he lifted his head, he realized the crowd had quieted, finally.

They were all staring at him and her, and he realized there were a few still photographers there and that they were clicking away at the scene.

He didn't care.

"What the hell is going on here?" he asked, spotting Chloe's half sister, who'd always been the sanest one of the family.

"They want their money back for their dresses," she said, glaring at him.

"Write them checks, if that's what it takes to get them to leave," he said.

"I'll take care of it," said Adam, who'd fought his way to James's side. Adam, who had a check James had just written in the car, a check with lots of zeroes on it. Let everyone think Adam was covering the new debts, too. James would find a way to explain exactly what was going on to Chloe later.

His first thought was to get her away from this crowd, inside, maybe even carry her upstairs to her cute, quirky attic apartment, where he'd bumped his head on the low, sloped ceilings more than once. To the big cream-colored iron bed he used to share with her.

He hesitated, wondering if he was making a mistake by not taking her to his apartment in the city. Here she could kick him out whenever she pleased. When she got her second wind, she'd start her whole I-don't-need-anyone routine. But he couldn't risk giving this mob a second chance at her. That settled it. He took her inside.

Reluctantly, he set Chloe on her feet just inside the doorway. She seemed so slight standing there in front of him, so sad and defeated. He put his hand to the side of her face, tilting it up toward the light.

"Is it just this?" he asked, finding a slight swelling at her cheekbone. "Or are you hurt anywhere else?"

"I'm fine," she insisted.

But her face was pale as could be, a few tiny, light brown freckles that he knew she hated spread across her nose and cheeks. He used to tease her that her freckles looked like fairy dust and kiss each one. God, he'd lost his head completely over this woman the first time and was clearly in danger of doing the same thing again.

He couldn't help it.

He leaned down, his face lingering against hers, the tip of his nose pressed against her skin, soaking in the sweet, wild essence of Chloe, drawing his other hand through her pretty blond hair. It was even longer than it used to be and hanging loose and messy, the way he remembered it from rare mornings when she'd arisen from her bed before he left.

She was not a morning person, had always said she did her best work late at night. He didn't mind. It was fine to get up and dressed and be able to stand there and stare at her in a rumpled bed, her hair all wild around her face, those little sprinkles of fairy dust on her bare cheeks.

How had he ever managed to drag himself away?

How would he do it again?

Was he not going to think of saving himself from her a second time? Self-preservation was usually one of his strong suits. But he just couldn't bring himself to care at the moment.

He picked her up once again and carried her upstairs.

Chloe was still thinking it all had to be a dream.

Monkeys escaped from zoos at times and attacked people. Bears walked out of the woods and into camping areas. Every now and then an elephant got loose from its ankle stakes.

But who got attacked by crazy, garment-bag-wielding brides?

Didn't happen.

She'd never heard of it happening, never read about it, never imagined it. What made it even more improbable was that James Elliott IV would show up, charge into the crowd and rescue her from them. Yet, in her muddled mind, that's what had happened.

He laid her gently on the unmade bed in her little attic apartment, then sat down by her side, looking concerned and strong and tall and absolutely gorgeous.

She whimpered and then said, "Pinch me."

He frowned, touched his hand to the side of her face, feeling the spot where she thought the shoes in one of the brides' garment bags had gotten her. "Do you need a doctor? I'll take you."

"No, I mean…I think I'm dreaming…" Then thought how that might sound to him.

I was dreaming you came charging to my rescue, after a year without a word from you….

No, not going there.

Not with James, especially if he really was here.

"I dreamed I was being attacked by brides with bouquets," she said.

Which had him looking even more concerned. "Flowers? Chloe, those were garment bags—"

"No, I know that! I'm just confused," she said. "Not in that concussion sort of way. In that this-is-really-weird kind of way. You know?"

"Yes," he agreed, still looking worried.

God, he smelled so good, so familiar.

Chloe winced.

Not now. Her life was falling apart already. She could not do this now with him. She looked at him warily.

Collapsing in his arms the minute she saw him again was not how she'd ever imagined any reunion they might have. She was supposed to look her best, maybe all done up for a show, and he was supposed to look bleak and sad and lonely without her. He was supposed to say he missed her terribly, that he had never stopped thinking about her.

That's how it was supposed to go.

"All of that really happened just now?" she asked him.

"Yeah, it did."

"Pinch me," she said. "I have to be sure."

James smiled for the first time since she'd seen him again, looking heartbreakingly sexy and so appealing she thought about dragging him down into the bed with her right that minute.

"I'm not going to pinch you," he whispered, ever so slowly lowering his head to hers.

Her whole body started trembling before he even touched her, and she could have stopped it. Truly, she had time. And some sense of self-preservation that was still alive inside of her.

After all, her most recent ex-fiancé had just been outed as a sometimes-gay man, having an affair with Chloe's model's boyfriend, outed on the runway at her Fashion Week show. Even Chloe, stupid as she could be about men, knew that the last thing she needed was for James Elliott to kiss her, even just once.

But he'd charged to her rescue like Prince Charming, saving her from hysterical, rioting brides, after all. She still wasn't convinced this was real. So she let him kiss her. It wasn't the stupidest thing she'd done lately, and it was one thing she actually wanted to happen.

He let his whole body sink into hers, those chiseled abs, the hard chest, wide shoulders. They sank into the feather mattress on her bed like they used to do. He'd loved this bed with her in it. She whimpered, a rush of hurt and longing washing over her, sending her arms around his shoulders and pulling him closer.

"Don't be scared," he said, tenderly, sweetly, his mouth merely a breath from hers.

And then he finally closed that last bit of distance between them, his lips soft and firm, heartbreakingly familiar, and yet as tentative as he'd ever been with her. As if he knew how much this meant to her, and he truly didn't want to hurt her. As if he knew what they were both risking, and yet just couldn't stop himself.

She let her eyes drift shut, drew in that wonderful man scent of his. Her hands came up to frame his face, to slide into his hair. He had beautiful, thick black hair. He took his time with the kiss, didn't attack with his mouth as so many men did. He coaxed. He soothed. He smiled against her mouth, teasing ever so softly with his tongue, while she wanted to open up and devour him whole.

He had to know that.

It had always been that way between them.

He took little nibbles of her, her mouth, her ear, her neck, back to her mouth, so carefully, so sweetly, with a kind of power and control that drove her crazy at the same time it left her in complete awe of him.

He could seem so cool, so reasonable, so strong. Was this some sort of game to him, a corporate takeover he'd planned out in minute detail and executed to perfection? But then she caught a glimpse of his face, his eyes, and she saw. He was burning up inside, as desperate for her as she was for him.

Was he still desperate for her? Had he missed her? Thought about her? Could he possibly want her back? At this, the worst moment in her life?

She lay there beneath him, in complete awe, her head still spinning, that perfect, hot, hard body of his pressing into hers, which was positively purring with pleasure.

He'd finally stopped teasing. Now he was kissing her for real, his body thrusting ever so slightly against hers in time with the thrust of his tongue in her mouth, everything about this, about him, as exciting as ever.

He could have her clothes off in seconds. She knew it. She could be naked beneath him, wrap her legs around him, open herself up to him in every way, and he could be inside of her, hers again, at least for a few moments. She wanted it, and so did he.

It would be so easy, and so good.

And then they'd be right back to where they'd started, everything that had gone wrong between them still there for them to deal with. She couldn't trust him. She knew it. She'd caught him with a model named Giselle, seen it with her own two eyes, and that had finally been the end of her and James.

Chloe drew in a big breath of him, of everything he was, everything she felt, everything she'd missed so much about him, and somehow found the strength to turn her head away, to break the kiss, kill the moment.

He went still on top of her, slowly raised his head and looked down at her, passion blazing from his dark, beautiful eyes, along with a million questions. And he had that dazed look that had her thinking he was as confused as she was.

Had this really happened? Were they sure it wasn't all a dream? A bizarre but very good one?

"You saved me from the brides?" she asked tentatively.

He cocked his head to the side, looking truly worried, then carefully, slowly, raised himself off her to sit by her side. His hand came to her face, tenderly working its way over her head, his eyes searching.

"Chloe, are you hurt?"

"No," she whispered. "Not really. I was dreaming about my show. Did you see the video? It's all over the internet. Everyone's watching."

"Yes, I saw it."

"The way Bryce kept turning in a circle to try to get away from Eloise's fingernails, and how her veil floated around them in circles, so you saw the whole thing through this gauzy haze, even the blood?"

"Yes."

"If they made horror movies for fashion designers and brides, that's what it would look like."

"Chloe, you're scaring me," he said.

"And that dress? I loved that dress. I loved it more than any other dress I've ever designed, because I looked great in that dress. That was going to be my wedding dress. Why did it have to be that dress Eloise was wearing when it happened?"

"I don't know, Chloe. I'm really sorry. About everything."

"All I have left is the sleeve. Bryce grabbed at Eloise to get her off of him, and all he got was the sleeve. He just ripped it off the dress. Robbie found it on the runway after everyone left and brought it back to me. It's all I have."

"You made it once. You can make it again," he tried.

"No. Not after what happened. It's cursed, too, like me."

"Chloe, you are not cursed," he insisted. "You know that."

"My poor dress. Do you think it ended up in jail with Eloise? Because I just hate thinking about that beautiful dress being dragged across that filthy floor at the jail. Do you think maybe you can bail a dress out of jail? And leave the person wearing it there?"

"Chloe?" He looked really scared then, like she was freaking him out. She tried to get up, but he wouldn't let her. "Not now, okay? The brides are still downstairs. We need to wait a while, until they leave."

"Okay. I don't want to see them again. They were mean brides."

"Chloe, did any of them hit you? Other than the one

who got you here?" He touched her poor cheek. "Did anyone hit your head?"

"I don't think so."

"Do you know where you are?"

"I think so." She was with him, in her bed, even though
that made no sense. "In my house. In my bed."

He smiled encouragingly. "Good. You scared me for a
minute."

So it had happened. It was real.

"I don't understand," she whispered.

Why was he here? Why did he care? Why was he being so nice to her? Why had he kissed her like that? She
thought he hated her, if he felt anything at all for her anymore. She'd hated him as best she could for as long as she
could, because that was the best way to get over him, to
try to forget him. Not that it had worked all that well.

"Chloe, have you been getting any sleep the last few
days?" he asked, looking like he wanted to haul her off to
the hospital and have her head examined, at the very least.

"Not much," she admitted. "I keep having nightmares.
Very strange nightmares."

"Okay, maybe you just really need to sleep," he said,
forcing a smile. "How about this? You stay here, close your
eyes, and I'll stay right here until you go to sleep."

He took a couple of pillows and piled them up against
the headboard, kicked off his shoes, pulled off his tie and
suit coat, then sat down on her bed, settling her against
his side, her head against his chest.

"I just…I don't understand," she said one more time.

"I know. Just go to sleep. I won't let anything bad happen to you."

It was the sweetest, most welcome thing he could have
offered her. Rest, peace, safety, with him right beside her,
watching out for her, just like in her dream.

* * *

He waited until she was asleep, and then waited a little bit longer, taking it all in. Being in her bed again, kissing her, holding her, wanting her so bad he ached with it. The smell of her, the joy, the absolute chaos, all still there, all just the same.

Except she was more vulnerable now than she'd ever been, and he'd come charging in like a man who had every right to be here and to protect her, sweeping her off her feet and fighting his way through a frenzied matrimonial mob to save her.

It was the charging-in thing, the every-right-to-be-there thing she'd most certainly object to, once she wasn't dazed and sleep-deprived and maybe concussed. He hadn't been able to find any evidence of a head injury, but she certainly seemed a little out of it, even for Chloe.

James was tempted to stay with her, but he had no idea what might still be happening with the riot downstairs. So, though it was the last thing he wanted to do, he disentangled himself as gently as he could, leaving her asleep, curled up against a pillow instead of him. He tucked covers around her like she was a child who needed to be protected from the cold, smoothed down her hair, kissed her forehead.

Then he dragged himself away.

Downstairs in the kitchen he found Addie and Chloe's twin cousins, Robbie and Connie. Adam was still there, too.

They all looked up as James entered, giving him the thorough once-over. Too late, he straightened his tie, smoothed down his jacket and then his hair, trying not to look like a man who'd just crawled out of bed. *Oh, well.*

"Is she all right?" Addie asked finally, clearly having a hard time believing what she was seeing.

James nodded. "She's asleep. Did she get hit on the head?"

They discussed it for a moment, then determined that no one had actually seen Chloe take such a blow.

"She was confused," James said.

"She might still think this whole morning was a nightmare," Robbie said, then looked at James, and mouthed, "I didn't mean seeing you, exactly, was a nightmare—"

"It's all right," James said.

Had she kissed him back only because she'd thought she was dreaming and been confused about who he was? James had no way of knowing, so he concentrated on the business at hand.

"You took care of that crazy mob?" he asked.

Addie nodded, looking from James to Adam and then back to James, like she knew they were both up to something. "We wrote a lot of checks."

"Okay," James said, as if that settled that. If there was going to be a fight about the money, it was between him and Chloe, no one else. "I think you should post a security guard outside for the next day or so. You don't know if you've reached the end of the crazy brides. We don't want anyone getting hurt."

He realized, too late once again, that it wasn't his decision to make, and looked at Adam to save him.

"I was thinking the same thing," Adam said. "I'll just have to find—"

"I know someone," James said, pulling out his phone. "Good guy."

"Good," Adam said. "Thank you."

Addie had obviously heard enough. She turned to James and asked, "What are you doing here?"

"I was…with Adam," James said. "We were having a business meeting nearby when we heard about the riot at

Chloe's. Adam was concerned, so he came over to make sure everyone was okay. And I came with him. That's all."

"That's all?" Addie laughed out loud. "What did you do to Chloe?"

"I just got her away from the mob out front and brought her upstairs to rest. Nothing more."

"And she just fell asleep?" Robbie was indignant now.

"I didn't hurt her," he claimed. "I wouldn't do that."

But he had.

They knew it. He knew it, too.

She hurt me, too, dammit.

He thought it, but didn't say it.

"She's perfectly fine," he insisted. "Just a little confused, and she said she hadn't been getting much sleep since the runway thing."

"You know about the runway thing?" Addie asked.

"Half the solar system knows about the runway thing," he said, which was true. He just wasn't normally in the half that followed tabloid news. But still... "Just let her rest. I'm going to call the security guy I know."

"I won't leave until a guard gets here," Adam offered.

James was so grateful for the out, he could have kissed Adam for offering, but then everyone might think that for some reason every man Chloe was involved with eventually turned to other men, and that was publicity she certainly didn't need. So James merely thanked Adam and left.

He'd lost his mind tonight.

That was the only explanation possible for all of this.

He went back to his office and forced himself to work until midnight, then went home and tossed and turned until he finally fell asleep.

Chapter Three

Chloe had no idea how long she slept, waking, if possible, even more disoriented than before. She'd barely turned over in her bed to squint at the clock, when her bedroom door opened slowly, quietly.

Addie and Robbie peeked in, whispering furiously to each other.

"I'm awake," she said.

They nearly tripped over each other getting inside, then just stared at her like she might have dropped in from a spaceship or something. She looked down at herself in the bed. She was in her favorite sleep attire, cotton spaghetti-strap camisole and pajama bottoms, nothing out of the ordinary about that.

"What?" she finally asked.

"She's dressed in her PJs," Robbie said. "He wouldn't… you know…and then dress her again afterward."

"Maybe he didn't take the time to undress her at all,"

Addie argued. "It's not like it's completely necessary. Maybe he's that kind of guy. You know. In. Out. Done. Over. Outta here."

"I bet he's better than that. You know. You can tell—"

"I can't tell. How do you tell just from looking that a guy will take the time to undress you completely first?"

And then it was all starting to come back to Chloe.

The crazy brides with the bouquets, but really with garment bags, probably with shoes in them, because they were heavy. Especially when people were swinging them at her. And then...then...

"Oh, my God! He was here?" she cried.

Addie and Robbie fell silent and solemn, just looking at her.

She started gasping for breath. "I think I might hyperventilate. He was really here?"

They nodded.

"He saved me from the rioting brides?"

"He did," Robbie confirmed. "It was like something out of *Gone with the Wind*. Rhett and Scarlett on the stairs and all."

"James Elliott was here, and he carried me up the stairs? To my room? This room?" She tried breathing faster and faster, conscious but in that fuzzy-headed way of one who's slept too long and can't really wake up.

"We followed as soon as we could," Robbie said.

James must have been here for a while. She vaguely remembered him touching her softly, sweetly, his body pressing hers down into the mattress, his mouth on hers, just as hot and sexy as ever.

Chloe lifted up the covers and peeked beneath them at herself. Yes, she was completely dressed, and he was definitely a man to completely undress a woman in those kinds of situations, though she wasn't confirming or denying any of that to Addie or Robbie.

So, he'd just kissed her? And held her? And then left?

"How long was he in my room with me?" she asked finally.

"Thirty-seven and a half minutes," Robbie said.

They'd timed the visit? Of course.

"We were thinking of breaking in—"

"Because we thought…I don't know, maybe you'd lost your mind or something, and we should try to save you from yourself," Addie finished. "Should we have been saving you from yourself?"

"Probably. Yes." Then she had a new, even more horrible thought. "He knew why those crazy brides were here?"

"Oh, yeah."

She looked up into their equally worried faces and felt anew the sinking feeling of complete humiliation. Not just the rest of the known world, but James, too, knew her ex No. 3 had a thing for men, and he'd been here to witness the aftermath of her latest disastrous relationship.

"What in the world was he doing here?" she asked finally.

"He said he was having a business meeting with Adam Landrey when they heard about the riot. Adam was here, too," Addie told her.

"I still can't believe it. It doesn't make any sense."

He was here? Yes, she could still smell him in her bed. That fresh, clean, citrusy smell of him. She thought she could feel his arms around her, her body snuggled up to his, could remember feeling safe and cherished and so turned on. Why would he charge in, rescue her from the crazy brides and then carry her up here and kiss her? Then leave without a word?

Addie frowned at her. "He thought you might have been

hit in the head, that you were a little out of it, a little confused."

Oh, perfect. At least she had an excuse for whatever she'd done.

"Do you need a doctor?" Robbie asked.

"A mental-health professional. We should probably keep one on call."

James was whistling as he approached the newsstand the next morning, then saw that Vince was waiting for him, tabloid in hand.

Uh-oh. Did they have photos of the mob scene from Chloe's?

But as he got closer, he saw that Vince was beaming at him. "Today, it's on the house! This and your *Wall Street Journal.*"

This, it turned out, was a tabloid with a cover shot of him saving Chloe from the mob!

"You're the first one of my regulars to make the cover of a periodical I carry!" Vince said. "How 'bout that? I've been telling everybody this morning that I know you, that I see you here every day!"

James groaned and looked again. Could anyone—except maybe people who saw him every day—tell that was him? In the photo, his head was bent down toward Chloe's as he carried her through a sea of rioting brides. She looked like a waif, a beautiful, fragile, helpless waif. And he was mostly just a dark suit with dark hair, he thought.

"So, you and that designer get back together?" Vince asked.

"Not exactly."

"Hey, come 'ere." Vince motioned for James to lean

over the counter, closer to Vince, who'd pulled out his cell phone and held it out in front of them.

"No!" James pulled away as the flash went off. He could only hope he'd gotten out of the way in time. "No pictures. Not today."

Vince looked mightily disappointed. "I was gonna put it up on the newsstand. You know, to show people that I really know you."

"Yeah. I'm just not ready for that, Vince. And I really hate having my picture taken," he said.

"You date that crazy girl, you're gonna get your picture taken."

He hadn't thought of that when he'd charged to her rescue, but he couldn't really say he regretted it, either. Because he'd gotten to see her again, to hold her again, to kiss her. He'd gotten into her bed again. He grinned at that thought. Not in the way he'd really like to be back in her bed, but it was certainly better than not being anywhere near her bed.

"I gotta ask you," Vince said, grinning wickedly. "Once you carried her off like that, what did you do to her then?"

"Nothing," James claimed. "Absolutely nothing."

"Yeah, right," Vince said.

A gentleman didn't kiss and tell, after all, and he prided himself on being a gentleman.

He got to his office to see Marcy waiting for him, looking as freaked out as he'd ever seen her and carrying a rolled-up copy of a tabloid.

"Let me guess." James went into his office, Marcy following. "You've never worked with anyone who made the cover of a tabloid before?"

Her mouth fell open. "You've seen it?"

"If it's the one I'm thinking of, I have. Please tell me I didn't make the cover of more than one?"

"No, just the one." She laid it down in front of him on his desk. "We're probably going to start getting calls—"

"From the tabloids? They know who I am?"

"Suspect, at least. The Bride Blog piece yesterday did mention you by name in connection with Ms. Allen, and if we're going to get calls, I need to know what to say."

She waited, looking so eager and excited.

"You mean, you want me to tell you what happened yesterday?"

"Only so I can do my job," she claimed.

Yeah, right. She was practically salivating at the thought of getting the tabloid news before anyone else.

"There is something seriously wrong with you, Marcy," he said.

"I know. Believe me, I do. I'm so sorry. Everyone has a weakness, a dirty little secret, and this is mine."

And Chloe was his.

His weakness, but not his secret. Not anymore. He didn't think he'd left any room for doubt about how he felt about her.

"She was in trouble, and I helped her out. That's it. End of story. I'm not going to stand by and watch anyone I know get attacked." He made it sound perfectly reasonable, he thought, like he was some sort of freelance do-gooder.

Marcy didn't look like she was buying a word of it. She'd seen him charge out of the restaurant like a crazy man to get to Chloe yesterday, after all.

"So, that Bride Blog thing yesterday…I never actually saw it."

"You're not going to like it," Marcy warned, handing

him a printout with the pertinent parts highlighted in yellow.

He scanned the article. It referred to him as Fiancé No. 2 and mentioned that stupid eligible bachelor list he'd been on, then got to the she-just-wanted-him-for-his-money part.

Well, that hurt.

Still.

He'd hurled that particular accusation at her after they broke up. Sometimes he believed it, sometimes he didn't, but it still had the power to make him seriously annoyed.

"Well, I've never been happy being No. 2 in anything," he said, handing that piece of trash back to Marcy. "And please tell me they're wrong about that stupid bachelor list. I can't be on that thing again!"

Marcy looked a little nervous. "The Single Woman's Guide to Bachelor Hunting in New York? I called. I'm afraid you're going to be on it again."

James cringed. He'd made *New York Woman'*s annual bachelor list for the first time a few weeks before he and Chloe had gotten engaged. Truly rotten timing, because women could be so aggressive these days. They'd been all over him. It had been a constant annoyance and a major source of tension between him and Chloe. So once again, this was the worst possible timing.

"What do I have to do to get off that stupid list?" he asked.

"Lose all your money or get married," she said, demonstrating that logical Marcy was still in there somewhere. "Or I guess you could leave New York."

No good options there. "Maybe we could just buy the stupid magazine and do away with the list."

Marcy paused, pen and pad in hand, like she wasn't sure whether she should write that down or not.

"I'm not that desperate yet. Still, there has to be something we can do."

"Well, it seems obvious. You need a girlfriend," Marcy advised.

"No, I don't." He was still smarting from the last one. *Chloe.*

"A very public girlfriend," Marcy insisted. "Take her out, smile for the photographers, just as that stupid list comes out. That way, women will think you're taken and leave you alone."

No, they wouldn't. He was painfully aware of that. Of course, it might be even worse, even more women, more aggressive, if he appeared to be completely available.

"I guess that would be less of a hassle than buying the damned magazine. When does the issue come out?"

"Next week. You'll have to date fast."

A very public girlfriend?

One of those women who needed three hours to pull herself together to walk out the door, who wanted every moment of her life gossiped about, speculated about and, best of all, captured on film.

Which made him think about Chloe. Vince had said that morning, *Date her, you're going to get your picture taken.*

Chloe as his very public, fake girlfriend.

As if reading his mind, Marcy continued. "You've already got a good start on it. Your rescue of Ms. Allen was like something out of a fairy tale." She sighed heavily. "It played very well in the blogs today, the way you took her in your arms and fought to get her to safety. People already want to know about the two of you."

Marcy got a particularly dreamy look on her face. James didn't want to admit that Chloe's behavior might be attributable to a slight blow to the head that left her disoriented. It would ruin the whole fantasy–fairy tale element, and he'd seldom seen Marcy look so happy—and maybe a little goofy.

He feared he'd looked the same way when he'd finally seen Chloe the day before—just plain goofy-giddy-stupid with happiness. Hopefully Chloe was too confused to remember.

"Marcy, come back to me," he said.

"Sorry. I was just thinking, from that photo, you might be able to convince people you and Ms. Allen have been seeing each other for a while, and that maybe she wasn't engaged to that secretly gay photographer."

Okay, James couldn't deny that would be useful, if his purpose was truly to keep Chloe's business from going under and maybe…to get to spend some time with Chloe while doing it. And he wanted some time with her. No lying to himself about that anymore. Or he was just nuts right now. Chloe Derangement Syndrome. He'd had it before.

"If anyone asks about Chloe and me, don't deny it," he told Marcy.

Marcy brightened instantly. "That you and Ms. Allen are involved?"

"Right. Tell them that we have been for a while."

Marcy was positively rapturous now. James wouldn't be surprised if Marcy had suggested this whole scheme because he and Chloe would end up in the tabloids some more. Marcy would love every moment of that.

"I want a full briefing on how the riot played in the blogs, the gossip sites…. You know, all that stuff."

"Of course." It was a dream-come-true assignment for Marcy.

"I have to go. Cancel my morning meetings. I'll call you later about what to do with my afternoon schedule."

He had to pitch the plan to Chloe. The one to save her business. She'd do anything to save her business, wouldn't she?

Even pretend to be dating him again?

"He's coming!" Addie whispered furiously to Chloe soon after they unlocked the salon doors that morning, happy to find no rioting brides and only a few tabloid photographers outside.

But now *he* was coming, and there was only one *he,* as far as she was concerned.

"How do I look?" Chloe asked, because she couldn't help herself.

She was still seriously annoyed at how she'd just crawled out of bed, her hair a mess, still wearing her PJs, when he'd seen her yesterday. Every woman had fantasies of how great she'd look the next time a man who broke her heart saw her again, and in all the fantasies, she looked fabulous. He would be shocked at how good she looked, sad he ever lost her, and beg her to take him back. It was a universal female fantasy, and Chloe feared she didn't look good enough for him this time, either.

"You're good. You're very good," Addie said. "Just pinch your cheeks a little bit. You could use some more color. And wet your lips. That's it. You want to look kissable. Very kissable."

"I do?" Chloe wasn't sure she could stand it if he kissed her.

"You're right. It's James. You don't."

Chloe sighed. "Why do you think he's here?"

"I have no idea, but he photographs well, especially in rescue mode. So I think, despite everything else, we should be nice to him."

"Okay. I can do that."

"But not too nice," Addie said. "I don't want him to hurt you again."

"Right. Me, either." She was such a wimp where he was concerned. "Addie, I don't know if I can do this."

"Of course you can. You just had your whole career and your love life land in the toilet, and half the world saw photos and video of it, but you survived. You can handle seeing this man again."

"You're right." He couldn't possibly humiliate her as much as she'd already been humiliated. She had that going for her.

He walked in looking characteristically gorgeous and uncharacteristically unsure of himself. Or maybe he was afraid some disaster might strike at any moment, like the riot he'd been in the midst of the day before. Even Chloe was scared of walking into her own shop right now, so she could understand how he would be, too.

Addie gave her a smile and disappeared, probably just to the other side of the door of the showroom, if Chloe knew her sister. She'd be close if Chloe needed her—and she'd want to hear what James had to say.

Chloe summoned up every bit of courage and confidence she had and put a smile on her face as he slowly walked up to her. Hands stuffed into his pockets, he stood and smiled, just looking at her for a moment.

"Feeling better today, I hope?" he said finally.

She nodded, thinking she really didn't have to speak just yet.

"Good. I was worried about you. You were kind of out of it last night."

"Oh…well…the whole thing was pretty surreal." The mob attack, seeing him again, having him lift her into his arms, carry her up the stairs, put her gently on her bed, kiss her so sweetly, let her fall asleep in his arms….

"I imagine it must have been," he agreed. "I mean, how many people get attacked by angry brides?"

"Even for me, that's weird." She'd always been a different sort of girl, and he knew it, even seemed to enjoy it at times.

"So, things are better today?" he asked. "No mad brides so far?"

"Not this morning."

"Good. I was hoping some good would come of us making the cover of one of the tabloids."

Chloe winced. "I am so sorry about that. I know how much you hate that sort of thing."

He shrugged as if it meant nothing at all to him, when she knew it did. He was a man who liked his privacy, liked peace and quiet in order to be able to concentrate on what he truly enjoyed—his work. He was as much of a workaholic as she was. It had been one thing that worked for them—that devotion and understanding of ambition and long hours.

"I was afraid they were going to hurt you," he said. "And I would never stand by and let someone hurt you, Chloe."

She looked him in the eye then, surprised and terribly pleased.

"I mean…" He shrugged once again and smiled. "I wouldn't just stand by and watch anyone get attacked like that."

"Of course. I knew that. I knew…what you meant," she lied. So all it had been was good manners and being in the right place at the right time?

"So," he said finally. "Marcy says you and I are all over the internet gossip sites today. They liked the photo of us."

"Marcy?" He had a girlfriend looking up everything she could find about him and Chloe on the net?

"My assistant. Brilliant woman. Wharton grad. Well-organized, efficient, careful. She just has a bad habit, embarrassing, really. She loves the tabloids. Please don't tell her I told you so. She'd be horrified that anyone knew."

Chloe laughed, trying to imagine anyone working for him and having a secret tabloid addiction.

"I know. It's ridiculous, but there it is. I guess we all have our secret...weaknesses."

Chloe wanted to hide. Was he talking about her? Did she know that he might be her most guilty secret of all? That her heart still did that crazy little jittery dance just seeing him again? And she was perfectly clearheaded today. She had no excuses.

"So, anyway," he said, "Marcy says the photo of us seems to have stopped the worst of...you know? The stuff about you being cursed in love and your dresses being cursed."

Okay, this was getting worse by the minute. "Well, I appreciate that. That the photograph did that. Thank you."

He nodded, still looking uncomfortable.

What did he have to be uncomfortable about? His life seemed to be going along just fine, no scandals, no business on the verge of collapse, no humiliation.

"So...remember that silly...magazine list I made back when we were together?"

She frowned. "Up-and-Coming Young Businessmen of Manhattan?"

"No, the bachelor list."

"The Single Woman's Guide to Bachelor Hunting in New York?" He'd been outraged by the whole thing, and soon she'd hated it, too. All those women, so pretty, so polished, with money and breeding, seemingly so much more suited to a romance with him than she ever would be.

"Yeah. That." He looked like it truly pained him. "It's

coming out again any day now, and…I'm afraid I'm going to be on it again."

"Oh." Of course he was. He was likely even more successful now than he had been before and still single, as far as she knew.

"So I'm probably going to have some photographers hounding me for a few weeks, like they did the last time."

"You poor thing," she said, hoping her tone didn't come off as too mean or bitter. She really hoped she wasn't bitter.

He shot her a look that said he knew from where she stood, his problems weren't that big or that bad.

"Sorry," she said. "Really. You've been…so nice, and I'm just…sorry."

"Chloe, the thing is…if one photograph of us together was enough to stop women from rioting at your shop… Well, I thought, some more photographs, more gossip, might be enough to turn things around for you and your business."

Her mouth fell open at that, and she feared she heard a tiny whoop of joy from behind the showroom door, where Addie was no doubt hiding. She really couldn't believe it. He'd charged to the rescue like Prince Charming the night before, and now he was offering to try to actually rescue her business?

"You'd do that for me?" she asked, simply unable to stop herself.

He looked uncomfortable once again. "I know how much your business means to you. I know how hard you've worked, what a chance that show at Fashion Week was for you. It's not fair to have it all taken away by…by…"

"Me being stupid enough to fall in love with a guy who has a thing for other guys?" She closed her eyes the second she got the words out. Sometimes her mouth just ran away on her and something like that came out, something so bad and so humiliating.... Now she really, really wanted to disappear.

"We all make mistakes," he said finally, which had her thinking about the end of him and her, that awful argument and then Giselle. Always Giselle.

God, that still hurt. He'd denied it so many times, denied that anything was going on between them, and then, finally, she'd caught them together, and just wanted to die right then and there.

"Look, Chloe, I wouldn't want my mistakes trotted out for all the public to see, and you don't deserve that, either."

She shook her head, staring at the floor, completely unable to look him in the eye. "I don't know what to say."

"It's no big deal," he claimed. "Like I said, I'm going to have photographers following me and taking my picture for a while anyway. Why not give this a try? We go out a couple of times, very public events. People get the idea that we're a couple again. I don't have women hunting me down. At least, not as many women, hopefully. And maybe we can save your business at the same time."

Chloe stood there, thinking that of all the things he could have come here to say, this was the least expected. He was ready to help her? And no matter what he said, he was talking about helping her.

"I can't believe you'd do that for me."

"It just so happens that being linked romantically would work for both of us right now," he insisted.

She wouldn't look like the unluckiest woman in the world in love, not if she had him escorting her around the town. If she were cursed, she wouldn't be able to get anywhere near him.

But she wasn't buying the whole good-for-both-of-us thing. Chloe hadn't seen him in a year and a half. Their breakup had been wretched, at least for her. After catching him with Giselle that day, she'd turned and walked away, returning her engagement ring by messenger, not so much as talking to him again.

He hadn't tried to see her, either, not in all that time. He was a proud, stubborn man, used to getting anything he wanted, to making things work.

Which made her think he had to be up to something. But what?

"James, that's really nice of you," she began. "And I appreciate it, given how badly things ended between us. I just don't think—"

"Chloe!" Addie shouted, bursting through the door and into the showroom, grabbing Chloe by the arm. "Sorry, James. I need her for a minute. I'll have her right back to you."

She dragged Chloe through the door and into the kitchen, then said, "You have to say yes."

"Addie, he's up to something—"

"Maybe—"

"Oh, he is. And we have no idea what that is," Chloe finished.

"Right. We don't. But we also know one other thing. You cannot afford to turn him down. Not now."

Chloe made a face.

"No," Addie insisted. "It is that bad. But yesterday, Prince Charming came to your rescue, looking romantic and absolutely perfect doing it. And thank God someone got a photo of it, and it made the front page of one of those stupid tabloids. Rule No. 1 in PR disasters: you have to change the story. You know, the icky one. He changed the big, icky story."

"Okay, so he changed the story."

"Yeah. Nothing I had thought of would've worked like

that. Nothing I could do. You're not pitiful anymore. You're not cursed. Because a rich, gorgeous man wants you. And now, everyone wants to know who he is. I'm going to make sure they do."

"Addie!" She knew Addie was right, always bowing to Addie's business sense, which was so much stronger than Chloe's. Still, it was hard to hear that right now they needed James.

"Don't worry. No one will know I did it. That awful Bride Blog lady has already told everyone the two of you were engaged once. People are going to figure it out. I'm just going to make sure they do it faster by dropping a few hints into the comments sections of a few gossip sites."

"And then what?"

"Whatever I have to do," Addie claimed. "And he said he's going to be on that bachelor list again. That's perfect. You'll have captured one of New York's most sought-after men. You'll go from Chloe the Cursed to having all the single women in New York envy you. It's perfect. We couldn't buy publicity like this."

Chloe wanted to hide. "But I'll have to see him again."

"Yeah, well, if this doesn't work we may be all selling ourselves in the streets to get operating capital for next month. Which do you want to do?"

"I...I...ahhh!"

"Believe me, if we had time for me to be more sympathetic, I would be," Addie said. "But we're desperate. Now get out there and tell him yes."

She practically shoved Chloe back into the showroom.

James was still standing there, still looking every bit as perfect as before, while she felt bedraggled, rumpled and freakishly cursed.

He frowned at her. "That bad?"

"Hmm?"

"The news Addie had to share with you right away? Was it really that bad?"

"Oh, that." Chloe sighed. She didn't even have the energy to lie to him. "There wasn't any news. She just…she told me I had to tell you yes, that I'd pretend we're back together."

He nodded. "And it sounds that awful? To have to see me again?"

Chloe's eyes came up at that. He sounded oddly vulnerable when he said it, and one thing James Elliott was not was vulnerable. Not ever. She still couldn't figure out what he'd ever seen in her in the first place. They were just such different people. Him, so polished and successful and careful, and her, so…flaky and disorganized and always perched on the brink of insolvency, with a big dream and her whole family depending on her to make things work.

"You don't do anything without a good reason, usually lots of good reasons, and I know you. You could just stay in your office for a few weeks, working practically around the clock on some deal and be perfectly happy, until this whole list thing blows over. You'd probably be happier that way."

"Okay, you're right," he admitted. "There is another reason. I feel guilty."

"Why? Nothing that's happened to me is your fault," she claimed. If she'd gone into her relationship with Bryce too quickly, still stinging from what happened with James, that was on her. Not him.

"No, not about you. About Adam. I talked him into taking over my interest in your business. He did it as a favor to me."

"Oh. Right. And now, if we go under, he's going to take a financial hit from that," Chloe realized. One more person's fate on her conscience. Her whole family and one Adam Landrey, nice investor guy.

"I hate the idea of him losing the money he put into your company. I mean, I hate the idea of you losing everything, too, Chloe. Honestly, I do. None of you deserve that. But with Adam, there's the added guilt that he's in this mess because of me."

"I thought he was loaded. That what he put into my company was nothing to him."

"It was at the time. But times have changed. Lots of people are hurting…." He swore softly. "I have no right to tell you this. Understand? Please, don't ever tell him or anyone else that I told you. But Adam really needs for this to work right now."

"Oh." She felt like a complete failure then, like some kind of plague upon those who loved her and had the supreme misfortune to get involved with her in business. And she couldn't handle ruining one more person's life. Really, she couldn't. If there was a way to stop it, she was going to take it. "Okay, I'll do it."

Chapter Four

"I think this is a really bad idea," Chloe said early that evening, as she stood in front of the big mirrors on the dais in her own showroom, dressed in one of her own bridesmaid's gowns that Connie had just finished altering to fit Chloe.

Chloe could make a gorgeous bridesmaid's gown. None of that awful the-bride-must-be-the-only-beautiful-one-on-her-wedding-day crap for Chloe and anyone serving as a bridesmaid to her brides. So she looked good. Or as good as she could look, considering she wasn't five-ten and twenty pounds underweight, like models were.

But she was seriously freaking out.

Connie knew it, too. She put her dress pins and tape away and said, "I'm going to get Addie." Because in their family, when things got tough, Addie got them through it.

Addie arrived and without any sympathy at all for Chloe, she asked, "Do you want to be bankrupt?"

"No," Chloe insisted.

"Do you want your entire family, all of whom depend on you for work, to be bankrupt along with you, all of us huddled together for warmth, living on the street corner, going through garbage bins to try to find some scraps to eat?"

"No!" Chloe said.

"Then you're going out with that man. You're going to look great, and like you're absolutely thrilled to be by his side at this charity ball, and that's all there is to it!" Addie said, sticking another pin in the gown and catching Chloe's side just a bit, as she tried to make the gown fit perfectly.

"Ouch!" Chloe protested, then tried to explain. "He's up to something! You should have seen his face when I agreed to his little plan. He was so happy—"

"Well, we don't want him looking miserable—"

"But why would he be so happy to go out with me? He must have a reason."

"He does. He said he doesn't want his friend to be eating out of garbage bins with us."

"Adam Landrey isn't going to end up eating out of garbage bins. At worst, four-star restaurants instead of five-star, which means James has to have some other reason for doing this!"

"What if he does? You don't have the luxury of saying no to him, no matter what," Addie insisted.

Chloe's eyes flooded with tears. "Addie, he broke my heart!"

Addie stayed stern. "Don't you dare cry! The makeup artist has already left. If you ruin all her hard work and don't look absolutely radiant in the photographs tonight, I will never forgive you. Do you understand me?"

Chloe sniffled, managing to hold back the tears, but just barely. "I'm scared," she finally whispered.

"We all are. But someone has to be strong. I'm trying to be the strong one now, and once it comes time to actually go out with Prince Charming, you'll be the strong one. Our financial lives depend upon it. I mean, do you really think any of us could function out there in the real world? Working for anyone else?"

"You could." Chloe was sure of it.

"I think I could. Could you or anybody else in our little enterprise?"

"No, I don't think so." They all had their little quirks. Together, they took care of each other, compensated for each other's weaknesses, understood and forgave and moved on. Most people wouldn't, especially not in business.

"Okay, so you have your higher purpose, and you are a brave, strong, wonderfully creative woman, and you're very lucky—"

Chloe sputtered with outrage at the world *lucky*. Addie could be fierce in fighting for the family business, but she went overboard at times.

"I am not lucky," Chloe said.

"Yes, you are. You have a way out. He offered us one. Before he showed up, it looked like we had no chance at all. Now we have one, slim, I admit, but a chance. Don't forget that."

"Okay. You're right. I'm sorry," Chloe said, feeling properly chagrined. Addie always knew what to say, and she was always firmly on Chloe's side. "I just…I can't fall for him again. Addie, I can't—"

"Then don't."

"Easy for you to say. He's never kissed you."

"Don't let him kiss you, either. I mean…those little pecks on the cheek for show in front of the cameras, but that's it. Nothing else."

But he already had. At least Chloe was pretty sure that he had. And that it felt every bit as incredible as it had before, maybe even better. "I just don't want to get my heart broken again. I don't think my heart could take it."

"Look at me," Addie the drill sergeant said. "I know you can do it. Now, let's see what we can do with your hair."

She was still fiddling with Chloe's hair when the little bell at the showroom door tinkled, announcing an arrival. Chloe turned around, braced to see *him* again, only to find a doll-like figure of a woman, her face a splotchy red, eyes brimming over with tears.

Which could only mean… Hysterical Bride.

"Oh, crap," Addie muttered. "I could have sworn Robbie locked that door fifteen minutes ago."

They both pasted on their everything-is-fine faces and walked toward the poor, sad thing. Chloe recognized this one. Denise? Dani? But she knew the dress, a graceful shantung silk due to be finished any day now.

Addie got to the girl, smiled and said, "Hi. What can we do for you?"

"Uhhh…I'm interrupting something."

"No, no, Chloe is all ready. She's wearing one of her own gowns. Doesn't she look great?"

The teary bride nodded slowly, then asked Chloe, "You're going out?"

Chloe nodded.

"Really? I just thought…well…it just sounded like…"

Like Chloe wouldn't be caught dead out in public right now? Yeah. She knew.

"She's going to the big charity ball at the Metropolitan Museum tonight," Addie bragged.

"Oh," the little bride said.

And if I can do this, you can walk down the aisle in one of my dresses, Chloe thought.

"Well, I just…I'm Daniella Santini. I ordered a dress a while back—"

"Of course. A fitted champagne-colored bodice with a full ballerina skirt in shantung silk. I bet you're so excited." Chloe put on her calmest, most reassuring, dealing-with-Hysterical-Brides smile. "Your big day is so close."

"I am." Daniella's bottom lip quivered and she looked a little guilty. "I'm sorry. It's just that…the dress isn't going to work!"

"Of course it will. It's going to be perfect," Chloe claimed. "Remember how you looked in the sample? So perfect with your complexion."

Not at the moment, because poor Daniella was all splotchy, but as long as she didn't bawl on her wedding day, she'd be gorgeous. Chloe whispered urgently to Addie to go get Robbie. He was the best with Hysterical Brides.

"I thought it was what I wanted," Daniella admitted. "But…well…it's just not. And I came to tell you I don't want the dress."

"Did you and your fiancé have a fight? Daniella, I can't tell you how many couples fight in the days leading up to their weddings—"

"No, it's not that. Mark is…well, he's a beautiful dresser, a better one than I am, and he's fussy about his clothes and has a really good eye for color. He loves Broadway musicals and has no interest at all in sports. Not that it means anything, really. I mean, he loves me. I know he does."

"I'm sure he does," Chloe claimed, getting a bad feeling about this.

"But my great-aunt Margene, who's helping pay for the wedding… She's always had some reservations about Mark. I told her she was being ridiculous but she met the best man yesterday, and Tom is absolutely gorgeous." Daniella sobbed the last part.

Gotta watch those gorgeous best men.

"He and Mark have been best friends forever, room-mates in college, and after that thing with your...your... you know what I mean!" she cried. "My aunt thinks Mark likes men! She says I'd be crazy to get married in a gown designed by you. That it would be tempting fate. I'm sorry. I just can't do it. Someone told me you were giving people their money back for dresses?"

Chloe's humiliation, feeling as fresh as if it had just hap-pened minutes ago, washed over her anew, as she heard the little bell over the front door again.

Of course James chose that moment to walk into the shop, smiling with the confidence, grace and take-charge attitude that seemed to carry him throughout every mo-ment of his life.

"I'm sorry." He came to Chloe's side, slid an arm around her waist and kissed her softly on the cheek, like a man with every right to do so, and then said, "Am I interrupt-ing?"

Daniella just stared at him.

Chloe stepped in. "Daniella, this is my...friend James Elliott. James, this is Daniella Santini, who's getting mar-ried soon in one of my gowns."

"I'm sure you'll be perfect in one of Chloe's gowns." James took Daniella's hand, bent over it and kissed it in a way that didn't look silly at all. That looked as natural and charming as could be and rendered Daniella momentarily speechless.

She looked from James to Chloe, then back to James again, no doubt wondering what in the world this beauti-ful, polished, important-looking man was doing looking down at Chloe like she was the only woman in the world. Chloe sincerely hoped Daniella's fiancé looked at her in just that way.

The look seemed to work for a moment, and then it just didn't anymore.

Daniella started to stammer, clearly trying to get rid of James, who played dumb and stayed where he was. Then Addie and Robbie showed up.

Daniella finally blurted out, "I'm afraid my fiancé's gay!"

Chloe felt like a balloon that had just sprung a giant leak. If she could just deflate to the point where she disappeared, that would be great.

"Oh, honey." Robbie, who was gay himself, jumped in and tried to save the day. "I remember your fiancé. The man knows how to dress and knows his art and modern theater. But I know a gay man when I see one, and believe me, he's as straight as they come. Gorgeous, but straight."

Daniella sniffled a bit, then asked, "Really? You're sure?"

"I'm sure." Robbie patted her shoulder and handed her a tissue.

Daintily, she wiped her tears away. "But, did you know...that other man...Chloe's other man... Did you know he was gay?"

Chloe gave a little yelp.

"You know," James said, coming to her rescue. His smile hadn't diminished one bit. If anything, it radiated with even more confidence and charm, as he pulled Chloe even closer and told Daniella, "You can't believe everything you read."

Daniella looked truly bewildered, but she'd stopped crying, at least. "Uh...you mean...the two of you are... together?"

Chloe felt herself smiling, hopefully not one of those kill-me-now smiles.

"Does she look like a woman who's devastated because she just found out her fiancé is gay?" James asked.

"Well…no," Daniella admitted. "I guess not. It's just… I—I can't have anything like that happen to me. I'd just die if it did."

Or wish you could, Chloe thought.

"You are going to be so beautiful in the gown Chloe made for you that no man would ever dream of leaving you for any reason," James claimed.

And after a few more minutes of reassurance, Daniella seemed to believe it. She dabbed at her eyes once again, told James how nice it was to meet him and said she'd be in to pick up her gown next Wednesday. Crisis averted, at least with poor Daniella.

Chloe still had James to deal with.

He eased away from her as Daniella left, and the arm that had been around her waist, anchoring her to him, dropped to his side. He shot Robbie a pointed look that said without a word, *Go away now.*

"We'll just…leave you two alone. Have a great date," Robbie said, giving Chloe a little kiss on the cheek and whispering, "You can do this."

He and Addie walked out of the room, leaving Chloe all alone with James.

"Well," she said, "that was good timing."

He nodded. "How many Hysterical Brides have you had today?"

"Daniella was the first," she admitted.

"Good. This is going to work, you know?" He stood back and looked her over from head to toe, taking in the simple, shimmery silk crepe gown in a barely pink color called blush, and finally said, "You're lovely."

"Thank you."

"Will I do? Or do you want to dress me?"

Chloe knew Addie had called his assistant—the previously mentioned Marcy, who was indeed very excited about simply talking to a relative of Chloe-from-the-tabloids fame—to give James some direction on what color shirt and tie to wear. The object, after all, was for the two of them to look great in the photos or video of them going into the event.

No doubt about it, the man knew how to dress. His suits were impeccably cut and fit like a dream, but he seldom ventured from the same color palette—white dress shirt, dark-colored tie to match his dark-colored suit of the day, which he was in now.

Chloe studied him, trying to look with the eye of a designer and not a woman at his near-perfect body. She took a breath, feeling tired and overwhelmed at the moment. It really wasn't fair that he still looked every bit as good as ever.

"Robbie pulled a couple of shirts and ties for you. Nothing too threatening, I promise. Just a shirt the same shade as my gown." She would not mention the words *blush* or *pink* when dressing a man.

"I am not threatened in the least by colors. At least not those colors," he said, looking at the rack of shirts in the corner. "They're all white. Or nearly white. I'm already wearing white."

"Then you shouldn't be afraid of any of these shirts. Just think of them as white. And you can keep your tie, if you want."

"You still think I'm color-blind, don't you?" he asked, loosening the tie and then pulling it off, shrugging off the suit jacket, as well.

"You can afford to have at least one flaw," she said, as he started unbuttoning his shirt right there in front of her. No big deal. At least it shouldn't be. She'd seen him without his shirt. Many times. It was just…she really didn't need to see him calmly, methodically undressing right now, taking her back to that first night they'd met.

She'd been coordinating a charity fashion show, and her model groom was missing. She'd hired him for the show based on a headshot, so she knew his face. When she'd walked out the back door and seen a man she thought was him, rushing down the street like he was late, Chloe had grabbed him. Before he could protest, she'd dragged him inside, scolding him all the way and telling him to get out of his clothes, that the show was starting.

She'd literally been undressing him herself—the tie gone, the shirt buttons in progress—when she'd noticed his grin, so dazzling, so potent and so clearly heterosexual and interested. *In her.* Chloe had been around a lot of male models, and this was not the way they looked at her.

Her hands froze on his chest, and she made a slow study of him, the dark hair, dark eyes, sexy grin, the very expensive cut of his suit, the sleek build that hid an unexpectedly muscular chest, the way he just stood there, a model of cooperation, waiting to see what she would do.

Three people shouted questions at her. The show was literally about to start. She answered them all, made decisions, shouted orders, and all the while he just stood there, waiting, making it nearly impossible for her to so much as drag her eyes away from him.

Finally, she said, "You're not my missing model, are you?"

He shook his head, never taking his eyes off her, a look of pure appreciation on his face.

"Then why didn't you say so? Why did you let me drag you in here and start taking your clothes off?" she asked, only then realizing she was still touching him. She jerked her hands away, like she'd had them on a hot stove. "And I swear, if you say something stupid and utterly predictable, like, 'I never refuse when a woman grabs me and tells me to take my clothes off,' don't bother. I don't have time."

He shrugged, still grinning. "I was just trying to be helpful. You need a man? Can I help?"

"I...I...you're not a model?"

"No."

But he did look the part and was willing. She frowned, studied him again. "What size suit do you wear?"

He laughed out loud. "Thirty-eight long."

"No. The tux we brought wouldn't fit. Although the suit you have on is not bad." Italian silk, and it fit him impeccably. This man did not buy off-the-rack. "Can you walk?"

"Since I was eight months old, I'm told."

Chloe nodded. "Overachiever, were you?"

"Right from the start," he bragged.

"Janie, come over here and let me see him walk with you," she called out to one of her brides, then as they waited for the female model to arrive, looked back to him. "I just need you to walk down the runway with her. On, off, over in a moment. Will you do it?"

"If you'll have dinner with me," he shot back.

Chloe gaped at him. "You can't be serious."

"I'm almost always serious. Women seem to think that's a fault."

Chloe had trouble believing women found fault with him at all. Still, the show really was starting any moment. "Look around. You're in a room full of models, absolutely gorgeous women, and you want to go out with me?"

"If you'll notice, I haven't taken my eyes off you since the moment you grabbed me on the street and dragged me in here. I haven't wanted to look at anyone else."

Chloe thought he was nuts. "Why?"

"I think you're interesting. And adorable. And different than the women I normally date—"

"Don't tell me. You normally date the models?"

He shrugged easily, as if it didn't matter at all. "I think you'll find I'm very clear in what I want and very good at getting it. I'm also known to have excellent negotiation skills. I want you to go out with me, and I'm willing to walk anywhere you want to make that happen. Do we have a deal?"

"Unbelievable!" Chloe began, ready to bawl him out for daring take advantage of a crisis in her show to bribe her into going out with him.

But right then, her missing model had shown up. She'd turned all her attention into getting him out of what he was wearing and into the tux.

She'd stood in her place just behind the curtain, coordinating the show, the last person who saw the models before they walked out onto the runway, making sure they were perfect. When it was over, James had still been standing there in the background, watching her and grinning that sexy, tempting grin of his, looking even more handsome and appealing than the missing model she'd mistaken him for.

And she'd agreed to go out with him.

Chloe finally dragged herself back to the present. He'd undone the last button on his shirt and stood there with a strip of skin showing between the sides of the open shirt, taut, tanned, perfect skin, a sprinkling of hair on his chest, fine ripples of muscles on his firm, flat abdomen.

"You're thinking of the first night we met," he said.

She didn't even try to argue. No way she could have pulled off a denial. All the old feelings were too close to the surface, the scene too familiar.

"I was interested from the moment you grabbed me and

told me to take my clothes off. What man wouldn't have been?" He shrugged easily, grinned that same potent grin. "But what really got me was that by the time I'd stood there and watched you work, pull that show together in this crazy frenzy of intensity, passion, sheer joy...I couldn't take my eyes off you. It's like you bewitched me on the spot."

"Don't say that. Don't do that."

"It's true, Chloe." He got his cuffs undone, one by one, and then shrugged out of the shirt, never taking his eyes off her the whole time.

Maybe she was just weak, she decided.

Weak and stupid.

She'd just never made good decisions about men. She tried. She really did. Tried to be careful and smart and take her time. She really didn't want to be hurt, to have her heart broken. What woman did? It was like she lacked some vital strand of DNA. The part that helped women choose a good man, one that would stay. One that knew how to love. One that had an attention span that lasted longer than it took for him to get a woman into bed.

If a woman couldn't be trusted to exercise common sense in choosing a man, then she had no business with any man. No matter how good James Elliott looked without his shirt.

"You look like you're about to be sick," he said, seeming concerned.

"Just coming to some decisions," she said, walking over to the rack of shirts. She had to get him dressed again, fast, before she did something stupid.

Like grab him and kiss him silly.

"So, what did you decide?" he asked, taking the shirt from her.

"That I'm done with men," she said.

He frowned, pausing once he'd gotten the shirt on but

not buttoned yet. "Going to start playing for the other team?"

"What?" She didn't play any kind of sports, but then realized he wasn't talking about sporting teams. "No, I'm not…switching teams. Although, I guess that was one possible story we could have tried. That Bryce was actually gay, and I was a lesbian, and we were just seeing each other to cover up the fact that we were both gay. We didn't think of that. I wonder if straight women would have a problem buying a wedding dress from a designer who was a lesbian?"

James looked at her like she'd lost her mind. "I have no idea."

She shrugged. "You've got to admit, it's better than buying a wedding dress from someone who doesn't believe in love."

"You believe in the tooth fairy, the Easter bunny and Little Mermaid, Chloe. Of course you believe in love."

Her mouth had run away with her once again, or maybe it was that lack of a certain decision-making gene. She admitted softly, "I don't think I do."

He came closer, too close, took her by the arms and just waited there, right in front of her, until she looked up at him, hoping he couldn't see just how badly her heart had been broken, hoping, and failing badly, she feared. He took her face in one of his hands, rubbed his thumb back and forth across her chin like he needed to know if her skin still felt the same to him.

"He really hurt you. I'm sorry, Chloe."

She was outraged at first, then so very sad and then mad all over again, and she just had to save herself, at least this time.

Did he realize that he'd hurt her ten times worse than Bryce ever could have?

Chloe was still thinking of what to say to him when she saw a flash of light behind her. Before she could turn around to see what it was, James took her firmly in his arms this time, his head bending down low to hers like he was going to kiss her any minute.

Chapter Five

"Don't look," he said, his lips practically on hers. "It's probably just a photographer."

"Staking out my showroom again! I thought they'd at least given up on that for the day. And Addie tipped a few of them off that we were going to the benefit. Why aren't they there, waiting for us?"

"Maybe one of them wanted something no one else would have. Isn't that always their goal? To see the thing no one else sees?"

"And he sees us having a fight—"

"No, he's going to see us make up."

Chloe practically growled, she was so mad.

James laughed. "It's a moment, Chloe. We just need to give him a moment that looks really good."

And with that, he slipped one of the skinny, slinky straps of her dress off one of her shoulders and dipped his head down low, like he was nibbling on her shoulder, her neck.

He didn't.

Not really.

But he got close enough that she knew with everything in her that his mouth was less than a half an inch away from her skin. His warm breath skimmed over her. She sucked in a breath and tried not to feel…anything.

Like that had any shot of working.

God must just hate her, Chloe decided. First, he didn't give her that not-stupid-around-men gene, and now she was supposed to stand here with James all but nibbling on her neck and not feel anything? Not do anything to give herself away?

It was too much to expect from any mortal woman.

"Remember, you're supposed to at least look like you like this." James moved over to the other shoulder and took down that strap with his teeth.

She grabbed at the bodice of her dress before it could fall down. "I'm not willing to show that much skin, even if it would save my company."

He laughed, his nose skimming along her collarbone, into that little hollow at the base of her neck. He spent a long moment there, and then worked his way up from her chin, along her jaw and finally stopped just shy of her ear.

Every nerve ending in her traitorous body was on high alert, silently begging him to touch her, really touch her. She feared she whimpered aloud.

"Chloe, you're acting like a statue. Put your hands on my shoulders."

"I'll drop my dress. There's nothing left to hold it up."

"Don't worry." He pressed his body firmly against hers, his chest now leaving nowhere for her dress to go. "I've got it."

She closed her eyes, her dress safely in place, but her breasts now nestled firmly against the wall of his chest.

This close, his body felt even better than before. She willed her hands to his shoulders.

"That wasn't so hard, was it?" he asked.

She slid one hand to the side of his face, the other into his hair and gave it a hard tug.

He laughed, the rat, and took a little nibble of her neck for real. "You want to play nice or not?"

"Nice, please," she said, still feeling those warm, soft lips on her neck, her nerve endings practically dancing with joy, the sensation shooting all the way down her spine.

"Okay. We'll play nice." He skimmed his nose up and down the side of her neck, inhaling deeply.

That was not her idea of nice. "James—"

"Just another moment. We want to make sure the guy gets a good shot."

"He got the shot already! He got dozens of shots," she said, pushing him away. "I just broke my engagement to a secretly bisexual photographer. I know how long it takes to get a dozen good shots off."

She was distracted by her dress nearly falling down, catching it just in time before the stupid photographer really got a shot.

"You were really engaged to a guy who was secretly bisexual?" James asked, either in disbelief or astonishment.

"I don't know what he actually was. I don't know if anything he ever said to me was true. He could just be one more man who lied about who he was sleeping with, claiming that he wasn't sleeping with anybody but me. I don't know. Men should come with those little GPS microchips you can have injected into your dog, so you can check at any moment and know where they are. It would make things so much simpler for women and stop so much lying."

James just looked at her. "I didn't go near another woman in the time we were together—"

"That's certainly one way to put it—"

"Chloe, I swear to you—"

"I guess, in your mind, you didn't go near any of those women. They all came chasing after you."

And she knew that was unfair. Because women did chase him. She'd watched it happen again and again. Women wanted him. Some of them weren't shy about that, even with her standing next to him. It had amused her at first because she'd had him. Or at least, she thought she had him. For a while. Eventually the whole thing had become infuriating and then simply impossible.

He let her have her say, waiting with a grim kind of patience, and then said, "We're going to have to talk about this, Chloe. You don't believe me right now. I know that, but—"

"I don't believe anything any man has to say right now! I mean, would you, if you were me?"

"All right. I guess not," he admitted.

She glared at him. "In fact, now that I think about it, that's exactly what Bryce said. That he'd never been unfaithful to me. He just forgot to mention that his idea of being unfaithful involved being with another woman. He claimed he hadn't done that. He just needed a man every now and then!"

"Oh," James said.

"Yes, oh! Now you know everything. I hope you're satisfied—"

"Hey!" Addie opened the showroom door and yelled at them. "You're not supposed to be fighting, remember? You're supposed to be happy. Chloe, I don't care if it kills you. Be nice to him."

And then she disappeared back into the kitchen.

Chloe stopped yelling, stopped doing everything except glaring at him. He knew every humiliating secret now. There were none left. Except the awful possibility that she wouldn't have fallen for Bryce in the first place if she hadn't been still reeling from her breakup with James.

Please, God, let her keep that one secret, at least.

"I'm sorry," she said finally, utterly defeated and still facing an entire evening with him.

"Me, too," he said.

"This is really hard."

He nodded, then smiled softly, sweetly, showing her his most charming self. "I'll behave. I'll be so good, you'll have trouble believing I'm me."

So if she asked him not to really touch her, not to hold her, not to kiss her, he wouldn't? Unless there was a camera in their faces? Or he'd do it, but not mean it? Was he capable of kissing a woman and not making her turn to mush inside? She couldn't ask because then he'd know her awful secret.

"Come on," he said. "Let's go save your dream."

To fool everyone into thinking they were in love. That no one's heart was broken and that little girls who for their whole lives had imagined they'd one day walk down the aisle to their very own Prince Charming were safe in entrusting part of their dreams to Chloe and one of her gowns.

She had to admit, he was a perfect gentleman from that moment on, as attentive and solicitous as could be when in the public eye, and quietly helpful and considerate— nothing more—when they were alone in the back of the limousine going to the party.

When they arrived at the museum, she took his hand and let him help her out of the limo, then stood there beside him, smiling like she absolutely adored him as they posed together for the cameras.

Inside the party, populated by the minor celebrities, politicians, New York socialites and rich financiers he'd come to court, she tried to feel like she belonged, dressed in silk and bits of vintage jewelry, with a beautiful, rich, powerful man at her side.

She danced with him, so close she breathed in the scent of him with every breath she took. She could feel all those lovely muscles of his pressed up against her, hear people whispering about them, feel them watching, but no one said anything horrible to her face.

He brought her fancy chocolates and champagne—just enough to try to help relax her a bit, no more—and introduced her to dozens of people. All the while he smiled broadly, a hand draped casually at her back, like he couldn't stand for her to stray from his side.

It was exhausting, and after an hour of mingling among the rich and fashionable, he escorted her back to the limo for the drive home.

She eased over as far to the other side of the limousine as possible, liking him a little too much at the moment. He sat on his side, looking like he was up to something but not making any move toward her.

"You're very good at this," she said.

"You make that sound like a bad thing, Chloe."

She frowned. "And I still think you're up to something."

"All I was thinking was that those shoes look great, but they're probably killing your feet. I could do something about that."

"See? There you go. Definitely up to something," she complained.

He held his hands up in mock surrender. "You're perfectly free to stay way over there, and I'll stay here. I think even you have to admit I've been a model of good behavior so far. Don't want to ruin that this late in the date. I was just offering to help. That's all."

"You're being too helpful."

"Maybe you're just too suspicious," he countered. "Did you ever think of that?"

"Of course I'm suspicious. All women should be suspicious around men. It should be automatic behavior, taught from birth. Trust no man. Especially the ones who seem nice."

"Okay, I'll work harder to find the perfect balance between being nice but not too nice. Anything else?"

She sighed. Her feet were killing her. She'd been thinking of slipping off her high heels before he said anything about her feet. She got so tired sometimes, trying to keep everything going, make things work for everyone else, and it seemed like no one took care of her. Ever.

Her family looked out for her, and they were definitely on her side, ready with advice and encouragement. But care was a different thing. There were times when she so wanted someone to take care of her for just a few moments in time. Little pampering, indulgent things. And then James did the most awful thing, a devious, disarming thing.

He reached over and took her hand in his.

Just held it in his big warm one.

Nothing else.

Like he'd read her mind once again and knew she was so tired, so sad, so alone.

He was a magic man, she'd decided when she first met him. There was some mystical quality to him that let him see right inside of her, that left her with no defenses against him, left her thinking he was perfect and put on this earth just for her. His hand felt like a lifeline, like strength and safety and an unlimited supply of support and kindness. How was a woman supposed to resist that? Especially when her life was falling apart.

"Slip your shoes off," he whispered through the darkness of the limousine, his voice like a spell.

It was what she wanted. She toed off her sandals and eased sideways, angling her body toward his so she could lean her side against the back of the seat. Then she drew her legs up and let him pull her bare feet onto his thigh.

Chloe closed her eyes and just let herself feel. He did nothing but smooth his hands slowly from her right heel to her toes at first, warming her foot with his hands. And then he stroked softly with his thumbs, finding little sore muscles and trying to smooth them out.

She clamped her lips shut so she wouldn't groan out loud. Because it felt so good. Kind, caring and sexy as could be, an incredibly potent combination.

"You took lessons in that, didn't you?" she asked finally.

He laughed softly, started to say something, then caught himself and gave her a small, sad smile.

Not lessons.

Okay, private lessons, maybe.

From a woman.

Not Chloe. In his post-Chloe period, hopefully, not during-Chloe. But they weren't going to talk about that.

She made the mistake of closing her eyes, as if that would stop her from thinking about exactly who had taught him to touch a woman this way, and it actually worked, kind of. Because closing down one of the five senses always intensified the workings of the others, and she seemed to feel what he was doing that much more intensely.

"Someone once told me you can get a woman to do

practically anything you want with a good foot massage," he said finally.

"She was right," Chloe said, trying not to glare at him as she said it.

He put her foot down and then said, "Give me the other one."

And she did it, because he asked, and because it just felt so good.

She could have those hands all over her whole body, she knew. He could be very kind, very patient when he wanted to be, always a very attentive lover. He could make her purr like a satisfied kitten.

And then where would she be?

Crazy about another man who'd break her heart in the end.

"It's just too hard sometimes, you know?" she whispered.

"Life?"

She nodded.

"Sometimes," he agreed softly. "And sometimes, it gets better."

"You really believe that?"

"I do, Chloe."

"Well, I'm not sure I do."

"You're just tired, and you've had some tough times lately. That's all," he said, those firm, warm hands of his squeezing slowly down the sole of her foot.

If her feet could talk, they'd be singing, it felt so good. It was getting harder and harder to remember why she had to stay away from him.

He went on for a glorious eternity, and when he finally stopped and let one hand rest on top of her left foot, the other slid ever so slowly up her leg, just to the point above her ankle, cupping that muscle and squeezing ever so slightly, his thumb moving lazily back and forth against the side of her leg, her whole body singing the please-touch-me song.

She was more relaxed than she'd been in weeks, felt a little pampered and more than a little turned on. Those magic hands of his could slide up her legs, up her dress, and soon he'd have her laid out flat on the seat with him on top of her.

Just like that.

And she was a fool.

"So what do you really want?" she asked, lying limp against the back of the seat, her feet still in his lap, his hands on her but still now.

"I already told you."

"You lied," she insisted, but without heat. "What's in this for you?"

"Assuaging my guilt over bringing you and Adam Landrey together."

"What else?"

"You just can't believe I would simply want to help anyone?"

"No. Not that," she said truthfully. "Just that you're… so focused, so driven, you hardly have time to think about anyone else. You're always five steps ahead of everyone—"

"So I'm too self-centered to help you and Adam?"

"I didn't say that. I'm just trying to understand."

The limousine slowed down, then stopped. Chloe glanced out the tinted window. She was home.

James got out. He must have told the driver to stay put, because he was the one who opened Chloe's door, her shoes in his hand.

"Want to walk?" he asked. "Or should we go for the Prince Charming, scoop-her-up-and-carry-her-inside treatment again? It did work really well in the first photos, I thought."

"I can walk," she insisted.

So he eased down onto his heels, took one foot in his hand and carefully slipped one sandal on, then the other, then took her hand and helped her out of the limousine.

He walked her to the door, took her keys from her hand and unlocked it, then gave her the keys back and gathered her in his arms. She stiffened, not expecting that, trying to hold herself just a little bit away from him and that alluring heat of his, the strength, the way he smelled.

She must be the strongest woman alive to resist him, she decided.

He leaned his head down to hers, his lips right at the side of her mouth. But he didn't kiss her, just whispered, "We don't know who might still be watching."

And then stayed there, perfectly still, his arms wound around her in a way that had to look possessive, like the perfect way to end a perfect date, just shy of being invited to come upstairs.

She let herself snuggle against him just a bit, easing just a little closer, her senses enveloped just a tad more completely in him. All she had to do was ease her mouth a fraction of an inch to the right, and he'd be kissing her, devouring her, she suspected. Or she'd be devouring him.

Two flights of stairs, down one hall, inside one door, and they could be in her room, in her bed. She shivered, thinking of them there, the way it had been so many times.

"I remember everything about what it was like to be with you," he whispered, sounding like a man who ached for her, and yet not moving one tiny millimeter closer, the discipline as astonishing as it was frustrating.

She finally broke the spell, not strongly enough to pull away from him but to let her head fall to his shoulder, to nestle into that wonderful hollow between his shoulder and his neck.

He breathed deeply, slowly, easing her body more firmly against his, wrapping her more tightly in his arms, like he was a man who'd stand between her and the entire world, if necessary.

And that's really what he was doing at the moment.

"You're going to have to tell me to leave," he said finally, his voice low and sexy, like he was as reluctant to go as she was to have him go.

The only problem was, she was even more scared to have him stay.

"I am an absolute mess right now," she said.

He grinned, laughed just a bit. She could feel the sound rumbling through his chest. "You're always kind of a mess, Chloe. But you're so much more than that. You always have been. And you never understood how appealing that could be."

"You can't be telling me that you've missed me," she insisted.

He eased back and nudged her head up, so he could look her in the eye. "I have missed you. Terribly. Tell me you've missed me, too."

Silly tears glistened in her eyes, coming on in a rush. "I've missed you, and I've been furious at you. I've cursed you and the day you were born, your mother, your father, every ancestor you ever had and now that damned woman who taught you to rub my feet that way! I've cried and cried and cried over you. I had a giant bonfire in the backyard and burned everything you ever gave me—"

"Okay, that's a little scary, Chloe—"

"I've done everything I could think of to get over you, to forget all about you, and now you come waltzing back into my life at the absolute worst possible time, looking every bit as gorgeous as before and being impossibly nice and saying you just want to help, and I can't say no to that help—"

"Good," he said.

"I can't say no, but I want to. I want desperately to just say no and tell you to go away because…because…"

"Yes? Because…why?"

She backed up until she couldn't anymore, her back against the shop door. Then she nearly yelled, "You know why!"

"Tell me," he insisted, following her until he was right up against her again. "I need to hear it, Chloe. Tell me. Because you—"

"Ahhh!" Chloe yelled as she nearly fell backward into the shop as the door behind her gave way. James nearly fell on top of her. He caught himself with one hand on the doorframe, caught her with his other hand and managed to keep them both on their feet, barely.

"What is the matter with you two?" Addie stood there holding the door open, glaring at them both. "You can't spend a few hours together without fighting? You're supposed to be crazy in love, remember? Prince Charming and that whole stupid fairy-tale courtship thing? And here you are yelling at each other before you can even get inside the shop!"

"Sorry," James said.

"You're never going to make this work at this rate! We'll fail miserably, and then we'll all end up living on the streets, begging for loose change and wrapping ourselves up in very expensive silk wedding gowns for warmth, because no one will want to buy them. Because we're all cursed! We can't even pull off a decent illusion of love for two stupid hours!"

"Addie, honey. It's okay. Go back to bed," Chloe said.

"No," she insisted. "Not until he's gone."

"Okay. I'll go," James said, giving Chloe one long, probing look.

He likely wanted to pin her to the wall and torture her until he got her to admit she needed another chance with him. He had to know how close he'd come to getting her to do just that.

But Addie could be scary when she was mad or scared herself, and James was a patient man, a wickedly patient one when it suited him. All as a means to getting what he wanted eventually. That was another truly scary thing about him—how he almost always got what he wanted in the end.

He leaned in, the perfect gentleman once again, kissed Chloe softly on the cheek, whispered, "Good night," and left.

Chloe collapsed on the showroom floor and buried her head in her hands, Addie fussing and wanting to know what was wrong. But Chloe couldn't even get the words out.

He wants me back.

Chapter Six

James was whistling as he approached the newsstand the next morning and Vince presented him with a tabloid with a photo of him and Chloe on the front page. Shot through the windows of her darkened shop, it was a shadowy impression of the two of them in an embrace, looking downright erotic as he nibbled on her neck.

Damn.

He got a little hot just looking at it, and he knew there hadn't been that much to the whole interlude. He hadn't actually touched her delectable neck.

"Looks like she's a lot more than your ex. You've been holdin' out on me," Vince said.

James shook his head. "I haven't."

"The hell you say," Vince insisted. "Come on. It's me. Was she really engaged to that photographer guy? And if she wasn't, what was that big fight on the runway about?"

"Vince, just out of curiosity, how much of the stuff do you think they print in these tabloids you sell is true?"

Vince shrugged. "I don't know. How much of the stuff do you think that's in the regular newspapers is true?"

"Okay, you've got me there."

James put the *Wall Street Journal* and his money down on the counter.

"You don't even want copies of the tabloids you're in today?"

"Nope." No doubt Marcy would have copies waiting. He couldn't deprive her of the pleasure of sharing all the news with him.

He was still whistling when he walked into the office. His secretary, his secretary's secretary and Marcy all stared at him like he'd lost his mind.

"What?" he asked finally.

"We thought you wouldn't be happy today, because of the photographs," Marcy said. "You have seen the photographs, haven't you?"

"Yes, I've seen the photographs."

Still, they stared.

"You just usually hate being photographed and showing up in the paper. Especially the tabloids," Marcy said.

"Oh, right. Yes. Awful, isn't it?" He tried, knowing even as he did that he wasn't selling it the way he should. He couldn't even pretend this morning.

Now they really looked at him like he'd lost his mind. *Oh, well.*

"Marcy, in here. Now," he said, pointing to his office. That was a little more like it, at least. He always started his day by ordering Marcy around.

She practically ran into the office, a little folder clutched to her chest, closed the door behind him and then stood behind his desk and to his right side.

"I have everything ready for you to review," she said, putting the folder down in front of him and opening it to a photo of him and Chloe arriving at the benefit. "This is the sort of shot used most frequently, correctly identifying you and Ms. Allen, mentioning that you had been involved previously. Many of them noted the prior engagement, and they all mentioned the runway brawl, but usually in questioning whether previous stories about it were true."

"Excellent," James said.

"Yes, it is. And then we have…this…particular photo…."

The shadowy shot of them in each other's arms in her shop.

He grinned, couldn't help it.

Marcy stared at him, waited and waited. He wasn't talking.

"This…uhhh," she finally continued, "one of the tabloids had this, claiming it's you and Ms. Allen, although it's hard to tell for sure. I wasn't sure if I should deny that it's the two of you or…"

"This is like a dream come true to you, isn't it?" he asked. "A front-row seat to front-page tabloid news?"

"I'm just trying to be prepared," Marcy argued. "The shot is out there, and if someone asks me about it, I have to know what to say."

"You don't have to say anything," James told her.

She pouted a bit, but went on to the various Chloe news items on the internet gossip sites, from "Chloe doesn't waste any time moving on" to "Chloe doesn't look like a woman with a broken heart."

"This one notes that Chloe may have already captured one of New York's most eligible, and that the list is coming out any day now."

"I can live with that."

"And then there's the Bride Blog lady."

James groaned. "What is wrong with this woman?"

"I think she hates Chloe. She's so mean. This morning

she says that Chloe's ex, Bryce Gorman, is being treated by the best plastic surgeon in the city but is likely to be scarred for life, that his boyfriend is either waiting tearfully by Bryce's side, pleading with Eloise to take him back or heavily medicated in a psychiatric ward in upstate New York, his life ruined. All while Chloe goes blithely on with her life, picking up where she left off with you, because she needs you for your money once again."

So, she was supposedly using him for his money? Something like that was always in the back of his mind when he was with a woman, but not Chloe. Maybe ninety-five percent of the time he was sure Chloe wasn't like that, and the rest of the time, he was just plain mad about the whole question of women, money and trust.

"This is just trash, Marcy. Don't believe a word of it," he said, then went to work.

Addie called James's office first thing the morning after Chloe's outing to the Met, ready to give him a piece of her mind, but was told quite snottily that he was in a meeting and could not be disturbed. It was a full hour before the phone rang again, caller ID telling her the call was coming from James's office.

"You rat! What did you do to her last night?" she said, not even bothering with "hello." They were long past pleasantries.

But it turned out it wasn't even him, just a woman who said she was his assistant, Marcy. She promised to messenger over the press clippings and internet postings of the day about Chloe and James, showing the initial success of their quest to prove Chloe was not cursed in love.

Then she started talking about how happy James was that morning, smiling—whistling even—despite that steamy photo of him and Chloe in the shop, where it looked like he was undressing her with his teeth.

"Oh, that rat!" Addie said. "He needs to understand that they are most certainly not back together. They're just pretending. That's it. She doesn't want him back for real, and he can't have her. He has to know that, if he has a functioning brain cell in his body."

"Oh, well—"

And then Addie got the worst feeling. "He's up to something, isn't he? He's got some hidden agenda with her, and when I get my hands on him, I am going to kill him!"

"I don't think he's up to anything. I mean…you wouldn't really hurt him, would you? Because he's a brilliant man. A financial genius and…a little different, but he's not evil. Besides, I don't think I've ever seen him really care that much about a woman. They come. They go. It doesn't really matter to him. Another one will come along sooner or later. They always do—"

The line went dead, suddenly nothing but silence, then a dial tone.

That was odd.

Suddenly, Addie had a bad feeling about the whole conversation.

James lunged for the phone, reaching around Marcy to slam his finger down on the disconnect button.

Marcy gave a little yelp, hung up the phone and slowly turned to face him.

"Another woman will come along? They always do?" he yelled. "Did you really just say that?"

She nodded shakily.

"What the hell did you just do, Marcy?"

"I'm sorry. I am so sorry. I was trying to help—"

"Help? By telling Chloe I don't give a damn about her, much less any woman?"

"No, no, no. It wasn't Chloe!" she cried.

"Oh, thank God," he said.

"It was her assistant, Addie."

James winced. "Addie's not just one of her assistants. She's her half sister. And she hates me! Absolutely hates me."

"She did say something about wanting to kill you." Marcy frowned. "But…she's not really dangerous, is she? I mean, if she shows up…should I call security or something?"

"Don't do anything!" he yelled, knowing he had to get to Chloe, fast. "I'm leaving. I may not be back today. Don't say anything to anybody. Not a word. Or I will fire you so fast—"

Marcy clamped a hand over her mouth, nodding still.

Around the same time as Marcy was being read the riot act, Chloe had just gotten out of the shower. She could hear Robbie bursting into her room, calling her name. She tucked her towel more securely around herself and opened the bathroom door. "What's wrong now?"

"You tell me," he said. "Addie's having some sort of fit about James. What did he do?"

Chloe frowned. "He didn't do anything."

"You are such a bad liar. Why do you even try?" He took her by the arm and led her over to her bed, pushed her down and then sat facing her. "Now tell me everything, so I can tell you what to do."

"He…he just…he rubbed my feet."

Robbie gave her a truly odd look, like feet-rubbing might be some euphemism for an odd new sexual behavior. It wasn't. Was it?

"Chloe, no foot massage is that good," Robbie claimed.

"He just has these great hands, and the way he touches me.... You know how some people just know how to touch you? How fast, how slow, how soft, how hard, just...so it feels exactly right?"

Robbie looked wistful and a little depressed. "Not anything I've experienced recently, but yes."

"Well, James knows. Do you think he makes every woman he touches feel that way? Or is it just me? That there's something about him and what he does that fits with something in me and exactly how I want a man to touch me?"

"I have no idea," Robbie said, looking really freaked out now.

"Because, if it's just him and me? And it wouldn't feel that perfect with anyone else, I don't know how I can give that up, because it just feels so good."

It was a horrible thought. Just him. Nobody else?

"Ahh, dammit," Robbie said, but he gave her a big hug at the same time.

"How does a woman give that up?" she said. "To know there's someone in the world who can make you feel like that, and to just...walk away from it?"

"You do it because he makes you miserable everywhere but in bed," Robbie explained. "Because you can't trust him, and he's pushy and overbearing and selfish and couldn't stay with the same woman for a month if he tried."

Chloe shook her head, her tears falling now despite her best efforts not to cry. "He says he never cheated on me."

"Of course he said that. All men say that when they're trying to get you back."

"You're right."

"And then there's that whole question of what, exactly, equals cheating to certain people. What body parts can come into contact with what other body parts without cheating occurring? Hands? Mouths? Anything else? These are questions you want answered in detail by a man who claims he never cheated on you."

"Robbie, stop!"

"Too much information?"

"Definitely too much."

"Sorry."

"I have to remember how awful it was in the end," she said, feeling bleak. "How awful he made me feel."

"Yes. That. Keep that thought in your head, and you'll be fine. If that doesn't work, come and get me. I'll remind you. And Addie'll beat him up for you. What in the world did you tell her?"

Chloe sniffled, feeling especially pitiful about that. "That I know what he's up to. That he wants me back."

Robbie swore. "Well, he can't have you!"

Robbie finally left, but not ten minutes later, as Chloe was searching for something to wear, she heard a commotion, pounding feet sounded on the stairs, men's voices, and then James burst into her room.

"Chloe, you can't believe her, okay? At least not without hearing me out," he said.

Robbie came into the room and glared at James. "You want me to get rid of him?"

James scoffed at the idea that Robbie could make him leave.

"Oh, stop it, both of you! I thought we were being invaded by crazy brides again." She turned to Robbie. "Thank you, but I can do this, I promise. I'm feeling much better now."

"At least put some clothes on," Robbie whispered to her as he walked past her.

"I will," Chloe promised, clutching her towel to her with both hands.

He left, and James just stood there, looking oddly mussed up and just not as perfectly put together as he normally was. He was breathing hard, too.

"Don't believe her, okay? Just promise me you won't automatically believe her."

"Believe who?" she asked.

"Marcy. She doesn't know what she's talking about."

Marcy? He'd mentioned her before. "I haven't talked to your assistant."

"I know. I didn't think you did. Addie did. And I know what Marcy told her, and I'm telling you, please, don't believe it. Because she doesn't know what she's talking about this time."

Chloe frowned. "I don't know what your assistant told Addie."

"You don't?" He looked like he'd love to believe that, but couldn't quite bring himself to. "Really?"

"Really," she told him.

He let out a long, slow breath and then looked her over slowly from head to toe, like he'd just figured out she was standing there in nothing but a towel. And like he was really glad, either that she didn't know what this Marcy woman had told Addie or that Chloe wasn't wearing anything but a towel.

"I just…I couldn't stand the idea of you thinking that about me," he said.

"Thinking what?"

"That I didn't mean what I said to you last night. I really have missed you. I wish we could go back in time, and everything between us could have been different."

"James, you don't mean that."

"I do. I meant it all. Every word. You know, the happi-

est day of my life since we broke up was when your customers rioted at your store—"

"Oh, gee. Thanks."

"No. No. Not like that! I mean, that was the moment.
The moment when I gave up on staying away from you.
Ever since I saw your picture in the tabloids for that crazy
runway brawl thing, I've wanted to come see you again."

Chloe wanted so badly to believe that.

"Before that, even. I did. But I fought against it," he said.
"Because it hurt so much to lose you. And I kept fighting
with everything I had until the bride riot, and then I just
gave up."

She wanted to give up, too, and just be happy he was
back.

"When I knew I was going to see you again, I was
so damned happy. No more fighting it. No more holding
back."

Then he pulled her into his arms like he'd die right then
and there if he didn't. He backed her up against the wall
and pinned her with his body. She let him take her face in
his hands, nuzzle her cheek with the tip of his nose, nibble
on her ear a bit, and she could feel the smile on his lips,
lips that were waiting patiently a breath away from hers.

She whimpered and shifted against him, something
that only served to make her more aware of every inch of
the big, solid body pressed up against hers. She put up her
hands between them to hold him off, but mostly all they
ended up doing was soaking up the warmth of his body
and then slipping beneath his jacket to wrap around his
waist and hold him to her.

He teased mercilessly, the tip of his tongue messing
with her ear and making her shiver, his teeth taking a little,
bitty bite of her earlobe, tiny kisses making a path down
her cheek, to her chin, then back up to the tip of her nose

and finally landing on her mouth. His tongue teased ever so gently against the seam of her closed lips.

"Chloe, let me in," he whispered.

She shook her head just a bit.

He took her top lip and pulled it into his mouth, sucking on it, stroking it with his tongue, so sweet, so gentle. "Let me in."

Inside, her heart thrummed like a big bass drum, the beats echoing all through her body, her breathing shallow and fast. She had no defenses against the man, and it was so unfair, and yet it was wonderful. Like more feeling than anyone could stand, like drowning in it, being carried off by the current of it.

"It's not fair," she whispered finally.

"What's not fair?" he asked, his forehead resting against hers, his nose nuzzling against hers, his lips right there, waiting for her.

"How much I want you," she admitted.

"But that's a good thing."

"No, it's not. It makes me not able to think, not remember to be careful and protect myself from you."

"Chloe, I swear, the last thing in the world I want to do is hurt you. And the thing I want most in the whole, entire world right now is to have another chance with you. And I think you want that, too."

"Because of some weird ego thing? Because women don't say no to you, and I did?"

"No! Because when we were together, it was so good. It was a little bit crazy and scary, and I didn't handle it well. I freely admit that. But it was so good. If I hadn't been so stubborn or so proud, I'd have been back here a year and a half ago, begging you to take me back. I was just so stupid about the whole thing."

She shook her head. "You're not stupid about anything."

"I am about this. About women, I am—"

"You breeze through relationships with women—"

"Okay, women who don't mean anything to me," he admitted. "Women I can take or leave without really caring. Those, I can handle. I'm good at that."

She knew that. Sore subject.

"But with a woman who's truly important to me," he said, "one I really care about? One who scares me and makes me furious, and makes me feel like there is a life outside of work and that maybe I want one? With that woman, I'm a complete mess. And you know how much I hate to admit not knowing anything, not being able to handle anything, so you know what it costs me to tell you that."

She scoffed at that. "So you're telling me that I'm different from all the others? That's the oldest line in the book, James."

"It's not a line. It's the truth. Is it so impossible for you to believe I was crazy about you? And that I still am? I mean, look at me. I was a mess with you. Do you think that's how things normally are between me and a woman?"

"No—"

"Okay, there you go. That should tell you something."

Chloe blinked up at him. Either she really wanted to believe him, or he was starting to make sense. She honestly wasn't sure which.

"I don't know how to handle you—"

"I don't want to be handled," she said.

"Okay, what do you want? God, just tell me, and I'll do it. I'll do anything, Chloe. I swear, I want this that much. Just tell me what to do."

"Don't…don't scare me," she said finally.

He frowned. "How do I do that?"

"Don't push so hard."

"Okay," he said, backing off so that he wasn't touching her at all.

She grabbed at her towel, still between them but not as securely around her body as before. "And don't rush me."

He took a breath and let it out in a big whoosh. "You want to go out or something? Dinner? Drinks? A walk? What?"

"I don't know. I just...don't grab me and kiss me. Don't rub my feet. Don't look so damned perfect and get me alone in the back of a dark limousine with that privacy window up between us and the driver."

"Okay," he agreed, but he was grinning now, thinking he'd won.

"And don't...just don't...make me want you so much."

"Chloe, I swear, I want *you* so much I can hardly breathe. Just to hold you, to put my nose against your skin and breathe you in, to have my hands on your skin, any little bit of skin...."

"Okay, that's not the way to do it. To keep me from wanting you so much."

"Sorry. I'm completely out of my element here, I swear. It's not some kind of fake line. I don't know what to do. I'm worried I'll mess things up so badly in the next moment that I ruin everything, and I can't stand to do that. It's taken so long just to get back here and to think we'll have another chance together."

"Okay. Enough." She held up a hand to stop him from saying any more.

"I'm sorry. I just don't know how to do it. That whole normal relationship thing—"

"Well, I don't know how to do it, either," she said. "You know I don't! Nobody in my family knows how to do it. We didn't get that relationship gene. We got the relationship-disaster gene."

"So what do we do?"

"I don't know. Go slow, maybe?"

He looked like the thought was extremely painful. "Okay. I probably shouldn't touch you then."

Chloe nodded. That sounded reasonable. It made her a little sad, but she couldn't argue the wisdom of it.

"We could…take a walk," she suggested. "In public. No public displays of affection whatsoever."

"Okay. I'll do it."

"Have some coffee, talk…. I think that's the place to start."

"Okay. God, I've missed you."

He said his world had nearly come to an end without her, and there'd been a time when she'd felt the same way without him.

"That's really not the kind of talk I meant," she told him.

"You're right. I slipped, but I'll do better."

"Okay," she agreed.

He nodded. "So that's it? We're going to try this? You're going to give us another chance?"

"Yes."

She watched as the most beautiful smile came across his face. He had dimples in his cheeks, and they were irresistible. He looked like a thousand-pound weight had come off his shoulders, like the sun had come out after a thousand and one incredibly dreary days.

Did it really mean that much to him? To have her give them another chance? Even as cynical as she was, Chloe didn't think anyone could fake that look of complete joy.

And it scared her even more.

She swayed a little on her feet, her head spinning.

He really meant it?

"Hey? What is it? Are you all right?" he asked, beside her but not touching her.

"Yeah. I mean…"

And then she fell into his arms, all the strength going out of her limbs.

He caught her to him, lifted her easily and had her on the bed in seconds, feeling her forehead. "Do you have a fever?"

"No, I don't think so."

He stretched out on the bed beside her, lying on his side, and held up two fingers in front of her face. "How many?"

"Two. I just got dizzy for a second. That's all." He'd been so honest with her. She felt like she owed it to him to be honest in return. "You scare me, too."

"Oh, Chloe," he said, reaching for her, then pulling back.

"And it's not easy for me, either. It's so hard. Like being on top of a really tall building and someone wanting you to walk out onto the edge and stand there." She felt it again, the room tilting on its axis. "You make my head spin."

"Don't look down."

"I can't help it."

"I'll be so careful this time, I swear."

"Okay."

And then they both went still, smiling at each other, staring, thinking. Hearts pounding, breath ragged, something that felt like static electricity zipping between them.

If she touched him, she'd feel that little spark she'd felt the very first time, she knew it. The first time he'd kissed her, too, there'd been that distinctive electrical jolt when their lips met. She'd lain in her bed later that night, alone, her fingers on that point on her lips, still feeling that little buzz.

It had been like something out of a fairy tale, something

that definitely couldn't have been real, she'd reasoned with herself. Those kinds of things didn't happen in the real world.

"The first time you kissed me," she began, because she just had to know. "I know this sounds crazy, but...did it feel like—"

"A little buzz of electricity, except in the best possible way," he admitted. "I told myself I must have imagined it."

"Me, too."

"And it's still there. I can feel it right now."

She nodded. "It is. Maybe we're both just crazy, but..."

She lifted her hand up and he did the same until their hands were spread wide, lined up palm to palm, fingertips to fingertips, but not quite touching, and there it was, like a force field all their own, tingling between them.

"It's a trick," she tried to tell him. "Some trick kids do. I can't remember exactly how or why it works, but...it's just a trick."

He pushed his hand forward, and she pulled hers back, feeling a push not of him but of the energy between them. He looked very satisfied with himself when she stopped pulling away.

"Tell me to go, Chloe. Tell me right now."

"You have to. Really. You have to just go."

"And I shouldn't...maybe...get just one kiss? A goodbye kiss? Before I go?"

"You'll go then?" she asked. "Really?"

"I will. I swear."

The problem was, what exactly constituted one kiss?

He nibbled on her, so delicately, with his lips on hers, and then teased with his tongue. She didn't move, couldn't move, didn't want to. Not ever.

He spread out on top of her on the bed, his body a glorious weight, the scent of him, the heat, enveloping her, and still, he was barely kissing her. He'd dip his mouth down to hers and then retreat. She started lifting her head off the bed, chasing his mouth as he pulled away from her, and finally, she took his head in her hands and with a groan, pulled him to her.

He still moved with excruciating gentleness, still ever so slowly.

Heat bloomed inside her, a million senses coming to life, like he'd flipped a switch and she was immediately an achingly sexual being once again. She'd forgotten just how much he could make her want him.

He finally kissed her for real, fully, deeply, wickedly, and she thought she might die from the sheer pleasure of it, that there was no hope for her, no way she was letting him leave without both of them getting naked right here, right now.

"You are a wicked man," she said.

"Yes, I am, but I'm also leaving," he claimed, breathing hard. "You made me promise, and I'm not going to start out by breaking a promise to you."

"I take it all back! Don't go!"

"Chloe, I've waited too long for another chance with you. I'm not going to blow it now," he said, rolling over onto his side next to her.

"But…but—"

He tugged her towel up higher on her chest, tucked one end into the top edge, to hold it there. She hadn't quite lost the only thing she had on, but she'd come close.

"I'm a man of remarkable restraint. Remember that. I think I should get two kisses the next time we're together."

"Two?" He'd had about a thousand, tiny, sweet ones, and at least one gigantic, luxurious one. What would two of those be like? "Okay, two."

"Good. Tell me to go. Make me go, now, please."

She kissed him instead, thinking it was goodbye, after all, and a man should get a goodbye kiss. So she took his face in her hands and leaned onto her side and took his mouth with hers, needing one more time to feel that magic little zing of happiness and desire that was uniquely him.

He was being very, very good, not pushing, not rushing her at all, just letting her take what she wanted from him, and then she felt his hand on her thigh, sliding slowly up under the towel.

"Oops," he said.

She laughed. "Oops."

The hand stopped moving, but stayed where it was.

"It's really not fair that you've been naked this whole time. I mean…not fair! I'm just a man."

"Of remarkable restraint. You just told me so."

"Yeah, and then you had to go and take advantage of me."

"Yes, I did," she admitted. "I'm very bad."

"Chloe, I swear, if you don't shove me out the door soon, I'm going to have my hand on your bare bottom. You know how much I love that cute little bottom of yours, and then your towel is going to be gone completely, and I'm going to have my mouth all over you. Your choice. What's it going to be?"

She thought about that big, hot hand cupping one of her hips, rubbing along that curve. It would feel so good. He swore softly and was reaching for the towel, when she became aware, vaguely, of footsteps on the stairs, racing up the stairs. What in the…

The door to her room burst open, and Robbie stood there once again.

Chapter Seven

"I just got the most bizarre phone call from the police station—" Robbie stopped midsentence when he saw the two of them there, rolling around on Chloe's bed, Chloe in nothing but a precariously positioned towel. "What… are you doing?"

"I…we…arguing, mostly," Chloe said, securing her towel once again and sitting up on the bed.

"Yeah, right," Robbie said, glaring at James.

"Did you say the police?" asked James, who'd gotten to his feet and was straightening his tie.

Robbie blinked once, then again, like it was all just too much for him. "Yes, the police. Am I dreaming?"

"I don't think so," Chloe said, although now that she thought about all the things James had said, the absolutely perfect things, maybe they were all dreaming. She looked to James. "Are we dreaming?"

"I've dreamed about you," he admitted, looking very, very happy.

Okay, that was not helping. Chloe turned back to Robbie. "Tell us what you think the police said."

"That they had Addie there," Robbie said. "And that she'd been arrested at James's office building. He owns the whole building?"

"I'm in a partnership that owns the building. I'm the managing partner," he said. "Why would Addie be at my office? Why would anyone there arrest her?"

"Something about a disturbance, a security guard and another woman," Robbie said.

"Addie has a thing for a security guard at my office?" James asked.

"No," Chloe said. "She doesn't have a thing for anyone at the moment. If she did, I'd know."

"So why would she be at my office?" James asked.

"She was really mad at you about last night," Chloe said.

"Wait," Robbie jumped in. "What happened last night?"

"Nothing," Chloe and James said at the same time.

"Oh, right!" Robbie didn't believe that.

"Hey, I didn't do anything last night," James protested.

"You…you…you rubbed my feet," Chloe said.

He threw his hands up in the air. "Like that's some sort of crime?"

"It is when you do it to…you know why you did it! You wanted me all relaxed and happy, so you could…you know!" Chloe insisted.

"No, I don't know. You wear those silly shoes all night, and your feet are bound to hurt. I know that—"

"From all those other women you date. You rub all their feet? You think I want to hear about other women you've been with, rubbing your feet and teaching you how to rub theirs? I don't want to hear that. No woman does—"

"Wait a minute," Robbie cut in. "Rubbing your feet? Is

that some euphemism for some kinky thing I don't know about?"

"No. At least, not that I know of," Chloe told him, then turned back to James.

"I'm not into anything weird. You know that," he protested.

"You know exactly what you were trying to do last night. You wanted me all relaxed and unsuspecting, so you could try to make me admit…what I admitted today!"

"No, I did not! I just thought your feet must hurt, and that they were one part of your body you might actually let me touch. And…yeah, maybe I thought I'd start there and end up…touching other places, and if that happened, I wouldn't have objected. But it would have just happened. That's all. That's what men are like. That's what we do. Start touching here, maybe work your way there."

"Okay, he's right about that," Robbie agreed.

"Yeah," James said. "Besides, I wasn't thinking about trying to get you to admit anything until you made me mad, and then…well, I was just mad."

"Well, I was mad, too, and Addie knew it. I guess…she might have…come up with some of her own ideas about why I was mad and about some things she might want to say to you about it."

"Okay, but that still doesn't explain her ending up in jail," James said.

Chloe frowned, then looked to Robbie. "They really said she was in jail?"

"Unless I imagined the whole thing. Weird thing to imagine, though."

"Yeah," Chloe said.

James's phone rang. He looked at it and said, "Hang on. Caller ID says it's the police."

As he listened, he began to look as confused as Robbie

when he'd first burst into the room. When he got off the phone, he said, "Okay, they say they've arrested Marcy, too."

"Addie and your assistant?"

"Well, we've never had anyone arrested in the lobby before. So, I'd say the odds of it happening twice in one day—in unrelated incidents—are highly unlikely."

"Addie's really going to hate you now," Robbie said.

It took an hour and a half to find them and pay their bail. The wait for them to actually be processed out was even longer.

The police didn't say much, just something about a woman wanting access to James's office, James's assistant refusing to allow that, and a security guard stepping between them, and then some sort of minor scuffle.

"Cat fight," one of the officers had told James and Robbie, grinning.

When they were alone, waiting, James said, "Marcy's father is a friend of mine and a business associate. When she got out of school, he begged me to give her a job, and I did. She's a little weird. She can be a little high-strung at times, but she's never been violent."

"Neither has Addie."

James's assistant got out of jail first. At least, Chloe assumed it was his assistant. She hoped he didn't know anyone else in jail today.

She was wearing an expensive if very boring suit, her long brown hair in a knot, but with more of it falling down now than actually in the knot. She had big, black streaks of mascara running down her face, was wearing only one shoe and looked terrified as she walked slowly toward them.

James looked incredulous. "Marcy?"

"I am so sorry," Marcy whispered furiously. "So, so, so sorry. And I know you're probably going to fire me. I understand that. I just…I just…I…"

And then she started sobbing pitifully.

James, looking exasperated, put his arm around her, patted her shoulder and let her cry it out. When her sobs finally slowed, he said, "What the hell happened?"

"It was Wayne, the new security guard. You know, the big, not-so-smart one who kind of has a crush on me?"

"No, Marcy, I don't know which one has a crush on you."

"Well, he can be kind of—" She stopped, mouth hanging open. "Oh, my God, it's you! You're Chloe! I've been wanting so much to meet you—"

"Marcy, not now!" James said.

"Oh, right. I'm sorry. I just, I've never met anybody who was on the cover of all those tabloids before. Or on *Entertainment Tonight*."

James winced and mouthed, "Sorry."

Chloe nodded and managed a smile for poor Marcy, who seemed a little flaky, but mostly just terribly young.

"You're so much prettier than you were in those pictures or the videos of that awful brawl—"

"Marcy, shut up about all that!" James told her.

"Oh, right. Sorry. I just…" She kept staring at Chloe, then got all worried again. "Oh, my God, was that really your sister I got arrested with? Please, please, please tell me it wasn't."

"If it wasn't, the police say she had my sister's driver's license and looked enough like her to pass for Addie," Chloe told her.

Marcy looked devastated. "I just don't know how this could have happened."

"Neither do I," James said. "Start talking, and stick to the subject this time. What happened?"

"I spoke with someone this morning claiming to be Ms. Allen's assistant, needing urgently to speak to you, saying among other things that she…wanted to do bodily harm to you—"

"Sounds like Addie," James said.

Marcy looked even more hopeless than before. "And I was a little uneasy about the conversation. So I called downstairs to security and got Wayne…." Marcy sighed heavily and looked at Chloe. "Why can't men be both intelligent and great-looking? I mean, I couldn't go out with anybody like Wayne. What would we have to talk about? But sometimes, I think I could just sit there and look at him for hours and—"

"Marcy, nobody cares what's going on with you and Wayne!"

"Right. Sorry," she said. "I told him to watch out for a suspicious woman who would try anything to get to see my boss, and Wayne said that someone had been lurking around downstairs all morning, not trying to get upstairs to any of the offices, just watching everyone go in and out. And I thought that sounded like someone from one of the tabloids, you know, spying on us all."

"Of course," James said.

"Then, a few minutes later, Wayne called back, and I…I—"

"Despite me ordering you not to do or say anything to anyone—"

"I know." Marcy winced. "But I thought if you were going to fire me anyway, I might as well at least try to fix things. So I went downstairs."

"And made them so much worse," James said. "I can't

believe you graduated from Wharton. Did you really, Marcy?"

"I did. I swear!" Marcy's lower lip started trembling. She was going to cry again, right here in the police station. She mouthed to Chloe, behind James's back, "Please, ask him not to fire me. I love my job."

Chloe nodded that she would, feeling sorry for the young woman and knowing what it was like to watch your career hopes dashed.

"Thank you," Marcy mouthed.

And then Addie burst into the lobby, looking as disheveled as Marcy and more mad than scared. She zeroed in on Chloe, then spotted James, and it was like smoke was coming out of her ears, she was so enraged.

Marcy slid behind James, whimpering, "Please don't let her hurt me."

Addie marched over, got up in James's face, pointing at Marcy. "This idiot child and that hulk of a security guard work for you?"

"Yes," James admitted. "Could we please not do this in public? That's all I'm asking, Addie. Please."

"Because some tabloid reporter might be lurking around?" Addie scoffed at that. "That's what she kept saying! That's what started this mess."

"You scared me, and Wayne thought you were going to hurt me! That's really all it was, I swear, Mr. Elliott. She came charging toward me, and Wayne was just trying to protect me," Marcy said, peering around James's shoulder just long enough to put her two cents in.

"That big buffoon of a rent-a-cop grabbed me and literally picked me up off my feet!"

"He just didn't want you to hurt anybody!" Marcy whined.

"I don't hurt people! I'm not some kind of nut! I'm

Chloe's sister! All I wanted was for the hulk to put me down!"

James stood between the two of them as they leaned left and right to yell around him. "This is a nightmare!" He turned to Marcy. "Say one more word, and you're fired. I mean it."

Marcy slunk down behind him and stayed there.

To Addie, he said, "Please, I am begging you. I have a car and driver outside. Could we please just get in the car and finish this there?"

"Not with her," Addie said, trying to look around him to get to Marcy.

"Fine. Marcy, go home. Right now. I'll hail you a taxi and talk to you tomorrow." He looked to Chloe and Addie. "Ladies, this way, please."

They marched out of the police station together, Addie still fuming, Marcy pouting, James exasperated, Chloe thinking her life could not get any weirder. Tabloid reporters, YouTube videos, the Bride Blog, Bryce, Eloise, her beautiful dresses that people believed were cursed.

They made it to the car with only a few more pointed comments from Addie, Marcy pouting and slinking away into a cab idling by the curb. Chloe just wanted to hide, and definitely not be caught between Addie, James and the fight she knew they were going to have.

"James," she said, "Addie and I are going to get a taxi and go home."

"No, he and I are going to talk. I was attacked in the foyer of his office by some rent-a-goon and his crazy assistant!" Addie yelled.

Chloe held up her hand. "Okay. You can tell me all about it. I just…I can't listen to the two of you go at each other right now. Please?"

James, looking like he absolutely hated the idea, leaned

in close and whispered, "She's going to give you a million reasons why you should run as fast as you can away from me right now and never see me again."

"I know, but she won't convince me to stay away from you. I promise."

"I'm going to hold you to that," he said, leaning in to talk to his driver for a moment, then holding open the car door for Chloe. "Here, you two take my car. The driver has the address."

"Thank you," Chloe said, not looking forward to the ride alone with Addie, either, but grateful to avoid all-out war between Addie and James.

But Addie wasn't done. She stood there, glaring at James.

"Addie, get in," Chloe said.

"No!"

"If you don't get in, I'll ask James to, and we'll leave you to find your own way home."

Addie gaped at her. "I just got arrested because of him!"

"Get in or I'm leaving you," Chloe insisted.

Addie got in. She was furious, but inside the car.

James shot Chloe one last worried look, closed the door and watched them drive away.

"He is like poison to you," Addie said, delivering her opening salvo the minute they pulled into traffic.

"I know. Don't you think I know that? I just can't help it. I'm crazy about him."

"Yes, exactly. Crazy. No one should be crazy over a man. It's a bad thing. You should know this by now."

"I do. I just…I've missed him so much. You were right. I latched on to Bryce so fast because I wasn't over James. I felt so bad, and I needed so much to forget about him, and then there was Bryce, trying to go completely straight for some reason. I bet it was that aunt of his with all the money and no kids of her own. He was always trying to impress her, and she's ultraconservative." Chloe felt even worse now. "Maybe he was going to marry me to make his aunt think he was straight, so she'd leave him all her money."

"Who knows why he did it? He's a man. They'll lie about anything."

Chloe shot her a look that said she was not helping right now. "Anyway, I jumped right into a relationship with him, and now I'm paying for it. But it brought James back into my life, and…God, Addie, I just can't be sorry about that."

Addie gaped at her. "It's that bad? Already?"

Chloe nodded, admitting it.

"I went there to tell him that he couldn't do this to you again, that I'd hurt him if he so much as tried, and it's already too late?"

"It is. I'm sorry. I tried so hard to get over him, and I tried to resist him. But what if…there's no way to really resist him? I mean…what if he's the one? The only one?"

Addie shook her head, silent for a moment, speechless.

Yeah, it was that bad, that big and overwhelming and scary.

"We need to get you on a plane," Addie said finally. "To anywhere. Anywhere but here."

"I can't leave now. We have to try to save the business. And besides, even if I did leave, he'd just come find me. He really wants another chance with me—"

"And you believe him? You think he actually means that?"

Chloe nodded.

"You know that's crazy. You know how he is with women. Admit it—you've been secretly keeping track of all the gossip about him and whatever ridiculous, beautiful woman he's dating at the moment."

"Yes, I have."

"And last time, in the end, you caught him red-handed with that model, Giselle—"

"I know."

"Men don't change," Addie said softly, taking Chloe's hand in hers as she said it, the awful truth.

"But it's not…impossible for a man to change," Chloe tried.

"Oh, God! He's got you again. He's got you right where he wants you."

And to that, Chloe couldn't say anything.

It was true.

James awoke refreshed, renewed and determined to see Chloe and make sure Addie hadn't convinced her that he was the devil incarnate, come to ruin her life in every way possible.

He put on his favorite suit, then added a shirt in the palest of blues, because Chloe used to always try to get him to mix it up a little with some colors. Going with a very pale blue instead of white was big for him. He was trying to show her he could be flexible and a little daring. He even put on a striped tie instead of a solid-colored one—another huge wardrobe concession.

He walked up to the newsstand that morning happy, confident, excited for the day to come and what it would bring.

Vince gave him an odd look, he noticed, but he wasn't worried. It was probably because of the striped tie. Then James saw that Vince had another tabloid waiting for him.

For just a moment, James felt a little jab of anxiety.

But no. Everything was fine. He was sure of it.

He stood directly in front of Vince. No mistaking that odd look now. And Vince laid the tabloid down on the counter in front of James. The headline read Chloe in a Three-Way (Fight) for One of New York's Most Eligible! Her Sister and His Assistant Caught Naked With Him, Financial District Brawl Results.

James went absolutely still, barely even breathing.

Just the day before, things had been going so well. He'd been in Chloe's bed, kissing her, hearing her promise to give him another chance, and then Robbie had burst in talking about Addie being in jail.

Now, somehow, there was a picture of him, Chloe, Addie and Marcy outside the police station, Addie looking like she was going to kill him, Marcy pouting and Chloe... poor Chloe, looking so sad. Below that was a smaller one of Addie and Marcy in handcuffs, being hauled out of the foyer of James's office.

Chapter Eight

"No, no, no!" James shook his head. "It can't be. Tell me you made it up, Vince. Tell me you have a friend who can put things like this together, and that the whole thing is a really bad joke! Please, tell me that."

Vince looked like he even felt sorry for James. "Tough break, man. The three of them finding out about each other like that. What are you gonna do?"

"I didn't do it!" James held up the stupid tabloid. "I'm not sleeping with my assistant or Chloe's sister. Hell, I'm not even sleeping with Chloe yet."

"No way I believe that," Vince said. "I saw the picture of you and that Chloe girl where it looked like you were undressing her with your teeth!"

"Well, I didn't. Okay, a little undressing with the teeth, but that was it. She doesn't trust me yet. God, she may never trust me again."

James just stood there, stunned and furious. This was a

disaster. There was the whole public humiliation aspect of it for Chloe. Having tabloids blaring to the world the news that the man who was supposed to love you was sneaking around behind your back would no doubt mean a reprisal of the whole cursed-in-love thing for Chloe and her business.

"I'm telling you, sex with a relative or a best friend of your lady? Strictly off-limits," Vince said.

James didn't even try to explain. And perhaps for one time in his life, he had no idea what to do next. It was the most horrible feeling. He always knew what to do. He always had a plan. The highly developed sense of logic he'd always counted on, the ability to step back from any situation, weigh the information, the variables, the probabilities and know the right thing to do… It was gone. Just… gone.

It was Chloe, Chloe World, Chloe Chaos. Logic did not apply. Plans went horribly awry. Confusion reigned. And yet he desperately wanted to be with her. He felt utterly defeated in that moment, James Elliott IV, a man who believed he could do anything, solve any problem, make anything work.

"I was supposed to fix things for her. I was just trying to help."

"By sleeping with her and her sister?" Vince gave a dismissive huff.

"I am not sleeping with her sister!" James yelled.

People on the street were starting to pause and stare. And that's when James saw the flash.

Right in his face.

A camera flash!

Some tabloid photographer was tailing him now!

"Oh, you bastard!" James yelled, taking off after the

guy, who continued snapping shots in James's face and backing up furiously as James charged toward him.

He was going to grab that camera and shove it down the guy's throat if it was the last thing he did. That was all he was thinking about. Get the guy, get the camera.

James took off, fury and maybe the flash of the camera blinding him at first. He stepped off the curb. The next thing he knew, a bike messenger was practically on top of him, people were screaming and he felt oddly like he was flying through the air.

Marcy felt certain Mr. Elliott intended to fire her after the incident with Addie, but she went to work anyway. He said they'd talk today, presumably so he could bawl her out in detail and then fire her. She wanted that to be a face-to-face meeting. Not that she'd rather be fired in person. She'd just rather be able to plead her case to keep her job in person. Marcy wasn't above begging.

On the way, she made her usual newsstand stop for copies of all the relevant tabloids, and that's when she saw it, right there on the cover of the *New York Mirror.*

"Oh, my God, that's me!" she yelled.

People started staring, whispering.

The newsstand guy took the tabloid from her hands and held it up next to her face. "Yeah, I guess it does look a little like you."

"No, it really is me!" There was a zing of absolute glee at first. Her picture was right there, like she was some kind of celebrity!

But then it occurred to her that the only potentially tabloid-worthy thing she'd done was end up in jail the day before with Ms. Allen's sister.

Marcy gaped at the photo, a horrible feeling of dread moving through her body. It showed her, Addie and Chloe outside the police station, with a headline that implied they were all sleeping with Marcy's boss, and that poor Ms. Allen was, indeed, cursed in love once again.

"Sleepin' with your boss. Never a good idea," the newsstand guy said.

"I am not sleeping with my boss!" Marcy yelled back, which only made more people turn and stare.

She rushed down the street and into her office building, where she came face-to-face with Wayne, who looked quite miffed at her.

"You're sleeping with Mr. Elliott?" he yelled.

"No! I'm not," she claimed.

"I can read, Marcy," he said, holding up the offending tabloid.

Marcy whimpered. Her cell phone rang. When she grabbed it to avoid seeing the condemnation in Wayne's eyes, the caller ID indicated it was her mother.

"Oh, no!" she cried. "My mother's seen that!"

Her mother didn't read silly gossip, but she had friends who did.

Somehow she got herself upstairs and walked into the office, only to find everyone there staring, too, and shooting her many disapproving looks.

"I didn't do it!" she cried. "I swear!"

They kept staring. She grabbed a ringing phone. To have something to do. And that's how she found out that her boss was in the emergency room.

Chloe and Addie were in the kitchen waiting for the first pot of coffee to finish brewing, when Addie's phone rang.

"I can't believe she has the nerve to call me again!" Addie said.

"Who?" Chloe asked.

"That crazy Marcy woman who works for James." Addie clicked a button to answer the call and said, "What in the world could you—"

Chloe watched as Addie frowned, then looked seriously freaked out and then just yelled, "What?" And with that, the familiar ooze of dread started working its way through Chloe's body.

Addie clicked off the phone and said, "Okay, try not to freak out."

Chloe's mouth fell open. "Freak out? There's nothing left to freak out about! Please, tell me there's nothing left!"

"Marcy didn't have a lot of details, at least none that made sense. But James is in the E.R., and he's asking for you."

"James is hurt?" That was worse than anything she had imagined.

"Come on," Addie said, taking her by the arm. "I'll go with you."

After what seemed an eternity, they got to the E.R.

"You have a patient here, James Elliott, who's asking for me," Chloe told the desk clerk, who immediately put up a hand to tell her she'd have to wait to even ask a question.

Addie leaned around Chloe to stare into the corner. "Wait, there's Marcy."

They hadn't gotten anything out of Marcy that made sense before a nurse found them, asking Chloe to follow her. Chloe left Marcy and Addie whispering furiously to each other, definitely hiding something.

Gulping, she finally asked the nurse, "What happened to James?"

"Apparently, he stepped off the curb and got hit by—"

"Oh, my God!" Chloe cried.

"—a bike messenger," the nurse finished.

Chloe started to breathe again. Not a car. A bicycle.

Still, those guys rode like lunatics, zipping in and out of traffic the way they do.

"Yeah, I'd take one of those over getting hit by a car. Still, it's no picnic." The nurse headed down the hall, motioning for Chloe to follow.

She stopped at a cubicle, drew a curtain aside and there was James, lying on a stretcher, looking bruised and battered, scrapes here and there, a white bandage on his head, an IV line in one arm and cardiac leads on his bare chest, which also had a big red bruise on it.

Chloe gasped. "Are you sure it was just a bike?"

"Yes. There were several witnesses," the doctor, who was standing by the bed, told her, steering her to the side of the bed and a waiting stool. "Sit. I'm Dr. Morgan."

"Chloe Allen. What's wrong with him?"

"Hopefully just a concussion and some bruises, but we're still waiting for the scans to be read to be sure there's no internal bleeding. There are no obvious fractures, although I don't know how. His BP's okay. Might have a cardiac contusion—"

"Wait, his heart?"

"It may be bruised, yes."

That sounded like such a scary thing, a bruised heart, and so sad. Chloe felt like her heart was bruised, too, right then, just from looking at James.

"The main point of impact was the chest," the doctor said. "But right now, the EKG is fine. He was unconscious at the scene, which we never like when someone's taken a blow to the head. But he woke up in the ambulance and has been in and out here. And he really wants to talk to you."

"But he's going to be okay?"

"I want to see his scans come back clean, but right now,

I'm not too worried," the doctor said, then hesitated, giving Chloe an odd look.

"What? What is it?"

"We had a hard time calming him down when he got here," the doctor said. "So please don't say anything to upset him."

"Of course. I would never want to do anything to make him worse."

"Good," the doctor said, then turned to James. "And I think he's figured out that you're here. Mr. Elliott? We found Chloe for you. She's right here."

James turned his head slowly toward Chloe. Beneath the stark white bandage on his left temple, his gaze wasn't quite focusing and one eyelid was swollen. He reached for her, and she took his hand in hers, putting her other hand on his shoulder—the one that didn't have road rash on it.

"Chloe?" he said weakly. "I didn't do it, I swear."

"Okay." Chloe looked to the doctor, who nodded that yes, this was what she needed to do. "James, I'm sure whatever it is, it's fine."

"I really didn't. You have to believe me."

Chloe squeezed his hand, trying to reassure him. "I do. I promise."

"I didn't sleep with either one of those women, I swear."

The doctor froze at that. So did the nurse, both looking at Chloe worriedly.

James, now that he'd gotten all that out, gave her a little smile. Then he drifted off, helped along by whatever medication he was on.

Women?

What women?

She looked at the doctor, who seemed like he was still waiting and worrying about what Chloe might do or say.

The nurse seemed as if she'd just had a little lightbulb moment, looking at Chloe. "Oh, my God! You're her! That runway brawl woman! The one who's supposedly cursed in love? Wow, you really are, aren't you?"

Chloe couldn't say a thing. Not one single word.

Yes, she was *that* woman, wasn't she?

The doctor took the nurse by the arm and practically shoved her out of the cubicle. "I'm so sorry for that. It's the last thing you need right now. And thank you for being so calm and not upsetting the patient."

Chloe nodded, having absolutely nothing to say at the moment.

Who could he possibly have slept with?

And not one woman, but two? How did he find the time?

He'd seemed so sincere this time, and just crazy about her. Why bother, if he didn't really care for her at all? What was the point? Chloe sighed, looking down at that beautiful face of his, that hand she still held in hers.

She was cursed, no doubt about it.

Chloe was trying to stay calm as she headed back out to the waiting room, to not remember every other time in her life when she'd found out a man she thought she loved was sleeping with someone else. Then she heard what sounded very much like Addie's raised voice saying, "No, no, no. We don't need security! We'll behave."

She followed the sound of raised voices and found Addie, Marcy, two security guards and James's doctor, who looked horrified when he spied Chloe.

"What's wrong now?" Chloe asked.

"Nothing. It's all a misunderstanding," Addie tried to reassure her.

"That's what you said yesterday, when we ended up bailing you both out of jail." Too late she realized that might not be the best thing to say in front of the security guards, then added, "They're annoying and ridiculous at times, but not dangerous."

"You are not helping," Addie complained.

"Well, neither are you! Can't the two of you get along for five minutes while I'm trying to make sure James is okay?"

"Yeah. About James—" Addie began.

"Not now," Marcy cut in.

"Yes, now. It'll be even worse if she hears he's supposedly sleeping with two other women and doesn't hear that we're the two women in question."

Marcy thrust a copy of today's tabloid into Chloe's hands.

"Oh, that's perfect. Just perfect," Chloe said, humiliated anew as the doctor, the security guards and seemingly everyone in the waiting room was staring at her, some with curiosity and some in abject pity.

"I swear, I've never slept with him," Marcy said, then shot Addie a look.

"She knows I didn't sleep with him. I can't stand him," Addie said.

"Wait, the two women he supposedly slept with are you and Marcy?"

Marcy nodded, looking a bit scared. "He told you?"

Chloe laughed a bit, some of her tension dissipating. "It's really supposed to be the two of you?"

"I would just never do that! It's been awful already, having people think I did," Marcy said, then looked like she was about to cry. "My own mother thinks I did it!"

"Okay, enough," Chloe said. "The two of you get out of here, before you get into another fight and we all end up in jail or in another tabloid."

They left, finally, Marcy offering to return with clothes

for James to wear home. The doctor gave Chloe an odd look as he said, "You lead a very interesting life."

James was having absolutely bizarre dreams.

There were people fighting to hold him down, poking at him, shining big lights in his eyes, taking off his clothes, and then he woke to find himself on a stretcher in what looked like a hospital. *Weird. Very weird.*

He felt the IV needle in the back of his hand, the little pads on his chest hooked up by cables to a heart monitor. He didn't have a shirt on. He might not be wearing anything except a thin sheet. It hurt to breathe and to move his head. Just having a head, in fact, hurt.

Then he saw Chloe dozing, curled up in a chair by his side and holding his hand, which made everything better.

The last thing he remembered was walking down the street, on his way to work. Things came rushing at him in disjoined flashes. Vince at the newsstand. The tabloid. Him, Marcy, Addie and Chloe. Good God!

There was a beeping noise nearby, getting faster and faster.

His heart?

A nurse came in, checking the monitors. A doctor came in and did the same. Chloe woke, sat up and looked worried.

"Just relax," the doctor said, putting a stethoscope to James's chest and listening. "Lots of people come to in the hospital a little disoriented. The heart rate kicks up. No big deal."

"I'm on a heart monitor?"

"Just a precaution. Hurt to breathe?"

"Yes."

"That's probably why. Head hurt, too?"

"Yes."

"We think you hit your head when you landed. Remember anything?"

"I was…" At the newsstand. *God.* Did Chloe know what was in the tabloids this morning? He looked at her. She was holding his hand, looking concerned but trying to smile at him. "Uhh…I was walking to work. I stepped off the curb, and then…I was in the ambulance."

"Okay. Not bad. Sounds like you only lost a few minutes. Not unusual with concussions. You were hit by a guy on a bike. Could have been a lot worse and from what the witnesses said, not your fault. He was going the wrong way on a one-way street. Right now, you look good. We're going to watch you for a little while, wait for your scans to come back and then we'll know for sure."

James frowned. "What happened to the other guy?"

"Already walked out of here. He was wearing a helmet. And he landed on the trunk of a parked car, which is much more forgiving than asphalt."

"Okay. Thank you," he said to the doctor.

The doctor sent a cautious smile in Chloe's direction, then took the nurse—who looked like she might be taking notes for the tabloids tomorrow—by the arm and hauled her out of the cubicle. Then it was just James and Chloe, with all the privacy a curtain could provide.

He took a cautious look at her.

"You were on your way to work?"

"Yes." He nodded.

"Maybe buying your *Wall Street Journal?*"

"Yes." She knew? Wait a minute. Had he told her himself?

"James, please don't tell me you nearly got yourself killed over the tabloid shot of the four of us outside the jail yesterday."

Yeah, he had told her. Right here in the hospital.

"Chloe, you know it's not true, right?" He rushed on. "Me sleep with Addie? That would be like sleeping with a porcupine. Plus, she'd never agree to it, unless… To keep us apart? Oh, damn. She might actually do that if she thought it would keep you and me apart!"

"If she was truly desperate to keep you away from me and couldn't think of any other way… No, even then, I don't think she'd sleep with you."

"Addie hates me, and for once it's a good thing," he said, relieved. "Now, Marcy is really smart when it comes to finance, but at the same time, wacky and annoying. I'd rather jump off a building than sleep with her."

"She was horrified by the idea, herself. Poor thing. Apparently, her mother's seen the story. I think we may have cured Marcy's tabloid addiction."

"So, you and me? We're okay?"

"James, you can't have seriously believed I'd think you were sleeping with either Addie or Marcy—"

"I knew it would hurt you. That it would be humiliating for you and bring up bad memories of how we broke up the first time." He looked absolutely grim. "And I knew you probably wouldn't believe I'd have anything to do with Addie or Marcy, but what about anyone else?"

Chloe just looked away.

"Yeah, that's what I was thinking. That's what I was so afraid of. I know exactly how fragile this whole thing between us is right now," he said. "We've never been good at trusting each other. Hell, I'm not good at trusting anyone, and you just can't seem to trust men, and I know I'm part of the reason."

Chloe shook her head. "You're right. It's never going to be easy for either one of us."

He nodded. "If it had been anyone but Addie and Marcy I was supposed to be sleeping with, you'd have believed it and walked away from me again. That's what I thought when I saw that tabloid."

"I'm sorry. I'm so sorry you were hurt—"

"I'm fine, Chloe. And all I need to know is that we're going to get the time together we need to learn to trust each other again. I couldn't stand it if anything happened and we didn't get that time."

"We'll have time," she promised.

"I can control what I do, what I say, where I go, but those tabloids? They can say anything. We've already seen that. I'm scared of what they might say, and the last time we were together... Chloe, you would have believed I was sleeping with half the population of Manhattan."

She shook her head. "We're different people now. This is a different time—"

"No, it's not," he insisted. "I'm afraid, in many ways, we're the exact same people, making the exact same mistakes, and I don't want to do that again. Do you really want to do that all over again?"

"No," she admitted finally. "It was too hard. It hurt too much."

"Yes, it did."

Her gaze darted to his, old hurt still in her eyes and a little bit of a challenge, a little bit of disbelief. Did she really think it hadn't nearly killed him to lose her? Had he really made it look like he hadn't cared that much about her the first time they were together?

"We have to talk about this, Chloe. We have to talk about Giselle—"

"Not now. I can't do it now. It's been an awful day. I was so scared when I got the call that you'd been hurt."

He should make her listen. He knew it. But he was just so damned tired. Every bone in his body hurt. Hell, it still hurt to breathe.

"Come here, Chloe," he said, pulling her against him.

She came slowly, easing down to snuggle into his side, her palm flat against his chest, working its way between the leads of the EKG, then pressed a tiny kiss to his shoulder. "You really scared me."

"I know. I'm so sorry," he said. At times, she could be so fierce, such a little fireball, and at others, she could feel so tiny and vulnerable. He loved both those sides of her.

"This whole thing is getting out of hand," she argued. "You're just trying to help me and you almost died out there today."

"I didn't almost die—"

"Do you know how many pedestrians are killed in Manhattan every year—?"

"Okay, yes. But I'm fine. I swear." He felt her take a breath, deep and slow, and gave up on making her listen to him right then. "One day, when you're ready, you're going to listen to what I have to say about the night we broke up, and you're going to believe me, Chloe. And you're going to trust me again. And then, everything is going to be better."

"Okay. One day—"

"Before you leave. Promise me," he insisted.

"Okay, I promise. But right now, you're supposed to rest, not get upset. The doctor said so."

"All right." He let it go for then and finally started to relax, both reassured and comforted by the feel of her head against his shoulder. "Stay with me?"

"Of course I'll stay."

He could make it if she stayed.

Today had been so bizarre, so unbelievably bad, that feeling of flying through the air out on the street. The sound of people screaming now. Thinking he had to land at some point, land hard. People working over him on the street, in the ambulance.

He remembered being scared, and that all he'd wanted was Chloe. She was here now, cuddled up against him. So he closed his eyes, locked his arms around her and let himself rest.

Chapter Nine

After spending the entire day and part of the evening under observation in the E.R., James was finally discharged. He and Chloe sat side by side, holding hands and uncharacteristically silent in the car on the way to his apartment.

Chloe soon saw that it was the same one he'd lived in when they were together, as stark, modern, functional and completely impersonal as before. Colorless, too. How did anyone live without color?

He hesitated just inside the doorway, wincing as he flipped a switch and the light hit him. Chloe turned it back off. With the big expanse of windows in the living room, there was enough light from the street and surrounding buildings for them to see.

She was exhausted from the day, so she didn't really understand how he was still standing. Guiding him straight to his bedroom, she pulled back the covers of his starkly modern platform bed and gave him a pointed look.

"Don't even think about arguing with me on this."

"Chloe, I've wanted you back in my bed for a year and a half. Believe me, I'm not arguing."

She shot him an incredulous look. "You can barely move. I don't know what you think you're going to do in that bed tonight—"

"Hold you, if I'm very, very lucky," he said, then made the mistake of trying, too quickly, to slide his jacket off, and ended up grimacing.

She pushed his hands away and took it off him herself, hanging it up in his meticulously organized closet. She knew exactly where it went. When she came back to him, he'd loosened his tie. She took that, too, and hung it up. She was simply overcome by the need to take care of him. It was something he'd never let her—or anyone else, that she knew of—do for him.

She began undoing the buttons of his shirt, as she'd done that first night they'd met, when she still thought he was her model groom. And she could swear that touching him now, her fingertips barely brushing against his poor, bruised chest, was every bit as unsettling as it had been that first time.

"Going to tuck me in, too?" he asked softly.

"If you're lucky."

He grinned at her through the dim light in the bedroom. "I'm feeling very lucky right now."

Which unfortunately brought back the memory of the doctor telling him how very lucky he was. *Get pitched into the street instead of the sidewalk, and a car would likely have gotten you before you hit the ground. And you could have landed the wrong way.... It's a miracle you didn't break anything.*

Chloe felt a shiver work its way down her spine.

James's hands closed over hers, holding them against his chest for a moment, as he breathed in and out. Then he brought her hands to his lips, kissing them softly. "Don't think about it, Chloe. I'm fine."

She found she couldn't look him in the eye, concentrating again on unfastening the remaining buttons on his shirt, then undoing his cuffs. She eased the shirt off his shoulders, and before she could go put it away, he took it from her hands and dropped it on the floor.

His arms came gently around her, drawing her slowly and cautiously against him.

"I should go," she said. "You need to rest."

"So do you." He kissed her forehead, stroked a hand through her hair. "I don't think you should be alone tonight—"

"You don't think I should be alone tonight?"

"I think neither one of us needs to be, and I for damned sure don't want to be. Stay with me, Chloe. Just sleep beside me in the bed. Let me hold you all night, and in the morning, we'll talk. You promised we would. You promised to hear me out about Giselle."

She closed her eyes against the notion of the talk, that there was anything he could say that would truly make a difference. Was he going to lie to her again? Even now? Because, honestly, she'd seen him with that witch of a model, Giselle, seen them in each other's arms. It hadn't been some innocent embrace, and it had been the end of him and her.

How could she possibly want to be here with him this much when he'd hurt her the way he had back then? How could she think anything had truly changed? It was like getting run over by an eighteen-wheeler and just lying there on the street, asking the driver to back over you one more time for good measure.

She really wasn't that stupid, was she?

Okay, yes, she was that stupid, because she wanted to be in that bed with him.

James stood there with her in his arms, not letting go. If need and determination could keep her here, she wasn't leaving. But he knew, too, that he could only push so far before she either pushed back or ran away from him. He was damned sick and tired of her running away.

So he stood there, waiting, an odd kind of nervous energy buzzing through his body, years of reserve and caution, that supreme need not to ever truly be vulnerable to anyone, rearing up inside of him.

He tried to push all thought away, except the fact that at the moment, she was still here, and she was in his arms. He thought about how small and vulnerable she was, about the fine trembling running through her body, the sweet smell of her hair and the way it felt when he slipped his fingers into it at her nape, to cup her head and hold her face pressed against his chest.

Breathing as slowly and easily as he could manage— because even that still hurt—he dug deep for the patience not to push her, not to rush her, not to mess this up.

Finally, in a small, shaky voice, she admitted, "Honestly, James, I can't think of anything you could say about the last night we were together that would make any difference."

He winced at that, knowing it was only what he deserved. "Let me say it anyway, please? Decide for yourself if it makes a difference, and then if you still want to go…"

Damn, he couldn't even say it. That she could go anytime she wanted to, that this chance for them together could disappear at any time.

"I can't make you stay," he finally settled for saying. "I never could."

"This is ridiculous," she said, pushing gently against his chest, careful of his bruises but insistent as she stepped away from him. "You're exhausted."

He thought she was going to leave then, but instead, he felt her hands on the waistband of his slacks, undoing the top clasp and then matter-of-factly drawing down the zipper.

At her touch, he sucked in a breath, which hurt, dammit, and just stood there while she slid his slacks over his hips and let them drop to the floor.

"Sit," she said.

He put a hand on the headboard to brace himself and eased down to sit on the edge of the mattress. The soreness in his abused muscles was definitely setting in, as the doctor had warned.

She knelt at his feet and slid his shoes off, followed by his socks and slacks. Then she stood up, holding the sheet and comforter out for him as she ordered, "In the bed."

It took a moment but he complied, easing farther onto the mattress and then getting his legs onto the bed. She fluffed up pillows and stacked them behind his head and back, propping him up at an angle as the doctor had suggested.

Finally satisfied, she helped him ease back onto the pillows and asked, "Better?"

"Yes, thank you."

"I left your pain pills in my purse on the hall table. I'll go get them—"

He stopped her with a hand on her arm. "I don't want them."

"Don't be such a stupid man about it. You're hurting. Take the pills."

"If I can't sleep, I will. I promise." But they were strong and made him fuzzy-headed. At least, he thought it was the pills doing that to him today. If he could get her to listen to him about their breakup, he'd need a clear head.

"You are so stubborn," she complained.

He laughed. "And you're not?"

And then they both fell silent.

She'd jumped up to go get his pills, and now she stood there, uncertain and clearly warring with herself about what to do next, looking as tired and vulnerable as could be.

Still, he held out his hand to her, which she took, and told her, "Just curl up on the bed with me, and let me hold you. I'm not sure if I could manage any more than that tonight."

She looked truly annoyed with him at first. Sweet, worried about him, but annoyed. And when he watched very, very closely, he would swear she was swaying slightly on her feet, toward him and then away from him, as if the need to be closer to him was warring with an equally strong desire to get away.

He waited, honestly thinking she was going to leave, braced for it, telling himself not to beg, when she finally asked, "I don't suppose you've acquired a pair of pajamas since the last time I was here?"

"No," he said carefully. Did that mean she was staying?

"T-shirts still in the same place?" she asked.

He nodded, closing his eyes, honestly not sure if he could have gotten any words out at that moment. He had these white, cotton undershirts he wore under dress shirts in the winter, when it got cold, and she liked to sleep in them. They were the simplest things, short-sleeved with a little V in the neck, hitting her at about midthigh. He'd watch her so many times, her hair loose and free and a little bit wild, her face scrubbed clean, wearing nothing but one of his shirts and looking sexy as hell as she walked over to the bed to climb into it with him.

He heard footsteps, drawers opening and closing, and then a moment later, when he opened his eyes, there she was, backlit for just a moment by the soft light coming from the bathroom, looking even more beautiful than the image he'd been able to conjure up in his mind.

She flicked off the light and became nothing but a shadowy image, walking across the floor and sliding into his bed, not nearly as close as he'd like her to be. It was a damned big bed, something he regretted right that minute.

She leaned over, kissed him on the cheek and said, "Go to sleep." Then she rolled onto her side, facing away from him.

Okay.

He could work with that.

He eased onto his side, slowly and carefully fitting the front of his body to the back of hers from head to toe, nerve endings coming alive, humming with happiness, lush expanses of naked and nearly naked skin against naked skin.

One of his arms slid beneath her head as a pillow for her and one went around her waist. He groaned, letting the weight of his body sink against hers, tucking that perfect little bottom against his groin, sliding his hand beneath her T-shirt and onto the bare skin of her stomach.

There, that was perfect.

He sighed in pure contentment now that he was close enough that he could bury his nose in her hair and inhale that perfect Chloe scent of hers. And despite all he'd been through, he was getting hard from wanting her.

"Not as worn-out as you thought?" she asked.

"Apparently not," he said, grinning for all he was worth, letting his hand slide lower on her belly, using it to press her bottom more firmly against him. She wasn't wearing any panties, and it was heaven and hell at the same time.

And if he wasn't completely out of his mind, he'd swear that she was pressing that perfect bottom against him ever so slightly.

He turned his face into her hair, kissing her shoulder, slowly, softly, giving her time to object if she wanted to. When she didn't, he kissed his way down to her neck. Chloe loved it when he nibbled on her neck.

She shivered and started rocking her bottom against him, the pressure exquisite and absolutely perfect.

Finally, she rolled over in his arms, looked him in the eye and said, "You're supposed to rest, remember? To not exert yourself."

"Then be gentle with me," he said.

She looked like she wanted to smack him.

He grinned. "You can do as much or as little as you want. I will have no complaints."

Taking a breath, she tentatively touched her lips to his, like she didn't trust herself to really kiss him yet. Her hands on his chest were trembling, as was his whole body.

"You rat," she said. "You tricked me, Mr. Too Weak To Try Anything."

"I haven't done anything yet," he said as his hands slid beneath the hem of her shirt to cup her bare bottom, which felt every bit as perfect as he remembered.

"You got me into bed with you," she reminded him.

He grinned. "Yes, I did."

"You even got me to take your clothes off of you."

"Wasn't even trying for that, although it was a nice surprise."

She sighed and pouted a little, looking adorable. He wanted her. Finally, she kissed him, fiercely and yet with a gentleness that just broke his heart. There were tears seeping out of her eyes, and he thought she was still a little bit mad at him for scaring her at the hospital and maybe now for making her want him again.

After a long moment, she pushed him gently onto his back and threatened him. "Don't you dare let me hurt you."

Then she peeled off her shirt, grabbed a foil packet from the nightstand drawer, which she handed to him, and then helped him out of his briefs, putting the condom on him herself.

She sat up, braced her hands carefully on his shoulders and shifted to straddle his hips, draping her beautiful, naked body over him with extreme care. It was an all-over Chloe caress.

He groaned, his hands clenching on her hips, rubbing her body against his, and she let him, helped him along, moving in time with the push and pull of his hands. Her breasts nestled against his chest, and her lips settled onto his, and suddenly, the world was a beautiful and perfect place.

She kissed him for a long time, so softly, so sweetly, until he nearly lost his mind. Finally, she raised her hips, arched her back ever so slightly and then took him slowly, carefully inside of her, her body pulsing, easing, working to make room, to let him in.

All the air came out of him in a rush, and then he drew in a deep breath that hurt, but he didn't care, because there was the most exquisite sense of wholeness to the moment, of coming home. To her.

His hands pressed hard against her hips, halting their movement.

"Does it hurt?" she asked, going absolutely still.

"No, just give me a minute," he said through clenched teeth. His body was throbbing away inside of hers. "I just need to feel…everything, and I don't want it to ever stop. I know that's impossible, but I just need it so much."

She nuzzled her cheek against his, kissing him ever so softly, holding his face between her hands, trying to stay still, to give him time.

"I've missed you like crazy," he confessed. "There were times when I was convinced I'd never have you like this again, and that I'd regret that every day of my life."

Her eyes came open, her gaze locking on his as he got the last part out, her look part hurt and part mad.

"Believe me?" he asked.

And she looked away.

He swore softly, and then while he was still trying to figure out what else he could say to her, she started rocking her body against his until he couldn't think of anything else but what was happening between them in that moment. He felt everything so intensely, need, regret, hurt, anger, sadness, love….

He loved her. He did.

He couldn't deny it any longer. He wanted a hell of a lot more than her back in his bed, glorious as that was.

She came in a long, drawn-out clenching of her body around his, going completely boneless in his arms when it was over.

He groaned, held her hard against him for a moment, then another, and then, there came that perfect point in time when the whole world fell away, dissolving into pure sensation alone, when nothing mattered except the two of them, and how they made each other feel.

The world was perfect.

Everything was.

She was his again.

* * *

Chloe didn't regret it.

Not exactly.

She'd missed him too much to regret it completely. But she really wasn't ready for this, either, because she didn't really trust him. And what kind of woman went to bed with a man she didn't really trust?

A stupid one.

Still, she let him hold her in the dark cave of his bedroom, let him stroke those big, hot hands of his lazily over her body as he kept trying to get comfortable during what was a restless sleep at best.

And when she finally felt bad enough about what she'd allowed to happen, she got up, slipped on his T-shirt and headed for the kitchen.

"Where are you going?" he asked softly, before she'd even made it out of the room.

"To get your pain pills, so you can get some sleep." And she could run away and hide in her attic at her house and think about what she'd let herself do with him. She was back a moment later with the pills and some water, hoping she looked every bit as stubborn as he did at the moment. "You're taking these. You promised you would, if you need them. And you obviously need them."

"You promised we'd talk, too."

"Now?" She sat down on the side of the bed, facing him. "James, it's the middle of the night."

"So? You're here. I'm here. We're both awake. We've avoided it long enough, don't you think? Besides, you promised."

"You promised, too. You said you'd take your pain pills and get some rest."

"Fine. I take those, you and I talk. Now. Before they

make me feel like I've got cotton balls for brains and can't think," he offered.

It was a terrible bargain. No bargain at all. She felt ridiculous and cowardly and…scared. Scared of what he was going to say.

He held out his hands for the pills and the glass of water, and she gave them to him. Could she stall until they took effect, and he fell asleep? She wanted to.

He swallowed them and gave her back the empty glass, which she put on the nightstand. "James, I'm tired. I know you're tired, too. Can't we just—"

"It's the biggest issue standing between us, Chloe, and you won't even let me say how sorry I am or how terrible I feel about it. Why won't you let me even tell you about that last night?"

Oh, she hated this. Absolutely hated it. Hiding from the past was so much easier. "Because…it doesn't really matter anymore—"

He scoffed at that. "Oh, it matters. How can you even say that?"

"I mean, it doesn't matter because…I just have to forget about it. I have to move past it, because I want to be with you now, and I can't do that if I'm still holding on to everything that went wrong between us before. So there's just no point in reliving it all anyway, when I know what I have to do—"

He stared at her, and she watched the carious emotions flickering across his face. From trying and trying to figure out exactly what she was saying, what was behind the words, to hurt and finally to out-and-out fury.

"You think I'm going to lie to you again?" he asked incredulously.

She shook her head. "I…I just—"

"Oh, my God, you do! Even now, that's what you think

of me. That I'm just another in a long string of damned lying men."

"No. I just…I can't imagine anything you could say that would really make it better."

"You thought I'd lie," he insisted.

"I just didn't…want to know. I thought we could just… never talk about it, and after a while, it really wouldn't matter anymore. Because I don't want that to stand in our way of being together now. I don't want anything to take that away from us."

"We don't stand a chance of any kind of lasting relationship if you don't trust me." He took her by the arms and pulled her to him. "Look at me, Chloe. Look at me."

She finally did.

He was furious. Why was he so mad? She was the one who had the right to be mad.

"Ask me what happened," he ordered her.

She shook her head.

"Ask me!"

"I know what happened," she told him.

"Do you? Do you really know? Are you absolutely sure I'm as guilty as you think I am? Ask me!"

She cringed at the quiet fury in his voice. "Fine. What happened?"

He took a breath, winced because it obviously hurt him to do so and then began. "We had an awful fight that day."

Chloe nodded. She remembered it well.

"It seemed like we'd been doing nothing but fighting about one thing or another for weeks," he said.

Her business. The money he'd invested. The way she felt as if he was taking over, that she was losing control of both the business and her life to him. And the other women. There seemed to always be women throwing themselves at him, one more persistent than all the others. A model

Chloe knew named Giselle, someone she'd never liked and a woman who'd never liked Chloe, all over some supposed slight to Giselle in a show Chloe had done years ago when they were both starting out.

"We went to that party, and Giselle was there," he said.

Chloe had wanted to leave on the spot. She didn't think she could take any more, that she could see that woman and not be half-insane with jealousy over what she feared James had been doing with her.

"You and I argued again there," he said. Chloe nodded. She remembered.

"I ended up on the terrace, and there was Giselle, following me. And I was mad, Chloe. I was so tired and angry, and I just… What did you say to me just a few minutes ago? I just didn't think there was anything left that I could say to you to change things, to make you believe me. That I hadn't been sleeping with her behind your back all along. Even though I hadn't."

Chloe winced. "James—"

"The only times I'd put my hands on the woman were to push her away. I won't say she didn't try. She did. But I—"

"You didn't push her away that night. I saw you, dammit! I was there. I know what I saw," she cried.

"I know you were there. I knew it all along. I have a kind of radar where you're concerned, Chloe. My whole body goes on alert. I knew you were there," he insisted. "And I also knew that I was making you miserable and that you didn't trust me, and I thought to myself, why was I still even trying to make it work between us? And I just gave up."

He took in a ragged breath and let it out slowly.

"What you saw was me giving up on us," he said. "Right then and there."

"No," she said.

"I gave up on the idea that I could ever get you to trust me to be faithful to you or to stay with you. That we could make our relationship work. That I could make you happy." He shook his head. "You saw me giving up, and there she was. I knew if you saw us together, we'd be over, right then. No more fighting, no more trying, no more feeling lousy for not being able to make it work. Just over. So I did it. I kissed her, and I made sure you saw it."

Chloe could see it. She hurt more right then than she thought she had on the terrace that night, watching him with Giselle in his arms. He'd looked up at one point, seen Chloe standing there and gone right back to kissing Giselle.

Chloe had wanted to claw the woman's eyes out, right there on the spot, but hurt soon overrode anger, and she'd simply turned around and left instead.

"I'm sorry," James said. "I'm so sorry. I didn't realize until it was too late, what I was throwing away."

"You two were together for weeks afterward," Chloe remembered.

"I know," he admitted. "She wasn't you. And if I wasn't going to be with you, it really didn't matter to me who I was with."

Chloe squeezed her eyes shut, wishing it was as easy to shut the image out of her mind of the two of them together. "I saw pictures of the two of you together for a while. It was awful."

"And you were engaged six months later," he said. "I wanted to come find the man and tear him limb from limb. I still do."

Chloe let her tears fall onto his shoulder, felt him drop a little kiss on her forehead. "I'm not saying I was a good guy. I'm saying I wasn't the rat you thought I was, who'd been cheating on you all along, and I hope to God you can believe that and that it makes a difference to you. And that you believe me when I say I know what I gave up when I walked away from you, and I've regretted it practically every minute of my life since then."

"I missed you, too," she admitted. "So much."

"So, that's it. That's what I wanted to tell you. I hope you believe me, although I'm not sure you will, even now, and it scares the hell out of me."

To which she said nothing, just let him hold her against him. And when he finally fell into a deep sleep, she got up, got dressed and, like a complete coward, ran out of there.

Chapter Ten

Chloe slipped in the back entrance to her house, not seeing any actual riots out front at that hour. But inside, once she'd showered and dressed, she was confronted with the evidence of what had happened in the days since the infamous runway brawl.

Dresses. Her beautiful dresses. Ones she'd poured her heart and soul into, rejected by superstitious brides and left in a heap in the storage room. Poor, sad, abandoned dresses. She sat there with them, feeling like she should apologize for all those broken dreams. At some point, she must have fallen back to sleep.

Addie found her there, hours later, hidden away with the poor, rejected gowns. "Okay, this is not good for any of us."

"Do you think they'll go on with their weddings? All these brides who brought their dresses back?" Chloe asked.

"I don't know," Addie said, looking truly worried about Chloe.

"Because I love our brides, and I want them to be happy, even if we can't be. I hope they all find another dress and go right on. I'd hate it if my lousy luck in love was enough to put them over the edge, too."

"Over the edge? Chloe, what—"

"You know, like you're trying to hang on, you're trying to believe, but you're really scared and one more bad thing is enough to make you just throw up your hands and give up. I feel like anybody getting married these days has to be barely hanging on, barely keeping all that fear at bay. I mean, who really believes in love anymore?"

"Dammit, you slept with him, didn't you?" Addie cried.

"Yes, I did."

"Battered, bruised, concussed, and the man can still get you into bed with him? Amazing."

"He is amazing," she admitted. There was no denying it. "Infuriating and frustrating. Sneaky, scary and amazing."

"Okay, so you had great sex with him—"

"We didn't have great sex—"

"Oh, come on. You don't look like a woman who had bad sex. I hate him, and even I don't think a woman could have bad sex with him."

"We didn't have bad sex, either. We had…sad, needy, overwhelming sex. I wouldn't let him move. No, I barely let him move, and there was nothing to it because I was trying not to hurt him and yet, I just had to be with him. There's nothing we did that should have felt that good, that amazing, but it did, because…it was him. That's all I need for it to be amazing. Just him." She stopped to take a breath, to look over at her sister. "And, at the same time, I still don't trust him."

Addie honestly looked like she was at a loss for words, which happened maybe once in a decade.

"In my own defense," Chloe said, "I did realize how wrong it was, and once he fell asleep, I got up and ran out of there."

"Too late." Addie shook her head. "Way too late. And this is the first place he's going to come looking for you when he wakes up."

"I know. We talked about Giselle. I finally let him talk about it." She went through the whole thing with Addie.

"So, do you believe him?" she asked when Chloe was done.

"I want to. And I think, too, how much of what happened back then, what I felt, what I thought was happening, was about him and anything he was doing, and how much of it was me and all my insecurities about relationships? Me thinking like I always have. 'What would a man like him be doing with someone like me? Why would I ever believe any man could be faithful or that any relationship could last?' I mean, did I give him a fair chance before the whole Giselle thing? Do I give any man a fair chance? I'm not sure I ever have."

"No, we never have," Addie conceded.

"The end was coming for me and James. I knew that before I saw him with Giselle that night. It was coming because we didn't trust each other. If he'd never done a single thing to deserve my doubts, I still wouldn't have trusted him. Not because of who he was. Because of who I was. I'm no good at this."

"Yeah, there is the whole family curse thing." Addie shrugged, shook her head. "And I hate to admit it—you know how much I hate this—but I can see how a man would decide to end a relationship by doing something like making sure you saw him with someone else. I can see a man thinking that was a chance to end things quickly, once and for all, and taking it."

"I hurt him, Addie. I mean, he hurt me. You know how much he did."

Addie nodded, giving Chloe a little hug.

"But I hurt him, too. I believe that. I believe he regrets the way he hurt me, the way he ended things."

"You just still don't know if he was faithful to you until the night you saw him and Giselle together."

Chloe groaned and buried her head in her hands, "I know. Believe me, I know. That's why I left. So I could try to figure it out."

"And you haven't yet?"

"No, not yet."

"Well, I hate to add to your misery—especially with this, and please know, I'm embarrassed that it ever came to this. But you have to talk to James, because that idiot Marcy has really lost it this time, and she has a plan to try to save her job and explain away the whole photo/jail/fight thing between me and her that doesn't involve either of us sleeping with James."

"What's so bad about that?" Chloe asked.

"Her explanation is that Marcy and I are both crazy in love with the security guard, Wayne, and we're both having his alien baby."

"Alien baby?" That had to be some kind of sick joke.

"Marcy says to the tabloids, nothing beats an alien-baby story, and she's been devouring them since she was nine. So Wayne's supposedly from another planet, and we're both having his alien baby."

Chloe just shook her head. "I don't think there's anything I could possibly say to that."

"Apparently, even alien men can't be trusted to sleep with only one woman at a time. I'm cynical enough to believe that. And you were upset in that photo outside the jail because…I mean, you would be upset to find out your sister was being two-timed by an alien, wouldn't you?"

"No one is ever going to believe a word of that—"

Addie shrugged, looking resigned to their collective fate. "I figure if it's too late, and she's already put out the story, you could issue a statement saying that naturally, you'll love your half-alien niece or nephew, because…you know…everybody needs and deserves love. No judgments here. Just love."

"We're doomed," Chloe said. "That's all there is to it. We're doomed."

"Yeah, probably, we are." Addie looked sad and worried and a little bit mad. "And if that wasn't enough to make your day, there's someone outside who insists on seeing you. I was going to try to deal with him myself, but…right now, I think I'll leave that up to you."

"Who?"

"You're going to have to see for yourself to believe it. He's out front. Robbie tried to get him someplace less conspicuous but he wouldn't budge."

Chloe couldn't imagine who was waiting for her, but decided if it wasn't James, she could handle it. Bracing herself, she went into the showroom.

Robbie was there, looking truly astonished and pointing to the front doors. "I begged him to leave, but that's as far as I could get him."

Begged? Who did he have to beg to leave?

She opened the big front door and walked out onto the porch and saw Bryce pacing back and forth.

Chloe just stood there with her mouth hanging open.

Bryce?

"Chloe!" he cried, rushing to her side.

He still had a bandage on the side of one eye, but otherwise he looked fine. Not scarred for life, it seemed.

"What in the world are you doing here?" she asked.

"I just had to see you." He grabbed her by the arms and positively beamed at her. "Chloe, I am so, so sorry. For everything. I never meant to hurt you. Please believe that."

Chloe wanted to point out that given the fact that they had been engaged and he'd been cheating on her with another man, she was bound to end up hurt, but she just didn't have the energy for that whole conversation.

"Bryce, what do you want?"

"To see you. To tell you how sorry I am, Chloe."

"Okay, you've said it."

Still, he just stood there, holding on to her and, if she wasn't seriously mistaken, looking like…like he… Surely, he didn't want…

And then he pulled her against him and kissed her. She was too shocked to stop him, and when she didn't make any response at all, he finally stopped.

"Chloe, I'm done with Reginald."

"Who?"

"You know, Eloise's boyfriend. It was a huge mistake right from the beginning. I don't think I realized how much we had until it was gone. I miss you, Chloe, and I want you back."

"You're insane," she said.

"No, I'm not. That story about me in the mental hospital was all a lie. You know how those tabloids make up things." He frowned then. "Although I have to say, I hope the latest one about James…I kind of hope that one's true."

"No, it's not. James is not sleeping with Addie or his assistant."

"Not that story. The one that said you left him over it, and he was so upset, he's on suicide watch after trying to kill himself by walking into traffic yesterday."

Chloe groaned out loud. It was all she could do not to scream.

"Yeah, I know, that's not very nice of me, to hope he's in such bad shape," Bryce said, looking a bit sheepish. "I really wasn't hoping he was suicidal, just that he was sleeping around, too, and you were done with him. And that you might take me back. I mean, you gave him a second chance. You're a kind, generous woman. Give me another chance, too. I won't blow it, I swear."

"I don't believe this," Chloe said. "I just honestly can't believe it."

"Please, just think about it. Let me see you every now and then. I need you, Chloe. We were good together."

God must hate her, Chloe decided. God, the universe, every living entity must hate her and be in on a plot to torment her right now for some reason she could not understand.

"Bryce, you lied to me, over and over again. You slept with another model in the show, and because the whole thing came out in that hideously public way, my life as a designer is probably ruined. I'm probably going to lose everything. So, no, I'm not going to give you another chance."

He looked shocked at that.

How could he possibly be shocked?

Then he reached for her again, and just as he got his hands on her, she heard an absolute growl of outrage from behind her.

James had been absolutely furious when he woke up and she was gone.

No note. No explanation. Nothing. He shouldn't have laid a hand on her the night before, shouldn't have pushed. He knew that. He'd just missed her so damned much, wanted her so much, and it was more his fault than hers that she'd run out on him. But he was still mad. Especially because she'd finally let him tell her about what really happened between him and Giselle, but hadn't said a word about whether she believed him or not. And then, she ran out on him, which he thought was probably a bad sign.

He'd calmed down a little bit by the time he got to the street in front of her shop, but then he looked up and saw...

Chloe kissing another man!

He felt like he was hit by the bike messenger again, taking a blow to the chest, to his already-bruised heart. He couldn't move at first, couldn't so much as speak.

Chloe was kissing another man!

James wanted to kill him, right there on the spot. She'd crawled out of his bed sometime last night or early this morning and run home to kiss another man!

Deciding not to kill first and ask questions later, he walked slowly and deliberately toward them. They were done kissing, and were now talking. He couldn't see Chloe's face, but from what he could see of the guy's, he looked the way James imagined he had with Chloe lately—desperate to make her understand something he was trying to tell her. Maybe it was wishful thinking on James's part, but he didn't think the guy was having any more luck with that than James had.

Then the jerk reached for her again to kiss her.

No way James was going to stand by and watch that happen again.

He lunged forward, got himself between the two of them and shoved the guy back with all his might. Chloe gasped. The guy looked confused, scared and somehow familiar. James might have actually growled. He couldn't be sure.

Then he got up in the guy's face and snarled, "You touch her again and it'll be the last friggin' thing you do—"

"James?" Chloe said, tugging on his arm, trying to get him to back off. "What are you doing?"

He didn't turn to face her. He wanted to see the look on this guy's face when he said, "I woke up this morning and was surprised you weren't still there in bed with me, Chloe."

She growled herself. "James, honestly—"

Her guy looked mad and more than a little scared. "Wait, this is James? The guy who's supposed to be suicidal over you? Yeah, I saw him in the tabloids. You're really seeing him again?"

"Yes, she is!" James was definitely growling in outrage. No other word quite fit the sounds coming out of his mouth.

Chloe got herself between the two of them, looked at James and yelled, "Shut up!"

Then she turned her back to him and faced his rival. "Bryce, leave now. Leave right now—"

He looked like he was going to pout. "Are you at least going to think about getting back together with me?"

"What?" *Get back together?* Wasn't he seeing one of Chloe's male models?

"No, I'm not. I have other men to torment me, to break my heart and help prove to the world that I am, indeed, cursed in love. Your part is done. You can go now."

He started to argue. But James loomed over her shoulder, trying to look as mean and scary as he could while Chloe held him back. After a moment, Bryce seemed to get the message.

They stood there together watching him leave, and then Chloe turned and faced James looking mad as hell.

"Nice caveman act," she said.

"I'm not acting. I saw him kiss you, and I wanted to kill

him right there on the spot. What's he doing here, anyway?"

"Apparently he wants me back."

James was truly baffled. Her ex-secretly-gay-fiancé
wanted her back? "Why?"

Chloe was fuming then. "I don't know. My sparkling
personality, maybe? My ability to bring chaos into the
lives of everyone around me? My failing business? I have
so much to offer, you know?"

"Okay, you know I didn't mean it like that. I meant…
the guy was sleeping with another one of the models at
your show. He ruined everything for you. How could he
think you'd take him back after that?"

"Funny you should ask. He said he read in the tabloids that I'd decided to give you another chance—despite
knowing how things ended between you and me—and he
thought, what the hell, cheater or not, maybe I'd give him
another chance, too."

James felt like he could breathe fire at that, he was so
damned mad. Mad at her for running away this morning.
Mad at that other guy who'd dared touch her, who'd been
engaged to her. Mad at the world for what had happened
to her business, her dream. But mostly mad at himself for
giving up on the two of them a year and a half ago and
bringing them to this point.

"Chloe, please," he began, but before he could say more,
Addie stepped between them and whispered fiercely.

"This may not matter anymore. We may have given up
completely on saving ourselves," she said, "but you have at
least one audience member with a camera pointed at you.
I thought I should at least ask if you'd like to go upstairs
and fight."

In James's mind, the words *given up completely on sav-*

ing ourselves hit, and hit hard. Who the hell was giving up? And why?

They couldn't give up. If they did, Chloe had no reason to see him again, nothing he could use to push her into seeing him, and he felt like a man who really needed a reason for her to see him right now.

"I would love to go upstairs," James said, as calmly as possible.

And once he got inside, he'd just refuse to leave.

Chloe gave him a wide berth in the house and even on the way upstairs to her bedroom. She didn't want to be anywhere near a bed with him, but her room was the most private place in the house.

He stood in front of the only chair in her room, waiting, looking positively grim and still very, very angry.

Chloe couldn't say she minded the angry part that much. He deserved to feel bad after the way things had ended with them before. And she had to admit, it was a little flattering, thinking he was so jealous of her and any man that he could hardly get words out. Still, jealous of Bryce? Did he seriously think there was any way in the world she'd get back together with Bryce?

"Could I sit down, please?" he asked.

She nodded, watching him as he did. He had a black eye. He looked like he was hurting a lot more today than he had been yesterday, and she began to feel the urge to cut him some slack because of that. She sat next to him on her bed and faced him, trying to figure out what she wanted to say. Things were just so crazy. She didn't know where to start. Apparently, he did.

"What did Addie mean about giving up on saving your business?"

Chloe blinked up at him. "That's what you want to talk about right now? Business?"

He threw his hands up in the air. "I want to talk about a lot of things. This is just a place to start."

"A place to start?" she repeated.

"Yes. Can we start there, please? You love what you do. I know you do. You can't give up on saving your career."

"Everything we've tried to do has only made things worse. Apparently, we're just really bad at pretense. Do you even know how ridiculous it's gotten? Yesterday, while you and I were at the hospital, Marcy wanted to try to make people believe that she and Addie weren't sleeping with you, they were both sleeping with Wayne, the security guard, instead—"

"What's so bad about that?"

"And that Wayne's an alien, and that she and Addie are both having his alien babies!"

"Alien babies? Okay, yeah. That's bad—"

"Yeah," Chloe insisted. "There's no coming back from the double-alien-baby claim. We can only hope it's not already too late to stop her, because otherwise, we'd have absolutely no credibility about anything. People would either think we're lunatics or liars. So if you want to do something, go find Marcy and make sure she doesn't say anything else to anyone about aliens. Honestly, even without that, things seem pretty hopeless."

James seemed to take that particularly hard. He looked like a man in serious pain. She was starting to really worry about him.

"Are you okay?" she asked finally.

"No. I said I was going to help you, and I've done nothing but make things worse—"

"Oh, that reminds me, in case you haven't heard yet, you're supposed to be so upset over how I've treated you, that you deliberately walked into traffic yesterday and now you're on suicide watch in a Manhattan mental hospital. I've driven another man to the brink of suicide."

"Oh, no," he groaned.

"Yes. The whole Chloe-cursed-in-love thing is going full steam again. Brides are still freaked, and we're doomed."

"We are not doomed," he insisted. "Although, obviously, it's going to take something truly drastic to overcome this."

"Drastic? You got run over. There's nothing more drastic than that," she explained.

"It doesn't have to be something bad," he said. "It could be something good, something happy."

"We've been trying to pull off happy, and it's all turned out awful."

"Chloe, I think we have to get married." He paled a little as he said it, but looked determined.

She just stared at him at first.

Married?

Then she laughed a bit, because… Another man claiming he wanted to marry her? That was where all her troubles started, and the idea of getting engaged for a fourth time… There was something really pathetic about that, especially when she'd never yet made it to the altar.

"No. I am never getting engaged again—"

"I didn't say anything about being engaged. I said married."

"Well, I can't get married without getting engaged—"

"Of course you can. Skip the whole engagement part. Maybe that's the problem. Go straight to the marriage part."

"That's insane," she insisted.

His face turned grim, looking positively bloodless for

a moment. She thought he might collapse right there. But he rallied.

"First rule of disaster PR. Change the story. A wedding is a great, happy story and the only way I see to kill the whole notion of a curse."

She shot him an incredulous look. "You can't be serious."

James watched her and waited, looking more concerned with each passing moment. Finally, he said, "It doesn't have to be a real wedding. We can just make it look real. We'll go to city hall for a license, book a church, get you an engagement ring."

She shook her head, hurt, scared and so tired. Were they trying to save her business or starting a new relationship? Last night, it had felt like they were starting over, even though she still had issues—rightly so—about trusting him. Now he was acting as if this was all one big farce, and he was playing right along.

"Look, it's been a crazy week or so. I'm exhausted. I can't think about anything right now," she said.

He looked truly alarmed. "It's a good plan. It will work."

"It just sounds like more of what we've already tried."

He looked as if she'd stabbed him through the heart or something.

She got scared again. "James, are you sure you're feeling all right this morning?"

"I'm fine," he insisted. "But we don't have much time to turn this around—"

She groaned, feeling so weary. "I just want some time to think."

"Fine. I can be quiet," he insisted. "I'll stay right here, and I won't say a word—"

"No," she said, watching his jaw tighten as she said it, then tried to say it in a nicer way. "Please. I want you to go."

Chloe lay in her bed and cried for a while after he left, feeling like she deserved the indulgence of a few tears after the horrors of the last thirty hours or so. After about an hour, Robbie came in and handed her the tabloid claiming James was suicidal over her. He quickly left her alone.

She hardly glanced at the story. It was the photo of him lying on the street bleeding that grabbed her attention, that she couldn't get out of her mind. He'd been hit by that newsstand just down the street from his apartment, where he bought a newspaper every morning. She'd been there with him before.

So what had really happened yesterday? She'd bet he'd walked up to the newsstand, seen the tabloid with the claims of their foursome with Addie and Marcy and been so distracted he'd stepped in front of the bike messenger and nearly gotten himself killed.

It was too horrible for words.

She'd nearly gotten him killed, sat by his side in the E.R. that day and then ended up in his bed that night. Making love to him had been like ripping her soul wide open. And what had he suggested this morning? More pretense.

She was sick of the games. She was done. Whatever happened from here on out would just happen. No more lies.

Soon Addie knocked tentatively and opened the door to peek in. "Sorry. I know I hardly ever say anything else to you and it is a cliché at this point, a bad one, but…we have a problem."

Chloe sighed. "Tell me it's not Bryce again."

"No," Addie said. "Does he really want you back?"

Chloe nodded. "Please don't tell me how ridiculous that is or ask me any questions. I can't deal with that right now."

"You know, I'm going to make you some of that tea for PMS. It really takes me down a notch when I need it, and right now you need it."

"I need a whole lot more than PMS tea, believe me. Now, what's my new problem?"

"James. What happened with him earlier?"

"He came up with a new plan to save the business."

Addie looked puzzled. "We need a new plan to save the business. What's so bad about his plan?"

"It involves me marrying him," she said, trying to keep from showing just how much that hurt—to have him offer to marry her to save her business. Not because he loved her.

"You're kidding. He really wants to marry you?"

"Of course not. He wants to fake marry me. He doesn't do things for real. He doesn't know how," Chloe cried. "Okay, for a few hours last night, he knew how. He did. He just got it, the whole thing, so real it probably scared him half to death. Me, too. And now, we're back to fake courtship, fake love, fake marriage. No man will ever want to do more than fake marry me."

Addie paused, looking concerned. "You're right. This is a job for way more than PMS tea. I still can't believe he wants to marry you. To even pretend to marry you—"

"Gee, thanks, Addie. I feel so much better now."

"Oh, you know what I mean. Men like him…they get the willies even mentioning the marriage thing, let alone ever actually getting close to it."

"He asked me to marry him before for real. We were engaged! For real! At least, I thought it was real."

"Yeah, but neither one of you ever actually did anything to move toward a wedding date."

"Okay, you're right. You got us there. Maybe it never would have happened. Maybe I'm doomed. No, cursed. I forgot. What I am is cursed."

"You're kind of scaring me today," Addie said.

"I'm scaring myself today. I scared myself half to death last night, and he scared me half to death yesterday. If he'd bounced the other way after the biker hit him, he'd probably have been hit by a car and be dead now, and it would be my fault. After all the things we've done to try to save my business. And I am not doing it anymore. I'm done. Whatever happens to the business happens."

"Well, if that's how you really feel—"

"I'm sorry. I'm so sorry. Especially about letting you and Robbie and Connie down—"

"Don't think about us now. Because, as I said earlier, we have a problem. The reason I came up here? James is downstairs, standing across the street just staring at the house. He won't leave. I already went over there and tried my best, but he won't budge. He's starting to freak out the neighbors again. I tried to tell them he wasn't dangerous, but I'm still afraid someone will call the cops on him, and, as I now know, jail is not a fun place."

Chloe groaned. "I thought he'd left. I told him to go, and he acted like he was going."

"You're going to have to go talk to him. No matter what it takes, get him to leave."

Chapter Eleven

"So." James stood on the street corner across from Chloe's, talking to Adam, who'd agreed to meet James at Chloe's to try to talk some sense into him. "Have you ever done anything stupid because of a woman?"

"No," Adam said. "I'm the one man on earth who understands women completely. They make perfect sense to me. So I've never done anything stupid for one."

James frowned. "That is not helping. You said you'd try to help me."

"Well, ask me a real question at least," Adam said. "This is about Chloe, right?"

"Of course it's about Chloe. She's the only woman who makes me crazy."

"And the problem is?"

"She makes me crazy!"

"Well, yeah. I mean, that's just part of it, if you really love her," Adam said, like there was nothing unusual about that.

"That's…that's insane. Love equals crazy? What the hell kind of plan is that? You love someone, and it automatically makes you crazy?"

"If you're lucky enough to really love them, yeah. Because it means too much. It's too important then. It's everything. And that means, to all us control freaks out there, that we're not really in control anymore. That someone else has the power to make or break us, and that's what gets to us."

"I am not a control freak," James said.

Adam just laughed. "Seriously? You're going to waste your breath even saying that?"

James sighed, feeling truly ill. "I don't know how to do this. The Chloe thing. The love thing."

"Nobody really does," Adam claimed.

"Don't say that. Some people have to know. They're in love. They even manage to stay in love and stay married. I thought they just knew how to do it."

"I don't think so," Adam mused. "I think they just want it so badly, they get in there and fight and suffer and even though they're scared, they figure it out."

"I never thought of it that way," James said, then confessed, "I panicked earlier and asked Chloe to marry me."

"Why?" James asked.

"Because she wanted to give up on trying to save her business, and if she does that, I'm afraid she might not see me again."

"Oh." Adam frowned. "So what did she say to your proposal?"

"She kicked me out of her house."

"Not a good sign."

"No, it's not. I mean, what I actually asked is for her to fake marry me. I started with 'Marry me,' and when she laughed at that… Oh, God, she laughed."

He'd felt just how bruised his heart was in that moment.

"Hey, I'm sorry," Adam said.

"Yeah, anyway, when it looked like really marrying me was out, I said, 'Fake marry me.' But that didn't really go over any better."

Adam nodded, giving James a look that said, *Man, you are so screwed.*

"And I never even worked up the nerve to tell her that I'm into her business for a couple hundred grand, more if she goes under after I pay you off," James remembered. "That's not going to go well. I guess I could fake marry her without telling her about the money, but I can't marry her for real without telling her."

"And you really want to marry her?" Adam asked, still looking like he thought James was screwed.

"I just want her to…never, ever leave me, no matter what. I don't ever want to have to live without her. I want her in my house and in my bed and sitting across from me at dinner every night, and smiling and happy and loving me." James threw up his hands in defeat. "What do I do? How do I make that happen?"

"I think you have to tell her all that, just like you told me. Get the money part out fast, and then move on to everything else."

James grimaced. "I don't think there's any way she'd marry me for real. I was hoping she'd fake marry me, and then we'd have some time for her to get used to the idea, to see how good this could be. I'd show her there was nothing fake about a marriage between us."

Adam nodded sympathetically. "Well, I guess you could go that way."

"I'm pretty sure it's my only chance right now," James admitted.

"Hey, you saw the tabloid thing, right? Saying you're suicidal over Chloe?"

"No, but I heard something about it."

"You should know, I'm hearing things about that deal you're about to close with Davidson?"

"It's all but done. We're signing the papers this week."

Adam shook his head. "The man's seriously spooked. I think he's looking for another partner. A friend of mine saw him talking to Syd Greenberg today. They've done business together before."

James swore. Now this whole disaster with Chloe was screwing up his business?

"I know. Sorry," Adam said. "And that girl who works for you? Marcy? Please tell me you're not sleeping with her."

"No, and I'm not sleeping with Chloe's sister, either!"

"Okay. I just had to ask. Now go tell Chloe the truth."

James stood as tall and straight as he could, took a fortifying, if painful, breath and said, "Okay. I'm ready. I'm going in."

Chloe peeked out the front window, and there was James, standing across the street talking to Adam. Where had he come from? At least Adam could talk some sense into him. Maybe. She hoped so. But then Adam stayed where he was and James started walking across the street toward the house.

"Dammit," she muttered.

She thought about hiding. She used to hide from difficult things all the time as a kid. Why didn't grown-ups just hide more often?

But she waited too long, and then there he was, looking as reluctant to be there as she was to have him there. Maybe he wanted to hide, too, Chloe thought. It wasn't too late. Or he could just turn around and leave again without saying a word. She wouldn't object.

But he didn't leave.

Instead, he said, "You look like you're about to run away from me again. Or try to push me out of your life again—"

"I did not push you out of my life—"

"You damned well tried, not an hour ago. I should know. I was there."

Chloe fumed. He was mad at her? "You think you have some right to be here? Let me remind you that you just showed up here when my life was falling apart and said you wanted to help, that you had a plan, that it would work. And we have made a complete and utter disaster of it."

"I know! Don't you think I know that? I feel terrible, Chloe. I don't know how it happened. It all seemed so easy, and now, here we are, in a huge mess."

Yes, they were. And his big answer was a fake marriage to her? She was still reeling from that.

"James, I told you I just needed—"

"I have to tell you something," he said, looking way too serious for her peace of mind.

Nothing good ever came out of a conversation that started with the words *I have to tell you something*.

"You really don't," Chloe told him.

"I do," James said grimly. "Adam told me I had to."

Adam? What did Adam have to do with anything between her and James? Adam was just…James's friend, and someone who'd put a lot of money into Chloe's business.

Money?

"Is this about Adam's investment in my company?" she asked, afraid things were about to get a whole lot worse. One would think that wasn't possible, after all that had already happened. But Chloe had found things could always get worse.

"Yes," James said.

Chloe swore softly and took James by the hand, leading him to the storage room at the back of the house, because that's where she went to hide and to think sometimes. It had a door, and usually, if she was in there with the door closed, everyone left her alone.

They went inside, and she shut the door behind them, leaning against it both for support and to make extra sure no one came in. "Okay, talk," she said.

He took a breath and let it out on a sigh, looking very guilty. "I'm sorry. I'll say that first, because you might not give me a chance to say it later. I'm really sorry. I never wanted you to even know this, and if things had worked out the way I hoped, you never would have."

Chloe didn't understand. "This is about you? I thought it was about Adam?"

"It's about all of us. Chloe, when we broke up, you wanted me out of your business right away, and I did my best to make that happen. But a company in the fashion industry is a high-risk start-up, and the economy was already showing some troubling signs even then."

"But then you found Adam," she said.

"I did. He did it as a personal favor to me and because I made him certain promises about his investment."

She frowned. "I don't understand. What kind of promises?"

"He put up his money, became your investor, and if you'd gone on to turn a profit, the two of you would have gone on as partners, and I'd be no part of it. And you'd never know the rest. I honestly thought that would happen but—"

"But it didn't, and now, here we are. What did you promise Adam?"

"I guaranteed his losses."

"Which means…?"

"That if he ended up losing money on the deal, I'd pay him back whatever he invested. Look, no one else would put money into a start-up clothing designer. No one. I'm sorry because I know it's not what you wanted—to have anything else to do with me—but it was the only thing I could think of to do that would allow you to stay in business, so I did it."

Chloe crossed her arms and glared at him. "So, all this time, ever since Adam came along, you've been lying to me about my own business?"

"I guess you could put it that way. I mean, we weren't speaking to one another. We didn't see each other, until very recently. I really hoped it wouldn't even matter."

Oh, she was seething. "Okay, just to be absolutely clear, do you have any other secrets you need to tell me?"

He shrugged, looked one way, then the other. "I…don't know… Maybe."

Chloe groaned. "What do you mean, you don't know? You have to know."

"I'm not sure if it qualifies as a separate issue or just… details about the secret I've already told you," he claimed.

"I think at this point, you should confess all and let me decide. Spill it!"

"Okay…after the runway thing, the riot, you needed another infusion of cash to get through it, and Adam just didn't have it to give. I wrote him a check the day of the riot, and he turned around and wrote a bunch of checks to all those angry brides."

Chloe just looked at him, hurt and angry. "God, it never stops with you! You just charge in and take over—"

"You think I wanted to do that? After all the grief between us about me trying to take over your business the first time around? No way I wanted to do that—"

"But you did, didn't you?"

"You would have gone under that day, if I hadn't," he told her. "That's the only reason I did it."

"Well, maybe I should have gone under! And if I was going to, it was my decision to make. Did you ever think of that?"

"I did." He shook his head. "But more than anything, I just wanted to buy you some time to save everything. I really thought we could."

She laughed, because honestly, what else was there to do?

They had failed miserably, made things worse, even, which she would have thought wasn't possible, given how awful things had been to start with.

"So, that's everything? There's nothing else you've lied to me about?"

"Nothing else," he said grimly.

"Fine. Now it's my turn. I want you to know that I am absolutely and completely done with all your plans and schemes. I will not tell one more lie with you."

"Okay."

"I will not go on one more fake date with you. We will not have one more fake kiss or fake embrace. There will be no more fake neck-nuzzling or fake foot massages in a limousine. Nothing. Got it?"

"Fine," he said.

"And I am so not having a fake engagement to you, and I will never, ever, ever fake marry you!"

"Fine!" he said, gritting his teeth.

"Fine."

He understood. She was glad. So why were they both so mad? He looked like steam might pour out of his nostrils at any moment, and then he'd breathe a little fire and burn the whole place down.

Chloe was breathing hard herself, furious, too, and then just hurt, so very hurt. "I just can't pretend anymore. I can't stand one more fake thing in my life. It's a mess, a huge mess, and I'm going to deal with it. I'm going to do what I want, what I think is right. No more lies. It's all going to be real."

"Okay," he said.

"So…you should really go."

Because, if they were being real…she didn't know what was left, and obviously he didn't, either, because his response to the night they'd spent together was the offer to fake marry her, the jerk!

Chloe finally got through the absolute worst of her fury and found a world of hurt roaring in behind it. She felt as if she was the one with a giant bruise on her heart, not him.

She opened up the door of the storage room, shoved him out, then closed the door behind him, sank down to the floor and cried.

Chloe was still mad the next morning, though she felt a little bad when she saw that more of the tabloids had picked up on the idea that James was suicidal over her.

"Serves him right," Addie claimed in the kitchen that morning over coffee. "And really, the timing isn't bad for him to be taking a walk in traffic over you, because *New York Woman* is out today with its stupid bachelor list, and he's on it. Maybe this will cut down on the number of women coming after him—"

"Addie—"

"Well, he claims to hate that sort of thing."

"Not enough to want people to think he's ready to kill himself. I mean, surely there are easier ways to make yourself less attractive to women."

"With him, I'm not so sure about that. This might be

his only shot, if what he really wants is to keep from having women swarming around him."

Chloe grabbed a doughnut and started munching. This was a morning that required sugary, gooey carbs and lots of them, and the doughnuts were still warm. She might eat the whole box, especially if Addie kept this up.

"Who went out for doughnuts?" Chloe asked. "These are great."

"Adam brought them. We're going over some budget issues this morning," Addie said, making a face.

"Oh, perfect." Chloe hadn't been able to bring herself to tell Addie or anyone else about James's little deal with Adam yet. She still had that to look forward to.

Adam came in a moment later, carrying his laptop, which he put on the kitchen table, and a tabloid, which he put in front of Chloe. The headline blared Chloe Strikes Again: She's Made Another Man Want to Kill Himself.

Chloe felt a buzz of hysterical laughter bubbling up inside of her, which she managed to hold back, just barely, by taking another bite of her doughnut and gnawing on it.

"Might be a two-boxes-of-pastry kind of morning," Addie told Adam.

"I can go get more," he offered.

Chloe chewed harder. "Never in my life could I have envisioned my career as a designer ending like this. It's too bizarre for words."

"It's not over," Addie claimed.

"Oh, it's over. I told James yesterday, and I meant it. No more schemes. No more lies. No more pretense. No fake engagements, no fake marriages. Nothing."

"Well, that's good, I guess. I mean, given that we seem incapable of pulling off any of that," Addie reasoned. "And it means you don't have to see James anymore. I know that's good."

Yes, it was good. It had to be good, Chloe tried to tell herself. He was a liar, a manipulator, a man who got run over by a bike messenger for her, but the whole pretend romance had been his idea in the first place, so it served him right. Right?

"I'm going to get my laptop, and we can compare numbers, Adam," Addie said, getting up and heading for her office.

Chloe sat there, feeling guilty with Adam looking at her the way he was. She liked Adam. He was a nice guy. He'd just been caught up in a scheme James came up with, that was all.

He kept staring at her. Chloe felt guiltier and guiltier. Finally, she said, "What?"

"James didn't want a fake relationship with you, Chloe. He didn't want a fake engagement or a fake marriage. He didn't tell you that?"

"I…just…" She thought about it. She'd told him she didn't want any of that. But he'd most definitely suggested fake dating and a fake marriage. "It was all his idea. All the fake stuff."

"Well, it's not what he wanted. You should ask him about that. And don't worry. I'm sure he'll be able to save that multimillion-dollar deal with Davidson even if Davidson thinks he's mentally unstable over you. I mean, it's James. He always comes out on top, right?"

Chloe looked up warily. "He's got a big deal falling apart over this?"

Adam nodded. "Big one."

"Well, I am sorry for that."

Adam just waited, watching her, leaving her feeling more guilty with every passing second.

"What did James really want from me?" she finally asked.

"Why don't you go ask him?" Adam suggested.

Chloe went to James's office that afternoon and found Marcy packing her things and—oddly—not looking upset at doing it. She actually looked happy. That was truly weird.

Approaching cautiously, Chloe said, "Please tell me you didn't put out the double-alien-baby story, Marcy."

"Oh, no. Mr. Elliott said no way to that one." Marcy kept on packing.

"So, did he fire you?"

"No, he helped me see that I'm really not meant for a career in finance. Honestly, I don't think I ever really wanted it. But my father really wanted it for me, and I loved him so much. I tried hard to make it work. He and Mr. Elliott go back a long way. They've done a lot of business together over the years. I'm pretty sure that's the only reason I got this job in the first place. Or kept it this long," Marcy admitted. "But my father's been gone for over a year now, and I'm not doing this anymore."

"Oh. Sorry about your father, Marcy. What are you going to do now?"

Her whole face lit up. "Mr. Elliott knows someone who knows someone who works in television, who got me a job as an assistant on a TV show! I'm so excited!"

Chloe tried not to make a face. "A gossip show?"

"Yes! Can you believe it?" Marcy did a little happy dance. "On the condition that I never, ever tell them a single thing about you, Mr. Elliott, your company, Addie, the bike messenger, Wayne… You know, about anything." She made a little locking motion over her lips.

"Well...I guess I'm happy for you, Marcy. I need to see James for a moment."

"Of course. Go right ahead. I'm sure he wants to see you. He's just crazy about you, you know?"

Chloe nodded, not sure herself how much James might want to see her, but she felt like she had to see him.

She walked into his office and found him behind his desk, talking on the phone and scribbling down notes on a pad of paper in front of him. He looked...uneasy, she decided, was the best way to describe it, at seeing her. He held up a hand to signal that he'd just be a minute and offered her a chair.

Chloe took one of the big, comfy chairs across from his desk and a moment later, he put down the phone and came to lean against the other side of the desk in front of her. She wished he wasn't so close and that he didn't look so good at practically every moment of his life, even with a slightly blackened eye. She tried hard to wish that she'd never met him, but couldn't quite manage that.

"So," she began, "Marcy's going to work on a TV gossip show?"

James nodded.

"Do you think that's wise?"

"Not for the rest of the world, and I feel a little guilty about that. But she's happy, and she won't be messing with my life or yours anymore." He shrugged. "She had to go. I was afraid if I just fired her, she'd spill her guts about you and me on TV in a minute. I look at this as a major incentive for her to keep quiet."

"And...maybe as something that would make her happy?" Chloe suggested, because she thought deep down, he did like Marcy, crazy as she could be.

"People should do what they want, what they like. It tends to make us happy," he said, turning it all back around to him and her neatly and quickly. "What do you want, Chloe?"

And he didn't say it like, *Why are you here, Chloe?* He said it like, *What do you really want, Chloe?*

"Adam said you have a multimillion-dollar deal that's falling apart because your partner thinks you're mentally unstable. Because of me."

He shrugged easily, confidently. "Don't worry about it. I'll handle it."

"I can't help it. I feel really bad about that," she said.

Again, that easy, confident shrug, as if the whole thing meant nothing.

And she couldn't quite bring herself to say, *Adam said you didn't want to fake marry me at all, that you wanted something else. What did you really want?*

"I'm sorry about the money, Chloe," he said finally. "I didn't see another way to give you what you wanted—to be able to stay in business—without making that promise to Adam."

"You're saying that's why you did it? Just so I could stay in business?"

"Of course. Why else would I do it?"

"I don't know...."

"It wasn't some bid to keep me in your life or to still have some kind of control over you. I just wanted you to be happy. If you'd turned a profit, you and Adam would have been partners, and you never would have known about why he agreed to step in in the first place. Done deal."

"Really?"

"Of course. Did you really think I'd come back some-day and use it as leverage to get you to...I don't know. Let me back into your life?"

She shrugged. It sounded silly when he said it like that. "It just seems odd that...I mean, we'd just broken up. I was so mad. It seemed like you were, too. Why would you care if my business went under or not for lack of an investor?"

"Because it was your dream. Because you'd worked so hard to get to where you were. Because I couldn't stand to be the one who took all that away from you, when it was only money. That amount didn't mean anything to me." He shrugged. "So why would I take it back, when it would mean taking everything away from you?"

Which sounded incredibly generous and kind of sweet.

She always ended up thinking he was really a nice person, when he wasn't making her mad. He just confused her so much. She had a hard time staying mad at him.

Money. They'd been talking about money.

"So, what are you going to do now about the money?" she asked.

He looked confused. "I wasn't planning on doing anything. What do you want me to do?"

"Nothing, I guess." Now she was even more confused.

"I promise I won't do anything else unless you specifically ask me to. That's what you want, right?"

"Yes," she said. "The company is mine. If I mess it all up, run it into the ground, kill it with my love life, that's on me."

He nodded. "Okay. We'll let things play out. If you turn things around, turn a profit, you and Adam will be partners in whatever happens in the future, and if not...I guess we'll figure out how to handle things then."

"I'll owe you a ton of money," she said.

He shrugged, as if it was nothing. "Whatever you want."

"Promise," she demanded.

"I promise."

"Good."

She sat there and waited. He gave the impression of a man who was a model of patience, which she knew was far from true. Which made her nervous. She still thought he was up to something.

"I'm…sorry I yelled at you yesterday."

He looked puzzled. "When?"

"When I told you…you know…that I was done. No more pretend…anything."

He shook his head. "Chloe, I'm good with that."

"You are?" Because he'd seemed really mad at the time. Of course, she had been, too.

"I don't want to pretend anymore about anything," he said.

That was too easy. She blinked up at him. "What do you mean?"

"I mean, I thought we had started something real. There was the fake stuff we were trying to save your business, and then, there was us, again, together, because it was what we wanted. Isn't that what we were doing?"

"I… Well…I thought so," she admitted.

"How did all that get lost in the middle of things yesterday? You, me, what's real?"

"I don't know. You were so mad at me," she began.

"You ran out on me? One minute, we're in my bed again, finally, and you finally let me tell you how sorry I am about the way things ended between us in the first place and about Giselle. Then I wake up, and you're gone?"

"I'm sorry," she said.

"You drugged me to get me to sleep so you could run out on me?"

"I didn't drug you so I could run away. I brought you those pills because the doctor said you were supposed to take them, and you were obviously uncomfortable and having trouble sleeping," she said, defending herself.

"Well, it so happens I didn't want to sleep. I wanted

that night with you. I'd waited damned long enough for it. I wasn't about to miss it."

She took a breath. "You were hurt."

"It wasn't like I was dying." He got this awful look on his face. "I thought you were happy. I thought that night meant something to you. And then I woke up, and you'd run away."

"I…I didn't know how I felt about…what happened."

"Well, I get that, Chloe. I do. Just tell me that. But don't run away. Not from me. Not again. Please?"

That was kind of sweet, Chloe admitted to herself, at least until she thought about the things he'd said the next morning.

"Wait a minute, you were the one spouting off all the fake stuff. You wanted a fake engagement, a fake marriage. That wasn't me. That was you."

"Yeah. I guess I might have panicked a little myself that morning," he admitted.

She gaped at him. He'd admitted to an emotion like panic?

"You drugged me," he reminded her. "Ran out on me, and then I found you kissing another man—"

"He was kissing me. I was too shocked to stop him. That's all."

"Okay, he was kissing you."

"Why would you be in a panic over Bryce grabbing me and kissing me?"

"I wasn't. I was just plain mad about that, and then you said you were giving up. If we weren't pretending to be a couple to save your business, I was afraid you might not see me at all. That's when I panicked." He shrugged, looking not arrogant at all. Looking astonishingly gorgeous and oddly human at the same time.

"Oh," Chloe said, her heart melting dangerously.

She was so far from being over him.

"I was just looking for a reason for you to have to see me, even if it was a fake reason," he said, grinning at her.

She fought the urge to throw herself in his arms, at least for the moment. She could worry about all their issues later. After she kissed him silly. She was thinking about doing just that, and from the look on his face, she thought maybe he was doing the same thing.

"So, what are you doing tomorrow night?" he asked finally.

"I'm not sure. Why?"

"Because people seem to think I'm despondent over losing you, and one of those people is a partner in a business deal I've been working on for six months. He's getting an award tomorrow night from the mayor for all the charity work he does."

"You're trying to hold your business deal together?" she asked. "How are you going to do that?"

"The easiest way would seem to be showing my business partner I am neither suicidal, nor have I lost you."

"But, we said no more games, no more lies—"

He stood up, pulled her to her feet, cupped the side of her face in his palm and asked, "Have I lost you, Chloe?"

"No," she whispered.

"Well, there you go." He backed up, let his hand drop to his side, and she could breathe again.

"It just seems like the same thing we've been doing," she said, when she could think again.

"I've got a lot of time and money invested in this deal already. I really want to save it, so I'm going to this dinner," he explained.

"Of course. I understand that."

"And I'd like to have you by my side, because I like it when you're with me. I want to see you. I want to dance with you. I want to try to convince you to come home with me afterward and hope you don't run away this time. That's what I want. What do you want, Chloe?"

Well, when he put it like that, it was really quite simple.

They were doing what they wanted, what was real.

"I like it when I'm with you, too," she said. "I'll go."

"I don't understand," Addie said that afternoon, as they looked through a rack of dresses in the shop to find one Connie could alter for Chloe to use as a formal gown. "I thought you said you two were giving up. No more games."

"We're not playing games. We're going to the mayor's charity awards dinner," Chloe insisted.

"But, how is that not pretending?"

"We're just not. No fake stories leaked to the press. No tipping off photographers. No fake strategies to try to make me look as if I'm not cursed."

"But, how is that really different from before?"

Chloe was a bit perplexed herself. "When he explained it, it sounded perfectly reasonable."

"Of course."

"No, really," Chloe insisted. "I want to see him. He wants to see me. So we're going out together."

"To the same sort of event we would have picked if we were still playing the save-the-business game that's proven to be so disastrous for us all. Do I need to remind you of any of this?"

"No. But I still want to be there with him. Besides, I'd hate it if all this started messing with his business, too. I feel guilty enough about my business going under. I'm not going to let his be hurt, too," she said.

"Nothing is going to damage his business," Addie argued. "The man has a fortune. He'll always have a fortune. If it's not quite as big as it used to be, he'll get by just fine."

"I want to be the woman who's standing by his side helping him fix this. It's no great challenge to gaze up at him adoringly in the middle of a fancy party, and it's not any kind of a lie. I always want to be with him, Addie. I've wanted that ever since we broke up in the first place. I was just too mad and too hurt to do anything about it."

Addie groaned and buried her face in her hands. "Please, please, please don't say that—"

"Whether I say it or not, it's still true. I want to be with him."

"He will break your heart again—"

"Or maybe he won't. Maybe he'll take really good care of my heart this time. Maybe we'll be better with each other, better to each other. Maybe we learned something from the last time and the time we spent apart. I mean, people are capable of changing. I need to believe that for myself, that I can grow and learn and change."

Addie just stared, looking like Chloe had announced she had a terminal disease or something.

"And if none of that's true, and I really am cursed in love," Chloe said, "I want to be cursed in love with him."

Still, nothing from Addie.

"Please say something," Chloe begged.

"If he hurts you again…"

"I know," Chloe said.

And then she found the dress she'd been looking for, a heavy milky-white silk gown, deceptively simple in front, save for the heavy line of shimmery silver beading at the neckline, plunging into a daringly low dip in back, again simple as could be but lined in silver beading.

It was for a woman who loved her back and hips.

Chloe was okay with her back, but she couldn't say she

was all that crazy about her hips. James, however, was. If she could make it easier for him to gaze at her adoringly, she was doing her part.

"Do you want his hands all over you?" Addie asked when she saw the back of the dress. "Because this is a dress for a woman who wants a man's hands all over her."

"I want to look like a woman who would dazzle him," she said. "And I wouldn't mind tormenting him a bit. We'll be surrounded by people. The mayor will be there. What's going to happen at a charity ball?"

Addie shook her head. "If that's what you really want, let's go try this on you and see what kind of alterations Connie can do."

They were headed for one of the big dressing rooms, when Robbie stopped them, pointing out a deliveryman with what looked like an old-fashioned trunk.

"It's from him," Robbie said. He was avoiding saying James's name unless he absolutely had to.

"Oh, now he's going to start with fancy presents?" Addie was definitely skeptical about that.

Chloe wasn't sure how she felt about it. He'd tried that the first time, showering her with expensive things, until she'd put her foot down and made him stop. It just seemed too easy for him, too smooth, too practiced a thing, and one that didn't really mean anything at all. She suspected his assistant picked out most of the presents he'd sent.

This looked…different. Very different.

"It's from Italy," Robbie said, signing for it. "I feel like I should recognize the name of the town for some reason."

He gave the pronunciation his best shot.

Chloe gasped. "Lace. The area's famous for its gorgeous handmade lace."

They finally got the trunk open. It was, truly, an ancient steamer trunk, and there, packed carefully in thin tissue paper, was lace so delicate and beautiful Chloe almost cried.

Lace was the most expensive part of wedding gowns, the most intricate, elaborate, fanciful part. She indulged when she could, but this was a veritable treasure chest of various handmade laces from an area of Italy known for producing some of the best in the world.

It was like giving a painter the finest set of paints, like giving a child the most delightful and thoughtful present ever. Terribly extravagant, and yet, the perfect gift for someone in Chloe's profession.

Robbie whistled. "I have to admit, the man's stepping up his game."

Yes, he was.

Chloe took the lace out piece by piece, studying each one, exclaiming over the delicacy, the workmanship, the things she'd like to do with each one. And she was utterly charmed and touched by what he'd done.

James stayed away for the three days until the party. It just about killed him, but he did it. He feared if he pushed too hard too soon, she would only retreat further, and he didn't want that to happen.

He sent presents instead. The lace, which he'd heard was a big hit. A special blend of gourmet coffee that he drank, because while she called him a coffee snob, she always raved about the coffee he kept at his apartment. And today he picked out diamond earrings to go with the gown Addie said Chloe planned to wear tonight.

He got to the house a little early, because he still had some bruises from the accident, and Addie insisted he allow one of their makeup artists to try to cover them. When he objected, she said, "Do you want to go to this party looking like a man who took a walk in traffic four days ago?"

No, he did not, so he arrived early and let them do what they wanted to him. He had to admit when it was done, he could hardly tell he'd been in an accident.

Then he spotted Chloe halfway down the fancy, old-fashioned, curving staircase in a simple, glossy dress in a shade that made him think of milk. It was all but sleeve-less, with a wide but delicate band of sparkling silver beads and things following the simple V neckline. Connie came down the stairs behind Chloe and draped a matching cape over her shoulder that fastened with a little silver chain in front.

Addie had been right to suggest he get earrings, he saw now. A necklace would have been all wrong with this gown.

James took a breath and walked over to the bottom of the staircase to meet Chloe, who had her hair piled on top of her head in one of those effortless-looking knots she wore so often, which showed off her neck and shoulders to perfection. She looked a little nervous, a little uneasy as she caught her breath and smiled up at him.

"You're like a medieval snow princess," he said, catching her lightly by the arms and leaning down, intending to kiss her softly.

"No, no, no. You don't touch so much as a hair on her head until after you get past the photographers on your way inside the party," Addie told him. "You two may not care anymore, but I do. Promise me?"

He promised. He could wait. But barely.

He pulled the little jewelry box out of the pocket of his tuxedo jacket instead and held it out to Chloe.

She frowned. "We're going to have to talk about this, James."

"Okay, but for now, these, I'm told, will look perfect with your dress." When she shot him a questioning look, he said, "I had help."

Addie had sent a photo to his phone that showed the glossy white of the dress and a bit of that silver trim, which he'd shown to the clerk at the jewelry store, who'd then pulled out a number of earrings she said would be appropriate.

Chloe took the box and opened it up, staring down at what he'd thought was a very plain line of diamonds to hang from each earlobe. But having seen the dress, he understood. Anything more would have been too much.

Chloe looked inordinately pleased with them, and he stood there while she put them on, then let Addie, Connie and Robbie look her over.

Addie gave her a handful of sparkly silver bracelets that went on both arms. Connie handed her a very tiny, silver bejeweled purse, and Robbie fooled with the cape until he was completely happy with the way it draped. They finally proclaimed her perfect and turned her over to him.

He tried to be a model of good behavior and courtesy, helping her out the door and into the limousine. Then he settled in on the far side of the big backseat and simply stared at her.

"You look like you want to nibble on me," she said finally, staring back at him.

"I do. I want to do a lot more than that, but I promised not to muss you up. You stay over there, and I'll stay over here, and we just might make it. But you should know now, there won't be any room between us on the way home after the party."

She seemed as if she wanted to make it harder for him to keep his distance now, and he got the feeling that she was up to something. She and her coconspirators back at the showroom.

But she didn't do anything, just sat there looking regal, like a woman from another era. He was already thinking about just how long they had to stay at the party. She was coming home with him tonight—another thing he'd already decided—and she would not be sneaking out the next morning.

By the time they finally pulled up to the party, he was in really bad shape, having mentally undressed her at least a dozen times. He was doubting his own ability not to ravish her in the nearest small, dark, enclosed space he could find.

He stepped out of the limousine and into the lights. One of tonight's award recipients was a well-known Broadway star, and the mayor was toying with a run for president, so Addie had predicted an abundance of media coverage. She was right.

In their time in the spotlight, James had discovered that if he kept his attention on Chloe, he didn't mind the cameras so much. He smiled with genuine pleasure and pride as he reached into the limousine to help Chloe out. He was more than happy to show her off. He wanted the world to know she was his.

The gown's glossy fabric with its silver embellishments came alive under the lights, and she positively glowed as they posed together for the cameras for a long moment. Then she undid the catch on her cape and peeled that off. He leaned in to her side for one more picture, put a hand to the small of her back, where it had been moments before, and found...

Nothing but bare skin beneath his palm.

He sucked in a breath.

She shot him another one of those little secret, mischievous looks that again told him she was definitely up to something.

"Chloe," he said, feeling like he was choking. "Did you forget something?"

"I don't think so." She blinked up at him innocently.

"There's no back to your dress."

"Of course there is."

He let his hand ease lower and lower still—to skin and more skin. He found himself nearly cupping her bottom before he finally hit dress. And then he didn't know what to do.

She obviously wasn't naked. But he didn't think he could stand beside her all night—or even worse, have her in his arms, dancing—in this dress, with all this luscious skin to see and touch. He didn't think he could speak.

Chloe laughed softly, the sound reverberating through his body, and then turned around, one of her palms pressed flat against his chest, smiling over her shoulder as she showed off the back of the gown to the cameras.

There were a few appreciative whistles from the almost exclusively male photographers, and then they started talking to her, encouraging her to look this way and that, telling her how beautiful she was tonight.

He told himself not to look, knew it was the smart thing to do. His best shot was to stand there like a mute statue.

But then she turned back around. She was a step ahead of him now, and all he did was look down, and there it was, her entire back bared for him to see, framed with that wide band of delicate silver embellishment that ended in a V just a hint above her hips.

He saw that pretty curve of her neck, the delicate bones of her shoulders, the subtle outline of her spine, but the thing that was killing him—just absolutely killing him— was the way the dress followed the indention at the base of her spine and then flared out, cupping that perfect bottom of hers.

His first thought, when he was capable of thinking, was to wonder exactly how much or how little she was wearing under that dress. His second—even more unsettling—was that it seemed with no effort at all, he could slide a hand down the back of the dress and onto her bare bottom. He really thought she might be completely bare under the gown.

"Do you like it?" she whispered without looking at him, without interfering with the view he had of all that delicious skin of hers.

He grunted, words failing him.

She laughed softly, and he didn't care about the cameras or anyone else anymore. He pulled her into his arms for a quick, deep kiss.

Chapter Twelve

Chloe thought the evening went as well as it possibly could, all things considered. They posed for photos, looking, she hoped, like a normal, happy couple, no one suicidal, no one cheating, no one cursed in love.

Inside, people at the event stared, most smiled politely, many whispered furiously among themselves as Chloe and James walked past them. Chloe didn't like it, but it wasn't as bad as she feared, either. No one said anything outrageously catty to her face. The other women kept their distance for the most part, and even when they didn't, James kept Chloe plastered to his side. No one got closer than she did, which she found highly pleasing.

And her gown seemed to be a big hit, judging by the things she heard from the photographers outside and as she and James walked through the room. She was always happy when people were admiring one of her gowns.

But not even people's reaction to her design could hold her attention.

That was all on James.

He was practically eating her up with his eyes. He hadn't taken them off of her, and he'd hardly said a word to anyone else as they drank champagne, nibbled on appetizers, nodded to a few acquaintances.

Then he got her on the dance floor, in his arms, and kept her there. He was so smooth, so elegant, holding her so that their bodies were brushing against each other, just barely, just enough to drive her crazy. She tried to get closer, but he wouldn't let her. And having his hand on the bare skin at the small of her back, in public, was starting to get to her, to feel a little wicked and forbidden, in the same way she imagined he'd felt when he'd first discovered the way the dress was made.

He kept it up, advancing and retreating, looking down at her with that heated gaze of his, and yet looking so cool and controlled, and she started to get it.

"This is payback for the dress?" she whispered to him.

He leaned down and took a little nibble on her earlobe, sending a shiver all the way down to her toes. "This is just the beginning of payback for the dress."

She laughed. No sense in lying to herself. This was what she wanted when she'd chosen this dress. To be irresistible to him and to end up back in his bed. She wasn't going to fight it any longer. They were doing what they wanted now, and she wanted him.

His hand slid lower on her back, just below the edge of the fabric at her hip, just for a moment. She arched her back and pressed her lower body to his, felt the unmistakable pressure of his aroused body and sucked in a breath.

In the end, they didn't stay as long as she expected at the party. She wasn't even sure they'd talked to the man he'd come here to see. It was all a blur of his heated gaze and possessive touch and anticipation of what was to come.

He got her into the back of the limousine, in the privacy there in the dark, him in the far corner and her leaning into him, as he slid that hand down her back once more. This time the hand didn't stop, easing below the dress and pausing briefly over the wide swath of lace of her panties, then slipping inside those, too, landing in a sexy, heated possessiveness on her bare bottom.

He swore softly and at length, savoring the touch. She dared to laugh, and he silenced her with his mouth on hers. He kept his hand where it was and kept right on kissing her until the limousine stopped and they had to get out.

She saw that they were at his apartment building.

He led her inside the building, into his apartment, into his bedroom, turned her to face the wall and then leaned into her with that big, powerful, unmistakably aroused body of his and started nuzzling her neck like a man who had all night to do it.

Payback time for tormenting him with the backless dress.

Chloe was glad she had the wall for support as he fought his own impatience and hers and took his time working slowly over her neck with his lips, his tongue, his teeth, his hands on either side of her bottom, his body firmly settled into the notch of her hips.

It was an all-out assault as he slowly worked his way down her back, ending up on his knees, his mouth finally settling into that incredibly sensitive spot at the base of her spine.

She could barely stand by then, her legs turned to jelly, her whole body trembling, only the weight of his body pressed against hers keeping her upright.

His hands slid back up to her breasts, cupping them,

teasing at her nipples, one hand slipping between her legs. And there was something about that spot on her back and his mouth there, sending all those delicious sensations up her entire spine, that made it feel like his mouth was everywhere, all over her body at once.

He would not stop, kept going until she literally screamed with the pleasure shooting through her body.

And then, looking very, very satisfied with himself, he turned her around, stripped her bare, lowered her onto her back on his bed and then stood in front of her, methodically stripping off his own clothes piece by piece. She lay there naked on the bed, eating him up with her eyes and having to wait until he was done undressing himself to touch him.

Then he climbed onto the bed on top of her and slid that deliciously, hotly aroused body of his inside of hers, inch by wondrous inch. She whimpered. She begged, but nothing worked. He hardly even breathed, it seemed, until he was damned good and ready, pushing her effortlessly, beautifully up over the edge and into oblivion.

She slept blissfully, snuggling with him, opening her arms to him deep in the night and welcoming him back into her body for more, waking the next morning naked in that big bed of his.

Chloe rolled over and found him awake and watching her, his perfect hair just a little mussed up, a sexy shadow of stubble on his face, looking at her with a gaze that was both possessive and very, very satisfied.

He leaned over and brushed her hair back from her face, then kissed her cheek. "Good morning."

"Good morning."

"No regrets this morning?" he asked.

"No regrets. And I didn't run away, either."

"You wouldn't have gotten far. I had the place booby-trapped after the last time. You would have set off all kinds of alarms, which would have woken me up, and I would have stopped you."

"Booby-trapped?"

He grinned wickedly. "It was that or handcuff you to the bed, which offered certain advantages of its own. Maybe next time…."

Chloe put a hand on that stubbly jaw of his, thinking about how much she loved seeing him a little mussed up, because it was such a rare thing with him, always so cool and controlled, so polished, so self-assured.

She leaned in to kiss him, thinking to pull him down on top of her, not ready for their magical night to end.

The next time she woke up, he wasn't in the bed beside her, but she smelled his favorite coffee brewing and a moment later, he walked out of the bathroom, steam billowing out behind him along with a delicious, manly scent she always associated with him. His hair was wet, and he was wearing nothing but a formfitting pair of workout pants riding low on his hips.

She leaned back against the pillows and grinned at him, and he grinned back.

"Coffee?" he asked.

"Yes, please."

He was back a moment later with a steaming cup for her and one for himself. Chloe sat up in the bed, the sheet wrapped around her chest, her hair going every which way. He sat on the side of the bed, facing her.

"Could you just stay here in my bedroom for a week or so, just you and me, nobody else? We have coffee, and we can have food delivered. We won't starve."

"You would never stay away from your office for a

week. They'd think you died and send someone to investigate."

"I'd call in, tell them I'm okay—"

"They'd never believe it. Besides, you have a big business deal and I have a company to save."

"I don't want to let you leave," he confessed, leaning forward to kiss her softly.

"Believe me, I don't want to go. But I have to make a lot of money, so I can keep my company afloat and so you and I are never partners in business again."

"You don't have to do that, Chloe."

"Yes, I do. I should never have let you invest in my business in the first place. It was too much. Everything went downhill from there for us."

"I wanted to do it. I wanted you to have what you'd always dreamed of, what you'd worked so hard for."

She gave him another quick kiss. "I know you did, but it just got to where it all scared me so much. I was in love with you, and that already gave you so much power over me. To have the other big thing in my life—my work—dependent on you, too… It meant my whole life was wrapped up in you, and given the fact that I'd never had a relationship with a man that had really worked…I couldn't handle it. I felt like you had way too much control over me," she admitted.

He shook his head. "And I always felt like I had next to none with you. That you were a woman who does exactly as she pleases, and no man could ever keep you from doing that. It left me feeling a little vulnerable, powerless, even, which was not something I was accustomed to."

James? Vulnerable? It wasn't a word she would have ever associated with him.

"So, we were both scared of the power we had over each

other. I never would have guessed that. I felt so inept as a businesswoman next to you."

"Well." He shrugged, smiled. "I wouldn't want you to be my accountant or make my business plan, but there are plenty of people with those skills. You, Chloe...you're brilliant. You have an amazing creative mind. I always admired that so much."

She sucked in a breath. Brilliant? "Really?"

"Yes. I fell so hard for you that first night we met, at your fashion show, watching you work. All the energy you had, the intensity you brought to getting everything just right, the joy in seeing what you'd created. You are like no other woman I've ever known. Did I not show you that? Make you feel like that?"

She pushed her hair back behind her ear and looked away, tearing up a little bit. "I don't know. I think, mostly, you just made me feel so much of everything. It was so intense, so overwhelming. I got scared. I started looking for things that were wrong or sure to go wrong. I've been thinking a lot about the last few days we were together, and I know I was pushing you away—"

"Tell me you believe me about what happened with Giselle," he said, taking her chin in his hand and turning her face to his, his gaze locked on hers. "I am so sorry, Chloe. So sorry I hurt you that way. I will always regret it."

"I believe we were lousy at trusting each other, and I pushed you away, and if you hadn't done something like that with her to blow up our relationship, I would have blown it up myself before long. I've done it before."

"You believe me?" he asked again.

"I do."

All the breath went out of him. He dipped his head down low, and when he raised it again, his eyes were glistening with moisture. "I wasn't sure I'd ever hear you say that."

He kissed her softly, took his thumb and brushed a tear from her cheek.

"I love you, Chloe. I'll never stop."

Chloe felt like her heart flipped over in her chest.

James laughed just a bit. "You look like you were afraid I was going to say that."

"A little afraid," she admitted. "But happy, too. Very happy. I want this to work. I want that so much. I was miserable without you."

"Me, too," he admitted. "And that's enough for now. I won't push. The next time I propose, you'd better not laugh at me."

"You didn't propose!"

"I said, 'Marry me.' And you laughed. I remember. I was there."

"You weren't serious!"

"I was—"

"Two seconds later, you said, 'Fake marry me.' And that made me so mad!"

"Okay, I didn't handle it well. I freely admit that. But I didn't go to the fake thing until you laughed at the real thing, and I told you, I only did that because I thought you might not see me again if we gave up on the plan to save your business."

"You don't have to marry me to see me again," she offered.

He looked ridiculously pleased with himself, despite the whole fake-marry-me thing. "Good. And you don't have to answer me right now about marrying me for real. I just said it because…I wanted to say it. I want you to know how I feel, but not to freak you out. Please tell me I didn't freak you out too badly."

"I…I'm still here. I didn't run away."

"Okay, I'll accept that."

"James, I have to fix this mess with my business. It's just something I have to do."

"Okay. I want you to be happy, Chloe. I want you to have absolutely everything you want in life. And I want you to know, whatever it takes to get your business through this crisis, money-wise, it's yours. I won't let you go under."

"No, you can't do that. I have to do it myself. I can't be this pitiful, inept woman you bail out of trouble, every time something goes wrong with her company. You have to stay out of it."

He made a face. "I don't think you're a pitiful or inept woman. I just love you, and to me, that means I'm never going to stand by and do nothing when you're in trouble. I am always going to try to fix things for you. How is this a bad thing?"

She took his face in her hands. "That's sweet. It's very sweet, and if that's why you came to my rescue when the whole runway-brawl thing came out—"

"That and because I was dying to see you again."

"Thank you. Really. I mean it. I've never had a man I felt like I could count on to have my back that way, and it means a lot to me," she said sincerely. "But I still have to do this myself. And you have to let me. No matter how hard that is for you. My business can't exist just because I have a rich boyfriend who'll keep writing checks to let us stay in business. It's too important to me and to who I am."

"I never saw it as anything like a hobby, I swear."

"No more sneaking around behind my back to fix things."

"Okay."

"Promise me. We don't want to be the same two people, making the same mistakes all over again. Remember?"

"I promise."

James had his regular driver take Chloe home, and she sat in the backseat of the town car in her dress and her cape, feeling like Cinderella whose ball had simply never ended.

She made it home before the shop opened that morning, even managed to get to her room, shower and dress before anyone found her. She got back downstairs, got some of the great coffee made from the stash that James had sent over.

She walked into the showroom, finding Addie sitting on the platform viewing area in front of the big mirrors drinking her coffee, as well. Chloe sat down beside her, and Addie tossed a tabloid on the floor in front of them, with a picture of Chloe and James on the cover.

"Wow, the dress looks great," Chloe said.

"Yes, it does. And you have that sickening little glow about you that… Well, I have to admit, it works in the shot." Then she added another tabloid on the pile. "James looks like he might need someone to perform the Heimlich maneuver on him in this one. Not that it's a bad look on him. I don't think the man could take a bad picture."

"I think he'd just gotten a look at the back of my dress. He liked it," Chloe said, thinking about when he'd kissed his way down her back.

"Okay, don't go all gooey on me. I'm not up to that," Addie protested. "I'm just saying…last night worked for us. Not that it was your aim. I understand that. Really, I do. I just…don't know what's going to happen. We've stopped the company's nosedive, at least. Which is big. Of course, God only knows what might happen tomorrow, with our luck, and we have so little available cash, even with the last check Adam wrote us."

"Yeah, about that…" Chloe began, telling Addie it really hadn't been Adam. It had been James all along.

"And you're okay with that?" Addie asked when Chloe had gotten the whole story out. "With a man as secretive, as manipulative and as controlling as that?"

"He said he did it because he loves me, and he couldn't stand by and do nothing while I was about to lose something he knows I love."

Addie made a face and groaned.

"It was sweet, really, the way he explained it," Chloe protested.

"And you believed him?"

"Yes, I did. You make him out to be some kind of monster, Addie, and maybe that's partly my fault, because I was so mad and so hurt when we broke up the first time. But he's not a monster. He's someone who's not all that good at relationships or trusting people, and neither am I."

"That's what you think?"

"Yes, I think we were two scared, screwed up people in love, making a mess of things and hurting each other. I know I hurt him, too. I really did. And I know I did things I regret. But I'm still crazy about him, and I want this chance with him. That means forgiving and forgetting."

"Oh, that's convenient—"

"If it's about the money and Adam… If he hadn't made Adam those promises, Adam wouldn't be here. We'd either still have been partners with James all along or we'd have been out of business a year and a half ago. Did you think about that?"

Addie fumed silently for a moment, then said, "He lied to you about it."

"Okay, yes, but it wasn't malicious, and I don't see how

it was any kind of effort at controlling me. It kept us in business, and we never heard from him, not until a few weeks ago when all hell broke loose. You can't believe he had some evil plan to force himself back into my life and waited a year and a half to spring it."

That got Addie thinking at least. "I didn't see it that way," she finally admitted. "I'm afraid he really wants to marry you this time. What are you going to say when he asks?"

Chloe wasn't quite ready to own up to the fact that he already had. That was her own sweet, little secret for now. She wasn't even sure how she felt about it yet. "That there's something really pathetic about a woman getting engaged for the fourth time. I already told him I was never getting engaged again."

"Okay, but one does not have to be engaged to be married," Addie pointed out.

"I know that." Chloe sighed.

"Well, the upside is, this whole non-fake romance of yours is a big hit. You are no longer cursed in love, and we are actually limping along fairly well right now. Limping, but going in the right direction, business-wise. I think we may just survive this, and maybe, one day, even pay off your boyfriend for his sneaky, underhanded investment in the company."

"Why is it working now?" Chloe asked.

"Because you're not pretending anymore. You and James are crazy about each other, and it shows in every photo anyone's snapped of you."

"I am absolutely crazy about him," she admitted. "And I'm not as scared as I used to be."

"Well, that's progress," Addie admitted.

"Oh, did I tell you Marcy's gone? James got a friend

of a friend to give her a job as an assistant at a reality TV show. She's so much happier now."

"Wonder what that cost him?"

"He wouldn't say, just that it was worth every cent."

Addie laughed. "He really paid to get rid of her?"

"I think the producer's wife heads a children's charity, and he just gave them a really nice donation, and Marcy got a job. It worked." Chloe shrugged. "He really is a wonderful man."

"You should probably know that I'm prepared to tolerate him. For your sake," Addie said.

Chloe hugged her. With Addie, that was progress!

Now she just had to figure out what to do with the man.

Chapter Thirteen

They had a good week. An incredibly normal, very good week. James took her to the opening of a Broadway play, to a gallery opening where he wanted help picking out some artwork as an investment and for the bare walls of his apartment, and to a benefit for a children's hospital.

Brides stopped freaking out. They even had some walk-in traffic, women not ordering dresses, but trying them on and probably trying to figure out if things were truly stabilizing at the design house.

They were no longer a constant presence on tabloid covers or the subject of ludicrous rumors on blogs. It seemed a relationship going well was simply not tabloid fodder.

Tonight James was taking Chloe to a fancy cocktail party hosted by the investor who'd been so nervous about doing business with James a couple weeks before.

Chloe had taken apart one of her gowns, floor-length with a sheer over layer in pale gold tulle, heavily embellished with burnt-gold leaf and beading, which had looked elegant and very bridal over a long, cream-colored silk sheath. Instead she put it over a clingy, stretchy, fitted minidress, which turned the whole outfit into something sexy, elegant and unusual.

She loved the way James's eyes got that slightly dazed look, coupled with a blast of sheer heat, when he looked at her in it.

He would hardly touch her in the car on the way to the party. It had gotten to be a habit, his trying so hard to keep his hands off her on the way to an event, flirting outrageously with her while there. He'd be all over her in the car on the way back to his apartment, and they'd barely make it inside before he stripped her bare and had his wicked way with her. As foreplay went, it worked really well for Chloe.

He was such a beautiful man, so perfectly put together, so elegant, so controlled, which made it so much more thrilling to see how hard he had to fight for that control when it came to her and how satisfying it was when he lost it.

The evening was running entirely true to form. Little innocent touches here, a polite hand there, long, steamy, appreciative looks and wicked, whispered promises of things to come. Chloe suspected they would be leaving indecently early once again.

"Five minutes," James whispered to her. "I just have to talk to one more person, and then we're out of here."

Chloe nodded, nibbled on a cream tart and then saw a redheaded woman in a dress that was absolutely to die for. She sometimes stalked women in really great dresses to get a nice, long look at the designs, and ended up in a quiet hallway, spying on the woman in another room. The dress was asymmetrical, a design technique Chloe seldom got to play with.

As she stepped to the right, to maintain her view of the great dress, she bumped into one of the servers working the party.

"I'm so sorry," she began, then realized he looked familiar.

He did a double take when he saw her, surprised, highly appreciative and a little embarrassed. "Chloe! It's you! You look…amazing and all grown up."

Chloe just nodded. "Charlie, I can't believe you're here."

This was Fiancé No. 1, the boy she'd supposedly walked out on because she wanted her career more than she wanted him. Which wasn't exactly true. For a time, she'd wanted both. But Charlie hadn't wanted her to want anyone or anything but him. She felt the slightest flicker of unease, because this was really strange, having him showing up here now.

"I am so happy you're here," he said, handing his tray off to a passing server, and steering her down the hallway where it was quieter. "I actually wondered if you might be. It sounded like the fancy kind of party you might go to. I've been thinking about you a lot lately. Seeing your picture all over the place."

Chloe nodded. "It's been an interesting month."

"Miss me? Just a little?"

She smiled, wanting to be polite and friendly, at least. "Sure, I do."

He got a huge grin on his face. "I've missed you like crazy, Chloe. The time when we were together was the best time of my life."

He grabbed her by the arms and held on to her, smiling down at her with that goofy smile she'd loved in high school, when they'd first gotten together, and those sad puppy-dog eyes of his made her feel like she was sixteen again, at least for a moment. And then, before she realized what was going on, he pulled her close and started kissing her.

Chloe stood there, shocked into a kind of paralysis at first, and then finally came to her senses and pushed hard enough against his chest to get her mouth free of his. "What are you doing?"

"I think I might still love you, Chloe," he said, still hanging on to her. "I want us to have another chance."

She gaped at him. "Charlie…"

And then James was there, by her side, with a tight grip on her arm, pulling her away, and he looked absolutely furious. "James?"

"Are you two done?" he asked.

"Done?" she repeated.

"Yes, done."

"Yes, we're done," she said. "What is the matter with you?"

He shot her a murderous look and took off down the hall, dragging her along with him. He went through a door, turned down another hall and then pulled her inside a darkened room and shut the door behind them.

Then he started pacing, like he had too much energy shooting through his body for him to be still.

"What in the world was that?" she asked.

He glared at her. "Is this payback for what I did to you? Is it punishment?"

"No," she insisted.

"Because that's the second time I've walked in and found you kissing another man, and it's really starting to make me mad. And it makes me think maybe this is all a game to you. Maybe you never intended to give me another chance. Maybe you just wanted to pay me back for the way I hurt you a year and a half ago, and you know just how to do it. Just like that. Exactly what I saw in there."

Chloe was shocked that he could think that, that he could feel that way.

"James," she said, going to him, taking his face in her hands, to make him look at her. He looked devastated. "That was…he's a guy I haven't seen in five years. I had no idea he was going to do that. One minute we're talking about high school, and the next thing I know, he's kissing me. I was too stunned to even do anything for a moment. That's all."

"That's what you said about the other guy," he reminded her.

"The other guy was Bryce. You saw the video of the runway brawl, didn't you?"

He nodded tightly.

"Well, if I told you that guy would ever show up in my life again and want me back, wouldn't you be shocked, too? Would you ever think he'd have the nerve to say he wanted me back and grab me and try to kiss me?"

He didn't say a word.

"Oh, come on. Nobody could have seen that one coming. Even my life isn't normally as weird as that."

"And this guy?" he asked finally, calming down a little.

"I spent maybe two minutes with him. You probably saw the whole thing. We…we dated in high school. We were engaged right afterward."

"That's your first fiancé? Chloe, what do you do to us, that we just can't forget you? How many more of these guys are going to show up, wanting you back?"

"I don't—there aren't any more. Just the three of you. You're the only one left."

She kissed him softly on his mouth, thinking to soothe him, and he responded by hauling her against him and holding her so tight she could barely breathe. Tension radiated from him, and he was sucking in air like a man desperate for it.

When he finally let her go, she said, "James, you can't seriously think I'm playing some kind of game with you, can you?"

He still looked grim.

"You do? You're seriously jealous of me and a guy I haven't seen in years?"

"Hell, yes, I'm jealous!"

She'd hurt him. Really hurt him. And scared him. Which wasn't something she could do unless the feelings he had for her were every bit as big and strong and scary as the way she felt about him.

She hadn't really believed that until now.

James Elliott was crazy about her.

How about that?

"I'm sorry," she said. "I would never set out to deliberately hurt you. I couldn't." She took a breath, then admitted, "I am trying very hard not to let myself love you again—"

"I know you are. I absolutely know it. Hell, I'd have to be a fool not see it."

And he hated it. She could see that now, too.

He just stood there, a beautiful man in a perfectly fit tuxedo, hands in his pockets, sucking in air and staring at her, and she felt terrible about the way she'd hurt him.

"Will you take me home, please?" she asked finally.

He looked surprised and not happy.

"Your home, I mean."

They got out of there and into the limousine, where he sat holding her hand, watching her, not saying anything. When they got to his apartment, he made himself a drink and stood in the living room, slowly sipping Scotch.

"I'm sorry," she said finally. "I would never set out deliberately to hurt you or to trick you. I care too much about you to ever do that to you."

"Okay," he said, seeming to want to take the measure of each word she said and turn it over and over in his mind until he knew exactly what he felt about them.

She took the drink from his hand and then slid into his arms, which caught her to him so tightly. He was trembling, she realized, and for the first time, she truly believed that he was every bit as vulnerable and unsure of himself in this relationship as she was.

In this, they were equal. Finally. All the risks of being in love, being that vulnerable to another human being, were theirs to share. The rewards, too.

She reached up and kissed him softly, a kiss he turned hungry and urgent. She finally eased back and said, "Until tonight, I don't think I believed that everything you feel for me is every bit as big and overwhelming and scary as what I've always felt for you."

He stared down at her. "How could you not know that?"

"James, you're the strongest, most self-assured man I've ever met—"

"Not where you're concerned!"

"Well, I guess I didn't really believe that until now."

"That's all I had to do? Go nuts over some other man kissing you? I did that with Fiancé No. 3 weeks ago, remember?"

"I don't know. I just thought you were mad then. We weren't…in the same place where we are now. We hadn't talked through everything or spent as much time together yet, and I…I guess there was still that awful knot of fear inside me about letting myself go completely. About not trying to hold back and protect any part of myself from you anymore."

"And now?" he said urgently.

"I give up. We can be scared together. I love you."

He finally smiled. "Say that last part again?"

"I love you. I don't think I ever really stopped, even though I tried so hard not to."

"And you'll marry me? Because I need that. I need to know that we're both in this to stay this time. I want rings. I want vows. I want a signed piece of paper, and anything else I can think of. The whole thing."

"I was thinking we could start slowly? Like…maybe getting a marriage license?" she asked. "Because I looked online, and the thing is, you can get one and you don't have to use it. I mean, you can, but you don't have to. They give you sixty days, and if you haven't gotten married then, you can just go back and get another license and have another sixty days. You can keep doing that as long as you want."

"You want to get a marriage license and not use it?"

"It's a step. A first," she explained.

"Okay—"

"A statement of intent. How about that?"

He laughed. "I like that better. A statement of our intentions."

"I just…can't be engaged again. You have to understand that."

"But you're willing to get a marriage license?"

She nodded.

"Okay," he agreed. "That's a step."

"And I don't want to take months and plan some big thing. We'll just…go do it one day when we're ready. I want to make my own dress, and I'll use some of the lace you gave me. It's so beautiful. I want Addie to be my maid of honor. I need Robbie and Connie. Adam should be there and anybody you want. And you. That's it. Can it just be like that?"

"Chloe, as long as we end up married, I'll be happy."

"And I have to get my business back on track. I have to. Although, things are looking so much better lately. Being seen around the city with you has done wonders for business. And it's been weeks since anyone's said I'm cursed in love."

He kissed her long enough to leave her breathless. "No one will ever have a reason to say that again. I promise."

Epilogue

Celebrities About Town
A Channel 5 Web Exclusive
by Marcy Ellen Wade

Designer Chloe Allen always manages to surprise, and her spring show was no exception.

Instead of a mess of jilted lovers in a runway free-for-all, this time fashion critics and buyers were treated to a surprise wedding of none other than Chloe Allen herself to one of New York's most eligible bachelors, financial whiz James Elliott IV.

The couple had repeatedly denied being engaged, even though they'd been seen all over the city together. Public records show they had purchased multiple marriage licenses over the past few months, and Chloe had even been photographed wearing a gorgeous cushion-cut diamond on the third finger of her left hand.

Chloe's collection was particularly exquisite at this

show, elegant, polished and yet highly romantic, perhaps influenced by her newfound faith in love and that fourth engagement being the one that finally took for her?

Her collection came down the runway to massive applause, and then as guests mixed and mingled at a reception afterward, they found themselves invited back to the runway for the simple, surprisingly intimate and touching ceremony.

There, where it seemed Chloe's career and her personal life were left in tatters, stood the happy couple, looking radiant and simply unable to take their eyes off each other.

Ms. Allen's half sister and a partner in her business, Addison Grey, served as maid of honor. Her cousin Robert Allen performed the ceremony, and another cousin Constance Allen sang as the newlyweds had their first dance.

Rumor has it the couple first met when Chloe mistook James for a missing male model at one of her earlier fashion shows and tried to send him down the runway with a model wearing one of her wedding gowns.

Who would ever believe such a mistake would lead to a runway wedding of their own someday?

* * * * *

LET'S TALK
Romance

For exclusive extracts, competitions
and special offers, find us online:

 facebook.com/millsandboon

@MillsandBoon

@MillsandBoonUK

Get in touch on 01413 063232

For all the latest titles coming soon, visit
millsandboon.co.uk/nextmonth

JOIN US ON SOCIAL MEDIA!

Stay up to date with our latest releases, author news and gossip, special offers and discounts, and all the behind-the-scenes action from Mills & Boon...

 millsandboon

 millsandboonuk

 millsandboon

It might just be true love...

MILLS & BOON
MEDICAL
Pulse-Racing Passion

Set your pulse racing with dedicated, delectable doctors in the high-pressure world of medicine, where emotions run high and passion, comfort and love are the best medicine.

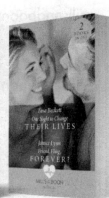

MILLS & BOON
True Love
Romance from the Heart

Celebrate true love with tender stories of
heartfelt romance, from the rush of falling
in love to the joy a new baby can bring,
and a focus on the emotional
heart of a relationship.

MILLS & BOON

MODERN

Power and Passion

Prepare to be swept off your feet by
sophisticated, sexy and seductive heroes, in
some of the world's most glamourous and
romantic locations, where power and
passion collide.